To Julie
with love
Shirley Battie x

CALLING EARTH

SUPERPOWERS FIGHT FOR DOMINION OVER EARTH

S M BATTIE

ISBN: 978-1-9995949-0-9

First published in 2018

CONTENTS

INTRODUCTION

Richard sighed heavily and pushed a large stack of papers to one side of his desk. He ran his fingers through greying hair, loosened his tie a little more and looked at his diary. He saw he just had one more person to deal with. It had been a long, tiring day and he was looking forward to going home and putting his feet up.

There was a sharp rap on his door. “Come in,” he called out.

As the producer of a popular TV programme he was used to people trying to get his attention. Their reasons were many, and more often than not he had to disappoint.

This won’t take long, he decided as he studied the wizened old lady hobbling into the room. “Please sit down. I’m all yours,” he said with what he hoped was an encouraging smile. She carefully lowered herself down on the chair facing him across the desk. Looking at her thinning white hair he tried to guess her age. He hoped she was not another nutcase convinced she’d seen flying saucers. His TV programmes leant towards connecting with space intelligence, and that brought out the crazy ones. From the look of her she could easily be over one hundred, but her bright blue eyes showed no signs of failing. There was something about her that was ageless, and it bothered him that he couldn’t put a finger on what it was. With a shock he realised that she was studying him back and was taking in every detail of his appearance. Embarrassed, he brushed his hair back with one hand.

“I’ve chosen you,” she said rather alarmingly. “It’s taken me a very long time to get here,” she said, as if it were his fault.

“Yes, yes, I know,” he said. “but I am a busy man. I don’t have a lot of time, but my secretary told me you’ve telephoned many times to see me. She said you told her it was vitally important.”

“It is, and what I have to give you will change your view of your world." She rummaged in a large bag and pulled out a package tied up with string. She slammed it down before him. "Please read all of this as if your life depended on. Indeed everybody's lives depend on it. Everything in there is true." She placed a thin bony hand on the bundle before her. "You can check up on much that is written there and find proof for yourself."

Richard half rose from his seat. "I'm very sorry but I don't have time ..."

She leant over the desk and a waft of lavender engulfed him. "Read it!" she commanded. The strength of her voice shook him. "And switch off your phones. Your future might depend on it." She thrust the package across to him. "It's all written in here. Don't lose it." She rose unsteadily to her feet, turned and left the room without another word.

Stunned, he stretched out an arm to stop her but she had already gone. Oh well, it was time to go home anyway. Richard shoved the thick bundle into his briefcase. Perhaps he would do as she demanded. What harm could it do?

Back in his apartment Richard settled down after a quick meal and opened the package. With a bottle of wine by his side he began to read.

CHAPTER ONE

A GREAT UNION BEGINS

Behold they are one people, and they all have the same language. And this is what they began to do, and now nothing which they purpose to do will be impossible for them. -- Genesis 11:6

Dorset UK

Seagulls screamed dipping and diving under an overcast sky and scudding clouds. It was late winter with spring just around the corner. Twenty-five year old Kate huddled in the doorway of the shuttered Hiker Café near the car park at Hengistbury Head, waiting for her father to arrive. Her fair hair escaped from her knitted hat and blew across her face in the gusty wind. The young woman had no idea that the next few moments and the arrival of spring would change her life forever, in ways she could not possibly imagine. A bitter wind gusted around her legs, and she shuffled her feet against the cold. Leaves and twigs gathered in drifts by the closed shuttered door. She silently cursed for she'd forgotten that the café would be shut for the winter.

Kate shivered and beat her arms against her wool coat and tried to stay warm. Though well wrapped up, the cold still cut through her clothes and despite her fur-lined boots, she had to stamp the ground to keep the circulation going in her feet. The grey sea lashed out in great surges, whipping up white-capped waves as if angry with the world. Few people braved this exposed headland in such wild, wintry weather and Kate longed to return to the warm cocoon of her car. It was a mistake to come out on a day like this. She wished her father would hurry up.

She heard a car scrunch over the gravel of the deserted and windswept car park. She turned to look. Two heavily built men wearing dark suits emerged from the darkened vehicle. Kate pushed down an uneasy feeling. They looked out of place, not the usual holiday makers, or the types to be out for a walk. Kate turned away from the men, but heard their footsteps crunching over stony ground as they got nearer. Suddenly, a heavy hand landed on her shoulder, and the cold steel of a gun pressed against the back of her neck. Her heart pounded and a rush of cold fear swept over her.

"Stay quiet and you won't get hurt. Scream and we'll shoot you." They grabbed her arms, fingers pinching her flesh, and dragged her towards the waiting car, its engine still running. Kate struggled and tried to scream but nothing came out. The men shoved her into the back seat next to a black-suited man who pressed a gun to her ribs. Kate didn't dare move. Her mind seemed paralysed. A pair of hands put a blindfold on her, and held a pad over her nose. Dread seized her. Was this end?

Her senses drifted and her mind fast tracked back to when she was four years old, oh so long ago. She felt as scared and submissive now as she had been then. That memory never completely faded and now came back to her in force.

"Let me out. Let me out." Four year old Kate screamed in the pitch black of the under-stairs cupboard. She banged and clawed at the door until her tiny fists bled. Sobbing, she put her hands to her head. Blood from raw knuckles ran into her blond hair.

"You will stay there until you stop this nonsense about tall blue men coming to visit you. You know full well it's not true," her mother Francine shouted through the door, as she walked away, high heels clicking on the parquet flooring.

Kate stopped screaming. It had happened before. Nobody would hear or care. She curled up among the clutter in the dark and rocked back and forth, sobbing quietly. She called for her tall blue friends, but they didn't come. She knew she'd stay in the dark, weeping and hungry, until her Daddy let her out; then she'd snuggle into his protective arms. This could take a long time to happen and was inevitably followed by a shouting match between her parents.

What she saw was true though and she wouldn't say otherwise. When alone— which was often— the tall wispy blue men talked to her many times. They'd become her only companions. Her cuddly Daddy had to work. Even at four years old Kate understood that. Only yesterday she'd stood unnoticed to one side in the kitchen as her mother yelled at him.

"Isn't it about time they gave you a raise? You've been there long enough. You ought to go and ask for promotion. Spineless that's what you are." Her mother tossed her head in disgust and flounced out of the room.

Her father's head hung low, and his shoulders drooped. Kate ran to him and clutched his legs. He patted her head.

Kate now twenty-five years old drew her mind away from that childhood memory, wishing she could erase it for good. She'd tried but in unguarded moments it still came back to haunt her. Somewhere in the fog of her mind, she registered the car raced along, screeching round corners and throwing her to one side.

Kate blinked, suddenly finding herself back in the cafe's doorway as if she'd day-dreamed the whole thing. But it wasn't the kind of thing she'd choose to dream about, and the experience had seemed all too real. Could it be real? A prediction of things to come?

The image had only lasted for a matter of moments before she came crashing down again from wherever it was that she had been, her mind reuniting with her body once more.

Kate squinted. Yes, she was still in the café's doorway. The same wind whipped around her legs, the seagulls continued to scream overhead as if nothing had happened. But what had just happened? One moment she was standing outside a café, the next, she was ascending into the clouds then watching a scene unfold where she was being kidnapped. She couldn't get her head around it. There was still the faint ringing sound but as it faded to nothingness there was very little for her to grasp on to – the only thing she could liken it to was an intense feeling of déja-vu.

Kate thought hard; she couldn't dismiss what had just happened, or file it under 'unexplained phenomena' because it felt so authentic, but she had to accept that it was baffling. Could it have been some kind of psychic disturbance, an elaborate visual hallucination? It felt utterly real at the time, but now she couldn't be so sure.

In fact, she'd been experiencing so many other strange mental images lately that she was beginning to wonder if she should be worried about it. Was it the onset of some kind of illness? One moment she'd 'see' crowds of people, all clamouring for her attention, the next she'd be transported to the empty nothingness of space, a clear expanse all around her, tinged with a beautiful azure blue. Sometimes the images in her mind's eye were so restful and reassuring that she felt wonderfully peaceful afterwards. Surely there couldn't be anything wrong with that?

It reminded her of the serenity she felt at the weekly spiritual circle she'd been attending for some time. She'd been drawn to go and find out more about it after seeing a poster advertising the gatherings, and she'd found that she felt remarkably comfortable there, despite being the youngest member by two decades, the only blonde head in a sea of greying hair. Thankfully, this particular group steered clear of the clichéd 'Dearly Departed' routine. Instead, they explored the wider reality of what they called, 'the spirit world'.

One or two members of the group were able to go into a light hypnotic trance, and channel information from their 'spirit guides'.

It seemed the over-arching message from these guides was that Love and Compassion were the attributes that humans should nurture. Something that spoke directly to Kate was the notion that there should always be 'Wisdom and kindness in your thoughts'. Kate certainly aspired to that and naturally detested the superficial celebrity culture and shallow political double-speak that pervaded the media. She knew attending the spiritual circle was an unusual interest for someone her age, but it just felt 'right' to be there. Perhaps this vision she'd just experienced was because she was beginning to open up to otherworldly possibilities – something that was often discussed at the 'circle'.

As she pondered these new and not altogether welcome experiences, given what she had just seen and experienced, she heard the very concrete and real sound of her dear old dad, pulling up in his trusty banger. Kate's father, Jacob, strode towards her, his longish, dark hair tied back in a loose ponytail, the beginnings of beard stubble on his chin and the beginnings of a beer belly too. He did so like his food. Her heart melted just a little as she looked at the only person who ever seemed to really understand her. Seeing him, she wasn't sure whether to mention what had just happened or not. Their traditional father/daughter relationship was so reassuring to her, and he had been such a rock her whole life, that she didn't want to trouble him with what must surely sound fantastical. But she didn't like to keep secrets from her father, and maybe he could help her explore the new visions in her head? He was always so open-minded and non-judgemental and of course, she'd have to frame them in a way that wouldn't totally freak him out!

Kate pasted on a smile, left the doorway and walked over to join him. "Hi Dad!" she said, giving him a big hug. "The wind's easing up a bit, but I hope you're going to be warm enough?" She mentally shook off the brief yet vivid episode and hooked her arm in his. "It's going to be a bit of a chilly walk. Ready for it?"

He smiled and nodded and they set off arm in arm.

After a while she broached the subject. "Dad," she asked tentatively, "do you ever wonder about your imagination? I mean, does it ever run away with you?

"Of course, my darling, I'm always daydreaming. Why do you ask?"

"Well, sometimes my daydreams are so vivid that they seem to leak into reality. Like, I can't tell whether something actually happened, or if I just dreamt it. What's that all about?" she laughed, to make light of what she was saying, then continued, "It quite often happens when I've been meditating. You know I've been going to the spiritual circle and practising my meditation, right? But, I don't know, sometimes, meditation and dreams and reality get a bit mixed up. Does that ever happen to you?"

He wrapped his heavy overcoat more tightly round his bulky frame. A sudden gust of wind knocked them sideways, threatening to blow them off the path. He caught his breath before replying. "The only difference between meditation and dreams is that in meditation you take yourself into that dream-like state deliberately. You've seen how people use the self-hypnosis method and they can have conversations and interact in a very real way with those they meet in their meditations, but in dreams you have no such control. What happens in meditation and dreams feels equally real, though – so what is reality?" It was his turn to laugh. "Reality is unique for each and every one of us, Kate. I would say to ask for guidance from a higher source. Ask for help and you will be helped."

"Thanks, Dad," she said, genuinely reassured, making a mental note to do just that at the next circle. "Shall we go back? This weather's atrocious and I fancy a cup of tea. I don't think we should stay out too long."

Jacob barely registered what his daughter had just said. His mind had cast back to the day when he discovered he was going to be a father. The moment that should have been a profound and moving one but in reality was far from it. He recalled walking into the house after a long day at work and seeing his wife Francine's face, which was blotched and puffy from crying. Francine was an emotional and challenging person at the best of times and being in a relationship with her was sometimes really tough. Jacob spent a lot of his time on damage limitation, shielding himself from the worst of her verbal assaults. He didn't know why she was upset but didn't dare ask for fear of setting off one of her outbursts.

"Look at me," she barked. "Can't you see I've been crying?"

Jacob nodded. "What's up?" he asked, genuine care in his voice.

She came up close to his face and almost spat at him. "I'm pregnant!" Francine gestured to what would become the bump with disgust.

Despite her fury, Jacob couldn't help but reach out to hug her, grinning like an idiot. "But that's wonderful."

She pushed him away, her fury rising. "It's your fault," she shouted. "You weren't careful enough. You knew full well I didn't want a baby." She paused for breath. "I'm getting rid of it."

Jacob stepped back, a horrified look on his face. "Oh, please no, you can't!"

His own feelings about the baby were clear: it had to be born, there was a place in the world for it, he knew. Over the following weeks, Jacob's certainty about his love for their baby fortified him, gave him the courage to give voice to his convictions and to persuade Francine not to terminate the pregnancy.

But, unbeknown to Jacob, Francine tried to erase what she considered to be the invasion of her body by using old wives' remedies such as herbal infusions and drinking lots of gin. They don't call it 'mother's ruin' for no reason, she thought – but nothing worked. The damn kid refused to leave her body despite all her attempts to be rid of it. Reluctantly, she knew she would have to go through with it and have the baby, but she spent the whole nine months looking aggrieved and grumpy. Where other expectant mothers felt proud of their growing bumps, Francine felt invaded, as if she were host to a parasite.

At last Francine went into labour and unsurprisingly, found the whole experience utterly appalling, telling Jacob she felt violated and that she hated him. Eventually, she gave birth to a perfect baby girl, and as Jacob bent over his wife, kissing her and thanking her for being so strong, he prayed that her mother's instinct would kick in when she saw their child, and that Francine would love the child as he instantly did. But to his dismay, her expression remained resolutely cold. She couldn't hide her distaste for him or feign love for, or even interest in the baby.

"What shall we call her?" he asked, gazing in rapture at the sleeping infant.

"Call it what you like," she said. "It's no business of mine." She turned on her side so they were both out of her sight and began to weep for a life that might have been.

"I'll call her Kate, after my mother," he said softly.

Francine didn't react to his choice of name – she couldn't give a damn – but she thought she'd heard him sniff, and annoyance immediately ran through her veins. Was he crying? What had *he* got to cry about? She turned to see him leaving the room with the tiny baby cradled in his arms.

CHAPTER TWO

FIRST CONTACT

'The art of communication is the language of leadership.'

James Hulmes

In Kate's street, like most in England and elsewhere in the world, people carried on with their lives as if what was happening right in front of their noses didn't concern them. Sparrows squabbled in garden hedges and dogs pulled their owners along on daily walks. Helmeted cyclists pedalled hard over potholed roads. Everyone rushed to conclude their day's work and settle down to an evening of television. Weekends were devoted to doing the supermarket shop and housework or gardening. So many people simply endured or enjoyed their humdrum existence, while others questioned and sought for answers to the way the world was, and why.

Those whose lives were spent in blissful ignorance meant that they turned a blind eye to the chaos, violence and upheaval they saw on the news. If they weren't directly affected, they didn't really think about it. The endless conflicts and civil wars throughout the rest of the world barely caused a flicker on their radar. Why should they care? There was the crossword to finish before bedtime. But, just beyond their garden gates, the world was rapidly changing and they were oblivious to it – worst of all, they weren't prepared.

Unbeknown to Kate, she *was* being prepared – her radar was being finely tuned by energies she couldn't explain. She sat, her blue eyes closed, in the peaceful stillness of her garden at Number Six, the silence broken only by the twittering of birds and the sound of an occasional car engine in the distance. Although it was still early in the year, it was a mild enough day to sit outside, her hands warming around a mug of tea. A blackbird's song rang from a treetop, sending a thrill through her as it always did. What was it about that particular bird's song that filled her with such a sense of nostalgia? The creatures of the air had always delighted her. A slight breeze ruffled her long fair hair. Usually tied back neatly, today it fell loosely around her shoulders, a symbol of the freedom she felt during her precious weekends away from the confines of her office job. She didn't mind the hardness of the wooden garden seat, tucked away in a corner surrounded by early daffodils, nor the slight nip in the air.

Kate felt something brush at her feet and opened her eyes to see a sheet of newspaper, blown in by the wind. She bent over and picked it up and a school photograph stared back at her from the page. School...what a long time ago that was. Uncalled for, she had a sudden memory of the girls from her class huddled in a group by the lockers, as if it were yesterday.

"Her mother never comes to pick her up, you know," the leader of the gang sneered. And then, deliberately, she added, "Maybe her own mother doesn't like her either?" She looked around at the others for confirmation, daring them to disagree.

"She's so boring! She's always got her nose in a book. Stuck-up know-it-all!" said another, chewing on a cola bottle sweet.

Kate's blue eyes brimmed with tears. Just as they'd hoped, she'd heard every word, and it hurt. If it hadn't been for her sweet, prim-and-proper friend, Poppy, who stuck close to her and defended her from these bullies, Kate would have been very lonely indeed. Her mother's coldness had left Kate unsure about how to act in a group, how to make friends – but Poppy has seen through that and had come to Kate's aid, and although it didn't occur to her until years later, Poppy was like the sister Kate never had.

Throughout Kate's childhood, Francine's main priority was to make her as self-sufficient as possible, as quickly as possible, so she could have even less to do with her daughter. Kate had been expected to get herself ready for school and make her own way home from a very early age and it was made clear that friends were certainly never to be invited back. Only the visits from the tall, shadowy blue men alleviated those early hellish years, but she could not, and would not, talk about them to anyone – not even to Poppy or to her beloved father – but then his job took him away from the family home, sometimes for days on end, and he didn't know half of what his darling daughter had to cope with.

But it wasn't all bad. At least she'd learnt good dress sense from her mother. Kate often hesitantly stood in the doorway to Francine's room and watched her as she tried on different clothes, smiling at herself in the mirror. In beautiful clothes, Francine seemed a little happier, a bit friendlier to her daughter. It was as if she liked being admired; liked her daughter to see what a beautiful woman her mother was, on the outside at least. On rare occasions, Francine even took Kate shopping, choosing outfits and shoes for her as if she were an object that needed to be decorated. But Kate didn't mind, because her mother was preoccupied with other things and so her malice towards Kate was slightly diminished.

Then, one fateful day, Kate was asked to join her parents in the living room, where for some time, there had been muffled whispering and the occasional raised voice. Francine told her with a curl to her lip that her parents were getting a divorce, and that she was to live with Jacob. Kate's relief had been immeasurable. It was the best day of her young life.

Smiling to herself, Kate folded the newspaper and tucked it in her pocket ready for recycling. It'd done its duty in detailing some useless piece of information – as if anyone really cared. Getting up from the seat she went indoors to the cheerful little room at the back of the house that she referred to as her study, where she kept the paper recycling bin and sundry other domestic items like the laundry basket and brushes. Kate's many reference books lined a shelf above her cluttered desk. From there, she could look out of the window over her garden.

Kate sighed. She wished she could work from home – maybe she could get some freelance work via the internet? Poppy had told her about an online agency where you could list your skills and they'd match you up to companies that needed support. If truth be told, Kate had begun to tire of her current job. It wasn't demanding or stressful – which should be a good thing, she supposed – but actually, she was bored and that never sat well with her. There had to be more to life. She needed a new challenge and if that wasn't to be forthcoming at work, then maybe she should look for another job? The company was responsible for employing technicians and scientists who ensured efficient transfer of data using satellite technology. It was secret, specialised, technical knowledge, but of course, she was party to none of that.

Kate sighed again. Oh well – she earned enough to run an ancient white Mini, keep herself looking smart and pay the bills with a bit left over. Maybe she should be content with that for now? Though she held a lowly position, her office colleagues recognised her as a bright spark, so perhaps some kind of promotion would come her way? The security screening for the job had been intense, but she'd managed to hide any hint of childhood trauma. They might have considered her a risk if they'd known about her the trauma of her childhood relationship with Francine. No, she'd learned the hard way to keep her pain firmly to herself. Only Poppy had some idea about the reality of her life. While at work, Kate kept focused on the task at hand and never let her thoughts dwell on emotional matters.

Kate moved to the small, cosy front room and drew the rather chic patterned curtains closed against the growing dark. She squeezed past the lumpy old leather sofa to run her hands over the books that lined one wall, floor to ceiling, and then looked at all her precious things – her illustrated copy of *Alice in Wonderland*, given to her by Jacob on her eighth birthday, and her first guitar, a half-size one suitable for her little fingers, again a present from her father when she was ten. There was nothing in her house from Francine, who had never once given her a present. Her friend Poppy, sensible as always, told her that her overfull house needed de-cluttering and that it was the equivalent of a security blanket, one she'd never had as a child. Kate supposed she was right. Bereft of a loving mother, she'd spent many hours as a child sorting through her belongings, giving her toys names and making scrapbooks of pressed wildflowers and cuttings from her comics. Having her things around her was comforting. She just hoped she'd never have to move.

Kate recalled how a colleague had once called in to Number Six to drop off her coat that she'd left at work. Kate had made her a cup of coffee and they'd sat in the front room making small talk, when the woman had somewhat maliciously called her books "New Age twaddle" – but Kate found these spiritual books a lifeline in an uncertain and often lonely world. She particularly loved the work of Carl Sagan and had read nearly all of his books. She'd even had a quote from one of his books written out by a calligrapher and framed: *'Somewhere, something incredible is waiting to be known.'* That thought had kept her going through many a difficult day.

She reached for a book, then stopped and sat down on the sofa by the coffee table. Tonight, she wasn't sure what she wanted to read, or what she wanted to do for that matter. Deep down she felt an urge for adventure, but the thought of this also frightened her. Going outside her comfort zone was difficult for Kate who had led a pretty sheltered existence to date – the unassuming, orderly life she'd built for herself was all she knew – she never even been on an airplane or visited another country. One area that allowed her to feel totally liberated though, whilst remaining safely in her own home, was meditation, a skill she'd learnt at the spiritual circle. Actually, she hardly had to learn meditation – it came as naturally to her as breathing. Once the door had been opened into this new world, it was never closed to her again. She merely had to focus her intent and she was able to go beyond the confines of her thoughts and connect with something other, which she had no name for, but instinctively knew was the domain of the spirit. She felt her very soul was nourished through the act of meditation – it made her feel whole and more herself, and this was a huge comfort to her.

At first, she'd started off following the traditional meditation route they taught at the circle, of visualising a path down stone steps to a beach or through a sunlit glade, but as her ability grew, she discovered that she didn't need to do this, she could just 'connect' through her intent. She could step outside of the limitations of her own thoughts into other realms, other realities, until she realised she was actually travelling in her mind. The sights, sounds and smells were so vivid that she knew it wasn't just a daydream. She could talk to people, engage with them and fully immerse herself, all in her mind – just as Jacob had reassured her on that cold, windy coastal walk. She often wondered if anyone else could do this as easily as she could, and how she could prove that she too was a mind-traveller, but then her natural instinct to keep quiet about anything out of the ordinary would kick-in – the old self-preservation making her reticent on such matters. And in any case, outside affirmation of her newfound skills was not necessary to her. She was used to relying on herself and here was the perfect in-house entertainment!

And so Kate decided that meditation rather than reading was what she wanted to do. At once she slipped into a state of receptiveness and found she had mind-travelled to a beautiful place that she knew to be South America. She was soaring above the clouds from the (dis)comfort of her sofa, enjoying the sight of the distant Andes when she heard a whisper in her ear.

"Beautiful, isn't it?"

She was so shocked, she could feel herself reeling, but the most surprising element of all was that the voice was her father's.

“Dad…? Is that you?”

“Yes, it’s me, Kate.”

“So, you can do this too?

“Oh yes – and this is a favourite spot of mine. I’ve been mind-travelling here for years. I’m so glad that you’ve found you can too.”

Kate immediately took herself out of her trance-like state and sat reeling on the sofa. What on earth…? She reached for the phone and rang her father.

“Hello, Kate,” answered Jacob, before she’d even said anything. “Yes, it’s true. I joined you in your mind-travel just now. I knew you had discovered how to do this and waited until you were expert at it before revealing that I can too.”

“But how did you know?” said Kate.

“I could sense it,” he replied. “Having well-developed psychic abilities makes me very sensitive to other people’s astral movements. I’ve known that you had the same abilities Kate, from the moment you were born – but these things are not to be rushed. You have to come to them in your own time. Once you decided to join the spiritual circle, for me it was just a matter of patience.”

“Oh, Dad!” exclaimed Kate. “That’s just the best! I need someone like you to help me make sense of it all. I love being able to do this, but it’s not normal, is it?”

“Who decides what ‘normal’ is Kate? Everybody is born with innate gifts, but some people don’t access them for many lifetimes. Was Beethoven normal? Was Van Gogh normal? You were born with this gift for a reason, though you don’t know what that is yet – and nor do I for that matter!”

"Oh Dad. What would I do without you?"

Jacob explained his own experiences of mind-travel to Kate over the next few days, and it was fair to say that Kate was greatly relieved to know that her beloved father, the person she trusted most in the world thought it was perfectly acceptable to hang out with his daughter in another dimension. It was all so new to Kate that on occasion, she doubted her sanity, but knowing that Jacob was with her, reassuring her and guiding her was all she needed to step out of her comfort zone and mind-travel with him to other realms. And so they began to go on psychic trips together, exploring new areas and showing each other where they'd been. It brought a closeness and connection to their relationship that hadn't been there before. Now that her gift was strengthening by the day, Kate felt herself spiritually unfurling, as if from a chrysalis. She marvelled at what she was able to do and pondered on Jacob's words, almost a warning, that she'd been born with this gift for a reason. She wasn't too sure she was ready to find out what that was quite yet.

It was a weekend some days after the life-changing revelation that her father was a fellow mind-traveller, when Kate found herself back in her garden, mug of coffee in hand, enjoying the last of the early spring sun as the golden rays bathed her in a glorious, warm light. In the deepening shade she warmed her hands on her mug and daydreamed about the year ahead. At the back of her mind she knew there was something she was meant to do, but she couldn't grasp what that something was – perhaps she was going to find a new job, or perhaps she would find some fulfilment in her mind-travel? Whatever it was, there was an insistent energy in her mind's eye that urged her to be alert to any change, to see the doors of opportunity opening and to have the courage to step through to her future.

To her dismay, Kate's mother Francine entered her thoughts, unbidden and unwelcome. Unlike her shorter, fair-skinned daughter, Francine was tall, darkly beautiful and elegant, the ideal of womanhood in the eyes of many people, but Kate knew that behind the façade lay a heart of stone; a woman who had a child that she didn't, or perhaps more accurately, couldn't love. Her mother hadn't wanted a daughter at all, and had done everything she could to be rid of her as soon as the opportunity arose. These days, they kept out of each other's way. Francine could hardly tolerate having a grown-up daughter, because Kate reminded her that she was ageing, a mere mortal. She preferred not to be called Mother, or heaven forbid, Mum and to do so in public was to invite rage – and she insisted that the same rule be applied to Kate's father. In her presence, he was to be called Jacob, not Dad, although they'd divorced many years ago. Now uneasy friends, they lived quite close to each other, but moved in different worlds. Kate hoped her mother was happy in her world, though she doubted happiness was something that came easily to Francine.

Suddenly, a voice interrupted her reverie.

"Transmission open! Sechem here." The words had a melodious bubbling quality to them, an almost musical sound.

Kate's senses shot to high alert, and she leapt to her feet in alarm.

The voice in her garden repeated: "Transmission open!"

Kate jumped again. It came as a clear announcement, but to whom? Was it someone in next-door's garden? But the neighbours were away...it couldn't be them.

"Who are you?" Kate whispered into the growing darkness. Instinctively, she picked up a spade and held it like a weapon, scything the air in front of her. She looked around, eyes straining, but saw nothing in the gloaming. Yet someone had definitely spoken, loudly too – a male voice if she was not mistaken. She held her breath, shaking with anxiety.

"Hello Kate."

She whirled round, trying to detect the source of the voice, but there was none.

"Yes, I'm talking to you. You seem surprised, yet we gave you lots of signs and hints that you'd be visited. Don't you remember?" The voice chuckled. "Did you not think it strange? All those visions you've had, all the mind-travelling. They weren't daydreams, Kate; they were rehearsals for what's in store." The disembodied voice came in waves, ebbing and flowing.

Kate relaxed her grip on the spade realising that the voice, wherever it came from or whoever it was did not seem threatening or malevolent, yet still she could see nothing that helped her to connect with who was speaking.

Then it came again, this time more strongly, like a thundering crash of waves on a shingle shoreline. She could almost imagine she was by the sea hearing the rattle of pebbles as the waves receded.

"So, now you're waking up, you need to prepare yourself. First I'll give you a little background information to help you get started."

Kate let the spade drop. Trembling, she felt for the seat behind her and sat down, her legs shaking. This was what Jacob had hinted at, she now realised. She was being prepared for something and she had to stay alert, despite every bone in her body wanting to run a mile from this unnerving situation.

The invisible voice carried on, seemingly unaware, or ignoring the effect it had on the young woman. "I'll tell you of beauteous things, of wonders that humanity has yet to comprehend. I'll tell you such things that you'll be inspired and you will feel great joy in the inspiration. Allow me to penetrate your mind. This is the beginning of a great union between us."

"A union? Penetrate my mind? What do you mean?" she asked, her voice shaking. She felt stupid talking to the air. But the unseen speaker ignored her, as if she'd never spoken. Perhaps this is only a one-way communication, Kate thought, but then an energy that was almost overwhelming filled her head. It felt as if her brain was being polished!

"In your understanding, the realms of possibility are very small. You exist in a bubble you call Earth, and your knowledge of what's beyond is very limited. I want to open your eyes to worlds of infinite possibility. Humans celebrate travelling to the moon as if it was a big achievement, but where I am from, this is a mere trifle. What you call a light year is but a moment for us. Our scope and vision is incomprehensible to humans. We have witnessed the birth of planets, including yours. Earth was recorded in our charts of the universe and we watched and wondered how this new planetary being would evolve."

"You were there to witness the birth of Planet Earth?" Kate said, incredulously. "Who… What are you?" She stared into the space before her, straining her eyes to see. A blue shimmering haze emerged from the midst of the shady garden. She shook her head and blinked several times, but the shimmer didn't disappear, it moved closer. Kate instinctively shrank back, scared now. She had no idea what it wanted from her.

Then the haze drew away, as if it sensed her fear. The garden resumed normality, and the birds began singing again. No sight of the blue light remained.

Kate sat there, her body still shaking as the adrenalin ebbed away. She could hear the echoes of the ethereal voice ringing in her ears and tried to make sense of what it had said, but it was just too enormous to comprehend. All she could do was turn over the sentences in her mind, searching for what they could mean.

"Your knowledge of what's beyond is very limited. I want to open your eyes to worlds of infinite possibility. Our scope and vision is incomprehensible to humans. We have witnessed the birth of planets, including yours."

Whatever just happened, Kate knew it was important and that she couldn't just ignore it. She understood from that moment on, her life would change forever.

After a while, it was obvious that this particular transmission had finished, but she was quite sure there would be others, and hoped she'd be less freaked-out by the next one. Silence followed and she could hear the birds twittering once more. Now it was over, she realised that she felt incredibly energised, like she was somehow cleaner, or lighter... It was hard to describe, but she felt different, less dense.

She decided to ring Jacob, she wanted to tell him all about it.

"Darling, that's incredible," Jacob said once Kate had recounted the situation to him. "Remember what I said about you having this gift for a reason? Well, I think you're about to find out what that is."

"But Dad… I don't think I'm ready for all of this. I don't know… I'm quite happy as I am really. It's all a bit overwhelming…"

"Don't worry Kate, you'll never be asked to do more than you're capable of."

"Really? Oh, I don't know Dad. Hearing voices in the garden, seeing blue beings, mind-travelling and the birth of planets… I think I'd rather just do my 9-5 job and watch repeats on TV in the evenings. I'm not ready for all this."

"You know that's not true Katie – what about last week when you were moaning about being bored with work? Don't deny this opportunity, embrace it."

"That's easy for you to say Dad, it's not you hearing voices!"

"Don't be so sure about that darling. I've got a feeling you're not on your own with all this."

* * *

For some time, Jacob had been joining Kate at her spiritual circle, where they were working on psychic development. He wanted to reassure her that she wasn't on her own with whatever was coming her way, and he was old enough and wise enough to recognise that she had extraordinary psychic talents. Kate welcomed his company and the opportunity to be able to discuss the sessions with him afterwards, and some instinct told her this was also his way of compensating for leaving her for days on end with her cold and hostile mother when she was little. She knew he felt guilty about this, but never really blamed him – after all, he had to work.

They sat close together on straight back chairs in the pleasant room where the sessions were held. Soft, relaxing music played in the background, and the curtains were drawn. Flickering candles cast strange shadows on the walls.

The main speaker addressed the group. "As we've established, the object of our training is to bring into the conscious mind what the soul is trying to communicate. As we know, this isn't easy and takes practise, but in this session, I want to talk about how we can further develop our faculties so that as well as accessing our own soul thread, we can also learn how to tap into messages from elsewhere, including from extra-terrestrial beings who are trying to assist humankind. With training, practise and true intent, it is possible for us all to connect with the angelic realm and those who are known as 'The Masters'. All have the ability to do this, but few succeed. It is not easy, but it is possible.

Kate sat up straight. This all sounded very familiar, it was just what she'd been told in her back garden. Relief and reassurance washed over her. She was not going mad, after all – other people had experienced the same things she had. Interestingly though, the speaker said that this was something that could take place with practise, but for Kate, it happened unbidden. She must be more receptive to these experiences than most, she supposed.

The speaker continued. "There will come a time in the future when practically everyone will use their inner awareness to a greater extent, and it will be normal to communicate in this way. The odd ones out will be those who haven't learnt to benefit from this soul contact."

Kate sat forward, eager to hear more, but instead of the speaker, another voice spoke, this time inside her head.

"What he is saying is true. We have told you that we are concerned about the planet and the souls of humans. We do not have much time to prepare Earth's population for events to come. We are training others like you to pass on the knowledge, so that a network of understanding is spread across the globe."

The voice faded away and Kate blinked, suddenly aware that the group speaker was thanking everybody for their attendance. The evening had come to an end. Kate still felt overwhelmed despite the reassurance from the speaker that others could communicate with spirit beings. But all these dramatic pronouncements from unidentified voices were mind-boggling. It was so much to take in and she felt completely out of her depth. Her father was chatting to some friends so she slipped away quietly into the night, her mind too preoccupied to join them.

CHAPTER THREE

THE WALLS HAVE EARS

'Most people never listen.'

Ernest Hemingway

Time-traveller Sechem's tall figure moved silently around Kate's garden, a rainbow haze gently wafting behind him. He liked this place more than he cared to admit, after all, he'd spent many lifetimes here, aeons ago. And in some ways, it reminded him of his home in The Pleiades. He sighed. What had possessed him to volunteer for this seemingly impossible mission? But then, how could he not? Unbeknown to the population of Earth, many of his kind still lived here without detection and wouldn't ever be able to leave until the vibrations and spiritual conditions on the planet improved.

Sechem's view of Planet Earth was massively different to that of humanity's – humans are still such infants in their awareness of the Universe. To humans, Planet Earth is 'home', but to the Pleiadians, Earth is more of a social experiment. Five billion years ago Earth was chosen by several otherworld species as the venue for 22 different intergalactic programmes. The aim was to create a paradise on Earth; the perfect residence where all, regardless of their origin – both human and extra-terrestrial – could visit or reside in peace. Planet Earth was uniquely beautiful in the solar system; it was a blue-green pearl of unparalleled complexity, a pristine utopia where harmony in all its many facets could unfold. Unfortunately, the ideals of the intergalactic programme had gone dreadfully awry, and wars and conflict were now rife. Extra-terrestrial time travellers like Sechem had remained incognito to all but the most sensitive of humans, but the different species had never managed to blend together satisfactorily as had once been hoped. The concept of Earth as a convenient place for otherworld species to occupy had continued, but not with such admirable intent. Recognising humans to be the guileless and vulnerable race that they are, ruthless invaders from other planets were at this very moment planning to take over Earth, no matter what the human cost, and use it for their own purposes.

Sechem sighed again and thought back to his own incarnations on Planet Earth long before he became a Pleiadean. He hadn't exactly been a highly-evolved human either, so how could he now judge others? As was the way of things, he'd had to reincarnate again and again, until he'd wiped his slate clean of karma. He'd done a lot of things he wasn't proud of, especially an incident that had been recorded in (Genesis) the human Bible, much to his dismay. His actions had resulted in a bloody, ruthless attack on his own people.

In time, he'd earned his right to return home to The Pleiades and act as advisor and intermediary between intergalactic organisations known as The Spiritual Council, The Galactic Command and those still incarnated on Earth. His main role now was as a spirit guide. Sechem shook his energy field vigorously as if to rid himself of his past. How many men had died because of his actions?

But it was no good looking back. He had a job to do. At least he wouldn't be alone. Others would join him after he'd prepared Jacob and Kate. He wasn't allowed to force or impel either of them do anything, though. That was against the rules. He had to wait until they themselves, by choice, wanted to do what was necessary. Their right to free will could not be violated.

He was grateful now to be in a guiding role rather than in the thick of it. Kate was his main charge and he had to prepare her for action. Although he couldn't actually command her to do anything, he could enlighten and encourage her and he strongly believed that when she saw how urgent the mission was, she would accept it.

Sechem enjoyed the delicate fragrance of the lilac that had just come into flower, and luxuriated in the rays of the sun. Anyone watching would perhaps catch a glimpse of flowing colours, almost like a heat haze, in their peripheral vision, but would dismiss it as a trick of the light. This is how Sechem moved among the inhabitants of Earth, with lightness and grace, ensuring that his presence went unseen.

Although Sechem regarded himself as a guide and educator, he was totally unaware that at that very moment he was also the object of scrutiny. He was being monitored by the same malevolent forces he was charged with protecting Planet Earth from, whose schemes were as dark as his aura was light.

* * *

Later that same evening, Kate couldn't shake off the feeling that she was being watched. A shiver ran up her spine. Despite it being almost dark, she opened the windows wide, as the air had suddenly become dank and oppressive in her house.

From the hallway, two grey, shadowy figures observed Kate moving around her little sitting room. To the untrained eye, they were invisible.

"So, contact has been made. This is not good."

"Well, at least she can't see us," the second indistinct figure said with satisfaction. "Her gifts haven't advanced that far."

The two 'viewers' didn't really know how far Kate had developed her abilities, but they did know they were breaking the rules by entering her space without permission from their headquarters. They'd picked up on Sechem's communication while trawling for anything out of the ordinary. It'd been a bit of luck, although they'd not followed the usual protocol.

"We should be sure though. The head at ISR (Intelligence, Surveillance, and Reconnaissance) needs to know if she is a threat to the organisation," the first said.

"It doesn't appear that she's had much of an awakening. Look how startled she was when he spoke to her. It has to be the first time she's experienced anything like that. We don't need to worry. What can he do? Nothing!"

The two forms merged into one and slowly dissipated and the air in the room freshened.

* * *

In a small building in Washington DC, a group of dark-suited men watched a screen.

A giant of a man stood among them, wearing a long, dark coat shouting.

"Those fools! Don't they know they too are being watched? Haven't they realised yet that we never send our viewers out unsupervised?"

"They're quite new," one of the watchers explained. "It was just luck they happened upon Sechem and the girl connecting. Quite good luck, I might venture," he added, but refrained from looking directly into the eyes of the gigantic figure. He'd done it only once and had almost fainted with fear from the images that had entered his mind as a result. The terrible being, known as Gork, held a prominent position in ISR. Where he had come from was on a need-to-know basis and no one on this level had the clearance for that particular piece of information. They were left to their own speculation, which they certainly never aired, because punishment from asking the wrong questions could be swift.

Another man bravely spoke up. "No need to worry, sir. Now we know Kate Greene is waking up we will watch her, using our best viewers who are already in place. These two are just fishing for intel – we'll pull them off."

Gork grunted. "You had better. And monitor the situation closely. I do not want the likes of her interfering."

CHAPTER FOUR

STAR TRAVELLERS

'Wherever you go, go with all your heart.'

Confucius

Far away on an orbiting spacecraft in a spacious, circular room lined with monitors, two tall figures in outfits of swirling colour discussed what had just happened at Number Six.

"Just as I suspected..." time-traveller Jamère said, leaning back thoughtfully, stroking his dark, short beard. His star-covered helmet failed to contain all his unruly, dark hair, which curled out from underneath. "Another thing to consider. Interlopers!" He reached out a thin hand and touched a button. The panel activated and began flashing.

His technicolour aura shimmered as a wicked smile spread across his handsome face. "I love a challenge." He exploded in irrepressible laughter, then scooted across to his colleague, Sechem in his chair. "Well, what do you think of that, Sechem? Who do you think they were?"

"Psychic spies from the military, for sure." Sechem worked on another screen, his expression serious despite Jamère's amusement.

Jamère groaned. "I didn't think they'd catch on so soon. I told you it was too early to approach Kate directly. She's just not ready."

The Time Traveller stood and raised himself to his full height. Colours enveloped him wherever he went, creating a brilliant display. To human eyes, the full effect would be overwhelming – film-star good looks combined with a mesmerising light show. Luckily, people from Earth couldn't see him.

"I suppose you think you'd have done better with all your funny voices and magical tricks," Sechem said defensively.

"She would've enjoyed meeting me – she wouldn't have picked up the nearest blunt instrument. Talk about white knuckles when she picked up that spade! You frightened the life out of her. Well done, Sechem," mocked Jamère. "And you weren't much better in the psychic meeting either. Instead of slowly introducing her to the idea of her mission, you launched into one of your grand speeches and completely freaked her out."

Sechem looked at his friend. He'd never have his charisma for sure, but sometimes Jamère's approach was, well...just less than professional. "Hopefully the next meeting will go better," Sechem replied. "Time is getting short."

"I'll be watching you," Jamère said, grinning. "Don't frighten her again."

Sechem nodded. "I'll have another go," he grunted.

* * *

Kate had promised herself a quiet night in front of the TV and try to forget recent events. Whilst all that was happening to her was exciting on one level, on another she felt vulnerable and somewhat out of control: it seemed that some kind of future had been mapped out for her, but she wasn't sure quite what it entailed yet. No, a simple supper and a night in front of the telly was in order, she had decided. She cooked herself a meal, washed and dried the dishes and put them away in the cupboard. She tidied the kitchen, then settled down on the sofa in the living room with her feet up, cosy in their slippers, on the footstool. In case the TV programmes turned out to be rubbish, as they so often were, she chose a book and placed it on the little table by her side. A nature programme or documentary of some kind would be good, something with positive human interaction and information about the planet. Certainly not a grisly detective series or hospital drama. Avoiding anything violent had become her rule of late.

Kate had recently noticed how violence had a way of pervading her mind without prompting. She hated how gory scenes surfaced unbidden. Once the eye has seen something, she realised, it's hard to forget it, even when you want to. It made her realise how impressionable we all are. Kate wished that parents, programme makers and video-game designers could see what was obvious to her: that allowing children to watch war games and violence meant they were more likely to develop those tendencies. The mind grows according to what you feed it, in the same way as the body grows according to what it takes in for nourishment. She cringed to think of children continually playing violent video games. It was sure to have repercussions in their adult lives, or even earlier.

Kate pressed the button on the remote, but instead of a nature documentary, squiggles and shapes covered the screen. She frowned at it for a moment and tried to change to another channel but the erratic patterns continued.

"Oh rats!" she said aloud. Trust the TV to be on the blink on this night of all nights. She got up to switch the television off at the plug, but despite doing so, the screen stayed on, crackling and fizzing as if it were alive. A cold trickle of fear crept over her scalp. What was happening? She clicked the TV on and off with the remote control but it seemed to have a life of its own.

Hoping it was a simple reception fault and nothing more, she decided to ignore the television for a bit and reached for her book. But it was not there. She got up and looked around on the floor and under the sofa, but there was no sign of it anywhere. Strange…

The sound of someone clearing their throat came from the screen. Kate swung round and stared wide-eyed at the fuzzy pattern of dots on the screen. How could this be? She was positive she'd turned it off just a moment before.

No, she *knew* she'd switched it off. The shiver started up again, this time down her spine.

"At last I have your attention." It was the voice she'd heard in the garden. "It isn't easy you know. You have no idea what we go through to get anyone to listen to us."

Kate blinked. She wasn't sleeping, so it couldn't be a dream.

"I hope I didn't frighten you this time?" the musical voice asked. "I didn't know what to do to help you feel at ease with me – I thought connecting through this contraption might be less disturbing for you."

Kate couldn't answer.

"Please don't be frightened," the voice continued, with the same mesmerising musical tone as before. "I am Sechem. I come with nothing but good will for you. As I said before, this is the beginning of a great union between us."

Kate gulped. "Umm… H…hello Sechem," she squeaked, feeling a bit daft speaking to the telly. "What do you want with me? Can you show yourself?" she asked, her voice still wavering with fear. "It's just that… I feel… I mean, I don't like talking to someone I can't see."

"You talk to people you can't see all the time on the telephone, don't you?" the voice retorted with amusement.

A blue hazy form materialised on the screen and slowly took the shape of a tall human-like figure. Ripples of coloured lights ran from top to bottom over the indistinct form. Kate trembled as the form grew larger, emerged from the screen and stood in front of her.

"Is that better? Oh, and don't worry about your TV – it will work perfectly normally next time you use it."

Kate sank back into the sofa and stared, dumbfounded. "Are you a hologram, or something? Are you real? Who are you?"

"As I said before, you have been chosen to pass on our message," Sechem said, ignoring her questions. "There's a lot I need to tell you, so please do not interrupt."

"You have to be a hologram," she murmured, her trembling easing off a little, "or a ghost?"

Again, he didn't respond. "We long ago learnt how to cross the barriers of time using inter-dimensional consciousness. In our earlier viewing, we took into account the distance between us in light years. By the time we saw your Earth it had already advanced from its birth. We were not able to connect however, until we ourselves had learnt how to cross the time barrier. This we now do."

Kate's mind raced. She was still trying to understand who this being was, let alone cope with the huge concepts he was coming out with. Inter-dimensional consciousness? Time travel? This was secondary to the explosive news that she had what could only be an alien in her front room. Her heart pounded as the reality of that sank in.

His voice went rippling on, oblivious to Kate's inner turmoil. "So here we are, communicating through our minds. Is it not wonderful? To make things easier for you I will explain. You have communicated this way many years ago, when you were too young to know it was unusual. Now, we have returned to make contact again, but this time you are strong enough to collaborate with us."

Was he referring to the blue men who kept her company in her childhood?

"They're still watching? You know them?" Prickles formed all over her body and inexplicably, tears came to her eyes. Why was she of such interest to this being from goodness knows what or where?

The previous visitors had filled her with comfort and warmth, provided a welcome diversion in a bleak childhood, but this person didn't. Instead of being undemanding and supportive, he seemed to want something from her. The thought filled her with dread. Whatever it was he wanted her to do, she didn't want to do it. As if he was picking up her thoughts he spoke again.

"Humans are in danger of destroying themselves. Do you not realise that you are the most endangered species on the planet? The Galactic Command wish to do something about it."

A distinct rumble like the sound of far off thunder came from the blue figure. Surely he didn't suffer with wind? Kate couldn't suppress a giggle at the idea, and immediately felt his disapproval.

He grunted. "As well as this, we wish our own species to flourish and expand further into the Great Cosmic Arena. You might liken it to your own human exploration and settlement in lands previously unknown to you. Like your continual movements from your homelands to discover and explore other parts of your planet, we too continue to traverse and explore the space between us."

As Kate listened, she couldn't help but be reminded of history lessons. Early explorers' behaviour in new lands was ruthless and dominating, the indigenous population becoming the minority, with little or no say as to how their country was run. Often the result was genocide. She shuddered. Was this what he was implying for the human race?

Reading her thoughts, he said: "Note, however, that our physical form, such as we have on our home planet, could not comfortably exist in your world. Therefore, we let our essence, our minds, our cultures, our abilities and our ethics to enter the newly conceived human. Entry into the DNA of one cell is all that is required to make the transition."

To Kate, this sounded extremely dubious, like some sort of uninvited parasite. "Is that even ethical, is that according to spiritual laws?" she asked.

Sechem disregarded her comment. He appeared to be good at ignoring her views. "My homeland is filled with music, laughter and joy." The shimmering blue figure smiled at the recollection.

"Why would anyone wish to leave such a place?" Kate asked.

"Simply the spirit of adventure. We don't all leave it behind. Many remain where they are. But others are drawn to travelling and furthering the species. When we do, we always take the joys and delights of our world with us. We try to give to other parts of the Universe some of the pleasures of our world."

"That's what our early explorers said when they took over new lands," Kate replied, becoming bolder as she relaxed a little. "Everyone always thinks that their way is the right way, but look what happened to the Native Americans and Aboriginal peoples."

Sechem spread his arms wide. "We have large populations on our home planets that do not travel through time and the stars. Like you, we have explorers and adventurers who are willing to share and teach, and like you we also have many who prefer to live unadventurous lives and are content to stay put in their comfort zones."

As she waited for the being to continue, she studied the prismatic colours emanating from the figure in front of her and without really knowing why she did it, she tentatively reached out her hand and put it into the shimmer. It went straight through, and sharp painful prickles ran up her arm. "Ouch!" She jerked back.

He also drew back. "Don't do that! It causes interference in our connection." Then he paused. "Let me tell you where I am from. You may have heard of The Pleiades, a cluster of stars in the constellation you call Taurus? There are more stars in this group than you've yet discovered. We Pleiadians are great travellers, so already walking among you are many thousands of us, conceived in the manner of which we have spoken."

Kate couldn't help but reveal a horrified expression.

"There is nothing to fear. Instead this should bring delight to your hearts, for with our coming, introduction of new genes is possible. Far, far superior genes. The genetic makeup of humans is forever altered and is to continue. It cannot now be eradicated. Who would wish to do so? As well as supreme physical attributes, we also contribute advancements in technology and science. We are humanoid and have form similar to you. Shall we call our home XX? Two kisses of love. My name is Sechem." He smiled proudly.

As Kate grappled with the fact that these other worldly creatures were already living on Earth, she hesitated before speaking with her mind to him.

"I would like to see your homeland one day, Sechem," she mused.

Suddenly she felt a seismic shift in perception – an energy that was like sunlight in her head momentarily overwhelmed her. Kate shook herself and looked around but at first, could only see a hazy blur of colours. Shock and alarm threatened to engulf her, but she quickly realised that Sechem had granted her request – the words 'be careful what you wish for' came to her and she smiled to herself. As her eyes adjusted to the vista, she saw indistinct figures milling around swathed in the most vibrant and glorious colours. They didn't take much notice of her, in fact, she wasn't sure if they could see her at all. She could hear the same musical notes that were present when Sechem appeared, chiming just on the edge of her hearing. The air was warm and denser than she'd experienced before but it felt somehow energising.

Although she didn't know how she was doing it, she sensed she existed between two worlds, one as Kate living on Planet Earth and the other with Sechem in the land described by him. She felt odd, spacey and not quite all there. She was totally at the mercy of her mind, which currently seemed to be comfortably coexisting in these two spheres. For some time she just observed the scenario playing out around her, unquestioning, just soaking in all that she was seeing.

Just as she had adjusted to this new reality her head jolted back, as if she were falling asleep on a train. She shook herself, feeling she had come out of a long and intense dream, blinking her eyes rapidly at the glare of the TV screen, which was now showing David Attenborough with a pair of binoculars.

What on earth just happened…?

From some deep recess of her brain, she remembered reading an article about quantum physics where it had been proven that an atom can be in two different places at the same time. Was that how she had managed to be both in her living room and in The Pleiades? Were mind-travellers merely more versed in the laws of quantum physics? She had no explanation for it, but also, she could not deny what happened.

CHAPTER FIVE

PREPARATION FOR ADVENTURE

'All that is necessary for evil to succeed is for good men to do nothing.'

Albert Einstein

Kate could hardly wait to tell Jacob about Sechem and her dreamlike visit to his homeland. Could it really be that she had just connected with an alien planetary being? The idea was so fantastical that she needed to say it out loud to someone, to explore it from all angles. Half of her worried how her father would react – would he think she had completely lost her senses? The other half felt curiously optimistic; her father was always receptive to her thoughts, whatever they were.

She punched in his number and waited as it rang.

"Pick up, pick up," she yelled at the hand piece.

The answer phone clicked in. "Please leave a message after the tone."

"Dad, you have to come here as soon as you can. I have something incredible to tell you. You'll never guess what's happened." Kate slowly and thoughtfully put the phone back on its stand. Maybe he'd also received a message from Sechem? He so often linked mind journeys with her. Her heart was still pounding with the adrenalin of the experience and she couldn't sit still. Instead, she paced around the room agitatedly, picking up books and discarding them seconds later.

Jacob was not one to hurry, however. 'Everything in its time' was his motto. An hour later he trudged up the path to her front door. He was a big man and although only in his fifties, he wasn't as quick as he'd once been. Kate opened the door long before he got to it. She pulled him inside and gave him a big hug.

"Dad, you won't believe what just happened!"

"Tea first. Let me get my breath back," he replied and lowered himself into an easy chair.

Exasperated, Kate went to put the kettle on. She knew he wouldn't do anything without a cup of tea. It was almost a ritual for him these days. She fizzed with excitement as she carried the tray in and set it down on the little table beside him. He took off his heavy-framed glasses, and placed them carefully and deliberately alongside the mug. Kate knew this ritual allowed him time to focus. He'd give her his full attention when he was ready and not a moment before.

Jacob spooned sugar into his tea and stirred it slowly while Kate told him all that had happened. When she was finished, Jacob looked grave and not at all surprised. He closed his eyes, deep in thought. This was not what Kate expected.

"Dad?" she asked.

"So, they've decided to make contact," he said quietly.

Kate eyebrows shot up.

"This is just the beginning. You'll certainly be introduced to others," he continued. His next words shook Kate to the core. "Sechem and I are old friends from a very long time ago. He was present at your birth. Invisible of course..." Jacob looked down, avoiding her eyes.

"You are being prepared for a great adventure, Kate. You need to be ready." At last he smiled.

Kate sat on the edge of her chair, and bit her lip anxiously as she watched her beloved father sipping at his mug, taking his time to formulate his thoughts. She yearned to hear what he had to say but knew from long experience that she couldn't rush him.

"I'll share just some of what I already know," he said. "You realise that Sechem is one of those blue beings that came when you were a child, don't you?"

Kate gasped. "You knew about them? Why didn't you tell me, Dad? I've been keeping them secret for years, I thought it was just me they visited."

"Yes, I knew about them." As he spoke, his blue eyes met her gaze. "I thought it best for you to think that they were just your special friends. I didn't want to fill your mind with too much cosmology or any kind of worries at such a young age."

This changed everything for Kate. A childhood spent having to deny the blue men's existence to her furious mother meant she had pushed the memory of them far, far inside her. If she had known that she had an ally in her father, things would have been very different. She looked at Jacob with fresh eyes, a mixed feeling of relief and disappointment brewing inside her.

"I wish I could've confided in you, Dad. I couldn't tell anybody, and I was so lonely. Why didn't you support me? Why didn't you tell me they were real?"

"You *knew* they were real Kate, despite everything Francine threw at you, and it was felt that gaining a degree of independence and self-assurance at such a young age would serve you well for the future."

Kate was struggling to take it all in. "So, you discussed me with the blue beings? You decided to let me suffer in silence for my own good?" A howl of pain welled up in Kate, years of suppressed grief and anxiety. Tears trickled down her cheeks as she remembered the loneliness of those hours locked away in the under-stairs cupboard, but it was as if the tears were washing away the memories, cleansing her mind of trauma, sweeping away debris to reveal a clean path. Before long her tears dried and she felt calmer.

Jacob watched his daughter with compassion. "I have always loved you Kate, and hard as it was, I did what was deemed best for you in the long run. You were different enough as a child from your friends anyway: your intelligence and your self-awareness set you apart and made life difficult for you at school. I didn't want to add to that."

Kate sniffed, and wiped her nose with the back of her hand.

Jacob continued. "As Sechem told you, the aim for this planet was for it to become a paradise on Earth, where all species, human and non-human, could co-exist in harmony, but events haven't unfolded that way. Earth could still be the most joyous place in the cosmos, but the future of the human race is still not firmly established among the stars. Humans will not die out, but their evolution is not assured, because they are distracted by violence and greed. You will find out more, much more, but not right now. In the meantime, promise me that you won't say a word to anyone about this."

"Of course, I promise. But Dad..."

Jacob interrupted her. "Kate, I know this is a lot to take in, but just ponder on our conversation and your time with Sechem. Let it settle in your consciousness and you will start to make some sense of it all. Trust that you are held in great love."

With this, he drained his mug, gave Kate one of his reassuring bear hugs and left the house more quickly than when he'd arrived, leaving her with her mind racing, attempting to process the momentous events that had just happened. She longed to pick up the phone again, but who could she talk to? She was sworn to secrecy. And who would believe her anyway? She couldn't imagine broaching the subject with Poppy – down-to-earth Poppy, who was so pragmatic and logical. Poppy would look at her askance, with her left eyebrow raised in that 'you've got to be kidding!' look of hers that signalled to Kate that she was on dodgy ground. When Kate once told her about the conspiracy theories she'd read about 9/11, up went Poppy's eyebrow. It was enough to stop Kate in her tracks and change the subject.

Oh, well. Kate decided to have an early night, and as Jacob suggested, just let the evening's experiences sink in. Work tomorrow would take her mind off things tomorrow, that's for sure. She was being moved to a different department, with a new boss – Helga someone or other – so she needed to be up bright-eyed and bushy tailed in the morning.

CHAPTER SIX

FRESH STARTS

'Follow your dreams, listen to your intuition –
your inner voice – to guide you.'

Katori Hall

Back in his little home Jacob frowned and paced up and down. It was all happening much too fast. How could he prepare Kate for what was to come with such limited time? He peered out of his front window, but what he expected to see in that darkened street he didn't know. The visitors he was familiar with didn't arrive by car.

Jacob thought Sechem had contacted Kate much too soon. Sechem had a reputation for being impetuous, but perhaps he'd initiated things sooner than intended because the situation had become urgent? He'd promised to wait until Kate was fully engaged and enlightened about her past, which was all going swimmingly with the meditations and mind-travel, but now things had gone off the scale and Jacob wasn't sure that Kate's inner resilience was enough to steer her through the upheavals she was to face. Goodness knows how she'd deal with the whole truth. He'd have to tell her sometime, but not yet. Jacob always preferred to let time take its course because things often settled into place of their own volition, but now there wasn't even the luxury of time, because Sechem's instructions had obviously been to bring Kate on board sooner rather than later. There would be a reason for that, Jacob was sure.

Clearly, he would have to move Kate's training along. She had still to learn to mind-walk and cross the barriers of time and space, and the sooner she did that the better. Everything had suddenly got very complicated, but trusting in the words he'd spoken to Kate earlier, he decided to let things settle in his consciousness, trying not to colour his judgement with parental concerns. Sometimes he felt the weight of responsibility was too much to bear and wished they could have chosen someone else, but that was not his path in this lifetime, nor Kate's.

Jacob now suspected that what had happened to him a year ago was no accident, and that it'd all been prearranged by Sechem and his co-time travellers, to enable him to evolve to Kate's level and support her mission. Of course, he didn't realise it at the time. He'd been busy at his desk at work when a portion of the ceiling had collapsed on him. It'd buried him in debris and a wooden lintel had knocked him senseless. Medics rushed him, covered in dust, to the nearest A&E where he lay dazed and confused on the hospital bed, only dimly aware of the bustle around him. He felt injections going into his arm and an oxygen mask on his face helped to clear his airways. He could sense the doctors were worried about him and all necessary precautions had to be taken in case he sued the firm for negligence.

Then he saw them. Outlines of tall misty blue figures wafted in and out of his vision. They were his old friends, whom he'd met many times before under different circumstances, but what were they doing here, in the hospital? They worked unseen around the hospital medics, but what shocked him was that they were changing the content of the drips, substituting hypodermics and adjusting valves. Nobody saw what was happening, and drifting off, Jacob tried to yell, but he was unable to speak. Jacob lost consciousness with the words 'Trust, Trust,' echoing in his mind.

When he awoke, he discovered that although he felt absolutely fine, fit as a fiddle in fact, his body showed some form of unknown infection. The doctors had no name for it and had never seen the likes of it before. All they could say was that his blood wasn't normal. The hospital staff noticed that he drifted off to sleep at inopportune moments, and they couldn't wake him. Over the next few weeks and months, they tried all sorts of treatment to no avail and in the end concluded that the change to his body was irreversible and discharged him. They obviously felt they had failed him by being unable to resolve the 'problem', but Jacob actually felt better than he had in years.

One morning a letter with his firm's official stamp came through the letterbox and dropped onto the mat. He'd picked it up and slit the envelope open instinctively knowing what was coming.

He skimmed over the niceties at the beginning of the letter and read:

> *We regret to inform you that your employment with us has been terminated for the following reason: your medical condition, which has not been and is unlikely to be resolved, means that you do not meet our minimum personal health requirements.*
>
> *We will be extremely sorry to see you go. We thank you for the service you have given us in the past.*
>
> *Please sign, date and return the enclosed form, which also acts as confirmation of receipt of this letter.*
>
> *Yours sincerely…*

Jacob had pulled the enclosure out of the envelope and discovered a form to be completed for payment of a generous annual pension straight into his bank account. They really didn't want him to dispute the termination and cause a rumpus. He'd laughed out loud and danced a jig round the room. He'd never liked working there in any case.

So now what? The space friends had done something to him in

that hospital, for sure, and he'd never felt so good – he patted his belly; he could do with losing some weight though – but he was wise enough to know there would be a reason for this turn of events. What had happened to him was obviously part of the pledge he had made at the beginning of this incarnation – the very reason for him being on the Earth in the first place – and the Galactic Command were calling it in.

Jacob faced his uncertain future with equanimity. Whatever they had prepared him for, he was ready for it.

* * *

Kate too was having to be comfortable with uncertainty – not just in her personal life and all that was taking place with the re-emergence of her blue friends – but at work as well. She'd been informed a few days ago that she was being moved to a new department, but had been told no more than that. She hoped it would be fulfilling enough to quell her growing desire to find a new job. Today, the reassignment was taking place, and she'd been instructed to clear her desk and take her belongings with her to the 'East Wing' of the building, a much smaller, modern block of offices and technical suites where all who worked were subject to a gagging clause, or a 'Non-Disclosure Agreement' as the form she was asked to sign called it. She wasn't allowed to talk to anyone about what she did there.

Kate wasn't entirely comfortable about signing the new contract, especially as she'd been having thoughts lately about finding another job, but she read through the Terms & Conditions assiduously and found the clause regarding termination of the agreement. She had to give one month's written notice, and similarly they had to do the same if they wanted to dismiss her for any reason other than gross misconduct. Fair enough. With a sigh, she realised there was no pay increase involved.

"Do hurry up Ms Greene," her new boss Helga Mortensen hissed.

When Kate first clapped eyes on her as she'd entered the East Wing, her heart sank. This was the woman who had given her an absolute grilling on her first interview, and now, she was her immediate line manager.

Kate signed the contract, which Helga Mortensen snatched away, and instructed a minion to photocopy.

"What will my new role here be?" Kate asked, determined not to be intimidated by the almost feline looking woman who was scowling at her.

"You'll do whatever I ask you to do."

"And what's that likely to be, Helga?" Kate insisted, feeling aggrieved that she was being treated like some kind of imbecile.

"Ms Mortensen to you," Helga spat. "Mostly data analysis, some research – don't worry, nothing too taxing."

It didn't exactly bode well.

CHAPTER SEVEN

A CALL TO ACTION

We of this evolutionary planet seek out the energy givers, those who can supply the needs of others without hesitation or self doubting. Here and now we are speaking to you directly, if you feel yourself to be such a one.

We seek selfless dedication to the task of raising mankind above its previous level of existence. When this has been successfully accomplished, man will have escaped the endless cycle of war, hate, greed, and all those things which degrade the soul.

To be elevated is to experience joy, love and such harmony in the soul as to be beyond expression in mere words. The value of this opportunity to raise your own soul is immeasurable. Count on us for full support. God bless you

It was only a matter of days before Sechem came again. Kate was in her favourite armchair idly glancing through a magazine, after what could only be described as the most boring day ever, at work. Helga Mortensen had tasked her with filing a mountain of data – mostly incomprehensible graphs – into the computer database. It was tedious work. Mind you, she found it hard to concentrate these days, as her thoughts were dominated by Sechem, and what it might be that he had in store for her. The irony didn't escape her that she had the dullest job in the world and the most exciting private life.

As she thumbed through the recipe section of the magazine,

suddenly there he was, standing in her front room, staring intently at her with his amazing warm eyes. Her mouth dropped open in astonishment. She saw him clearly this time and thankfully he did look quite human. He appeared to be on the verge of laughter. His appearance was still not completely normal though – whilst at first glance he was just a tall, slender man with a long, narrow face, when she looked more closely she could see a shimmering cobalt haze around him. Kate sensed he was giving her plenty of time to study him before he spoke.

He smiled, but his words shocked her to the core.

"It has been suggested by the Galactic Command and the Spiritual Council that we abandon Earth humans to their own devices and let them get on with the mess of their own creation, until they destroy each other. These great Lords have watched and waited patiently for so very long. They have sent envoys, people of special talent and with the highest spiritual values, many Masters...but what happened? Wherever the teachings were taken into the hearts of humans, it has had some lasting effect, yet instead of using this knowledge for bettering the planet, those same teachings have been misdirected and misinterpreted. In the present, as it was in the past, they are twisted and reinterpreted to instigate wars for selfish ends and power struggles. This is the tragedy of it all."

Kate leapt to her feet, her magazine falling aside. "Abandon us? You can't abandon us! Please, no. I've only just heard about this and now you're giving up on us..."

He smiled again. "I like your spirit but they're reaching the end of the road. They've tried the soft and patient approach, but it's had little effect. So, the Galactic Command and Spiritual Council are considering whether to terminate the Earth mission. It's either that or they'll try something that will shake everyone out of the complacency and ignorance that prevails on Earth. They are currently debating this dilemma."

Kate gasped in disbelief. What did they have in mind? "But what are we supposed to do? There's not much the average person can do, even if they wanted to," Kate protested. "Shouldn't you be making yourself known to the elected leaders?"

"Don't you think we haven't tried?"

"So, why you are telling me? I'm no one. I have no influence, no political clout."

"The majority of those in command are not open to communicating with time-travellers or spirit beings. They don't have the psychic abilities needed to connect with our vibrations, as you do, my dear friend."

Kate looked at him, scared at the meaning behind his words. "But, but..."

Sechem reached out to hold her hands, sending a huge wave of energy rushing through her, like that she felt in her head when she time-travelled to his homeland. "You have immense power, Kate, that you're only just becoming aware of. You can be an agent for change. Already I can see that there is a fire inside you that will burn ever brighter. You can be the conduit through which a massive transformation can take place. Even in the midst of corruption, war and greed, there remains a community that cares what happens to their planet, and you will guide them towards a brighter future."

Kate gazed at him desperately. It was so hard for her to comprehend the enormity of what he was suggesting. She felt so insignificant in the face of what was needed to be done. But whilst she struggled with this, part of her couldn't help but acknowledge that what he said was true: there was a growing awareness in ordinary folk that we couldn't continue to treat Mother Earth with such disrespect, and thanks to the internet we knew and understood more about the plight of humans and animals alike, so where there was injustice, there was often a group of people protesting and campaigning, fighting for a fairer world. There was less resignation these days, less willingness to accept the status quo, and a fate worse than death.

Kate slowly withdrew her hands from his, noticing that her energised state remained.

“People in general do care, I agree, but do those in power care? Remember when the whole world rose-up in protest about the war in Iraq, but those in power went ahead anyway. Look where that has landed us,” she said thoughtfully.

“This is true, but inside everyone is a potential goodness that can eclipse even the most negative character traits.” He paused and scrutinised her face for a reaction before continuing. “The good news is that the situation on Earth is monitored by Melchizedek, Paradise Sons, Elohim, Arch-angels and other commanders in a Space Alliance. They keep a watchful eye on those some of you call, The Illuminati, and the shadowy collection of political, military, banking, media, intelligence, business, and other globalists embedded throughout the centres of power worldwide. We call them the Secret Government.”

“The Secret Government? That sounds ominous.” Kate was getting used to speaking with her mind, without sounding the words aloud. It was becoming second nature now.

“Many within those groups are connected to and are currently interacting with negative, self-serving races from other worlds. This does not bode well for those on Earth who do not wish to be controlled by anyone other than themselves.”

Kate swallowed. The idea, though disturbing, was one she’d heard before. She remembered something she’d read in a BBC News online magazine where Jonathan Duffy reported that, ‘The Bilderberg group, an elite coterie of Western thinkers and power-brokers, has been accused of fixing the fate of the world behind closed doors.’ Kate had investigated further, and to her utter amazement, she saw the impressive list of people who attend the Bilderberg conferences. It encompassed well-known figures from politics, prime ministers, presidents, EU commissioners, and others from the military, financial institutions, corporations and the media. Were they working for the benefit of the world, or for themselves?

Sechem continued. “This by the way, is not where the only danger lies. Those who monitor Earth are extremely worried about the use of nuclear power and devices of war. Misuse could put your planet out of action for habitation for hundreds and hundreds of years.”

“It doesn’t bear thinking about,” Kate groaned and put her hand to her head. “Is this why UFOs are so often seen over nuclear establishments?”

Sechem walked over to the window and looked out. But the little street was empty of people. Kate noticed his interest.

“They’ll all be watching their favourite TV programmes,” she said.

Sechem turned back with a huge sigh. “Nobody is interested, that’s the problem. The danger also lies in the Dark Projects of the secret government – run by those who are *really* in control of your world, hidden behind your elected leaders. It does not help to simply point the finger and grumble. Those who already know of these things have done little about them so far.

“You may ask why would humans take notice of all this now? It is a rhetorical question of course, as there have always been dark forces for you to pit yourselves against. But remember, in this case, they are few and you are many. It’s time for humanity to wake up and stop being complacent.”

. “So, there is still hope, then?” Kate asked. “I’m not sure exactly how I’d go about changing the world, but if there’s still hope, I will do what I can. It will take a pretty charismatic figure to make an impact though, certainly not the likes of me.”

Sechem merely grunted and drifted slowly around the room, shimmering. He passed his long fingers over her books and ornaments.

"So many are willing to leave the most important work to others," he said. "That is the problem. All must take responsibility for the future." He stopped by her television set and peered into it and grunted again. "It's all too easy to do that, especially when it's dangerous to speak up. We are aware, sadly, that many who dare to challenge the establishment often suffer as a result. Freak accidents, supposed suicides, disappearances…Even worse, some have been subjected to mind control."

Kate blanched. "You're frightening me now. I feel totally out of my depth."

"Do not be afraid. The fate of these poor individuals was because they were on their own, and therefore weak. This is why they were scapegoats. There is strength in numbers. A strength that cannot be ignored. What's required is that *all* whistleblowers concerned with global interests get together, and *en masse* disclose and prove what they know. Why do you not have a Whistleblower's Convention? Then, it would be very difficult for individuals to be selected and damaged in the ways I've stated. The sheer numbers of people 'blowing the whistle' simultaneously, would be too obvious and if any harm came to them it could not be ignored and passed off as suicide or accident. We applaud the Exo-politics Group and the Citizens Hearing on Disclosure held in 2013 in America. This is helpful to us for it also provides concrete evidence of our presence on and around Planet Earth and discloses the fact that your elected governing bodies are aware of our presence."

"I don't know…" Kate protested. "I find politics so self-serving that I've kind of given up on it of late."

Suddenly, Sechem stopped speaking and placed a long finger on his lips. "Be quiet. Someone is listening."

Kate tensed, looking round and although she could see nothing, she could sense that the energy was changing in the room. She shivered as a cold wave passed through her body. Sechem had gone absolutely still. She watched spellbound as the glimmering blue haze enveloping him grew larger and denser and then engulfed her. At that very moment, she saw a black shape jump across the room towards her. Then another dark shape reared up behind Sechem. Long black tentacles reached around the still blue form of Sechem and Kate. Kate knew they were about to be attacked.

"Sechem, Sechem! Do something!" she pleaded with her mind.

"Stay calm Kate and repel them with your intent. Do not engage with them, but strengthen the shield I have cast around you. Do it now."

It was as if time stood still, for she knew not how long they battled with the dark forces; but imbued with his energy she found she could cloak herself with a protective shield of... Well what was it? Later the nearest she could come to describing the energy she surrounded herself with was love.

She watched as the dark energy lost its power and diminished, edging towards the corners of the room. A dog began barking in the street outside. It seemed to break the spell. Sechem's blue haze flared as it withdrew from her and he regained his form. The inky black shapes vanished, as if they had never existed.

Sechem let out a breath. "Well done, Kate. That was a close call. Now do you see how urgent the situation has become? Whilst I'm here trying to enlighten you, there are other, darker forces intent on turning you towards the path of evil. Next time, I won't be here to protect you, so we must develop your powers as quickly as we can."

Kate nodded mutely, terrified of what she had just seen, and also of what lay ahead for her, in the future. Events were unfolding so fast and all was so new to her, that it was hard not to feel overwhelmed.

* * *

Back in a dimly lit room in Washington DC the fearsome giant form was eyed with trepidation by the men gathered there. Gork, as usual had commanded there were to be no bright lights in the room. Despite the gloom, he was wearing dark glasses. The men were grateful for that. Anyone who had looked into his eyes experienced nightmares for months on end, sometimes for years, and there was a rumour of someone actually having to be sectioned after staring into the eyes of the creature. The men standing in the room also wore dark glasses but for a different reason; they naively believed that it prevented Gork from seeing their expressions of fear. They hadn't yet realised that he could read their minds as easily as reading a book.

Gork's words were harsh and guttural. "Have our latest mind-workers succeeded in reaching her yet? Tell me they have."

There was prolonged silence in the room followed by a shuffling of feet. One or two coughed quietly. At that precise moment, the door from the corridor opened and a tall thin man slid in. A shaft of light pierced the room as he entered.

"Damn you, whoever you are. Shut that door," Gork thundered, shielding his face from the sudden flash of light. "Who are you to come without permission?"

Before he had a chance to reply one of the group, a heavily decorated General festooned with medals stepped up to the interloper and put a hand on his shoulder.

"Sir, this is Silas Pearce. He's working with our intelligence team. He's invaluable as he can work under the radar. He can help us keep an eye on Kate Greene. We are placing him in the firm where she works."

Silas, looking smug, nodded and looked around the room.

His colleagues murmured greetings towards him, glad to have the attention lifted from them.

* * *

Kate sat down, trying to recover from the frightening experience with the dark shapes. Sechem appeared to be unconcerned and had regained his composure immediately.

"Now, where were we?" he repeated as if nothing had happened.

"Whistleblowers." Kate reminded him.

"Whistleblowers frequently face reprisals, sometimes at the hands of the organisation or group they've accused, sometimes from related organisations, and sometimes under law. Anybody who says anything that questions dictatorial institutions will never find another job, never have a career, will be harassed and hectored, will never find any peace, and likely may be assassinated. Edward Snowden did that, and the response was no diplomatic immunity, but no death sentence; no chance of living a free life and sanctions against anyone who might accept him as a responsible citizen."

Kate sighed. "I can't imagine anyone taking that chance… I remember reading about a 'Litmus Test' imposed by the Commander-in-Chief of the US on whether military commanders would lead their troops to fire upon US citizens during an event of civil unrest. Those who said no to that were dismissed. Doesn't this mean that dissent is impossible? That if we don't toe the line, we will be disempowered in some way?"

Sechem nodded. "Look what happened recently in the dispute over an oil pipe line on tribal land? The 'protectors' – those who still regard Mother Earth as sacred – were badly abused by the security forces. Happily, some of the military there withdrew from the battle and would not fight, but who knows what happened to them afterwards?

What I am saying is that it takes courage to stand up and fight for a more just and equitable world, but that if more and more people do so, a momentum could be reached that would be unstoppable."

Kate sighed knowing that what Sechem said was true, but where did she fit in? Sechem wasn't telling her all this just to pass the time.

"You were wanting me to change the world, if I remember rightly," she said, half in jest. Although she was still completely in awe of Sechem, signs of her fiery spirit were returning.

"Ah, yes, your role in the future of the planet." Kate saw that Sechem decided not to rise to her sarcasm and knew he was too wise and too patient for that. "Although you may not believe it now, you will learn that you have a great ability to influence others; that you can impart a message that will transform the way people think. Not just their views but their connection with each other. You will enable humanity to join as one."

"Er, will I?" replied Kate. "Any chance of a pointer as to how I'm supposed to do that?"

He sat opposite her and reached for her hands. Kate started, as she once again felt a shockwave of energy ripple through her.

"You see? You can feel it!" said Sechem. "Always remember that you are receptive to incredible forces, that you can channel them. It must seem impossible to you at the moment, but with time, you will learn the strength of your abilities and will realise what needs to be done. I am always here to guide you, but I cannot force you to do anything. The decision must always be yours." His blue haze intensified so much that Kate drew back from his energy and released her hands from his. Her head was starting to reel from all the information.

As she gathered herself, suddenly a memory came to her from a book, that she'd found utterly fascinating. Its relevance was astounding. She hurried over to the bookshelf and reached for it. It was a biography of the famous astronomer Carl Sagan. She pointed to a sentence with a trembling finger. Dr Sagan was once reported to have said, “Star visitors are here as missionaries.”

“Is that you? Is that who he was referring to?”

Sechem nodded, smiling.

“I have read this passage so many times, wondering what he meant by that, and now I understand!” Kate’s eyes shined with delight, a brilliant turquoise glint in them.

“I am glad to hear it, my dear. It will make my job a lot easier. As star observers, we’ve noticed several different sections of human society. Some have it good and are more than happy to let their lives continue as they are. Why would you expect any change in their attitude? Others have to struggle to achieve what they feel they need but are managing this reasonably well. They enjoy the adrenalin that drives them forward. So why would they change and jeopardise what they’ve worked so hard to gain? Then there are those who struggle and struggle and feel they are getting nowhere. They’re not making any headway, but they still try. But most people on your planet don’t see any hope at all. Their daily lives are just about existing, nothing more. A miserable fight for survival until they finally fail and release the soul.

“Often it is in these last two groups that great souls surface and work, for there is huge incentive and nothing to lose. What is not yet recognised by all groups is that there is a further motivation, the greatest of all: that of preserving the entire human species.”

Kate sighed, once again realising the truth of what he said. Most people have no reason to look further than their own little lives; they have no interest or connect to the wider world around them; they are so disconnected from Mother Nature and each other, that they think this is all there is: birth, school, work, death, the end. This collective apathy of society always frustrated her, she didn’t want to be part of it but was she really that different? Her own routine was like clockwork; dull as dishwater and only alleviated by the few friends she had, and now this otherworldly connection. Was she really ready to lead the ranks of whistleblowers and activists, making a stand for better world that seemed so far removed from the one she currently lived in? As she pondered this, to her astonishment, Sechem suddenly vanished.

Someone was tapping timidly on her front door, so quietly that Kate almost missed it.

"Who can that be?" she said to herself, making a mental note to get the doorbell fixed. Most of my visitors these days don't knock, she thought wryly as she opened the door.

Her grey-haired neighbour Mrs Thomas from across the road stood hesitating on the doorstep, an uncertain look on her face.

Kate smiled. She liked her neighbour even though they had only met a few times on the street, but as she registered her expression she wondered what was wrong.

"Excuse me for the intrusion," Mrs Thomas said, "but there's something I thought you ought to know." She plucked timidly at her sleeve. "I've been meaning to tell you for a while now, but didn't know if you'd like it."

"Why don't you come in?" Kate said gently.

Mrs Thomas took a hurried step backward. "Oh, I won't do that. I mean, I must get back, I've left my front door open..."

"Okay." Kate smiled. "What do you want to tell me?"

"Well, I'm not sure what it is, in fact I have no idea what it is..." She cleared her throat and soldiered on, obviously finding it difficult to have to impose like this. "Well, did you know that there are often coloured lights playing over your house, even when you're out? I went out into the street to see if I could find out where the lights were coming from, but I couldn't see anything."

Kate leapt out on to the pavement and craned her head to gaze above her house, trying to see what Mrs Thomas was referring to.

"Oh, it's not happening now, my dear, they've gone. But I just wanted to check that you're all right, and that you knew about it." Mrs Thomas peered at Kate, a quizzical expression on her face.

"Umm… Oh, thanks for letting me know. That's so strange, isn't it? I've never seen them and have no idea what they could be," Kate replied, not quite truthfully. She had a good idea what or rather where the lights emanated from, but she wasn't about to go into that with Mrs Thomas. "But thank you for telling me. Will you tell me next time it happens? I'd like to know as much as you as to what it could be."

"If you say so, dear," Mrs Thomas said. "Night night." The sweet lady gave Kate's hand a light squeeze, and retreated to her safe little house.

Kate closed the door and went back into the living room. Sechem had returned and was sitting in Jacob's chair. He got up as she came back into the room.

"What's all that about then?" she asked. "Were the lights because of you?"

"Yes, Kate. We're keeping a watch over you," he said. "Don't you realise you are important to us? Those lights are only visible to those with a clear vision, such as yours. Your neighbour has inadvertently revealed she has an affinity with you – don't forget this."

"Right, I won't forget."

Sechem hadn't finished what he had to say. Mrs Thomas' interruption was merely a hiatus. “I want you to understand that I speak for the Command, that is, *my* Command.”

“I see,” replied Kate. She didn’t, but she was getting used to feeling baffled.

“A little background information will help you to grasp our meaning. We’ll be as brief as we can and will restrict ourselves to your own universe, though you may know there are other universes quite unlike your own.”

Kate frowned. “Can I ask a question?” She felt the room getting hotter and hotter and wondered if it was his energy.

“Of course. Keep it brief, please.” He leaned in closer and she took a step back.

“Why are you telling me now? What do you think I can do as a person who has no clout and absolutely no interest or intention of getting involved with politics?”

“Those were two questions. The answer to the first question is: Now is the time.” He laughed and for a moment, his voice so dulcet Kate thought he’d break into song. “If we don’t do it now, it may be too late. The answer to the second question is: You are our human intermediary and can act on our behalf of those who don’t now, or who will never communicate with us themselves. You’ll be ridiculed of course, but that may be the worst that can happen to you. There exists disbelief in us and in uncomfortable facts. But others will listen. It is VERY IMPORTANT that they listen.”

Kate opened her mouth to ask another question, but he put up his skinny hand and stopped her.

“You have interrupted my flow. Where was I?”

“You were saying how important this was.” Kate replied.

"To understand what trouble the Earth is in, we need to go back to the beginning, to the very start of existence. All souls, and we mean *all* souls, began at Source, that which you call God or the Great Creator or whatever name you decide to give it. That was the 'I AM' moment, the start of a long journey to experience all things before the soul could return to Source. Each soul has an inbuilt need to regroup, to go back to Source and it's this need that drives it through the soul journey, going through deep space, until it reaches a cosmic body, a planet, and in your case a planet that is in your universe, and within your galaxy."

Kate had an image of little flashes of energy swimming towards a planet, just like sperm struggling towards an egg.

"To fully experience life and interact with others, these souls needed to develop a form. The form was light at first, and then became denser as the need to experience grew stronger. The forms developed bodies that grew according to environmental conditions and nourishment on each planet. This was also strongly influenced through genetic engineering by Celestial Beings who understood evolution." He moved about the room like some blue, ethereal ghost. Kate resisted the urge to touch him.

"It is the nature of existence in any form whatsoever, whether it is bacterial, plant, animal or viral to increase, expand, proliferate and reproduce itself. Would you agree?"

"Yes." Kate watched, fascinated by the stream of colours that came from him as he gesticulated. They went straight through anything he touched, proving to her that his own form was not solid but purely vibrational.

"Nature is always adapting to conditions in order to survive. Remember also that the whole purpose of existence is to grow and expand through experience. This need to continue evolving also took place on other cosmic bodies, that is, all planets. The time and extent for this to happen varied tremendously. Some became more spiritually advanced whilst others progressed technically but ignored spiritual directives. This resulted in fighting and disagreement and a split occurred into what we will call the 'Dark Hats' and 'Light Hats'. The old theme of good and evil."

Kate nodded obediently but these enormous philosophical themes were very hard to take on board and she wasn't sure where he was going with them.

"Did you know that your own species is among those that have divided in your evolution between spiritual and technical advancement? You too have your Dark Hats and Light Hats, and something in between. You know, the ones who don't care one way or the other. 'Sheeples' we call them. We'll talk later about these divisions within one species. Remind us if we forget. We know *you* will not forget and will come up with a question," he said pointedly. "Did you know you are often referred to as 'the one who asks questions'?"

"I think it is often the only way to get answers," Kate retorted, defensive now. She'd frequently been remonstrated for asking too many questions at school, but often those teachers didn't have the answers she'd sought. Asking too many questions had also put off possible boyfriends. "Don't spoil things," they'd said. "Enjoy the moment." She knew all too well what moment they wanted to enjoy.

"What do you want me to do? Where are you going with all this?"

Sechem ignored her and carried on. It was patently obvious he had his own agenda and wouldn't stop until he'd finished what he had to impart. Kate settled back into her chair, suddenly exhausted. She tried to stay awake, but her eyes drooped, like a child who tries hard not to go to sleep.

"Wake up!"

Jolted, she sat up straight.

"As I mentioned before, since we cannot communicate with those who are not receptive to us, we need you to disseminate our message to as many people as possible. A good place to start would be to learn public speaking, to become competent at addressing large numbers of people."

Kate opened her mouth to object, and then closed it again. It was useless to protest. She'd learnt that he usually got his way.

A lengthy silence followed. Kate's mind drifted again and her eyes closed. In her minds-eye, Sechem was floating around her room like a giant bubble, with liquid petrol-colours swirling on the surface. Much later, she realised she'd fallen asleep and he'd gone.

CHAPTER EIGHT

SEIZING THE DAY

Open yourself to possibilities, even existence in form other than the human body. Open your mind to other realms, other dimensions, other worlds. They all exist. Hold love in your being and you will know all.

The Ascended Masters

The next morning Kate woke to sun streaming through her window. She leapt out of bed full of good intentions – it was going to be a great day. Sechem's efforts had not been in vain, as Kate realised that she couldn't sit back and do nothing. He wasn't going to let her, for one thing, of that she was sure. Sechem's information should be shared, but how to do it was the question.

She started by telephoning her father before she left for work.

"Dad, I want to start to contribute more in at our spiritual circle and thought I could do a talk on what Sechem's told me about human evolution. I mean, it's bound to be a receptive audience, don't you think? I won't tell them about Sechem, just introduce a couple of the themes he's mentioned. Is it a good idea?" She waited eagerly for his answer.

"I don't see why not. They're always looking for different kinds of input, and it'll be good for you," Jacob replied, knowing that this was in fact a crucial next step for Kate. She had to feel competent speaking about these matters, eventually, even to sceptics.

Kate breathed a sigh of relief and put the phone down. If her dad approved, she'd share what Sechem had told her. She just needed a bit of time to think about how she could best present the information.

As she was putting her coat on in the hall, a brochure from the local borough's Adult Education Programme dropped through her letterbox. When Kate picked it up, it fell open at a section entitled Public Speaking Workshop. She grinned. Sechem might just as well have placed it under her nose.

She took his heavy-handed hint and the following week, she went along for the first session. Kate was relieved to see she was not alone in being a little fraught. A small group of people standing around looking anxious, were waiting to see what would be expected of them, so she went over to join them.

"Hi, my name's Kate. Are you nervous too?"

A young man of about twenty replied. "You're not joking. My boss has sent me because I've got to start doing presentations at work. I'm bricking it. What about you?"

Kate hesitated. What should she say? I want to learn how to speak about aliens?

"Well, I'm just hoping to learn a new skill in case it comes in handy," she said, side-stepping the question.

As it turned out, the course was just what she needed, full of practical tips on how to project her voice, keep an audience's attention and disseminate information in an accessible way. She found out that she was rather good at it, and so too was the young man, Gareth, who was a bit of a natural comic, which gave his presentations a light-hearted touch. Kate was quick to catch-on that it was possible to convey complex information with clarity, especially with a bit of humour thrown in. It gave her the courage and confidence to start thinking about what Sechem had asked her to do, even though she was still very unsure what exactly was involved.

Several weeks later, on the final night of the course, Kate picked up her bag ready to leave the hall, but the teacher stopped her at the door.

"Don't go just yet," she said. "How do you feel about taking a Public Speaking exam? It'll give you confidence."

Kate hesitated. She'd enjoyed the classes much more than she'd expected, but she didn't really need any qualifications in the subject.

Seeing Kate's reluctance, the teacher pressed on. "I'd like you to enter the London Academy of Music and Dramatic Art examination for speaking in public. I think you've got talent Kate, and who knows where it might lead? Here are the details." She handed Kate an envelope, smiled and turned away. "Think about it," she said.

Well, Kate was never one to turn down a challenge – and as a bit of an antidote to the grind of office life, which had gone from bad to frankly unbearable since her reassignment – she decided to enter. All too soon, the Saturday arrived when she needed to get the train into London and sit the exam.

The journey from Bournemouth to Paddington was only two and a half hours, and she'd got her iPhone and headphones so she could listen to some music on the way, and had packed herself a snack and a flask of coffee. She was enjoying herself. As she boarded the train, she noticed another passenger dart out of the station waiting room and jump on the carriage behind hers. She thought she recognised him from work, but couldn't be sure.

She had to hop on the Tube at Paddington and get the District Line to Earl's Court. The underground was absolutely packed with humanity, seemingly from every culture: Japanese tourists, a smiling German family, two women in full burqas, and an array of different languages to boot. Kate took a deep breath and headed down into the stairs to the platform, and so did the guy from work. Or maybe he was just a 'lookey-likey' as they used to say on the TV, a doppelganger? When she changed to the Piccadilly line, there he was again, at the end of the carriage, head obscured by a newspaper. If it wasn't so jam-packed, she'd go over and say hello.

Eventually, Kate found the Academy and was asked to wait in a rather dusty, narrow corridor alongside other hopefuls. As she looked around, she saw framed photographs of famous actors lining the walls. Most of the pictures were faded and had clearly been there for quite some time. She clutched a sealed envelope she'd been given containing a list of subjects that candidates could choose from. Every so often a door opened and a clerk emerged, his tie slightly askew, a flustered look on his face.

Each chair was filled with an applicant; some looked nonchalant, as if this was a normal day, others, clearly nervous, twitched and fidgeted with their notes. Eventually, the door at the far end of the passage opened and a middle-aged man sporting a goatee beard, a multi coloured silk scarf and rather large rings on his fingers stepped out, looking grand and important. Kate thought for one brief moment that he would start reciting Shakespeare, but he was to be their invigilator.

"You can all open your envelopes now," he said.

Kate tore hers open and read down the long, printed list of subjects they could choose from, such as 'Cottage Industries' and 'The French Revolution'. She stopped at 'Psychic Phenomena' and smiled in relief. 15 minutes later, she walked into the hall and took her stand. As she spoke, the man made notes but didn't look at her once. So much for eye contact, Kate thought.

"We will let you know," he said as she finished. "Thank you. Please let the next person in."

It was a bit of an anti-climax to be honest, but Kate thought she'd done okay. Just a couple of stutters and a brief hesitation, fluent nonetheless, but boy, did she feel shattered. She'd have to remember that this public speaking lark could be tiring, and make allowances for that.

On the train home, her eyelids began to droop, as the motion of the train lulled her towards a nap. When she opened them again, they were drawing into Bournemouth station, and as the carriage doors opened, she saw the man again, this time wearing dark glasses. He looked directly at her and she felt an air of menace exude from him. He wanted her to see him, to know she had been followed.

As Kate drove home from the station, she felt a little shaken, and kept one eye on the mirrors to see if he was still tailing her. It was all a bit odd, she thought, because she hadn't told a soul at work about her public speaking exam, and anyway, why would it matter? It didn't say in her contract that she couldn't have hobbies, for goodness sake. Over the next few days at work, Kate looked for the man again, but didn't see him, and eventually all thoughts of being followed were forgotten as she went about her daily routine.

At the spiritual circle the following week, she asked David, one of the regular hosts, if she could say a few words. He readily agreed, grateful to step back and allow others to take the lead. When the time came, David handed over to Kate – there was no need to rise from her chair or take the stage: the circle was very informal. She cleared her throat and spoke for ten minutes or so on her own methods of self-hypnosis to achieved deep mediation. She told them of her concerns about the future of the planet, hinting that we are all part of a greater planetary family and that we should respect our beautiful Mother Earth. She wanted to keep it short and sweet, and just see how she felt. She got a warm response from her friends in the circle and it helped her to feel more confident in her abilities.

A few days later, a brown envelope arrived. With her hands shaking a little Kate opened it to find a letter of congratulation and a certificate.

She had passed the public speaking exam. Sechem and Jacob would be pleased.

Kate had always tried to be mindful that as well as her dealings with Sechem, she had a full-time job to concentrate on, so when she was at work, she tried to shelve everything to do with her private life. She was good at compartmentalising things – a childhood trait – but the company she worked for was good at compartmentalising things too: she knew its main line of business was to design software that enabled efficient satellite functionality, but what those satellites were used for, she didn't know, nor was there much interaction between departments. Where she now worked, with Helga Mortensen as her boss, she found she was mostly responsible for administration – routine clerical work – and still she couldn't determine from the data she processed what *exactly* the company did. It was all rather secretive. Occasionally there would be details of technicians and scientists who were working on a specific programme in another branch or even in other countries, but any finer detail was coded or censored.

She mentioned this to Poppy one Saturday, when they met at their favourite café for lunch.

"You know what, Poppy, I don't even know what it is that SatData Consolidated really does, and even if I did, I couldn't talk to you about it, because I had to sign that NDA thingy. They could be launching satellites to spy on people for all I know."

"Doesn't that bother you, then?" Poppy asked, dipping her biscotti into her latté.

"Yeah, it really does. Now I'm in this new department, I feel really disconnected, like I'm just a tiny cog in a machine, but I don't actually know what the machine does. I just know that I'm keeping it all oiled for maximum efficiency."

"Well do something about it then. An intelligent girl like you could get a job anywhere. Life's too short to spend it doing something you don't enjoy."

"Yeah, maybe you're right. The only good thing about it is that it's easy, so I've got plenty of time for the spiritual circle. You should come along some time, Poppy."

"You're kidding me! You know I don't do all that airy-fairy stuff."

Her brush-off slightly hurt Kate, especially as Poppy knew how much it meant to her. Perhaps she didn't realise quite how much Kate needed to share what was going on in her life, but now obviously wasn't the time. Had she been able to speak more openly, Poppy may have pointed out the interesting parallels between Sechem's talk of interplanetary communication and those satellites Kate's company were monitoring, orbiting in space above them as they spoke.

Not only was Kate's work relatively easy, but the offices were based just outside town, the impressive modern glass and steel building incongruously tucked away down a long, tree-lined drive on what had once been a large private country estate hidden in the beautiful Dorset countryside. Purpose-built for the company, there was a good size car park shaded by trees and even a refectory selling decent coffee and light meals. When the weather was good, Kate sometimes walked to work – it only took her 25 minutes at a brisk pace.

Kate didn't have much to do with the head office in Surrey. All she knew was that her department had a supporting role in three new satellites due for launch that summer, that apparently were involved in monitoring and predicting environmental activity – that had to be a good thing, surely?

What irked Kate most was her boss Helga who never seemed to like her from the moment they saw each other. When their eyes had met during the interview for her original post, Kate felt a shiver of fear run down her spine, because it was as if hatred blazed out of Helga's eyes. The woman's body language was incredibly domineering and rude, and she was incapable of saying a courteous word.

Kate was surprised when she got the job and then when she started to work directly under Mortensen, the feeling of dislike became mutual, though Kate couldn't put her finger on why. Helga was a tall, lean woman with what could only be described as having vixenlike features in that her eyes were almond-shaped, her nose was long and blunt and her ears – which were always visible because she wore her hair in a tight knot – seemed to be set higher than usual and they had a certain pointed quality to them, in fact, Kate thought they were her best feature. She always wore grey or black and this coupled with her silver-grey hair gave her a steely quality. Kate wouldn't mess with this person for sure. As for cracking a joke? She'd never dare try.

Not long after her public speaking examination, Kate made the mistake of hitting the snooze button on her alarm once too often and oversleeping. Arriving late, she pulled up to a full car park and had to drive up and down rows of cars before finding the only free parking bay. Still hoping to get into the building before her lateness was noticed, Kate dashed through the large, automatic doors of the East Wing, crossed the polished hall, entered the lift, and pressed the button for the third floor, breathless and harried.

She stepped out of the lift to find Helga was waiting with a face like thunder. "You're late."

"Only four minutes..."

"That's four minutes too late, and it's nowhere near good enough." Helga bellowed, not waiting for Kate to finish. "Mr P wants to see you, now. Jump to it."

Through the separating glass partition Kate saw the big cheese – the Director of the East Wing – pacing restlessly up and down, his overhung belly wobbling like jelly about to slip off a plate. An unbidden thought flashed through Kate's mind: I'd hate to see him in bed. Horrors! She suppressed a giggle at her mental vision, and walked into Mr P's office with Helga.

He stopped his pacing and glared at them as they paused in the doorway.

"What are you smirking at, girl? This is a serious matter. Come in and sit down," he said, adding, "both of you."

Helga's mouth tightened as they did as they were told. She obviously wasn't used to being spoken to like this.

"There has been a data non-conformance issue which we've tracked back to your department Ms Mortensen. The tracking codes in the files sent to HQ were incorrect. Do you know how serious this is?"

"Apologies Sir," said Helga, surprising Kate with her obsequiousness. And then, "It was Miss Greene's responsibility to send the codes. It was just a matter of extrapolating them from the data entries..."

Mr P leaned towards Helga. "You run this department Mortensen, therefore it is your responsibility and yours alone. What we have now is the potential for orbiting irregularities and possibly an impact on some transmissions. This does not look good for SatData Consolidated."

He thrust a wad of files into Kate's arms. "Sort it out Ms Greene, without delay," he barked and waved them both out of his way. "Shut the door on your way out."

For the first time it occurred to Kate that perhaps her job wasn't as dull as she thought it was; maybe she found the work easy where others didn't? This was the first time she'd had any inclination that there were major implications if she got things wrong. Those tracking codes, though – she'd double-checked them all and had them passed by the new quality control guy…Simon, was that his name?

Helga pressed her lips together; clearly this dressing-down aimed at her wasn't what she expected. "Come with me, into my office. Now." She snapped her fingers, and Kate followed, her colleagues giving her sympathetic smiles as she closed the door to Helga's domain. Neither of them enjoyed being thrown together like this, but they went through the stack of files to work out where the errors were – but everything seemed to be in order. Helga frowned. This was most irregular.

Whenever Helga drew near, Kate's skin went all prickly, as if she'd entered some kind of electrical field. It was a most uncomfortable feeling, and one she couldn't explain. She forced herself to ignore her instinct to back away and worked through the files all day with Helga at her side, until the clock said she could leave. They still couldn't find the problem with the codes.

On her way to her car, Kate pulled out her mobile and phoned Poppy, who could be relied on to make Kate feel better in any situation, and after her trying day, Kate needed a good dose of calm.

"Fancy a coffee, Pops?" she asked.

"I'm on it Katie, see you at Tom's in five."

They met at Tom's Coffee Cabin on the way home, a favourite haunt half way between where the two girls lived. Poppy worked in the marketing department for *Living Dorset* an upmarket lifestyle magazine that, as far as Kate could tell, mostly sold advertising space to estate agents and interior designers. Poppy loved it though, and it seemed a lot more glamorous than Kate's job right now.

When Kate arrived, she found Poppy already seated and munching a sandwich with obvious enthusiasm. Kate loved the way she never worried about putting on weight. She was beautiful inside and out.

"Life is to be enjoyed, not suffered," Poppy said between mouthfuls as Kate sat beside her. "What's this all about then? I could tell you were stressed on the phone. That's not like you."

Kate sighed. "Helga is a *hellhound*," she said and pulled such an exasperated face that they both fell about laughing, the tension of the day ebbing away.

Kate gave her order to the waitress before replying. "You know Helga's my boss right? I just can't understand why she doesn't like me. She seems to loathe me whatever I do, and she blames things on me that aren't my fault. Mind you, I don't like her either. There's no love lost there – she's so cold… There's no warmth in her heart. She makes my skin crawl whenever she comes near me."

"Maybe it's a past life thing," Poppy teased. "You must've done something terrible to her in a previous lifetime, like stealing her boyfriend or something. Now she's giving you payback." She picked up the remaining sandwich and resumed eating.

"Yeah, like you really believe in all that stuff."

Poppy shrugged. "Who knows? It's one answer, and as good as any. Or maybe she really is just an old cow."

"She is!" Kate laughed, slightly choking on her cappuccino. It felt good to be with her friend. They sat, comfortable with each other, for nearly an hour. Kate couldn't really offload about work – she had signed a contract agreeing not to, but Poppy had an intuitive way of just knowing how she felt. Kate loved her for that. They went their separate ways, agreeing to meet up again soon.

* * *

Later that evening Jacob turned up at Kate's house. She watched from the front window as he extricated himself with difficulty from his metallic blue Lexus hybrid and puffed his way up the path. Even with only the street lamps to light him, she could see he was showing his age, his hair greying around the temples, and he was not quite as spritely as he used to be. He never paid any attention to her when she mentioned diet, and she did that regularly.

"I feel fantastic, Katie" he would say, but she felt worried about him nonetheless. He was her big old dad and she couldn't bear the thought of him being anything less than invincible.

"You ought to take more exercise," she said fondly as she let him in. "And eat less," she added for good effect.

"I've never felt better," Jacob said, and she hoped it was true. There was nothing any of them could do about getting older. Kate walked into the kitchen, put the kettle on and got the mugs from the cupboard.

"And you want to watch out for that hellhound," he called after her.

Kate came and stood in the doorway, a quizzical look on her face. "Have you been tuning in to me at work?"

"I must admit I have," Jacob replied. "I caught a vibration from you today that worried me a bit."

"Well, you needn't worry, Dad – I'm a big girl now," Kate replied, a smile on her face. "But actually, I did have a difficult day. Nothing to be concerned about – just work, you know how it is."

When the kettle boiled, she made the tea, put it on a tray and carried it into the sitting room, setting it on the low table beside him.

"You'll be glad of me one day when you need me to tune in to what you are up to," he chastised gently. "As I have in the past," he added, almost to himself.

Kate caught it but said nothing. She sat in front of him, took his strong hands in hers and prepared herself to listen.

"There is a battle going on between you and Helga," Jacob said.

Kate grimaced. "Don't I know it."

"It's quite unfair of her to treat you badly because the original grievance happened long before you were born."

"What? Dad, what on earth are you talking about?"

"Katie, this is not a new battle, but a continuation of an old one. I've had to intervene before but I hoped to avoid it this time round." He sighed heavily. "I'm afraid this is a little embarrassing for me."

"What happened, Dad?"

"I don't want to go into details, but it's enough for you to know that I chose Francine over Helga and she has never forgiven me for it, and as a consequence, she detests you."

"Oh my god! Are you saying you had an affair with Helga? Dad, that's…"

"She wasn't always so cold, Kate, believe me, and thirty years ago she was a very attractive woman. Sorry, I'm sure you don't really want to hear this. To cut a long story short, she'd prefer it if you didn't exist because somewhat irrationally, you remind her of what she lost, but it would never have worked between us anyway. She was delighted when your mother and I split up." Jacob sank back into his chair, glad to stop talking about this mortifying subject.

"I can't imagine you and Helga together, ever." Kate pulled a face of disgust. "So she knows you're my father then? Do you think I got the job so that she could torture me with her vitriol? To get her own back on you?"

"I don't know Kate – maybe." Jacob sighed. "Perhaps it would be best for you to look for another job after all."

"Well, maybe not," Kate retorted, "since now it's all starting to get rather interesting. And since you *chose* Francine, why does she also dislike me so much? My own mother can't stand the sight of me. Why?"

"Francine did her best in a difficult situation. My darling, it's all very complicated."

Kate pulled a face. "Don't patronise me, Dad, I can handle the truth."

"I know you can, but now is not the time for you to know it. I'm sorry but that's the way it is."

Kate saw the determined look on his face and knew it was pointless to pursue it any further. Kate still had many questions, but they would have to wait. It occurred to her that somewhat ironically, there was an element of truth in what Poppy had said earlier.

Jacob got up to leave. "I'm sorry my love," he said. "Have we had a row?"

"No! Of course not Dad, but don't keep me in the dark again. Will you promise me that?"

"I promise that I will tell you everything you need to know, when you need to know it. Will you trust me on that, at least – even if my choice of women leaves something to be desired!"

They hugged and Jacob left the house, looking lighter on his feet than he had on the way in.

Later that evening Kate's phone rang, and she heard some pip-like tones, immediately recognising that the call was from a public phone box.

"Hello? Kate speaking."

"It's me, Simon."

"..."

"Simon, from work."

"Oh, hi Simon!"

"Look, keep this to yourself, but after you left work tonight, I ran some checks on those codes. I think they were hacked."

"Really? You mean, someone wanted to deliberately derail the systems?"

"Looks like it. I'm not sure how they did it, or who did it, but I can't see any other explanation. I'm going to speak to Mr P about it in the morning, but I think you're off the hook."

"Oh, thanks Simon. That's really kind of you – I thought I was going mad, because I checked everything carefully. Will you let me know if you find out any more?"

"I will, but not at work, okay. Oh, and Kate. Be careful. Things aren't always what they seem."

"Hmmm – I'm beginning to realise that," she said. "You're a star. Thanks Simon."

"Bye Kate."

* * *

The next evening Jacob called on his daughter once more. He pushed past her as she opened the door.

"Do come in," she quipped and followed him into the front room. By the time she got there, he was already seated in his favourite chair.

"How long is it since you've been attending the spiritual circle?" he asked. "I'll tell you. Too long. Sit down, I have something to say."

"I gathered that, Dad."

"In all modesty, as you know I'm quite skilled at connecting with the spirit world, and you've inherited that skill. It's high time we started our own group. I should've suggested it long ago."

Kate looked at him, ready to reply, when she noticed a bright shimmering glow all around him, just like Sechem's.

"Dad, what's going on? I can see a… well, an aura around you. Are you okay?"

"I've always had it, my darling, it's just that now you can see it. It proves that your powers are developing beautifully."

"Wow, it's amazing, and absolutely huge – it extends you." Kate spread her arms to show how wide it was. "I'm liking this new ability, it makes life a lot more colourful. What else can I expect to see?"

"I know it's tempting to rush ahead but we have to tread very carefully here. Take things one step at a time. And that first step needs to be your own psychic development group."

"Okay, Dad. I know you're right, and it fits with what Sechem asked me to do. It's just that it's so exciting." For the first time, Kate's fluttering tummy and pounding heart weren't from fear and anxiety, but exhilaration. She was beginning to enjoy this whole different realm, safe in the knowledge that her father was there by her side "Let's run a group."

Jacob leapt up from his chair and hugged her as if his life depended on it.

"You won't regret it, sweetheart. I promise you. This is where we begin to educate others, and not a moment too soon. Now, let's get to it. I don't want to waste any more time."

They sat down together over a cup of tea and worked out a training curriculum for those who wanted to develop their psychic abilities.

"We'll run the classes weekly and see how we get on," he suggested. "Would it be okay to start off with the group in your house? If we get lots of interest, we can find a hall somewhere, but it's best to start small."

"Sure thing, Dad," said. Kate. "I'll circulate some fliers."

In the next few days they set to work, designing and printing fliers, getting the word out through the network of friends from the spiritual circle and buying some cheap and rather rickety kitchen chairs from the recycling centre. The following Thursday night was the date for the first meeting and it was upon them before they'd had time to stop and draw breath. At 7pm the doorbell began to ring repeatedly as people filed in, eager to begin their journey into the psychic world. There were all sorts of people among them: some old, some young, some familiar faces from the other group, keen to see what Kate had to offer. What connected them all was the light shining in their eyes; a light that showed that they were open to new experiences, exactly who Kate and Jacob had hoped for.

Kate began teaching, starting off with some easy meditation exercises before moving on to the more complex concepts of mind travel. As she taught, she learned almost as much as the students. With chairs crammed into Kate's living room, everyone sat totally absorbed, all eyes focused on her. Right from the start, some were more receptive to her guidance than others; but they all discovered abilities they never guessed they had and were delighted to discover that the more they practised, the easier it became. After the group had been running for a few weeks, some of them were able to tune-in and catch glimpses of the ability to mind-travel. None of them had

Kate's abilities but all felt motivated enough to practice with focused intention. It was phenomenal. It turned out that Kate was a natural at communicating and encouraging others. She realised that Sechem had seen in her something that had lain dormant for years, and only now was it being allowed to see the light, and fully blossom.

So many friends turned up to the meetings that at times it was almost standing room only. Sechem was absent, for which Kate was glad, as she felt his presence may have been intimidating and anyway, she wanted to introduce the concept of The Pleiadians and extra-terrestrials gradually, so as not to freak people out. She'd found it mind-blowing enough to know that the softly-softly approach was best. But many other spirit souls visited, sending positive messages. Not everyone in the group could see them, but they were certainly there, helping, guiding, and protecting. Jacob and Kate never knew who or what would come through.

"This is just the start of things to come," Jacob commented as he helped to clear the chairs at the end of one of the evenings.

"Yes Dad," Kate said. "I know. And I think we're going to have to find a bigger venue."

Across the street, Mrs Thomas had seen the coloured lights drifting over Kate's house again, but she she'd also seen two men draw up at her garden gate in a sedan car, take several photos with long-lensed cameras, and drive off slowly – and that was something that worried her. Should she tell Kate?

CHAPTER NINE

ENTER MASTER M

'The soul returns to earth in a body similar to its last one and has similar talents and inclinations.'

Plato

As Kate drove to work the next morning, she recalled something Sechem had said. 'It has been suggested that we abandon Earth humans to their own devices and let them get on with the mess of their own creation...There are darker forces intent on turning you towards the path of evil.' He was insistent about this but had been oblique too. Kate wanted to know more about it. While at work, her mind kept straying to the topic.

Helga passed Kate's desk and rapped it with her long fingernails. "Keep your mind on the job," she snapped. "We can't have satellites zooming off in all directions as before, can we?" She sniffed noisily, as if it were funny.

Kate wondered, not for the first time, how Helga seemed to know when her attention was drifting. She didn't like it at all.

* * *

Later that evening with Jacob watching her carefully Kate put herself into a trance and prayed she'd be able to handle whatever came up.

She had learnt long ago how to relax herself, by imagining a flight of stairs. Each step down would take her deeper into her subconscious mind, to the point where she forgot her body and operated in mind alone. She knew it was a good self-hypnosis method and often she didn't even need to do that.

This particular evening, after a few moments of visualisation, Kate began feeling less solid as she descended the stairs. Her form was wavering about, and was not clear cut. She was neither here nor there. The stairs were neither here nor there. They wavered in and out of reality. She moved in between worlds. At the bottom, a passageway beckoned. The scene before her transformed into a rippling field of wheat with paths going off in all directions.

She instinctively knew which way to go, almost as if an arrow had been placed before her. She followed, noticing other paths as she walked, and came to a clearing. Incongruously, a card table stood in the centre. A tall, slim but imposing figure sat at the table, waiting patiently. Kate studied him, which he didn't seem to mind at all. His broad nose angled downward, more like a sloping proboscis, or an oversized beak than a normal nose, and his head swept back in an extended dome shape. The intense gaze from his brilliant blue eyes held her entranced. A voluminous flowing cape covered him from shoulder to ankles, but somehow she could see straight through the purple velvet fabric. Beneath it he wore a close-fitting suit with a broad band diagonally emblazoned across his chest, very much like a comic-book superhero. He waved his arm, indicating the seat opposite him.

"Sit," he said in a soft, musical voice. "I see you have developed 'The Sight'," he said, sounding pleased. "That will save time. You can call me Master M."

Kate sat on the wooden folding chair on the other side of the table.

"The reason I have called you here is an important one. There is a plot to destroy or overpower the human race on Earth." The frightening words rang loud and clear.

"A plot to destroy the human race? Surely not?" Kate couldn't believe it.

"It is so. And you can play a vital role in preventing this, once you know who you are."

"I know who I am..." she replied, uncertain of what he meant.

"No, you don't. You are aware of your human existence, but this is only one aspect of you. You are also a soul worker between worlds, reporting on and influencing incarnated souls, wherever and whenever you are sent. You are a special envoy for extra-celestials and you are on a mission, acting as communicator between worlds. Your current assignment is Planet Earth.

"You have been told of the Celestial Galactic Command Council before, but not of your role in it. You have been assigned the role of helping the Council to determine whether to terminate the programme that is encouraging the human race as a whole to join the Galactic Federation, or to let it destroy itself. This it seems intent on doing at the moment, I may add."

Kate took some time to absorb this information. The things he was saying just seemed so incredible, so fantastical that she found it hard to believe him.

"Tell me more," Kate asked after a while, but infuriatingly at that very moment she was painfully jolted back to the real world by the telephone ringing. She was back in her room again where Jacob was in attendance. They had both forgotten to unplug the damn thing. This was a painful lesson to learn. They should have known better. It is definitely never a good idea to come out of a deep trance too quickly – it could even be damaging, akin to a diver rising to the surface of the ocean too quickly.

"Katie, are you okay?" Jacob asked, picking up the receiver and dropping it back down again. Whoever it was could wait.

"Yes, I think so Dad. Well... no, not really. I met someone called Master M. He told me how the fate of humanity on Earth is hanging in the balance."

"Ah, yes. Now we are getting to the crux of the matter," Jacob replied. "This is where your role lies my daughter. Can humanity be redeemed or will it be an evolutionary dead end?"

"I can't bear that thought, Dad. We humans get a lot wrong, to be sure. We fight wars over resources when there's enough to share; we've forgotten that Mother Earth is our only planet of choice and we defile her daily; we are greedy and selfish...but we can also make the most beautiful music, and create the most profound literature. The love a parent has for a child, or the joy that we take in a beautiful flower or sunset... the Earth would be diminished without our presence. A tree grows in stature when a human admires it. Humans help the Earth to be conscious of itself; if we weren't here a light would go out in the Universe."

"And so your role is confirmed, my dear heart. I am proud of you."

* * *

Early the next evening, sharp insistent rapping on Kate's front door brought her out of a pleasant reverie. Work had been particularly boring that day, as Helga had asked her to add contact details of hundreds of different telecoms companies to a database. It was laborious work and she felt tired from hours in front of a computer screen. She got up reluctantly and went to open the door. Who could be knocking so aggressively? She opened the door and her jaw dropped in dismay. Her glacial, elegant mother Francine stood there tapping her foot.

Kate stood stock still and stared at her. Francine had exchanged Jacob for a younger, richer model when Kate was still a child, and then a few years later, traded him in for a slightly older, even wealthier man, whom she married. Now, social engagements and fine dining filled Francine's life, leaving little time for her daughter, so a visit to her was rare. It wouldn't occur to Francine that Kate may have guests of her own, a boyfriend even or, god forbid, may not want to see her – but perhaps something important had brought her, Kate thought with resignation.

"You really will have to fix your doorbell," Francine sniped, using that special voice she saved for fools and naughty dogs. "Well? Are you going to let me in, or are you just going to stand there gaping like an idiot?" She brushed her daughter to one side and swept into the living room. She looked disparagingly at the décor and after sweeping some crumbs off what Kate called 'Jacob's Chair,' she sat down and arranged her designer dress around her.

Kate sighed and followed her in. "What brings you here, Mum? Is Johnny in trouble again?" Johnny, her husband's teenage son from his previous marriage, was always in some sort of trouble.

"Kate, for goodness sake, not 'Mum' please! Do you never remember?" Francine complained. "I don't suppose you have anything decent to drink?" She glanced around the room.

"I have tea or coffee. Would that suit? Or water," she added mischievously.

Francine sniffed. "I suppose tea will have to do. What kind do you have?"

"Builders or builders," Kate replied. She did have some fruit teas but knew her mother wouldn't like them on principle – too hippy by half – it was Darjeeling or Lapsang Souchong that floated her boat. When Kate returned with the tea, Francine patted her already immaculate hair into place and sipped tentatively at her teacup. Kate knew better than to give her a mug.

"Now, what's all this I hear about you talking to dead people and messing with the supernatural?" She placed her cup back in the saucer and glared at her daughter. "I'm appalled. Whatever are you thinking? I don't approve of this behaviour and I want you to stop it at once."

Kate's hackles rose. "Mother, you can't come swanning in here, disapproving of my life choices. You lost that right by deserting me when I was still a child."

"Oh, don't be so melodramatic, Kate," Francine sniffed.

"I'm older now, and you certainly can't start telling me what I should or should not do with my life, *Mum*. And anyway, how on earth did you hear about my meetings?" She knew the term of endearment would annoy Francine, and that's why she used it. Underneath her bravado however, Kate was quaking in her boots. Their meetings always made her feel this way – she couldn't remember ever feeling at ease with this woman. Kate didn't exactly hate her, but how could they be so different? You'd think they weren't related at all.

Francine took another sip of her tea before answering. "You know I've joined a bridge club, don't you?" She gave a smug smile.

"No, I didn't know that. How would I know?"

"Well, I've been going for some time now. I love it."

"Good for you." Kate said, impatiently. Why did everything have to revolve around her? Francine's ego had to be continually massaged.

"We get talking, you know, when there's a break in play. It was Helga Mortensen who told me."

Kate's stomach flipped. Here we go, the plot thickens, she thought.

"Did you know that your father and Helga were 'friends' before I came on the scene? She had ideas of marrying him! What a joke. She's used to getting what she wants though – have you noticed that? And she hated me when I took him from her. He was so good looking in those days."

"He still is."

"That's a matter of opinion. We'd been moving in the same social circle for some time, your father and I, and my parents decided he'd be a good catch for me. They encouraged the relationship and made sure we were thrown together at every opportunity. And so we fell… we got married. We were pushed into it really…"

"Why are you telling me all this now? I'm not remotely interested in your love life," Kate said deciding not to mention that Jacob had already spilled the beans.

"Well, Helga was hurt and upset, obviously. And when I produced a child – you – it turned the knife in the wound. She never married, or had children, you know." A gloating smile crossed Francine's face. "But over the years, she mellowed a bit, if you can use that word to describe Helga – ha ha!" Francine's chuckle was more of a choke, as if humour found it hard to make its way out of her. "We'd see each other at social occasions and had friends in common, so it was inevitable really that we'd become reacquainted."

"Yes," said Kate. "You're two of a kind."

Francine grimaced. Kate saw she didn't like that, but she continued. "Actually, we get on quite well, considering. We have the same good taste, although not in men it seems. Then by some weird coincidence, it turns out she's your boss. How odd is that? So, anyway it was Helga who told me about your 'Mystic Meg' activities."

Kate drew back in surprise and dismay. How on earth did Helga find out? Now that was creepy. She hadn't told anyone, certainly not at work, and everyone who attended the circles was asked only to share what they learned with like-minded souls. Worse still, the thought of Helga and Francine being friends and discussing her private life at bridge club – ugh!

Kate took another sip of her tea, then placed her cup back on the coffee table and gathered her wits together.

"It's nothing for you to worry about. I'm just exploring some ideas with a group of friends – it's a bit like your bridge club really, only more interesting."

"It's a slippery slope, that's what it is, Kate. You'll be a laughing stock. I've a good mind to book you in to see my therapist."

"No way! There is nothing wrong with me." Kate said. What a blessing they didn't know the half of what she was doing. "Anyway, Mother dearest, you really don't have a say in the matter. Dad, on the other hand, comes along to the groups with me." She just had to get that nugget of information in, and she could see it floored Francine, who had always been insanely jealous of their relationship despite not wanting it herself.

"Kate! I'm telling you not to get mixed up in all of this. Helga said it was bound to get messy."

"What does she know? And what's it got to do with her anyway? My private life is just that – nothing to do with her, or you for that matter," retorted Kate, getting hot under the collar. "I think you should leave Mum. I've nothing more to say on the matter."

At least Francine was in agreement with that, and swept out in a cloud of perfume. Kate's energy plummeted as it always did after seeing her mother. A feeling of inertia and sadness washed over her. She wondered if they would ever see eye to eye, or understand each other. She doubted it. More worryingly, she'd found out that the two people in her life who were the most challenging were friends, and were talking about her private life. It was an awful thought. She could just imagine Helga pumping her mother for information on her, relishing anything that could get her into trouble. She'd have to be careful. She didn't want that woman to know anything more than was absolutely necessary. Somehow she knew that was imperative.

^ ^ ^

As soon as she could, Kate invited Jacob over and told him about the visit.

"You're right to be concerned," he said after Kate had served the obligatory cup of tea. "Helga's a tricky customer and you know what your mother's like. Time to be extra vigilant, especially since we want to take you a step further. The Galactic Command is aware that you're opening up fast, so fast we can hardly keep up with you! How have you been feeling by the way?" He studied her anxiously.

"I'm fine, just a bit woozy from time to time." Kate hadn't missed the 'we', and his concern was obvious. She didn't tell him she frequently felt giddy, but it didn't surprise her, because after she'd mind-travelled it seemed to take some time for her mind and body to settle back down. It felt a bit like jet-lag, and she knew it would take her a while to adapt.

"If you're sure? We'd like to take things more quickly. There's much training to be done. Sechem would like you to experience remote viewing as soon as possible. Time is running short."

"But isn't that already what I'm doing?" Kate asked.

Jacob took off his glasses, settled his big frame deeper into the chair, and stared hard at her. The clock on the mantelpiece seemed to tick even more loudly.

"Not really. Remote viewing will help you fine-tune your abilities, sweetheart. It will be a positive experience, I'm sure," Jacob responded. "But now it's time for you to go into a trance," he said firmly.

Kate saw his jaw set and didn't object. She lit a candle and placed a large quartz crystal on the table in front of her. She began the usual 'walking down the stairs' technique and she was quickly in a trance, hardly needing the visualisation at all.

She found herself in a cave. Lights glistened around the sides. They seemed to be moving, alive energies.

"There is a plot to destroy or subdue the human race on Planet Earth." The frightening words rang loud and clear. "Master M here," the voice said.

Kate gasped and peered more deeply into the far end of the cave where she made out a tall glowing figure. As she focussed it took shape before her astonished eyes. Magnificent was the word that sprang to her mind. The cape still flowed around his shoulders but the light that broke through the folds was intense. His blue eyes held her fast.

"A plot to destroy the human race? Surely not?" Kate couldn't believe it. She wondered if she'd be allowed a peek under his cloak this time.

"Not yet," she heard him say.

Oops! He'd picked up her thought.

"I know you have many questions about the future of the human race on Earth," he said, "and believe us when we tell you that there are more intergalactic races interested in Planet Earth than you can possibly count. Do you know why there is such interest?"

Kate shook her head. "That's one of the things I want you to tell me."

"Of course," he smiled. "Many civilisations have come and gone since humans have inhabited the Earth, and some races have vanished completely, mainly because of warfare and genocide. We note that this is still happening, and it staggers us how little humanity has learnt."

Kate quelled the wave of irritation that surged up in her – she was tired of all the criticism of humanity but knew she couldn't express it.

"The answer to your question, however," Master M continued, "is of the greatest importance to you, if you truly love your current home. If the plan Sechem spoke of is implemented, then Earth is up for grabs by any galactic race that can exist within the same environment and can prove they can look after the planet better than the humans there. And why not? We have truly given enough time, aeons of time. We have sent spiritual teachers to show the way. We have communicated with you, given warnings. We have demonstrated our understanding and have been lenient with the actions of humankind..."

Kate stopped him in mid-flow. "I completely understand what you're saying, but what about all the people who have tried to make a difference? Don't they count? Some have even died trying."

"Yes, and many who did so stuck to their own particular and at times peculiar brand of spirituality. They refused to embrace another's point of view, creed or method of living. The result has been, and still is, war and hate. What is spiritual about that?

"It is spiritually dangerous to believe that everyone else is wrong and you are right. Granted, there are times when you go into a situation with the best of intentions, when you work hard, give your all, and things do not turn out the way you expected them to. It is even possible for it to appear that people are against you, out to get you, doing their best to destroy you. Even then, the most difficult adversary and the biggest obstacle can teach a powerful lesson. However, when you take up arms in opposition to people and conditions, you run the risk of missing the lesson. If you continue with the concept of 'an eye for an eye and a tooth for a tooth', then the whole world will be blind and toothless."

"That's true," Kate said. "And it seems to be getting worse not better. But one thing in favour of the human race is that difficulties and challenges have brought out enormous courage in many. I love the human race. I love people. And I love Planet Earth. Each human being plays an enormous part in the growth of this planet and there is potential for it to become even more beautiful. It's all down to human beings, the human species." Kate paused, realising that communicating 'mind to mind' was becoming second nature to her now. This was the theme Sechem had discussed with her, and she knew she was getting to the heart of what it was she was tasked to do. But Sechem was much more approachable than Master M, who just seemed to be pronouncing from on high, rather than advising her. Compared with Sechem's aura, Master M's was dazzling and far more impressive. Had they brought in the 'big guns' to make sure she got the message?

Determined to defend her race, Kate continued. "It may be true that there are many terrible things happening between individuals, groups and countries. But in our defence, look at the enormous courage and bravery shown by many in the face of adversity. Look at the individuals who help others, without thought of recompense, just because they want to do what they can. There is goodness in humanity. Some people do the most extraordinary things to raise money for charities, to help those less fortunate than themselves."

M nodded.

She was on a roll now. "In the midst of war, peace can be found. In the midst of hatred, love prevails. And love can be seen even in the direst, poverty-stricken places. Yes, many have to endure hardship and yet out of this comes greatness. Courage, compassion and love for others is what it means to be human. And not only courage in emergencies, but courage to face the trials of everyday life and the future.

"Some give their talents: musicians, artists, scientists and doctors, nurses and healers, to name just a few. It's amazing how innovative the human mind can be in creating new technologies to help the world move forward. Has there not also been an enormous growth in the evolution of the soul? I'm proud to be a human being!" Kate knew she had been speaking words of wisdom from her own heart, and that these were her true thoughts – not Jacob's or Sechem's – this was her passion, which she had verbalised perhaps for the first time in her life. Her eyes were on fire, azure and sparkling with energy. They locked with Master M's.

"That was quite a speech," Master M said, studying her closely and, it seemed to Kate, approvingly. "You need to channel that passion, it's very effective." He stood and paced up and down. Suddenly he stopped in front of her, as if struck by a sudden thought.

"Any black sheep in a family still has good points. The human race is currently considered to be the black sheep of the galaxy, but as you have rightly pointed out, nothing and nobody is totally bad. Because of the work we've already put in place to evolve a viable spiritual species on Earth, we're reluctant to allow humanity to fail and for other races to take over. We have the last word, but please be clear about this: from where we stand, the future of the human race on Earth is in the balance. The need for spiritual change is imperative."

Kate nodded. "So how do we go about it?"

"You need to understand the seriousness of the situation." He pinned her with his powerful gaze. "Do not ignore the seriousness of the situation. We beg you."

"Okay. Okay. I've got it. It's serious."

"There is much that you can do. We are aware that there are wonderful souls on the planet doing astounding work, but much more has to be done by others who are silent. It should not be left to the few."

"You mentioned before about my role as an envoy for the…er… the Galactic Command Council." Kate felt a little embarrassed saying this, as it still all sounded so surreal. "But what exactly does this entail?" Kate almost felt afraid to ask.

"Your role is to wake the others up, to help them to realise that it is time to step out of their safe little pockets of comfort and do something responsible towards helping their home planet."

"But how do I do that? I'm already giving talks."

"We have noted this, but you do it rarely and on limited subjects, to small groups of people who are already familiar with this subject, often the same people. You have to wake everybody up to the presence of interplanetary species surrounding and upon your Earth. Tell them what is going on under their noses. Tell them your planet is up for grabs. Be prepared."

"I will, if you'll help me," Kate said. "I promise, but I need to know how."

Master M paused for a few moments, his being undulating with shimmering colour, putting Kate in mind of those cuttlefish she'd seen on David Attenborough programmes. She waited watching his light show as the minutes stretched on and on. Kate wondered if his thoughts had drifted to another place. He no longer looked at her. Feeling that the meeting was over, she decided to get up and leave.

At that very moment, a huge black bird-like creature swooped over their heads. Instinctively Kate ducked and sensed an attack. She called out to Jacob.

Kate jolted back to her room and her world of normality.

“You called out to me, with your voice, not your mind Kate. What happened?” asked Jacob, visibly shaken.

“Oh Dad! I’m so glad you’re here. I don’t know… I had an amazing encounter with Master M, but then it was like this threatening shadow was about to engulf us. That’s when I called out to you. There’s nothing outside the house, is there?”

Jacob got up and peered out of the window. He saw nothing out of the ordinary, just the twitch of a neighbour’s curtains, and a black car turning left at the end of the road.

CHAPTER TEN

MEETING OF INTERPLANETARY LORDS

'Eyes that you do not see are upon you. Every move is noticed. Where your actions are to assist someone else, the eyes light up with joy and delight. We know then that all is not lost upon the Planet Earth and the heart is lightened.'

The Universal Brotherhood

Exhausted from her mind-travel and the sudden jolt back to Earth, Kate bade goodnight to Jacob and took herself off to bed, leaving him to wash-up the teacups and turn out the lights as he left. In bed, she began to consider M's request about how she might go about fulfilling her promise. The logical conclusion was that she should hand in her notice at work. If her spirit guides wanted Kate to reach more people and quickly, then just giving talks in the evenings when she got home from work would not be enough. She needed more time, and she'd managed to save enough money to pay the bills and rent for about six months. After that, who knows what she'd be doing? She fell asleep wondering where she'd put her photocopied contract of employment.

The next day was a Saturday, and before she'd even fully shaken off the drowsiness of sleep, communication happened again. It was coming thick and fast these days.

A sea of colours formed in her minds-eye.

"Wake up. Wake up. We have something to tell you."

Kate immediately recognised the authority and music of Sechem's voice. His hazy blue form emerging from the colours. He smiled, apparently pleased to see her.

"You asked about The Plan."

"Did I?" Kate said, still in a dreamy state.

"I see you do take note after all. Your impassioned speech reminded us about the brave and inspired souls on Earth, not to mention the artistic and creative talents that raise the spirits. We take note too, but remember you are the envoy between us and the human species."

"I am human too, remember?" Kate thought he was getting his wires crossed just a tad.

She raised her head when suddenly a new voice said, "Groth ET here. *Understand us.*"

Kate frowned at the interruption. The voice sounded like radio interference, as if she'd tuned into an unknown station. Strange, she didn't know thought-waves could be interfered with.

"We are all of us human in mind and thought," it continued. "We understand the temptations, joys and fears and what drives you. But do you understand us? We would all work better together if you could understand what our drives are. One day you might well be in our place of endeavour. Many of you have joined with us and been in conference with us between your lives. If you could awaken your memories once more to these moments of time, you would have a clearer view now of what is expected of you.

"Communing with the spirit world opens channels a little wider each time you connect. Think of it as a stream that continually runs over the same ground and eventually makes a permanent channel that is ready to fill up whenever there is water to flow through. We wish to help you and meet in unity once more."

Then with a crackle, the voice faded out.

"Did you get that, Sechem?" Kate asked. "Did you hear that, or was it just my imagination?"

He nodded. "Yes, I heard it. It was meant for you though, not me." He chuckled with a gurgling sound, like water bubbling along a shallow stream. Kate felt deep understanding and an overwhelming love coming from him. "Now for a little more history if you can bear it."

"I'll do my best to stay awake." Kate felt so relaxed, she wasn't sure if she might drift back into her sleep state.

Sechem picked that up straight away. "You forget that you're awake while you sleep and asleep while you're awake. Both states are real and are simply divided by levels of awareness. How long have we been teaching you?" he sighed in jest.

"You enjoy the banter between us, don't you?" she said.

"It's so human!" he replied, laughing in that delightful bubbling sound she was coming to love.

Kate shrugged and peered into the swirling colours that cloaked him. She wanted to get a more clearly defined view of her communicator. He was fading in and out of her vision, as if he had difficulty maintaining his presence strongly enough for her to see him at all. She looked around and realised she was sitting on a wooden, slatted seat, on a grassy bank overlooking a stream. Sechem stood a little way off leaning against a tree.

"Oh, do come closer, won't you," she said. "I have to strain my eyes to see you from here." She ran her hands over her face.

Sechem moved nearer and sat cross-legged on the ground. "Is that better?" he asked.

Kate nodded, enjoying the energising proximity of his presence. "Tell me about The Plan," she asked. "Where do I come into the plot?"

"The word 'plot' is correct. Master M has enlightened you about what's going on. The threat to humanity is very real. As we speak, there are large fleets of spacecraft circling Earth, waiting to pounce. In the past there was a time when the human race as a whole was deteriorating into violence to such a degree that the Galactic Spiritual Council held a meeting to decide whether or not to scrap the programme of colonising Earth with its progeny. If they'd scrapped the programme, other intergalactic races would've taken Earth for themselves. That time is now repeating itself. Everything goes in cycles."

She remembered seeing a video of Jaime Maussan's footage of hundreds and hundreds of clearly visible UFO's in broad daylight over Mexico. At the time, she didn't quite believe it; couldn't comprehend it.

"It's time for you to warn everyone. It's time the human race learned about this," Sechem said, "and that's where you come into the plot, or rather into helping undo the plot. You must teach them what they need to know."

Kate pulled a face as she remembered Master M's last communication. Sechem was making sure she got the point. She'd promised she'd help, but the subject of ETs and a plot to take over the Earth was a bit of a divergence from her usual subject matter of how to communicate with guides, teachers, and one's own soul.

"You do realise that most people are not at all interested in UFOs, ETs or deep space? In fact, they call it science fiction – 'fiction' being the operative word. They don't believe in beings from space," she said.

"So start telling them the truth."

That's easy for you to say, she thought, but knowing he would've caught that she said, "I'll do my best." In her heart, she felt quite downcast though. She was as open-minded as they come and even she was struggling to grasp the fact that not only do off worlders exist, they're about to attack and that only the Galactic Spiritual Council was keeping humanity safe. She didn't want to think about what the general public's reaction would be to that. Maybe Helga was right: this could get messy.

"Next time, I'll show you something you haven't seen before. But you'll need to have Jacob with you for protection. Arrange that please."

Her trance dissolved, and Kate regained awareness, back where she was, in bed on a sunny Saturday morning. She thought about what she'd promised Master M and Sechem, and realised that if she wanted people to take her seriously, she'd need to have something more than a conversation with a couple of invisible beings to back up her claims of the existence of extra-terrestrials. It was time to do some research.

After spending most of her weekend googling the topic of ETs and UFOs, she invited Poppy around for a chat. She thought she might practice explaining the galactic situation with her best and most sceptical friend. Poppy's reaction would be a gauge of the reception she might expect.

Kate wanted the evening to go as well as it could so she made sure the sitting room was cosy and comfortable. After the usual greetings, the two friends settled down on the sofa with a glass of Rioja.

"The wine's lovely," Poppy said after a few moments, "but what's the real reason you've called me round? What's the latest?"

Kate took a breath, then plunged straight in. "Poppy, I've got something to tell you."

"Let me guess... You've been visited by aliens?"

"How did you know?" Kate replied, flustered. This wasn't the first time Poppy seemed to have an almost psychic intuition, but she'd never admit to it.

"What the...Katie? Don't be daft – now, what do you want to tell me?"

"Have you ever heard reports of strange flying objects?"

"What kind of objects? The ones you throw in a temper?" Poppy giggled and Kate joined in, amused by the mental image.

"No, seriously, I've got really interested in UFOs lately and..."

"What, like ET? 'ET, phone home'," Poppy croaked in an impression of the film character. They both giggled and Kate topped up their glasses.

"No, not that exactly," Kate said when the giggles had subsided. "I mean actual spacecraft."

"Isn't that a figure of speech? *Actual spacecraft?"* Poppy sipped her wine.

"Listen Poppy," said Kate, desperate for her friend to take her seriously, "I was googling and came across these reports. They seemed really convincing, I mean, why would anyone make that kind of thing up? There was an amazing account in Russia almost 30 years ago in a city called Voronesch, or something like that, near Moscow. Like, *dozens* of adults and children saw spacecraft land and these giant beings moving about in the park. Seven UFOs landed in different parts of the city at the same time. One of them landed in a square where children were playing, and they watched a small alien with an egg-shaped head emerge from the UFO, followed by a 10ft tall humanoid alien. Don't you think that's amazing? They also saw people vanish and reappear near the tall alien. Thousands more people saw several large shining discs hover over the city's nuclear power plants and electrical generating station..."

Poppy looked at her friend with a mixture of concern and incredulity.

"It was all documented and verified." Kate said defensively, waiting for her reaction.

Poppy took more than a sip of her wine, a gulp really. "My god, Kate," she whispered. "You don't actually *believe* all that stuff, do you? And what's a 'humanoid' anyway?"

"As far as I know, well, from what I've read on the internet, a humanoid is a living being similar to us humans, but not quite the same. Two arms, two legs, two eyes and so on, but they may be quite different in size and shape, and have different kind of eyes." Her cheeks flamed, both with the wine and the memory of her own meetings with creatures from outer space. She longed to share them with Poppy, but instinctively felt she should hold fire and present the concept in a more palatable way. She inadvertently burped and they both giggled like silly schoolgirls, breaking the tension somewhat.

"Oops! Pardon me. I also found a most interesting case involving UFOs, in Zimbabwe in 1994. Children and teachers at a school reported seeing a UFO land. The student's ages ranged from 5-12 years and 62 children with one adult were outside the school during the incident. They described a small human-like being on the craft. It was about three-feet tall, wearing a dark suit, with a slender neck, long black hair, large eyes. Guess what Poppy? It walked towards the children, watched them for a while, disappeared and then the craft took off. How about that then?"

Poppy frowned and Kate saw the disbelief in her eyes. "Are you really saying that you believe some random website you looked at? I mean, it's interesting and all that, but whether it's believable is another thing all together. It's just mass hysteria, isn't it? Next you'll be telling me you believe the moon landing was real."

"But it was real!"

"Just kidding," said Poppy, topping up her glass.

"Yes, but Popsicle, if you believe in the moon landings, then why can't you consider the opposite might be true, and beings from other planets have visited us. Isn't that logical?"

"Well, I suppose so..." Poppy said thoughtfully, "but isn't this all just classic conspiracy theory fodder? If it's so convincing, why hasn't there been more media coverage of it? Why do you have to search for it on obscure websites?"

"The media know all about it but the news has been embargoed," Kate said. "The powers that be don't want us to know."

"Hah! The classic conspiracy theory explanation," laughed Poppy.

Kate held the almost empty wine bottle up to the light. "Better not have any more – we've both got work in the morning. Anyway, get this: at a conference in Washington DC in 1995, a man called Michael Hesemann quoted from a KGB file, saying that a UFO hovered for two hours over a Soviet nuclear weapons storage facility in 1989."

"How dare it? Kaboom!" Poppy giggled loudly.

"You're not taking this seriously." Kate snorted.

"Should I? The only thing I am taking seriously is your state of mind. What's got into you Kate, to start believing all the rubbish you read on the Internet? I thought you were more discerning than that."

"I don't think it is rubbish though. I know it sounds crazy, but give me a chance to explain. Steven Hawking believes in the possibility of extra-terrestrial life, and surely you don't doubt his intelligence?"

"Of course not, but you're no astrophysicist, Kate," replied Poppy.

Kate persisted. "Please listen, Poppy. The list of documented sightings corroborated by more than one person goes on and on, and still most people are simply not interested, or ridicule the information that keeps coming. There've been so many reports of clear sightings of spacecraft that to deny their existence and interest in our planet, is like pretending that gravity doesn't exist. I marvel at how disinterested people are, when the proof is out there that interplanetary beings are visiting and interacting with us." Kate refrained from telling Poppy that she'd actually *seen* beings from space – but then the most unexpected thing happened.

Poppy admitted, "My mum and dad saw a spacecraft once. It was after the Harmonic Convergence in 1987, I think it was, well before we were born, when they lived in that community in Devon. Anyway, they both told me separately about what they saw, and other people who were with them saw it too. What they described was like an archetypal spaceship – you know, oval-shaped with two tiers of windows, and completely silent. The thing is, I trust my parents implicitly. I just know they would never lie about a thing like that. So, I suppose what I'm saying is that I don't believe it, but I don't disbelieve it – I think I have to experience these things myself and then make up my mind. Anyway Kate, I'm off. I've got a busy day tomorrow at work. Thanks for a lovely evening."

After clearing the glasses, and tidying the room, Kate went to bed. Sechem was right, she was likely to be ridiculed, but some would be receptive. Poppy did listen and in the end, she shared something very personal with Kate that allowed their relationship to deepen.

Then, a clear message entered Kate's mind as she was about to drop off to sleep. It sounded like a prediction of things to come.

When the birds fly east the sun will rise hotly and the ill vapours of the earthbound will be released. The birds will be of another time and place that have returned yet again to offer their assistance. The fish of the sea will proliferate once more, to regenerate the waters from which all life comes. Waters will cover new lands cleansing them and purifying them. Lands that have never seen the sun before will emerge rich in promise. Peace will reign with a new spirit of fellowship.

From Spirit

Were the 'birds of another time and another place,' the Bird Tribe from Sirius, that she'd read about? And what about, 'Lands which had never seen the sun before will emerge'? What could this mean? Maybe underwater volcanic eruptions creating new islands?

Kate remembered reading other prophecies, including those of Mother Shipton born Ursula Southeil in 1488. The woman grew up around Knaresborough in Yorkshire and was a strange child, both in looks and in nature. She had a large, crooked nose, bent back and twisted legs, just like most people's idea of a witch. She spent her days around the cave where she was born preparing herbal remedies and foreseeing the future of those who visited. Years ago Kate had visited the cave where she lived, and remembered seeing an interesting prophecy that was credited to Mother Shipton.

She got out of bed and went to her computer, and googled the verse that'd had such a great impact on her back then:

But the land that rises from the sea
will be dry and clean and soft and free
of mankind's dirt and therefore be,
the source of man's new dynasty.
And those that live will ever fear

the dragon's tail for many year,
but time erases memory
You think it strange but it will be.
And before the race is built anew,
a silver serpent comes to view
and spews out men of like unknown
to mingle with the earth now grown
cold from its heat, and these men can
enlighten the minds of future man
to intermingle and show them how
to live and love and thus endow.
the children with the second sight,
a natural thing so that they might
grow graceful, humble, and when they do
the golden age will start anew.

It all had such a different meaning to Kate now. *'Spew out men of like unknown to mingle with the earth.'* Were these unknown men the intergalactic ones she was meeting? It made Kate think seriously about what Sechem and Master M were telling her, especially about how history repeats itself and goes around in circles, calling into question our concept of time as well as space. How interesting it all was, really.

She remembered what Sechem had said the last time he visited. "I will show you something you have not seen before. For that you will need to have Jacob with you for protection."

Kate made a mental note to arrange that with Jacob the next day.

* * *

The night after Poppy's visit, she picked up the phone and called Jacob.

"Dad, can you come around this evening? Sechem asked you to be present at our next meeting, and it feels important that I connect with spirit tonight."

"Well, I was going to go to the cinema, but I trust your intuition, so I'll be round soon."

"Thank you, Dad. I sense it's going to be a momentous evening."

Kate felt nerves she'd not experienced before. Something was about to happen. She felt it in her bones. She was sorely tempted to have a drink to calm her nerves, but knew she should keep a clear head. She recognised that was a slippery slope. She'd seen Francine take that route to calm herself down, with disastrous consequences. A stiff drink had become a habit when she felt insecure, and now the habit was so strong she couldn't let it go.

Kate dimmed the lights, drew the curtains, lit some candles and disconnected the phone. Having arranged and plumped the cushions to his liking, Jacob sat firmly ensconced in his favourite chair. Kate sat opposite him, prepared for whatever might occur. Not wishing to spoil things by being impatient, she took plenty of time getting into a deep state.

Her mind became fuzzy as an enormous energy in her head almost caused her to faint and tingling currents of energy ran up and down her spine. She clutched the sides of the chair until she became strong enough to focus on what was taking place within her.

Master M was with her. She knew that the energy field emanated from him. It held her firmly in place. She felt merged with him in some indefinable way, as if they'd become one.

In her mind, Kate sat on a soft padded seat at the side of an auditorium of immense size. Waving bands of light flickered erratically throughout the entire area reminding her of a mirage, like heat rising from the road on a hot summer's day. Kate watched fascinated as colours played in constantly moving patterns in mid-air. She wondered if the walls were solid as they seemed to be ebbing and flowing like the glorious light display in front of her.

"Is this because we're not totally or truly here?" Kate asked tremulously, in awe of the surroundings. But her question was unanswered and she was left only to gaze at the incredible rainbow display before her.

The coloured light thinned enough that Kate could see through it, and she realised that a mass of beings filled the room. In the centre was a huge crystal, shaped like a pine cone on a raised plinth covered in a rich blue cloth. Tables were placed in a triangle around it, with seats arranged to face the crystal. On one of them sat a heavily built, coarse-looking creature with scales. He stood and banged on the table with his fist.

"Why are we wasting our breath on this? We've given them plenty of time; lord knows it's enough. We ought to bring this experiment to a close."

A beautiful androgynous creature glowing in many colours rose from the other side of the triangle. "I do not agree."

This comment brought thunderous applause. From what Kate could see through the waving lights, these shining beings of luminosity and energy were a range of otherworldly creatures, not unlike humans, but not exactly the same. She recognised the blue Birdmen, and as she surveyed the crowd, she could hear Master M explaining who each being was: Greys, Blond Nordics, Lion tribe and races from star systems such as Lyra, Vega, Pleiades, Sirius, Procyon, Tau Ceti, Ummo, Andromeda and Arcturus. It was like a lesson in astronomy and she marvelled at this glimpse of the diversity of the universe.

On another side of the triangle sat a range of mostly humanoid beings, many like the one with them banging the table. Kate sensed heavy, dull energies emanating from that side. The third side of the triangle had a mixture of the other two. They surely must be sitting on the fence, Kate thought.

"No, Master M said in her mind, "they represent the Lords of The Universe, The Galactic Command Council and the Planetary Programme for the Grand Spiritual Experiment."

Kate stared at this third group with fresh eyes. She could hardly comprehend that the unusual group included such mighty beings and that she was allowed to be party to this momentous occasion. She suddenly felt very small and inadequate.

The heavy creature remained standing. "Like you, we need to expand, and to do this we need to use viable places in the universe. Why can't we use planet Earth? The races there have not evolved as planned and it looks like they will destroy themselves and that beautiful planet."

Another at his side lurched to his feet. "Don't worry, my friend. We already have many of our kind in human form down there making sure that the planet will be unsuitable for continued, comfortable human habitation. Those in power think they'll be safe within their tunnels and underground refuges. What a laugh! We have the upper hand. Wars, pesticides and pollution are fouling the air they breathe right now. They are already killing the seas and the forests. We truly do not need to do anything. They are doing it all for us." Those at his side laughed. A chill spread through Kate and she fought the urge to defend her beloved planet.

The lighter side glowed brighter and someone who shone with golden light stood slowly and majestically. He seemed familiar to Kate. "You are forgetting that the time allowed to them is not yet up. Do not be in such a hurry to take over. We still have hope for the human species on Earth. The hardships they are undergoing are producing amazing courage, kindness, love and great endeavour." He bowed in Kate's direction. "Wonderful souls are being born and are making a difference. This is now outweighing those who promote death, cruelty and destruction. You and your kind will be seen for what you are very soon."

The heavy one, who had remained standing, shouted, "Don't be so sure. We are securely cloaked and have been around for a very long time, since the very beginning of your plan to introduce a spiritual race on that soil. Many races entered through the Star Gate on Atlantis. We are skilled at infiltrating," he said smirking.

The Star Gate at Atlantis? What's that? Must Google it, thought Kate. She had heard of Atlantis, but what was this Star Gate? The more she heard about these previously fantastical places casually dropped into conversation, the more she was growing used to just accepting them as fact.

The light side's glow grew even stronger, and the golden being continued. "I do believe you are so convinced of your power that you have completely forgotten that we too have many of our kind in place." He looked straight at Kate. "They have been given their roles to play, if they wish to take them up." In spite of herself, Kate shivered. She understood what he meant by that and again felt a wave of inadequacy wash over her.

More wrangling took place until at last the other side of the triangle and the brightest of all, stepped in. Kate felt an immediate overwhelming immersion in a world of bliss, ecstasy, understanding and love. If she'd been fully physical it would've blown her over. Tears welled up, and threatened to spill.

The central figure, a Lord of the Universe rose gracefully to his feet. To her awestruck eyes, he appeared just as she'd expect a celestial of high standing to be, a being of calm, light and love. His head was triangular in shape, his skin shone with a golden sheen and he appeared to float rather than stand. Everybody fell silent in respect and reverence.

His words seemed to buzz into their hearts like a vibration rather than through their ears and washed over them like a wave.

"As you know, all creatures, every race from all spheres have both come from and are part of The Great Intelligence, the source of all things. This is true no matter how each soul, group or race appear to be in conflict. Therefore, we do not pass judgement, only direction. We have listened patiently at great length to your arguments. We have decided that there is sufficient good intent and love within the human race on Planet Earth to bring it into the vibration required to join the Galactic Family." He paused while this was taken in and understood.

"However, there is to be a time limit imposed, as well as a limit as to how far they are allowed to go in respect of damage to the Earth, and damage to space by their irresponsible use of nuclear energy and weapons."

A murmur of approval came from the gathering.

"Those of you who have the best interests of the human species as your goal, please train well those you have in place on Earth. We understand you have already sent special envoys from your own planets to aid in this. We watch with interest. If peace has not prevailed when the period of transition has passed there will be a re-think."

What did he mean by that? Kate wondered as he sat down. The meeting was over, the heavy ones grumbled among themselves.

"We're not finished yet," she heard one of them say. "We'll easily deal with those over there." He glowered in their direction. Kate shivered and cold flooded through her again.

"Planet Earth will be ours before too long," another said. "There are too many of us in place for our plan to fail."

Kate shuddered and came back to Earth with a bump.

"Well?" said Jacob.

For the first time, Kate just 'thought' the experience for Jacob; an instantaneous transmission of what she had seen and heard. It was quicker and easier for both of them, and was an admission to Jacob that her powers were growing stronger.

He nodded, hands clasped in thought. "You have done good work tonight my dearest daughter. We have to work smartly now – this was a multi-faceted message to us from Master M. I have found a small hall not too far away. We need to move our psychic development groups there so that we can welcome more people. Your house is too small – last week, people were listening from the hall! We will also ask those in the group to invite any friends who are interested to come along, and we will select the most advanced souls to set up their own groups to spread the word too. Time is most obviously of the essence. And you, my dear Kate, need to start disseminating the information you have been given in whatever ways you can, to whomsoever is receptive."

He got up and kissed her on both cheeks, and left for home.

CHAPTER ELEVEN

WHAT DO YOU KNOW?

'In the practice of tolerance, one's enemy is the best teacher.'

Dalai Lama

The visit to the Galactic Command Meeting had unnerved Kate. How did Master M expect her to tell people about *that*? No matter what they said, she was but an insignificant human – how could she fight against such dark forces? Also, the darker side of the triangle seemed to acknowledge her – a scary thought – and she felt as if they were plotting something to do with her, which was an even scarier proposition.

To distract herself from these worrying thoughts, over the next few days, she worked with Jacob on improving her remote viewing. The techniques were already familiar to her, but with practise, she was able to hold her focus and sustain concentration for much longer without feeling too drained. All she had to do was go into a deep relaxed meditative state, ask to go to a time and place and it happened. She was there. She had to admit Sechem was right as usual,.

They also worked hard to let all their regulars know that the meetings were now to be in Windmill Hall, a newly refurbished community centre with a kitchen, toilets, plenty of chairs and neutral décor. In the daytime, it was mostly used for zumba and slimming clubs, but they transformed it for their meetings with candles, incense and always, beautiful flowers for the centre table, where they put their leaflets, books and other information for people to peruse.

* * *

A few days after the Galactic Meeting, Kate was idly looking out of the office window during morning coffee break, and saw a fleet of cars pull up by the front entrance. Out climbed men who looked important but incongruous somehow: dark glasses and heavy coats on a late spring morning. What was going on, she wondered?

When she arrived for work the following day, she found another desk had been butted up to hers. Kate frowned, not only surprised, but a bit put out. Overnight, someone had repositioned her desk so that she had her back to the door – it was bad *feng shui* and Kate felt really uncomfortable about it. What's more, whoever was going to sit behind the new desk would be directly facing her.

Unhappy with this new arrangement, Kate was on the point of deciding how to approach Helga with her objections when the woman herself strutted in accompanied by a familiar man.

Oh my god…Kate thought, taken aback. That's the guy who followed me on the train, I'm sure of it. What the man lacked in height, he more than made up for with bulk. In any other environment, he'd be seen as a 'heavy'; more like a bouncer at a nightclub than an office worker.

"This is Marco," Helga announced with a smug smile. "He's from the US, and he's been sent here by Head Office. As you know we've had trouble recently with satellite tracking positions…" She looked meaningfully at Kate, so that anyone watching would assume it was Kate's fault.

"But I thought…"

Helga interrupted. “Our work with satellites and our government contracts are vitally important. We cannot allow any more silly mistakes to be made. So, Marco has been brought in to oversee some of the work we do.” She paused and waved an arm, indicating Kate’s desk. There was no mistaking her message. Why didn’t she put up a sign saying: ‘An idiot sits here’ and be done with it?

Marco settled in, opposite Kate. He made no attempt to cover up the fact that he was watching her and spent long minutes just staring at Kate as if trying to see inside her head. It was most unnerving. When he wasn’t at his desk, she often glanced up and saw him in deep conversation with Helga, nodding in her direction. And weirdly, she never saw him do any actual work. Would she have to put up with this every day? It was intolerable. Time to hand in my notice, she thought.

At lunchtime, Kate left her desk to slip over and see Simon, who, since he’d given her the heads-up about the hack that had been blamed on her, had become a good friend, one of the few she’d made in the East Wing so far. But he was nowhere to be seen.

“Looking for someone?” Helga sneered from behind her.

“Umm, yes. Do you know where Simon is today?”

“Gone. Marco’s taking over his work. He wasn’t exactly any good at it, now was he, letting those errors slip past me.”

“Gone where?” Kate asked, knowing she wouldn’t get a straight answer.

“Gone, is all you need to know, Greene,” said Helga, her eyes holding Kate’s own with what can only be described as malice.

The afternoon dragged on. At one point, Kate ventured making conversation with Marco.

"So, you're from the US?" Kate said. "Have you been to the UK before, to London perhaps?"

He looked over his ridiculous dark glasses at her – as if he needed them indoors – and with barely concealed disdain said, "First time for me, but sure, I've been to London. I flew in to Heathrow, didn't I?"

"Yes, of course," Kate said, no further forward in ascertaining if he was the man that followed her on the train. Maybe these guys just all looked alike?

Kate was mightily glad when the time came for her to go home. When she got there, she picked up a mind-contact from Jacob.

'You are not alone.'

Sometimes it really felt like it.

She spent that evening scouring her study and then her whole house, for her contract of employment, but couldn't find it anywhere. She was sure she'd filed it in her work folder, but it wasn't there. Oh well, she didn't actually need it. She'd just write her letter of resignation and hand it in on Friday, giving a nice, neat four weeks' notice.

The next day when Kate was busy at her desk, Helga called for attention. Everybody looked up to see, standing beside their boss, a tall, scrawny man with blank eyes and no discernible expression. Kate thought he looked like a well-dressed skeleton. She disliked him at first sight.

"I'd like to introduce you to Silas Pearce, who is joining us at managerial level. You'll see him around a great deal. If you see or hear of anything unusual you're to report directly to him." The new man said nothing but nodded at Marco, as if in collusion. That didn't escape Kate.

Kate wondered what would merit the label, 'anything unusual'. The fact that Marco never appeared to do any work? Or that Simon had disappeared? Or the increased number of visitors of late? Kate still hadn't found out what Silas Pearce actually did, but she sure as hell didn't trust him an inch. She kept out of his way whenever she could, but he seemed to silently appear when she least expected it, like when she came out of the restroom, or needed to get some water from the dispenser – there he was, like a curse. She saw him smooth his dark hair and almost preen whenever he passed a mirror or saw his reflection in a window. He was always smartly dressed and could be taken for a high-powered businessman any day. That is, until you looked at his empty, cold eyes. Impossible to read and dreadful to look at. They made you wonder what was going on in his mind.

* * *

When Friday came, Kate tucked her letter of resignation in her handbag and endured yet another day of scrutiny. Five o'clock could not come soon enough.

As her colleagues were packing up to leave for the weekend, Kate knocked on Helga's door.

"Come in, Greene," Helga called, somewhat to Kate's surprise.

When she entered the room, Marco and Silas were standing behind Helga's chair like two bodyguards.

"I'd like to speak with you in private," said Kate.

"What you have to say to me, you can say in front of them. We are all your superiors," Helga replied.

"Okay. Here's my letter of resignation. I'm giving you one month's notice to quit, as per my contract."

"What contract's that?" Helga enquired.

"Well, I couldn't actually find my copy…" Kate stuttered, feeling a bit stupid, "but I remember checking that I only had to give a month's notice. So here it is."

"I think you must be mistaken, Greene," said Helga. "I have a copy here, and it clearly shows that you signed a two-year non-negotiable contract." She pushed a document towards Kate which she had ready and waiting on her desk.

How did she know I was going to do this? thought Kate, picking up the paper with shaking hands. There was the two-year term and her signature in black and white.

"There must be some mistake, Helga. I would never sign a two-year contract. I didn't like the job enough to do that."

"Ms Mortensen to you – and are you calling me a liar?"

Both Silas and Marco took a step closer to Kate, flanking Helga and exuding an air of menace.

"No, but…"

"Then, I think this meeting is concluded Greene. Have a nice weekend and we'll see you on Monday. Shut the door on your way out."

Kate was in a daze of confusion and did as she was told, hearing a sneer of laughter coming from Helga's office as she closed the door.

Kate was dumfounded. What the hell just happened? She began to wonder if she'd been set-up, or if it was just some big joke and Helga would ring her later to sneer and tell her they'd be glad to get rid of her.

She felt the need to speak with Poppy about it and rang her mobile, but it went straight to answerphone; Jacob's did the same and Tom's Coffee Cabin was inexplicably shut, on a Friday night of all nights. Well, Jacob said she wasn't alone, but she certainly felt alone tonight. She resolved to go and see Mr P on Monday morning – he already thought she was useless so perhaps he would override Mortensen and co., and give her leave to quit.

* * *

About the time of Silas's arrival, Kate had a most intriguing journey of the mind, which literally, helped take her mind off the situation at work. She thought it was probably due to her new remote viewing skills that she was able to go so much deeper.

After taking her usual descent into a deeply altered state, Kate found herself walking along a long corridor several floors underground. She stopped outside a plain steel door and ran her hands over the surface, searching for the means to open it, but couldn't find any. Then she noticed a light cast across the floor on one side, and discovered a sensor. She stepped into it and the door slid silently open.

Kate stepped through the door and was flooded with a light so bright that she could see every little detail on her clothing and every pore on her skin, but nothing else, just white light all around. The door closed silently behind her. She sensed eyes watching and felt she was in some kind of screening mechanism. A beam of light moved down her body like it was scanning her. When it finished, Kate automatically moved forward, instinctively knowing that was what she was expected to do.

She stepped out of the blinding light and saw she was in a large, white room. It was humming with activity, but rather than the fascinating mix of beings from other planets, this time the group was made up of male military personnel, all from different nations. Some were moving around whilst others were sitting at desks filled with computer equipment and screens.

A voice instructed her to go down a passage on her right. She obeyed, and two uniformed men walked behind her. Kate knew she had to keep going. There was no return. She had a fleeting worry about where she'd end up. The setting was just like a science fiction film, something you might make up. But she wasn't making it up.

A door slid open beside her, and the same voice told her to enter. She stepped inside, but her escort remained outside and the door didn't close behind her. Kate looked around her. The white walls were blank, except for a large map of the stars on which sections of the galaxy were marked out with pins. They were the only coloured things in the stark room. A ceiling strip light flickered on and off. In front of the map-wall, a black-haired man in a dark uniform sat behind a desk. On either side of the tidy pile of papers were three telephones, one of which was red. Kate found these mundane signs of everyday life quite reassuring.

Without looking up, the man beckoned her to the only other seat in the room, on the other side of his desk. She sat down and waited for him to speak.

The man looked up and stared coldly at her. She felt a pressure to comply, but didn't know what she was complying with. All she could do was wait.

His eyes narrowed and his cheek twitched. "You know everything we need," he said bluntly, "and you will tell us everything."

Her mind became a complete blank. What the heck did he mean? Was he referring to her contact with other-world beings? She certainly didn't want to reveal anything inadvertently. She'd been warned often enough about being careful who she divulged information to.

"You will undergo a process similar to hypnosis, such as you yourself use. But this will go deeper than that. With our system you will reveal what we need to know." His cheek twitched again.

"What's this relating to?" she asked.

"Your galactic friends," he replied with an expression of contempt.

"I see." Kate still felt reluctant to share her knowledge with him, particularly because of his frosty demeanour. "I know nothing."

"But your deep unconscious does know. It knows much more than you think you can tell us."

Kate frowned. This sounded like something Master M would say. How did the military know about this? She'd no idea where this was going, but she tried to relax, reminding herself that she could come out of the trance when she wanted.

Two tall, thin and definitely not human females walked in. Kate stared at them, fascinated. It was incredible to see other-world people in this military setting. It confirmed everything she'd read on the internet – it isn't a conspiracy theory, as Poppy said. It gave Kate a wonderful feeling of relief, even though the situation was still utterly incredible to her, and if truth be told, slightly scary.

Though humanoid, the women were clearly not from this Earth. Like Sechem they had a bluish tinge to their skin. Their eyes were huge and unblinking. Unlike Sechem they wore long silky gowns in soft hues of pink. One of them touched Kate gently on the arm. Her long fingers felt soft, like powder. At the touch, Kate knew immediately that she could talk to them in their language, and they could talk back to her. They began communicating, and she felt something change inside, as if their language activated something in the brain. Kate marvelled at this – but she didn't have long to dwell on it as the woman plunged right in.

"Did you know that ET language activates the DNA code so that it functions more fully?" one of them said. "This is what we need. You will use our various languages during your talks and workshops. You will allow us to speak through you when you speak publicly."

Then the two females patted Kate gently on the head until she found herself drifting into a reverie.

Kate awakened back in her own room. It was over. What had they done to her, and more's to the point, what did they mean about ET language activating DNA? Then she remembered Jacob's words. "You are not alone." He wasn't referring to the trifling matters of her work, he meant during times like this. If she was in danger, Sechem or Master M would protect her. She was not alone in this. It was some comfort.

* * *

That evening was the first of their groups in the new hall, and it was very well attended. Though not by Jacob. He'd rung her earlier to say he couldn't come, that he had important work to do elsewhere. Kate was disappointed.

"What could be more important than this, Dad?"

"Do you remember when I had that accident at work, years ago, Kate? Well, it was spirit's way of clearing the path for me so that I only need to work with them. I don't have a job as such, I mind-travel all the time, helping other advanced souls like you – though not as highly evolved as you, I must say – to fulfil their part in this Great Work we are doing. Tonight, I'm at a meeting in Brasilia. My knowledge of Portuguese helps me to guide those present more deeply. It is a lovely place."

"Oh, I see. Thanks for telling me – that might explain why sometimes you look so tired."

"Perhaps, although I love my job!"

"I'm sure I'll be alright hosting the group on my own. I'm going to speak about the development of remote viewing, which I know will be so useful in the future. And by the way, Dad, I think it's really sweet that you still ring me on my phone instead of mind-contact!"

He chuckled.

"Oh yes, talking of language, remind me to ask you about ET language and DNA. Now that is something I'd like to know more about."

CHAPTER TWELVE

A BATTLE OF MINDS

We request that you listen to the knowing in your heart, that whatever seems to be going wrong, all is proceeding as it should. Your efforts are having results. We send our own energy fields to mingle happily with yours, to strengthen and heal wherever we find a thinning decolourisation or weakening of energies. Do not fear for the outcome of the Planet or yourselves. All is in hand. Believe it and it will be so.

The Universal Brotherhood with the Galactic Command

On the Saturday morning, Kate answered a knock on the door, and her mother Francine pushed past her. She strode into the room in her usual wave of perfume that Kate loathed.

"Hello again, long time no see." Kate exaggerated a deep bow.

"No sarcasm please. Tea first," she snapped. "Then we'll talk."

"Yes, Ma'am." Kate huffed. The woman, mother or not, was insufferable.

Tea was soon in place, china cups of course. They sat on the sofa, and after a cursory sip of tea, Francine lost no time with niceties.

"I went to bridge last night. I thought Helga was acting a bit odd with me, and anyway, when we had a break, she grabbed hold of my arm and took me outside and told me about a very disturbing dream she'd had."

"Mother, let me stop you there. I'm not interested in that woman's dreams."

"Well, you might be when I tell you about this one, my girl. She said she was in an X-ray room and she watched you go into another room and sit down with a man in uniform. She could see you were frightened of him, but you soon dropped off to sleep. At least she thought it was sleep, but when two weird-looking females came into the room and they shook you to make sure you were fully unconscious. You didn't wake up but began spouting a lot of strange sounds. The two females did the same and then picked you up and carried you out of the room. The man closed a file and rang a bell. Then Helga woke up. Don't you think that's weird? Anyway, then she started having a right go at me about you Kate, saying you were putting yourself in danger with your psychic groups and that I had to make you stop. Kate, look at me."

Kate turned slowly, trying to stop her trembling and control her expression.

"And why would this be of interest to me? I have no idea what you're talking about," she said. "It's a bit freaky for my boss to be dreaming about me but a dream's a dream, only that. Don't go all Freudian on me and start analysing it."

Francine frowned, eyes narrowing. "Why should your boss dream about you? Especially such a strange dream."

Kate shrugged. "I don't know. Why does anyone dream anything? I wouldn't worry about it."

"But Helga thinks you're dabbling in some kind of black magic or something. She's worried about you and thinks the dream was a warning. She's only got your best interests at heart. Look, I don't give a fig about all this New Age stuff, but Helga is worried about you and so, here I am, I suppose."

"Worried my eye! Maybe it's because Helga's been angry with me recently and she can't get it out of her mind. Let's drop it, shall we? It's nothing, just a silly dream."

Francine shot her daughter a peeved look. "Don't you think it's bizarre how fate brought you and Helga together in the same office?" she said after a few sips of tea.

Kate nodded. "Not fate, just bad luck." But alarm bells were ringing and she hoped to goodness it was just bad luck and nothing more sinister. Then again, Helga had somehow connected with her mind-travel, and that was infinitely more worrying.

"If Jacob had stayed with Helga, you could've been Helga's child. Just think about that."

"I'd rather not," Kate said. "Having her as a boss is bad enough. Anyway, that's a daft thing to say. I wouldn't be me, if I was her daughter, would I."

Francine stood, preparing to leave. "Hmm. What is it they say about a woman scorned?"

"Hell hath no fury…" Kate offered.

"Exactly," Francine said, then she swept out of the room and through the front door without another word.

Kate stared after her, frowning. She was pretty sure that Francine didn't have a clue about what was going on, and just saw the whole thing as Helga worrying about Kate's welfare. How ironic, but how on earth could Helga know about her mind travels? The very thought made the hairs on the back of her neck stand up. Kate had experienced her probing her mind at work, and the weird way she seemed to know what Kate was about to do, like when she tried to quit, but surely her boss didn't have anything to do with her other-world dealings? Could Helga mind-travel too? Had she been eavesdropping on Kate's journeys?

She shivered, suddenly feeling chilled. If Helga was involved, she knew it wouldn't be in a good way. At least she'd had the presence of mind to plead ignorance to Francine. It was the best option. Her mother could be like a dog with a bone and wouldn't drop the subject for long. She would speak about it with Jacob when he came over for the next meeting. He was sure to be able to cast some light on the subject.

* * *

Kate's weekend was pleasantly quiet. Lunch with Poppy on Sunday was the highlight. She'd been getting ready upstairs in her room and was walking down stairs engrossed in her thoughts when she suddenly felt a hand push hard on her back. Fighting to stay upright, she grabbed the banister just in time to prevent a tumble. When she turned to see who'd pushed her, the stairs were empty, yet she hadn't missed a step or tripped. Though it appeared no one was there, it felt just like she'd been pushed. Along with Helga's unnerving dream about her, it seemed that negative influences were beginning to make their presence felt. Kate felt her stomach churn with anxiety.

The next day at work Helga made one of her now infamous announcements.

"I'm so sorry to tell you all that Mr Peters had a stroke at the weekend. He's okay, but he's in hospital and he's not likely to be back at work for a few months. In his absence, Silas Pearce will take over his workload."

Kate's heart sank. So, there goes my last resort for getting out of this place, she thought.

At lunchtime as she entered the canteen, the room started to spin and she thought she'd be sick. Trying to hold on to her senses, she collapsed into a chair. People gathered round, but Kate assured them that she was all right and stepped outside for a breath of fresh air. It felt good to be out of the office. She sat on a garden seat near the wall and closed her eyes, enjoying the warm sun on her face, her head slowly clearing.

"Look out!" a man called.

Kate jumped up off the seat just as a piece of guttering crashed down, right where she'd been sitting. With her heart thumping like crazy, she went back indoors.

What on earth was going on? Kate felt incredibly jumpy. It didn't feel safe anywhere. Later a pounding headache came on out of the blue and over the following days it came back again. Kate took to carrying painkillers around with her but didn't like this change in her health. What was happening to her?

She told Jacob her fears as they sat in her garden enjoying a cup of tea before the evening's meeting.

"This all sounds like psychic attack," he said, his face stern. "Helga is powerful, but don't worry, she's no match for you."

"Helga? Dad... what are you on about? She's more than just my unpleasant boss, isn't she? Come on, Dad, you have to tell me," Kate demanded.

"Yes Kate, now is the time. You see, the universal law of attraction applies across all fields and all walks of life. Just as positive and negative have complementarity, so does good and evil. All those who work for the light are subject to attack by dark forces, as you have just found out. Helga was attracted to me because of who I am, not what I looked like! She sensed my spiritual path and would've done all she could to destroy it had we stayed together, and I knew it too.

"Poor Francine really was but a pawn in the battle. By marrying her, I could deflect the worst of Helga's energy, but she will never give up. She has an awareness of your power because she knows about mine. She's befriended Francine to get to us. Poor Francine," he added again. "She is not to be blamed in all this – she doesn't know how to love us, Kate. But just like Helga was attracted to me, the two of you have been thrown together by this same cosmic attraction; you have karmic battles to sort out between you. She knows something of our secret work, but not the extent of it, and believe me, she isn't on our side. She's working for the dark forces and you need to learn to protect yourself against her psychic invasions."

Kate was speechless. It seemed that every day her life was subject to seismic shifts.

"Here's what you can do. First, when you feel her negative energy, summon up an image of her and mentally put it into a tower." He chuckled and made a tower shape with his hands. Put her in it!" He giggled at the thought and Kate laughed with him, feeling some tension loosen.

"Her spirit won't like that, one bit," Jacob continued. "Seal it top and bottom so she can't get out. Then place the whole thing on the other side of a river. It will disempower her, although only for as long as your focus can keep her there, and you have such a lot of work to do that this can only ever be a temporary measure.

"As for her invading your mind, when you feel it happening, you can either just think gobbledygook, sing a song or 'tune-out' or place an imaginary tube over you and have it mirrored on the outside. Mentally of course, or you will look most odd! Any bad thing she sends you will be mirrored straight back to her." He chuckled again, pleased with himself.

Kate smiled, greatly relieved.

“Thanks, Dad,” she said, hugging him. “I’ll remember those tips in times of need. She really does scare me though! It must’ve been pretty tricky for you when she set her sights on you.”

“I was given help, Kate. As you will be. Come on, let’s go or we’ll be late for the meeting.”

CHAPTER THIRTEEN

SPREADING THE WORD

'Remember, each one of us has the power to change the world.'

Yoko Ono

Kate couldn't stop thinking about what she'd learnt during her mind-travels. Could it really be true that visitors from other planets were already amongst us? When she walked down the street, she began to see people in a different way and noticed some with features that didn't quite fit with a human face. Longer noses, bigger eyes, and pointed ears – really distinctive, now she came to think about it. Why had she never seen this before? Could it be that only now she was aware of it that they became recognisably different?

One day as she walked down the high street, she noticed a woman looking at her as if she were odd. Then she remembered what Sechem had said: "So you thought you were human." At the time, it was too extraordinary a concept to process, so she let it pass, but what did he mean? She must remember to run it by Jacob to see what he had to say on the subject. She was so grateful her father was party to everything that was happening; she didn't know how she would have coped on her own.

She knew she needed to focus on spreading the word about the threat to the Earth, as Sechem had said, and the new venues for meetings was a great start. She had to branch out, get more organised, expand the network of like-minded souls. She needed help, and she knew just the girl to ask, someone who was a whizz with event organising: her dear friend Poppy. She'd be amazing at networking and setting up a public-speaking circuit. All Kate had to do was persuade her. She winced at the memory of Poppy's scepticism last time she'd broached the subject of aliens.

"I'm happy to help, but what are the talks about?" Poppy asked as they sat over a cup of coffee at Tom's. "Nothing illegal, I hope! I do have my scruples, you know," Poppy joked. She paused. "Please tell me it isn't your little green men."

"Not green, no," said Kate. "Just the kind of things I told you about before."

Poppy rolled her eyes. "Oh Kate, I can't believe you're still going on about aliens. And now you want to spread the word? Seriously? I'm worried about you."

"You don't need to be, Poppy," Kate replied. "I'm fine. And I know you're not interested in the subject but lots of people are – that's okay isn't it? I just want to reach out to those people."

"Fair enough, I suppose," said Poppy, taking a slurp of her coffee.

"Thanks, Pops, you're a star. We can start with the Positive Living Group, that personal development and spiritual network based in town. They're used to way-out ideas!"

"You said it! What do you want me to do?" asked Poppy. "You sound like you've got it all worked out."

"I haven't talked in any major venues yet, or to anyone who isn't already on board with psychic phenomena. I just need help with the networking, and getting bums on seats. And mostly it's because you are so good at organising."

Poppy grinned. "Flattery will get you everywhere. Okay, count me in, just don't expect me to come to the meetings, right? When do you want to start?"

"The sooner the better."

They set to work on the fliers, first.

Do ETs and UFOs Really Exist?

Come and hear the evidence directly from the mouth of Kate Greene, who communicates with aliens. Discover all about this fascinating topic, and learn how you too can communicate with Spirit.

"Well, the mention of ETs should bring them in out in droves, just out of sheer curiosity, if nothing else. But shouldn't you have started with something less controversial?"

"I haven't got time for that, Poppy. As long as I have your support with the logistics, then I'm more than happy."

"Well, it could be fun seeing the weirdos who'd turn up for something like this. And brace yourself for some heckling. You have my support, girlfriend." They high-fived and got on with the job in hand, like back in the day when they were doing some homework assignment, like – well, like two giggling schoolgirls.

A week later Poppy received a phone call from the organiser of Bournemouth's Positive Living Group. Their speaker for the following week had cancelled and he wanted to know if Kate could step in at short notice. Kate agreed, hoping she would have her talk worked out by then.

On the night, a steady stream of people filed into their meeting room.

Kate stood nervously at the side of the stage, listening to the noise of murmuring voices. This was a far cry from the talks to a couple of dozen people that she'd given so far. This time she wasn't preaching to the converted. She shut her eyes and crossed her fingers, then remembered that Jacob told her to always ask for help if she needed it.

"Please, Sechem, help me with the words I need tonight. Please let me send the right message."

Not long after, the presenter introduced her, and the audience fell silent. Kate took to the stage and looked out over the sea of expectant faces in front of her – hundreds of them – and wondered why on earth she put herself through this. She stepped up to the front and, trying to control her shaking knees, rested her notes on the lectern to stop them quivering in her hands, and then she began.

"Do ETs and UFOs exist? Or are we alone in the Universe?" Kate paused and readied her notes. She took a deep breath. "I'm here today to tell you that indeed they do exist, and we are not alone – but forget the Hollywood archetypes of alien invasions; if they had meant to harm us they could've done so years ago." She shuffled her notes looking for the examples she wanted to share.

"I'll give you some examples proving how long they've been coming here, but there are many others which you can easily research on the Internet if you wish."

She looked down at her papers. "Did you know that former President Jimmy Carter and about a dozen witnesses saw a UFO in 1969? He said it was 'the darnedest thing' he'd ever seen. It was very bright. It changed colours and was about the size of the moon as seen from earth. He said, 'One thing is for sure, I'll never make fun of people who say they've seen unidentified flying objects.'"

Kate had attempted an American accent and the audience laughed. She relaxed a little and continued. "President Truman stated, 'I can assure you that flying saucers, given that they exist, are not constructed by anyone on our Earth.' Kate noticed a man standing at the back of the hall holding a Dictaphone. Why didn't he sit with the rest of the people? Concerned and puzzled, Kate tried to remember her thread.

"In fact, there is speculation that many presidents and other leaders have been aboard a UFO, here on Earth." Kate waited and watched the audience. She'd learnt a lot by watching the speeches of presidents and prime ministers, noting how they often paused between sentences. It kept the audience's attention, she realised.

Someone shouted, "Wouldn't surprise me one little bit, what they get up to."

Everybody laughed and began calling out. Kate raised her hand and waited till they calmed down. At least they were not hostile. She breathed a sigh of relief and carried on.

"In 1963 President John F Kennedy sent a memo to the head of the CIA, seeking documents about UFOs, just 10 days before he was assassinated. JFK wanted a review of all UFO intelligence files that might affect national security. On the same day, Kennedy sent a separate memo to NASA, indicating he wanted to cooperate with the then Soviet Union on outer space activities." There was a hush among the audience, and to her delight, she spotted Poppy sitting in the back row, fully attentive.

"In 1974, President Richard Nixon became part of UFO folklore when he allegedly took comedian Jackie Gleason to Homestead Air Force Base in Florida and showed him wreckage of a flying saucer, as well as the remains of several extra-terrestrials. The story was made public by Larry Warren, who had been involved in real UFO encounters experienced by many American military personnel at the RAF Bentwaters base in the UK, in 1980.

"As you see, I can list any number of top governmental figures all confirming the existence of aliens. You yourself can research more on the Internet."

A lot of murmuring came from the audience and several hands shot up. Kate held her hand up for silence.

"Questions at the end only, please," she smiled. "You're not as alone on this planet as you think. As well as historical evidence, I can confirm from personal experience that they're still with us today, and they have a message to share. They want us to become more spiritually attuned and to take care of the planet. It's such a positive message, I hope you can join me in following them.

"As the sci-fi movie poster says: 'We are among you.' Only this isn't science fiction. And there can be a happy ending – remember, they've been here for years and no War of the Worlds has happened! Can interstellar peaceful coexistence be in our future? Why not? It has already been going on for centuries.

"I hope that has convinced you of the presence of extra-terrestrials on our planet. And we are still unharmed. There is more to fear from our own people on this planet than ETs. They are only here to help us towards a brighter future. Come to my next meeting to find out more."

The response in the room was explosive. People actually stood up from their seats, applauding her. Then came the questions, a barrage of questions. Kate had obviously tapped into the zeitgeist.

"Will aliens visit me?"

"What should I do if I'm visited?"

"Are we safe from attack?"

"Are you an alien?"

Eventually, Kate was forced to call an end to the meeting, otherwise she could have carried on all night. The presenter closed the evening and ushered Kate out the back door.

"Wow you've really set the cat among the pigeons now. I hope you'll come and give a similar talk again."

* * *

The next morning dawned bright and breezy. Clouds scudded across the sky, and having done what she'd promised Sechem, Kate felt really good. She heard the local paper land on the floor with a thud, delivered as it was by the nonchalant boy on his bicycle who could hardly be bothered to walk up the garden path, and she went to get it thinking she'd read it in the garden with a cup of coffee. She bent down to pick it up and found her face staring straight back at her from the front page. It was a review of her talk. 'Local girl says Little Green Men have been coming here for years'.

"Oh, for goodness sake," said Kate aloud. "They couldn't even get the colour right!"

The review continued, mostly in a ridiculing manner. So that's who the man at the back of the hall was. Kate snorted at the closed-mindedness of his article, but she wasn't surprised. She knew she had a challenge ahead of her and couldn't expect the cynical media to be on board. However, the response she'd received in the meeting cheered her immensely, and that was what she chose to focus on.

Today, she didn't have to go into the office or face Helga and her cronies for a full weekend. What a relief. Dressed in her gardening clothes, Kate set about tidying up the vegetable patch before autumn passed and winter blew in. Already the leaves were falling and covering the paths and grass. When she'd finished in the garden she planned to take a walk in the park so she could breathe freely and enjoy scuffling her feet through the carpet of dried leaves.

Jacob however, had other ideas. From the back garden, it took Kate a while to realise that someone was banging on the front door.

"I'm coming, I'm coming," she shouted.

She raced through the house, only stopping to wipe her feet, and opened the door to find her father waiting.

"Oh, it's you!" she exclaimed.

"What sort of a greeting is that?" he said, kissing her on the cheek. "Aren't you pleased to see me?"

"Of course I am." That was true, but she had to resign herself to losing her walk in the park and some precious daylight hours. She never knew where they'd end up after a conversation with Jacob.

"Good. Any tea, my darling?"

"Sure. Let's sit outside. No point in wasting the lovely day, and, I'll bring the tea out there."

Jacob nodded and Kate led him through the house to the garden. She set up the folding garden chairs beside the little wooden table, ready for the tea tray. It was a pleasant, shady spot.

Kate waited a decent interval while Jacob sipped his tea, but before he could enlighten her as to the reason for his visit, a thought popped into her head.

"Do you remember me telling you about a meeting I had once?"

"What meeting?" Jacob, engrossed in watching a ladybird tackling the jungle of hairs on his arm, barely looked up.

"It was some time ago. I was in town for an appointment with the optician, and his wife walked in. Remember? I told you about it."

Jacob shrugged. "Vaguely… And, so?"

"Well, I'd never met either of them before, but as soon as his wife's eyes met mine we simultaneously said, 'I know you from before man was.' And we then both spoke in a strange language. Now don't you think that was odd? I certainly thought it was odd at the time. I didn't really know what it was we'd said to each other – I felt a bit embarrassed really! I quickly made an excuse and left. What was that all about, Dad?"

Jacob let the ladybird crawl onto his finger, then he lowered it gently onto Kate's favourite lavender bush, the one that was full of bumblebees in the summer. He looked at his daughter, perplexed.

"Oh Katie," he sighed, "in spite of all the messages and experiences you've been having, you still don't know who you are, do you?" He shook his head in an, 'I don't get it' kind of way. "But it's for you to find out for yourself, if you can."

Kate grimaced, somewhat miffed. A little attention to what she'd said would've helped, but Jacob seemed more interested in the ladybird. Coming second to a ladybird, eh? Now who'd have thought it?

"Dad… what do you mean?" she whined, somewhat uncharacteristically.

"It's important that things unfold as they should Kate, without me interfering, so I won't say more. But think about that conversation. Think about what it may have meant. I'll get going now, my dear." Jacob got up stiffly, made his way back indoors and exited the house, leaving Kate with no idea why he'd called. Perhaps he'd just been lonely? Did there have to be a reason? Perhaps he was just checking she was alright. Kate decided she liked that idea.

* * *

Kate began to receive messages almost every time she meditated or slept. She was fully invested in what they wanted her to do, yet the constant invasions into her thoughts were hard to deal with, especially when she just wanted to rest and centre herself.

"Damn it!" she complained one night in the early hours when once more, a voice woke her up and insisted she pay attention. She pulled the bedclothes over her head, tossing and turning to try and blot it out. But it wouldn't let up no matter how she resisted. She might just as well give in and listen.

It turned out to be Sechem. Did he never sleep?

"Spring is eternal they say. But not all areas have a spring, though it is the way your world works. The Earth will turn and the seasons will adjust accordingly. Do not fear for this is a natural event which has happened before," he said.

"I am not fearful of anything," Kate said, wondering if this may be some explanation of the changing climate the world had begun to experience. "I just want a decent night's sleep."

"Please do not interrupt me," he grumbled.

"Sorry."

"Whatever the powers that be on your planet try do, they cannot change these occurrences."

"What occurrences?"

"I've just told you. The Earth turning and seasons changing. Don't you ever listen?"

Kate screwed up her face and rolled her eyes. She figured he couldn't see her in the dark of her room.

“They think they’re all powerful,” he continued, “but they’re not. All you can do is be prepared, and most of all, do not be concerned. The existence of souls is paramount, all souls, whoever they might be. This is where those whose intentions are nefarious need to take note. Their continuation may not be what they had expected. Those who put themselves in high places have the furthest to fall. Pass this on. Transmission terminated.”

“Does this mean I can go back to sleep?” Kate asked the disembodied voice. But there was no answer. Sechem had cut the lines of communication, like switching off a light. There one minute and gone the next.

CHAPTER FOURTEEN

ENTER ADAM

Shifting sands, shifting sands. Smooth movement of land, vast land. Nothing is recognisable, nothing is left of former times. Move on, move on. The new is fresh, the new is welcoming you. Forget the past, forget the now. Look ahead. It is almost here. Can't you see it coming? Do not be caught unawares. Do not waste time. Get your mind settled in peace and readiness. The change is for you. You will do this with no company alongside except me. I am Ra, the greatest of all. Come with me. Be with me on my beam of life and you will know all.

Ra

The boardroom was packed. Colonel Adam Fenshawe didn't think he'd ever seen so many high-ranking officers and commanders in one place at the same time before. He began to fidget and repeatedly look at his watch. Time was running out. If he was going to make his plane, he'd have to hurry. The girl taking notes caught his eye and smiled. Clearly, she was interested in him. She often seemed to be where he was, and he suspected she organised it that way. She missed nothing.

"Do you have to go?" she mouthed silently and pointed to her watch.

He nodded and raised his shoulders in a, 'What can I do?' gesture.

What happened next took him by surprise. It took everybody by surprise. She fell off her chair and landed awkwardly, screaming in pain

"Oh! I think I've twisted my ankle," she yelled. Men rushed to help the attractive girl, and just before they surrounded her, she winked at Adam. He nodded his thanks and used the confusion to make his escape from the building. Now he'd be able to carry out his mission, and would no longer have to pretend to agree with the plans these military men had in mind.

Adam's highest security clearance enabled him to be anywhere anytime without questions asked. Everyone said he was rather young to be holding this position, but they didn't dare go into why he'd got where he was. Whenever they enquired, they were told,

"Secret stuff, you know. Best keep out of it."

Finally, free of the stultifying atmosphere of the meeting, Adam sank back into the leather seats of his official car, diplomatic flag waving as it sped through the heavy traffic of Washington DC. He had plenty of time to reflect on his mission, which had nothing whatsoever to do with the military meeting he'd just been attending. If only they knew. He chuckled. He had just enough time to change into civilian dress before going to the airport.

* * *

Adam was tall with wavy, light gold hair and he moved with both athletic grace and authority. His many female admirers saw him as a Brad Pitt look-alike, but he appeared to be oblivious of their overtures. They couldn't understand why he seemed to be immune to the wiles of the opposite sex. Rumours went round that perhaps he was gay. "That would account for it," was a common response, assuring all that his lack of interest wasn't personal.

This placement to Earth was the last thing Adam expected. Many months ago, before he left the Way Station in space — also known as the Mother Ship — the Galactic Command had told him about the body switch.

Adam had stood before a long table with a line of multi-planetary beings from the Galactic Command sitting on the other side. He waited for them to speak.

"We have a mission for you," the being in the centre said. "Since you have evolved sufficiently to be allowed to exchange places with an already incarnated person, you will exchange with Colonel Adam Fenshawe who, in accordance with the law requiring full agreement of both outgoing and incoming souls, has agreed that a switch be made. You'll be a 'walk-in'."

Adam raised his eyebrows. He'd never had a mission like this before. "What will happen to him after I step in?"

"He'll move his soul on to other experiences in non-physical worlds. Then, when he's ready, he'll reincarnate, just as he would if he'd gone through a normal physical death."

Adam frowned slightly, wondering what he was getting himself into.

"Why does he want to quit?" Adam asked.

"Colonel Fenshawe, the outgoing soul, has had enough of his involvement in the terrible affairs of the Black Ops military. If he blows the whistle, he'll be killed. He's against suicide, but is at the end of his tether, and since he's still a young man, he can't wait until retirement. There appears to be no way out for him, except this. During a very powerful dream his soul explained to his conscious mind that a switch could be made, providing he agreed. Since he has no family to miss him, he jumped at this solution. He's ready to go."

A bright glowing figure at the end of the table stood up. Adam recognised him as Master M.

"Do you agree?" Master M asked.

"When can I go?" was Adam's quick reply, so many months ago.

* * *

The night before the meeting in DC, Sechem had contacted Adam. He'd been in a deep sleep when he heard a voice filtering through his dreams. Adam gave up trying to sleep. He propped himself up on one elbow and watched Sechem wandering around his room.

"Well, you have my attention. What's so important that you have to wake me up?"

Sechem stopped exploring the room. "We want you to fly to England. Tomorrow would be good."

"Why do I have to fly to England in such a hurry?" Adam heaved a sigh. "You never give me tasks that are easy or straightforward."

Sechem sat on the bed, leaned close to Adam's ear and lowered his voice to a whisper. "Master M sent me to put you in the picture. There's a young woman over there who needs help."

Adam groaned. "Young women are always wanting my attention. What's new?"

"Ah, but this one is different. She's one of us; her father Jacob is too. Only she doesn't know it yet."

"If she's one of us, she ought to be able to look after herself."

"You're not listening. She doesn't know who she is, but she's giving talks on politically sensitive things – things that involve our inter-galactic colleagues. I've visited and talked to her about this, in fact, I asked her to give the talks to educate the populous, but she's being closely watched by our adversaries who have infiltrated her workplace. I'm afraid she is in danger. Her lectures are vitally important, but we need to protect her. That's where you come in. She's doing good work, but by going into areas that are meant to be hidden from the public, she's compromising her safety. There's a fine line between educating and revealing things that some would rather were left secret, and she hasn't yet learnt quite how to stay on the right side of that line. Your military people are gunning for her. She's being watched and you know what that means."

"My people? That's rich. They're not my people. You and the Galactic Command Council put me in with them." Adam groaned at the memory of the company he had to keep in DC in order to do his job. It was no wonder the original Colonel Fenshawe wanted to get out.

Sechem stared at Adam. "Yes, yes I know. You realise of course that the reason you're there inside the Shadow Government is to get them to consider the consequences of their actions and to report back to us. Some of what they do may be irreversible and will affect them too."

Adam sighed. "So what am I supposed to do with this young woman? By the way, what is her name?"

"Protect her. Her name is Kate Greene. We will brief you on the plane. Make friends with her. Get her to like you. That should be easy given your charms and looks." Sechem laughed his gurgling laugh.

Adam sighed. This was all he needed – another silly girl. He was tired of being judged by his appearance. It wasn't even his! Just the host's body that he'd adopted.

Sechem saw this and tut-tutted under his breath. "You'll not be on your own with this task. We are sending help from The Command."

CHAPTER FIFTEEN

AT FIRST SIGHT

Loved ones of this Earth. We wish to assure you that you are not alone in your endeavours to bring our reality into that of the Earth plane.

Osishoo ET

After the revelations about Helga's psychic abilities and her work for the dark forces, Kate kept more to herself at work than ever before. She sensed that Helga was on the lookout for information about what Kate might be doing out of the workplace, and as usual her instincts were correct. Kate never mentioned her talks to anyone at work, but they weren't exactly kept a secret, being advertised as they were on certain websites and magazines. It was only a matter of time before Helga cottoned on. But, withdrawing from the office chitchat made her feel very alone. She needed someone she could trust, someone she could confide in, but someone like that was in short supply.

One night, after work she called round to see Jacob, needing to vent her frustrations about work and her worries about the talks.

"You know Dad, I can't think what happened to my original contract of employment, but they definitely doctored it so that I can't leave – it's like at least when I'm at work, they can keep an eye on me. But what about the talks? They're bound to find out about them sooner or later, and that's going to really enrage Helga."

"Yes, I'm worried about that too. I think we need to ask Poppy to form an email database so we can contact people personally, without advertising the talks, and I think we need to vary the venue and the days you speak." Jacob looked thoughtful, his years showing in his greying temples, his furrowed brow.

As it had already been arranged, Kate arrived early for her public talk on remote viewing at the Positive Living Centre, who had invited her to speak again the very next day after her first lecture. She was fascinated to see who else was interested in this subject. Who would turn up was anybody's guess. She watched from the side of the stage as people entered the hall. People-watching was one of her favourite pastimes. The hall filled up fast. A couple of hairy bikers walked in followed by a tall, strikingly attractive man with blond hair. He strode confidently through the door, wearing a perfect and expensive suit. She thought him the most gloriously handsome man she'd ever seen: he carried an air of authority which commanded respect. Putting it mildly, she was smitten, and to say it made her nervous about her lecture was an understatement.

Kate's love life to date had been a bit of a disappointment. She'd had a couple of boyfriends at college but no one she had ever felt a real connection with. No one had truly 'got' her, seen inside her soul and understood her and so she had resigned herself to being single, at least for the foreseeable future. That is, until she saw this intriguing man, who made her heart flutter and her pulse race.

He sat down a row or two in front of her.

"Oh!" escaped from her lips, in spite of herself.

Whilst she gave her lecture, her eyes would inadvertently flit over to him and she felt unreasonably jealous when the person next to him made a comment and he replied.

At the interval, she made her way through the crowd to the little room at the back, where tea and biscuits had been set out. She stepped into the line for tea and, feeling eyes on her, turned. The blond god stood just inside the door, looking at her with a smile. Their eyes met, and Kate felt as if an electric current had zipped right through her. Then, while her heart skipped a beat, he strode purposefully across the crowded room to her side. Eyes followed him. He would never be inconspicuous.

"Come with me," he said softly into her ear, his words so quiet that Kate wondered if she'd heard correctly. He took her by the arm and drew her out of the room and into the passage. "I've come a long way to meet you," he said.

To her dismay, Kate was unable to formulate a word. She sort of grunted a bit and annoyingly, felt a blush emanate from her very core. How embarrassing, she thought – I hope my foundation covers it up.

"They told me where to find you, so here I am. Oh sorry. My name's Adam Fenshawe. I'm pleased to meet you."

Kate opened her mouth to respond but still found herself to be struck dumb. This sort of thing didn't happen in real life, did it? She raised her eyebrows and looked down at his hand on her arm. "Emm, p…pleased to meet you too," she stuttered. Then, regaining her composure she added, "Who's 'they'?"

"Let me reassure you with one word: Sechem." Then he surprised her even more by saying, "It's safe to tell me everything you know, everything."

Kate's was incredulous. This was just insane. "Err… can we go and sit down somewhere?" she asked, fearing her legs would give out.

"Of course. Let's sit over there." He pointed to a couple of chairs near the entrance. "I enjoyed your lecture by the way."

Kate nodded. "Thanks," she said, not quite sure if he was mocking her. Grateful they didn't have to go far, she knew that if she needed to call for help someone would hear her. He might be the most handsome man she'd ever met, but how direct and confident he was unnerved her. But he had uttered the word, 'Sechem'. That was a fact.

Kate stared at him, amazed and slightly bewildered. "How do you know about Sechem?"

He answered her question in an easy, agreeable tone. "We go back a long way, and he told me about you." Just then a black cat ran, yes, ran over to him and curled itself around his legs, purring loudly. He reached his hand down and stroked it tenderly. It gave Kate time to absorb that astounding piece of information, she relaxed. Crazy as it sounded, in the light of what she knew, it made sense. Somehow, she knew she could trust him. Meeting someone in everyday life who knew all about Sechem was incredible. It felt as if worlds were colliding: her world of aliens and her everyday life.

"Listen to me Kate. You're going to have to be very careful of Helga and her spies Silas and Marco," he whispered. "Very careful indeed. They seem to be one step ahead of you most of the time, do they not? Have you noticed?"

She gasped in surprise. "How on earth do you know about them?"

"We are watching your mind-travels," he said, "but so are they. They might look like imbeciles, but they are highly skilled operatives, and you are in danger every moment you're in their company, but also when you're lecturing. We must find a way to block them. I'll help you with that."

"Well, that would be lovely…" Kate winced at her crass response but she was so utterly thrown by meeting this knight in shining armour that her brain had frozen. Pulling herself together she added, "Well, I could just leave work altogether, go AWOL."

“That’s true, but have you ever heard the adage, ‘Keep your enemies in plain sight’? Life will be easier for you if you know where they are. They’re keeping an eye on you, but you’re also keeping an eye on them. Two can play at that game.”

“I see what you mean…” she mused.

“Look, I’ve booked a room nearby until I can get something more permanent. So, we’ll be physically close, and I can protect you.” He smiled.

Take me to bed, Kate’s thought inappropriately, raising another blush. Oh god, what’s happening to me? She hoped he wasn’t a mind-reader along with all his other obvious talents. A bell rang in the foyer.

“The lecture’s about to continue,” he said. “You’re needed. You’d best go in. I’ll be in touch.” He stood up and walked away, leaving her to take the lectern, her thoughts all over the place. But her heart ached at the parting. Is this what’s meant by love at first sight?

Unable to regain her composure, she took questions from the audience for the final session. Adam was nowhere to be seen.

* * *

That night all she could think about was the divine Adam with his blue eyes and blonde hair. She wondered briefly, very briefly, what Francine would make of him, and figured that since he clearly intended to stick around, she wouldn’t have to wait long to find out. That night she had a dream, but not about Adam at all. Pity, she thought later.

She stood to attention in front of a desk surrounded by walls lined with books. Was this a library? It appeared to be so. Behind the desk sat a man wearing a blue jump suit. Star Trek came to her mind.

Could this be Sechem's real outfit, she wondered? Perhaps, but it was unclear, as dreams often are. Maybe it was one of Sechem's race. The similarity was uncanny.

The man began to speak in the same musical tone as Sechem.

"From what I've learnt about you, child, you use Jacob the father to tell you what's happening. He knows about military bases on the Moon. However, what he has heard regarding the underground movement cannot be verified. See what can be done there."

"Is that a command?" she asked. "Or instruction?"

He ignored the question.

"Bring in the knowledge you are getting on underground water and sea bases, visitors from other planets, and the programme to infiltrate all areas of government, not just those of the Black Budget underworld. Bring in and report on as much as you can."

"Well I'm here and waiting for the connection. Is what I've done so far the correct way of acting and of thinking?"

He tilted his head as if pondering the matter. "It will do for now."

"That's not much of an answer, is it?" she said.

The man stood and moved away from the desk towards shelves of books and ran his hands lovingly over them.

"The apples from the tree keep falling. If too many fall there will be no more left. If they fall too soon then the Tree of Life will suffer as a result."

Kate raised her eyebrows. "Very poetic, I'm sure. What can we do about it?"

"The first thing is to nourish. Everything has to be nourished and that includes the Tree of Life. It has been denuded by wrong thinking, by ill-fated actions. It is time to put things right."

"Talking of rights," she said. "Everybody knows where we humans are going wrong, but nobody really knows how to rectify matters. We just end up with platitudes and no action. I need some advice please. I need to speak to someone who can assist me."

"We have sent Adam," came the reply.

Later when she awoke and analysed the intense dream she sensed it was some kind of message, a warning of sorts, but she wasn't quite sure what. At least she could tell Adam, but when and how? He hadn't even given her a contact number.

* * *

Kate could not wait to ring Poppy and arrange to meet for coffee at Tom's. As usual, they ordered cakes of all descriptions to go with their drinks. Poppy sat opposite, tucking in. After a bit of the usual chit chat, she stopped eating, observing her friend for a moment, then said, "Come on then girl – give me the low down! Don't keep it all to yourself."

Kate hesitated. "I don't know what you mean."

"You're like the cat that's got the cream – what's going on?"

"I've met a man, Poppy," she said, and blushed.

"Ooh! How exciting," Poppy said sarcastically. "I met several today too."

"I think I'm in love. I can't stop thinking about him and I've only met him once and then it was only for a few minutes. Crazy, isn't it?"

Poppy grinned. "Okay, spill. What's he look like? Where did you meet him?"

"Tall, blond and handsome. I mean it! Drop dead gorgeous. He came to the lecture yesterday, at the PLG – did I tell you they asked me back?" Kate said with a dreamy expression.

"A chat?" Poppy asked ignoring her question. "And you fell in love there and then? What're you like!" She clapped her hands soundlessly, delight beaming from her face. "What was the chat about?"

"I can't remember."

"Oh, for goodness sake, give me strength!" Poppy said, still grinning like a Cheshire cat, then she brushed the crumbs off her lap and checked her watch. "Look, Katie, I have to get back to walk the dogs," she shuffled in her purse, pulled out a note and placed it on the table to pay her share of the bill, "but I want to know more about this guy, right. And if you're that keen, then let him know. You're always so backwards at coming forwards! I'll ring you later, yeah?"

"Oh, it's early days yet, it'll probably come to nothing," replied Kate, but in her heart she knew that if Adam had a connection with Sechem, this certainly wouldn't come to nothing, even though it may not necessarily be romantic. She'd only met him the day before, but she felt sure that he was going to be someone special in her life.

* * *

The following morning, now that she knew that Helga and her cronies were well and truly on her case, Kate kept her mind carefully cloaked whenever they were around, and focused on nothing but work during the day. She'd discovered through careful enquiries in various offices that the visiting men were both from the US from some obscure government department in Washington DC. Satellites, my eye, she thought! Who were they kidding? She knew the company had other secret programmes that never made the public records, or the financial books. She knew too that the business was expanding, taking on more staff and offices to accommodate visitors from other countries. Intriguing indeed.

Kate was studying some figures at her desk when a shiver ran down her back. She looked up, and her mouth fell open. Through the glass partition, she saw Adam in a dark, expensive looking suit chatting to Silas.

Kate's first thought was that she'd been double-crossed. That he'd tried to gain her trust, get her onside – could she really trust him? What in heaven's name was he doing there and what was he saying to Silas, the living skeleton man? Adam glanced her way, then looked quickly back. She tried to keep a blank look on her face for the sake of Marco who sat facing her, though the urge to smile at Adam was overwhelming. She rightly guessed it would be a bad idea to let on they knew each other. But how much did she really know about him? Why was he closeted with Silas? Seemingly they were very friendly with each other. Did they know each other.

At last she could stand it no longer. "Who's that blonde man with Silas?" she asked Marco as casually as she could.

Marco scowled. "He's here to discuss a new monitoring satellite," he grumbled. "As if we don't have enough to do already."

Well, I've never seen you doing very much anyway, Kate wanted to say, but again thought better of it.

The day dragged on with Kate forever on the lookout for more signs of Adam. She lifted her head again and again to scan the corridors just in case, made trips to the loo and the water cooler in case he was lingering there. Honestly, she had it bad.

At last the day ended and she was able to escape. When she pulled into her drive after work she found him sitting on her doorstep. Holy

Moses, thank you god and all your angels, she muttered to herself a smile involuntarily wrapping itself across her face. Clearly, he'd been waiting for her.

"You'll really need to get your doorbell fixed," he said when she walked up the path.

"How do you know where I live?" she asked feeling a strange mix of euphoria and suspicion.

He grinned. "You forget we know all about you. Big Brother and all that."

Her face fell. Big Brother? "I don't think that's a laughing matter," she said. His comment, though jokingly said, dampened her delight at seeing him. "I'm not sure I can trust you, but since you're here you'd better come in." Kate surprised herself at the coolness in her voice. Poppy was right, she was backwards at coming forwards. She knew the net curtains in the street would be twitching with curiosity, nonetheless.

She unlocked the door and stood aside as he went in, admiring his physique as he passed her by, then blushed again at the thought that goodness knows who might be 'catching' her thoughts. She cloaked them quickly so they remained private – a technique Jacob had recently taught her, that took some doing – and wondered instead what he would think of her little house. She showed him into the front room and watched him as he studied her books and the small ornaments and crystals lined up on the mantelpiece. He looked around him at the shabby chairs but remained standing.

"Oh, where are my manners? Please sit down, you make me nervous," she said awkwardly, feeling hideously self-conscious.

Adam coughed politely. "Before we go on, I want to apologise. I'm sorry about that wisecrack. But Big Brother is more real than you think and they know what you are doing, Kate. Mind journeys and what you do in them are every bit as real as you and I being here together. No less real," he said with emphasis. "I'm here as a backup should anything happen to you."

"Oh dear," she said, genuinely worried now. "Please do sit down."

He chose the most dilapidated chair she owned, the one with the stuffing poking out but he didn't appear to notice how uncomfortable it was. She sat on the couch opposite.

Adam carried on, seemingly oblivious to her emotional turmoil. "We are, all of us, extremely concerned about nuclear warheads both on Earth and those sent into space."

"Yes, so am I," replied Kate, furrowing her brow in an attempt at gravitas, but wishing they could just talk about more normal things like music and literature, like ordinary people.

"There's also the problem of the accumulation of nuclear waste from all nuclear power stations. Dumping it is not the answer. If it continues, it will soon pile up into unmanageable amounts."

"A bit like our landfill sites and plastic in our seas," Kate said.

Adam grunted but said nothing. Then as if they were having a perfectly normal conversation, he said, "Any chance of a cup of tea or coffee? I'm parched."

"Coming up," she said quickly, relieved to have some time alone in the kitchen to think without his distracting presence. Should she trust Adam with things she'd never told anyone except her father? Was his presence at work really to protect her, or was he actually colluding with 'the enemy' as she now called Helga and her cohorts. She decided that she could trust Adam, if he could give her some proof that he was on her side. She couldn't bear to think he could be a spy who had intercepted one of her mind travels and was here under false pretences.

She laid biscuits, milk sugar and two mugs on a tray, then once the tea and coffee was made, added the tea pot and carried it in. She placed the tray on the coffee table beside Adam's chair, poured the drinks, then sat back on the sofa and watched him. He chose a biscuit, with great care, as if it were most important. Curious, she thought.

"Do you like them? The biscuits, I mean."

"Yes," he mumbled, with his mouth full.

"I have to be honest with you, Adam. It's good to think you're here to protect me, but how do I know I can trust you?"

He swallowed a mouthful of biscuit and took a sip of coffee before speaking. "I told you that we have a mutual friend, Sechem."

Kate studied him. "Yes, you did. Describe him and tell me how you know him."

Adam nodded and gave her a description of the being she knew as Sechem. As well as a physical description, he also described his musical voice. He tried to copy it but failed. They both laughed at his efforts. "He's also doesn't have a great sense of timing which is not the best for getting a good night's sleep," he finished.

"That's him alright!" Kate laughed. Convinced now, she couldn't wait to tell Adam her most recent journey into the mind, as it was definitely relevant to what he was talking about.

"Please do," he said when she asked if he'd like to hear about it.

Kate took herself there again. She spoke as if she'd entered some kind of time slip, as if she were still there.

"I'm in a kind of orange jumpsuit. There's a walkway sloping down. It's got handrails and isn't very wide, and it winds down, goes round in curves, no angles. This is really weird. I don't know where I am. I've come up against a thick wall. I remember that I'm only mind, and walk straight through it, no problem. But the wall is there for others. I can only walk through it because I'm in a non-physical state.

"I'm in a different place now. It's softly lit by emergency lights. I hear a gentle hum. I don't know where this is leading me, but it's going into somewhere that requires work, specialised work. Oh, I see! My mind keeps going to the nuclear disaster in Japan. This is something to do with that. That's why I have a protective suit. But this is a mind job. I must remember I'm not physical.

"I am in the heart of things now, in the very centre. It's a massive area. I see disconnected pipes. I put them together. I do this with my mind, but using my 'energy hands'. I snap them together and screw the rings tight. There are quite a few of these, and I must do them all. I'm now opening a conduit which allows the coolant, or whatever it is they use, to come through. I do this and it starts to flow. It's designed to bring the levels of danger down. Where all this is coming from I don't know, but this is what I must do.

"I stand watching it happen. The place feels extremely dangerous with massive levels of radiation, but I know I'm alright. There are switches; I turn some of them on. Things are starting to happen around me. There's a glow and a vibration, a physical vibration, caused by a noise. Gentle humming now.

"Things begin to change, become more settled, it's time to leave. I turn around looking to find a way out. I see a wall and step into it. It's very thick and eventually, I emerge on the other side, into a much cooler environment. The fresh air is a relief. I'm out of there. Hands come and pull me away. They belong to spirit guides, from the angelic realm. They pull me out and attend to me."

Adam snapped his fingers, bringing her out of her recall. "My goodness, you go in so easily and so deep. And it sounds like you're already working on exactly what we're concerned about. No wonder the CIA are frightened of what you can do and where you can go."

Kate frowned. The CIA? But in one way, his reaction was good as it revealed that the secret government didn't know the scope of what she did after all. That was a relief.

"You'll have to keep quiet about this," he said, "or you'll have more falling downstairs episodes, or worse."

"Oh, you know about them as well? There is much more," she said. "I've been to so many other places you wouldn't believe. How much time do you have?" She paused, remembering that she was putting a lot of faith in a complete stranger. "You are trustworthy, aren't you? I mean in the 'real' world." Knowing about Sechem was one thing, but he clearly had dealings with the firm where she worked.

His smile at her words made her go weak at the knees. How could she not trust him?

"I have a high-security position within the government. The best place to be, don't you think, to be 'in the know' so I can react? I have authority there and am well placed. I am what you would call a 'Light Hat', a Trojan Horse really." He reached into his pocket. "Here take my card. My private number is on the back."

She recalled Sechem referring to Light Hats as the beings who were concerned for the spiritual growth of humanity. Once again, he referred to something she'd learned only from her space friends. He really does know, she realised as she took the offered card. Suddenly she felt terribly tired.

"I can't do what you are doing," he said, "but we are watching. Keep safe. Do you hear me? I mean it." He gave her a quick peck on the cheek and left.

CHAPTER SIXTEEN

A DRESSING DOWN

Make haste and act before it is too late. Give of your best in all things with hope and trust in a perfect outcome. Now is not the time for sitting and waiting in spite of all you have been told. Do not be influenced by contradictory views for you are the one to make things happen, not another. Set your mind on your journey and plan the route. Take whatever path will get you there. Do not sit back and wait.

Our love goes with you.

The Universal Brotherhood

Helga and Marco filed into Silas' office and shut the door behind them. They stood waiting he fiddled with papers, ignoring them, playing 'the boss'. Suddenly he stood up and banged his hand down hard on the table. All the loose pens and papers jumped. Those standing in the room jumped too. Marco reddened and began to say something, then stopped. Silas swung round and faced him with flaring nostrils.

"You were supposed to find out more about this woman, but what have you done? Nothing! I've seen you leering at her across the table. You – you lecher!" Silas snorted in disgust. Marco reddened a bit more and fidgeted.

Silas sneered and turned to Helga. "And you're no better. We put you in this job so that you could monitor her thoughts and activities. But all you've managed is to make her aware of your own psychic abilities. That was the last thing we wanted."

Marco took a deep breath. "I don't know what you are all so afraid of," he mumbled, looking at his feet. "She can't do anything to us, or the firm. She has no inside knowledge. We've made sure she doesn't have access to sensitive material."

"No inside knowledge?" Silas almost screamed. "What do you think she's getting when she goes on her inner journeys?" He turned to Helga who'd taken a step back. "Come here," he ordered, his voice high. "You may be the one the people here are answerable to, but don't you ever forget who is the real boss, or where our orders come from. Without me you wouldn't have a job, and if you don't comply you'll never get another. Do you understand me?" he shouted full in her face.

Helga hung her head and muttered, "Yes." But fury built in her as she spoke. Someone was going to pay for this dressing down, and she knew who that someone was.

But Silas wasn't done. "Helga, from now on you will use your mind-reading abilities all the more and try to follow her activities, even when she's not in the office. By that I mean outside your office hours, do you hear me? You've been too lazy up to now."

"You mean use my second sight to enter her mind?" she stuttered. "I don't know if I can do that from a distance. I can do it while she is here. That's easy, but..."

"No buts. You'll do it. The matter is closed. You may both leave."

Marco hesitated by the door. "What about me?"

"What about you? Intimidate her. Scare her, make her realise who holds the power. You lack the brains to do anything else." With that put-down he waved to the door. "Leave. Get out of my sight, both of you."

* * *

Kate got no peace that night. Just when she was dreaming of Adam leaning in to kiss her, an unknown voice broke the spell.

"Reporting to base. People everywhere are waking up and opening their eyes. People in all countries are saying 'enough'. As each individual wakes up, he or she gathers with others en masse. Together they are becoming more powerful than those who would control the world. If you think that the human race as a whole will sit down and let creatures from outer spheres control them you are very much mistaken. Human beings of whatever creed or nationality are becoming more enlightened and spiritually conscious than ever before in their history. They always, without exception turn to a Divine Source when they feel the chips are down. Haven't you noticed this already?"

Kate sighed. She would have much preferred to continue her dream about Adam. But she realised there was something strange about this message. She was never sure if she was giving the report or receiving it. It just was! She appeared to be tapping into wavelengths of communication from somewhere else. At the back of her mind, she sensed she was giving the report to the Galactic Council, who she knew were watching closely before making their decision as to the future of humanity. Was it her voice she heard in her head? She didn't seem to have any control over it. Was she going mad?

It was time to involve Jacob in all this because she was concerned for her own safety.

The next morning, as if he'd read her thoughts (which indeed he had), Jacob called round to see her. "Dad, I've met a man," she said once he'd taken off his coat and joined her in the kitchen. The kettle whistle blew loudly and made them both jump. She made the tea.

"Oh yes?" Jacob said grinning. "What's he like?"

"Take the tray Dad, please." They wandered into the front room where they sat down together, then Kate told him all about Adam and how and why he'd turned up. She hardly knew where to begin, but she had to get a nagging thought off her mind.

"He's really nice, Dad, but he's here because of my work with Sechem. I know I'm in danger with what I do, and his presence makes that all the more real. I know what I'm doing is classified, top secret, otherwise why would the CIA be involved? I don't go to these real secret government places deliberately, but I'm guided to be there, in areas I ought not to be in, like a nuclear missile centre, for goodness sake. I just to do whatever I'm directed to do at the time. But I'm scared Dad, and to be honest, I don't know if this Adam chap is able to help me in the places I have to go."

Jacob munched on his biscuit, looking thoughtful and pondering how best to reply. "It's true there've been a great number of individuals working in these places who've disappeared or died in doubtful circumstances," he said, "but they were usually people in positions of authority inside the establishments, and who had proof and were able to blow the whistle effectively on whatever they had to expose. You don't have any concrete evidence or knowledge of wrong doing, so I don't feel you are in any danger."

"But I'm there on my own Dad and I know what I'm doing is dangerous. You hear about people dying in suspicious circumstances all the time – like, like… Marilyn Monroe," she said, the name unexpectedly popping out of her mouth. "She had an affair with President Kennedy, didn't she? What if she had been party to official secrets and had to be killed off? Then there was David Kelly who died in suspicious circumstances after investigating whether there were weapons of mass destruction in Iraq," she continued. "But what about whistleblowers, who could change events by disclosing how the establishments really worked, or even by hinting about things that are covered up? And what if anything *I* said started an investigation…?" her voice trembled as she spoke of her concerns.

Jacob held his hand up to stop her, mid-sentence and scratched his head while looking at the ceiling with a slight frown on his face. Kate watched and waited. He always did that when he was considering what to say, and it was always worth the wait.

"I see you've given the subject some considerable thought. Kennedy wanted more open dealings concerning space intelligence, you know. Marilyn Monroe had an affair with him and might well have had secrets they were worried she could reveal."

"See what I mean, Dad?"

"But that is something we will never know for sure," he added. "Maybe it would help if you read these reports." He produced a folder and thrust it in her lap. "This is a list of what hasn't been suppressed."

Kate's eyes widened.

"I knew you'd need them. Psychic, remember?" He grinned, pleased with himself.

Kate opened the file and read. They were official government documents from all around the world and page after page listed evidence of alien contact.

> J Allen Hyneck, Former Chairman, Department of Astronomy, Northwestern University; Scientific Consultant, Air Force Project Blue Book (1947-1969): 'Each wave of sightings adds to the accumulation of reports which defy analysis by present methods — we want some answers. When the long awaited solution to the UFO problem comes, I believe that it will prove to be not merely the next small step in the march of science but a mighty

and unexpected quantum leap.'

From an interview in *The Chicago Sun Times,* August 1966 by James E McDonald, PhD Senior Physicist, Institute of Atmospheric Physics, University of Arizona: 'The type of UFO reports that are most intriguing are close-range sightings of machine-like objects of unconventional nature and unconventional performance characteristics. The general public is entirely unaware of the large number of such reports that are coming from credible witnesses.'

In a letter to Clyde Tolson, July 15, 1947 from Admiral Roscoe Hillenkoetter, First Director, CIA, 1947-1950: 'It is time for the truth to be brought out...Behind the scenes, high ranking Air Force officers are soberly concerned about the UFOs. But through official secrecy and ridicule, many citizens are led to believe the unknown flying objects are nonsense — I urge immediate Congressional action to reduce the dangers from secrecy about Unidentified Flying Objects.' (Kate noted with interest that his concern was not for the dangers from the objects but the dangers from the secrecy.)

In known German antigravity programs, citing Werhner von Braun's mentor, NASA Space Scientist, Dr Herman Oberth, said, 'We cannot take credit for our record advancement in certain scientific fields alone. We have been HELPED. And we have been helped by the people of OTHER WORLDS.'

Dr Michael Wolf stated in his book, 'I met with extra-terrestrial individuals *every* day in my work, and shared living quarters with them while doing research at underground government research laboratories. Zetas work in underground facilities as requested by the US government, but governments have broken treaties by mistreating ETs and by trying to fire on UFOs.'

Kate put the file down.

"The list goes on and on," Jacob said, "but that should convince you that all is not as bad as you think. The question will be answered as to whether we are alone in the Universe or not."

"But Dad, don't you see? This all proves that there are off-world visitors who may or may not have designs on our planet. Some of them may be the heavy creatures I saw who said they have their kind in place on Earth."

"I can understand your concerns, really I can sweetheart. I think it's clear from what you've seen and what my research shows, that both benevolent and malevolent off-world creatures are visiting this planet. It's just a question as to who is working with the secret government and why."

"Dad, look, I want to tell you this. I found this report online, and I asked for permission to reveal it to our groups. It's by Alexandra Bruce of, *ForbiddenKnowledgeTV.com*. Kate went over to her printer and found the document she'd printed out to share with Jacob, and read from it.

> 'In 1997, Lance Corporal Weygandt was stationed in Peru, to guard an installation that was monitoring and shooting down drug-runners' aircraft from Bolivia. One night, he was asked to report on a crash site of a mysterious aircraft shot down into a mountainside. After visiting the site and communing with the large-headed, four-fingered beings inside, he felt like he was at a love-filled family event. They touched him and telepathically told him they would do him no harm, and they wanted his help to escape their mishap with the human military.
>
> Weygandt was promptly arrested and after a 15-hour interrogation, where his and his family's lives were repeatedly threatened if he were to ever speak of this event publicly, he was held in a cell for days. The camouflaged officer who threatened him said, "You're a Patriot, you love the Constitution; well, we're not like that. Over here, we do whatever we want and we could

> drop you out of a helicopter into the jungle and no one would ever find you."
>
> At the base in Peru, Weygandt observed military personnel from China and Germany, in addition to Peruvians and Americans from Special Operations and other military branches. He said it was a most peculiar base, which he guessed had been there for some time. He was certain that it was not about the 'war on drugs'; it was about monitoring ET craft. After his scary ordeal with these rogue elements of the military, he said he found himself wishing he could go away with the aliens.'
>
> Kate paused, then said, "I really do need to be careful, Dad. I'd hate to be interrogated like that. I know that Adam and Sechem and Master M and you are all there to protect me, but sometimes – well, quite often really – I just feel so alone."

Jacob agreed that prudence was necessary. "Remember Kate, in your dreams and journeys, the line between everyday human life and that of the other-worlds can become fuzzy, but you are mind-travelling and you can come back to the safety of your home at any time. To put your mind at rest, and mine too, we'll check for bugs before you begin any further sessions, and I will stay with you in the room to make sure you're quite safe."

Jacob then moved from room to room, unscrewing light fittings and inspecting them. He checked the phone and anything else he could think of. Kate wondered if he or she had gone completely mad. Bugs? Was her mother right after all? Should she see a therapist? But then there was Adam. Didn't that change things?

Kate made a fresh pot of tea and told Jacob how Adam had turned up at her house unexpectedly. "He turned up at work too," she added. "That's strange, don't you think?"

"It sounds perfectly logical to me. He is there for you at work and at home, and I believe it has all been arranged at the highest level

Kate," Jacob replied enigmatically. "You are that important to us."

* * *

Kate had to go to the office. It couldn't be avoided. She still had to pay the bills and it was true that it was in her best interests to keep her enemies in plain sight – but Kate was finding it more and more of a strain to be there, to be on her guard constantly.

That morning, when she got into work somebody had moved boxes of supplies into Kate's small office. What with Marco sitting there looking smug behind his desk, the space was even more restricted than usual. Eventually they would be taken elsewhere, she was sure, but until then Kate had to struggle through the gap between the wall and a wall of boxes to get to her desk.

Marco watched her efforts to squeeze through with a leer on his lips. He suddenly jumped up from his desk, shoving the boxes out of his way, and pushed her against the wall, pressing himself so hard against her that she could barely breathe. She felt him stiffen against her belly.

"What are you up to Greene?" he hissed. "What are you keeping from us? You think you're so clever, but you won't get anything past me."

"Get off me you *animal*," she said, her voice ice cold despite her heart beating ten to the dozen. "Leave me alone or you'll live to regret it."

"Ha! Says who? The office dogsbody? You're a nobody – a nothing!" He put his hands around her throat, tightening then loosening his grip. "You've had this coming from the first time I set eyes on you. You think you're something special, but you're not. You're expendable," he growled into her ear. "Behave yourself and enjoy it, or it'll be the worse for you."

Kate tried to scream but his mouth came down hard on hers. His hand groped her breasts roughly. His other hand reached up under her skirt. Kate struggled, bringing her knee upwards sharply, knocking him off balance. Then an office door slammed nearby and they heard Helga's inimitable tones.

"Greene – where are you? I need you to come with me."

Never before had Kate been so pleased to hear her voice.

Marco let her go, whispering, "Next time you won't be so lucky."

Kate almost collapsed, but refused to give him the pleasure, instead she summoned all the energy she could muster to look him in the eye and said, "There won't be a next time. Keep on your guard Marco, because you won't get away with this."

"You say anything to anyone and you'll be the one regretting it," he replied, a faint edge of concern in his voice.

"Oh yeah? We'll see about that," she said, then in a louder voice, "I'm just coming Ms Mortensen."

Kate straightened her skirt, shivering uncontrollably she headed out of the door. Oh my god, that was a close call, she thought. What if he tried the same trick again? Clearly he'd enjoyed wielding that kind of power over her. She'd have to tell Adam – he'd come to protect her, hadn't he? Well here was his first task.

Inadvertently, Helga came to her rescue that day as she asked Kate to go over to the main building and sit in on a meeting with some new clients. She was to take the Minutes of the meeting. As she left the East Wing and walked across the courtyard to the main building, Adam fell into step with her.

"Are you okay?" he asked, at the same time looking at his phone as if he were just checking his messages.

“Boy, am I pleased to see you,” she said, meaning every word. “Did you get that? What Marco was doing?”

“Not exactly, but I picked up that you were experiencing stress. What happened?”

“The low-life assaulted me. He set a trap that I walked straight into and he, well… he…God it was awful.” It was all Kate could do not to burst out crying.

“What a creep!” Adam was obviously repulsed. “Okay Kate. Leave it with me. I’m going to get him out of your hair. It won’t happen again.”

“But, what can you do? He’s on Helga’s team and Silas is our boss now Mr P’s out of the picture…. They’ve got me cornered.”

“You forget Kate, I’m from HQ and I’m senior to all of them. I’ll tell Mortensen that I need Marco as my driver, or something or other. Don’t worry. It won’t happen again.”

“Thanks Adam. It was a bit of a close call. I don’t know what he would’ve done if Helga hadn’t called for me.”

“Consider it sorted Kate, but keep a low profile for a while, okay.” He held the main entrance door open for her, then turned back towards the East Wing. Kate couldn’t help a huge smile breaking out across her face. She couldn’t quite believe she had a real live knight in shining armour.

CHAPTER SEVENTEEN

THE REVELATION

'The voyage of discovery consists not in seeking new landscapes, but in having new eyes.'

Marcel Proust

Kate's phone ringing drew her out of a deep sleep. Her brain felt as if it'd switched itself off, so as not to remember yesterday's events. Kate reached over and picked up her mobile, dragging herself into wakefulness. She saw it was Poppy calling.

"Hey Poppy, what's up that you're ringing me this time in the morning?"

"It's 11.15 Kate – are you still in bed?"

"Is it? I must've slept in. Thank God it's Saturday! What's happening?"

"I've just been asked if you'll give another talk, so I've said yes on your behalf. You will, won't you?"

"Yes of course. When is it?"

"Great! I knew you'd say yes. It's a bit of a hike – in Exeter, actually. There's a 'Mind Body Spirit' festival in a couple of weeks' time, and they want you to speak on the main stage. You'll be one of the 'Special Guests' that they're arranging. Sounds good doesn't it? They've even agreed to pay your travel expenses, and I've also got a free pass so I can come too. Maybe we can go the city centre afterwards and have a look round? I've heard it's got a lovely river walk."

"You're really enjoying all this events management, aren't you?"

"I have to admit I am rather good at it," Poppy chuckled. "We'll need to sort out some blurb for the flier."

"Okay, meet you at Tom's at 3pm," Kate said and turned over. She was asleep again in seconds.

The 'Mind Body Spirit' event came around quickly. The main stage was in one of several large marquees, set in a beautiful wooded valley near the River Exe, yet despite the tranquillity of the setting, Kate still felt a lurch in her stomach as throngs of people came in. But she had prepared her notes well and gave herself a quick pep talk, just as she'd learnt at the public speaking workshop she attended – which felt like a lifetime ago. Then, with a deep breath, she stepped confidently onto the podium. She noted with interest that there were several people in the audience who had been at her previous talks, and also more men in the audience this time.

"Welcome, everybody and thank you for coming. I'm glad to see some familiar faces as well as new ones. As you'll see from the programme, the title of my talk is 'Do ETs and UFOs exist – or are we alone in the Universe?" Kate opened her files, cleared her throat and forced herself to look out over the audience, despite her nerves. "We are not alone and have never been alone," she said. "Aliens have been visiting us for hundreds of years, and they're still doing so now. I noticed how at the last talk, many of the questions were regarding our safety. But you don't need to fear that visitors to our planet mean us harm, because they are being monitored by a spiritual force, a Prime Directive, that will not allow harm to come to us – however, we cannot take this protection for granted.

Humanity's future is on a knife-edge because we are yet to evolve beyond war and greed and profit at all costs. We are not treating our sacred Mother Earth with respect – instead we are befouling the air, the waters and the soil. Our planet is a jewel in the Universe, but humans are despoiling it. If we don't change our ways, our protection from other intergalactic species who would like to colonise the Earth will be terminated."

A lot of murmuring came from the audience and several hands shot up. Kate smiled, relaxing into the occasion. "Questions at the end, please."

"You may think, 'That's all very well, but how do we know UFOs are real?' Well, I'll give you some verified examples – there are many others which you can research online if you wish.

"In 2010, NH State Representative Henry W McElroy records a video on which he claims to have seen a briefing document from the 1950s that described how benevolent aliens were present in the US and that a meeting was arranged between them and former President Eisenhower."

This revelation was followed by a hubbub of noise; everybody wanted to have their say, but Kate again held her hand up for silence. "We're not as alone on this planet as we think," she said, then continued to read out what she'd researched.

"Paul Hellyer, Canada's Defence minister stated that UFOs are as real as the aeroplanes that fly over your head. He continues to hold these views and speaks at many conferences even today.

"Richard Boylan PhD, a very well-known and respected author and scientist said: 'The well-informed members of today's public can now know that US Air Force generals have been engaging in junkets to the Moon aboard Star Visitor-manned space craft for almost 40 years. The well-informed public is now also allowed to know, from a retired military serviceman, that Star Visitors are not only visiting, but some of them are in residence here and some of these Visitors have been resident on Western American soil since before the white man came." Again a ripple of whispers echoed around the audience as they tried to take in the enormity of what they were hearing.

"On April 17th 1897 a UFO crashed in Texas in a small town called Aurora, not far from Fort Worth. It was reported by the local press. The unusual flying device had previously been observed in other parts of the country. Eyewitnesses said it had been travelling slowly, perhaps ten to twelve miles per hour and gradually was descending as it passed over the town square. Moments later it collided with a windmill and exploded, scattering metallic debris and at least one small body around the area."

Some of the audience sat straighter and others took notes.

"Can you imagine that? This was over a hundred years ago. The Aurora UFO was remarkable because flight had not yet been achieved by humans." Kate paused to let it sink in. "This means that the Aurora UFO, which was clearly made of an unknown metal, could not have been built by humans. News accounts stated that many local residents viewed the wreckage that day, some collecting samples of the debris. The UFO occupant was said to be a small figure who was definitely not human. It was buried in the local cemetery, but all signs of the grave vanished. Little is known about what happened to the wreckage.

"This may have been many years ago, but it's still relevant today, because it proves that we have been visited consistently for millennia, and not one of these visitations has ended in the harm of human beings. But again, I reiterate that unless we mend our ways, future visitations may not be so benign. Now, I'll take questions from the audience."

One of the men she'd clocked earlier, stood up. His gaze unnerved her; it was like he was mocking her.

"Thank you for your talk Ms Greene. I found it enlightening. Can you tell us how we can protect ourselves from these less-than-friendly aliens you've been warning us about?"

"Yes, I can. Protecting ourselves is not a Hollywood-type solution of having more weapons or bigger armies – that will be totally counter-productive. The short answer is, we need to raise our vibrations and our spiritual awareness in order to protect ourselves. We protect ourselves by being kinder to each other, more loving and generous to our fellow human beings and our animal brethren; we need to introduce regenerative technologies that restore the Earth's ecosystems to their former glory, and we need to design our cities, towns and villages more wisely so that they each produce all the food and resources we need, without polluting the wider ecosystems. We can do this now – as another great intergalactic explorer once said, 'We have the technology, Jim.'" (Kate was relieved to get a laugh at this joke.) "It's ironic really that in order to protect ourselves from harm, we have to love more, show more compassion and live more harmoniously. It's not about conflict, it's all about balance."

The man thanked her and sat back in his seat. She noticed that he tapped his mobile phone screen as he did so, as if he were ending the recording of her speech.

After sharing more such information and answering further questions from the audience, Kate ended her talk by saying, "I hope that has convinced you of the presence of extra-terrestrials on our planet. And we are still unharmed. There is more to fear from our own people than ETs."

The audience erupted into applause, and some stood up, showing their appreciation with smiles and whistles. There were some shouts of, "More please!" and the invigilator nodded and put up his hand indicating that she had five minutes left in which to speak. She hesitated before going on and looked at the audience. Could they take what she had to say?

She took a deep breath. Here goes, she thought. "I would like to share with you that, in fact, last night I received a visit from a being not of our world. Luckily they didn't crash land." The audience gasped. "No, they share their messages directly into my mind." There were some expressions of shock and surprise, and even some of fear on faces in the audience. Kate quickly went on to reassure them. "I know – I felt like that when it first happened, but now I'm used to it, I welcome them. It's hard to believe but I really am receiving messages from aliens, and before you put me down as being deluded or hearing voices, I want to reassure you that it is true. How can I prove it? I can't. All I can do is hope that you have faith in me. You came along tonight because you're interested in the subject and you were right to, as here is a chance to have a first-hand account of what it's like to meet an alien." Kate paused for breath and glanced around the hall.

A cry came up from the front row. "I can see one. I can see one. He is standing right alongside you."

To her delight, all faces were directed at her, rapt. But she carried on. "I won't lie, I was afraid at first but I was soon reassured. It's a wonderful honour to be visited by aliens. You can sense their magnificent power and they're beautiful too." A few chuckles came from the audience.

"But you wouldn't believe the rainbow of colours that surround them, it's just mesmerising. They started to visit me because they wanted to convey a message. You too may start to receive messages if you allow yourself to be receptive to them. Some of you may already be receiving them but are unaware of what they are. They won't give up until you listen, so make sure you're receptive. Last night's message was one I thought I would share with you. It sounds to me to be a prediction and is clearly symbolic. So, for what it's worth, here it is:

"'Present man is dying and will die when the ice melts. Current man knows and accepts he is dying by degrees and that Mother Earth is killing him. She is waiting for the ice to melt. When it does, he will die and she will give birth to New Man.'

"Food for thought, eh? There are so many ways one can interpret that. It doesn't necessarily mean bad news, it could be a warning instead." Amongst the crowd there were murmured agreements and nods. Kate carried on, relieved that the audience was friendly.

"I also have contact through meditation and recently saw humans and aliens working side by side, all with jobs to do. They were manufacturing products, using energy drawn from the great energy source that is available to everybody. This energy is all around and can penetrate rock. They turn this energy into a denser matter to produce physical objects. In fact, this is what we all are – condensed energy. But this time, they were making survival equipment and nourishment and anything that a human being might need in the event of an emergency. They were preparing us for something. With the state of the world can you imagine what this might be? Think about it."

Kate eventually had to call timeout. She felt satisfied that the talk had gone well. The message was spreading and she hoped that Sechem would be proud of her.

The response in the room was explosive as the audience clapped enthusiastically and gave her a standing ovation. The presenter closed the meeting but as Kate was ushered out, she saw the strange man who'd asked her a question earlier, staring straight at her whilst speaking into his Bluetooth headset. She knew he'd been sent to spy on her, and that could only mean trouble.

As if picking up on her thoughts, the event manger said, "Wow you've really set a cat among the pigeons now. Did you know there were reporters present?"

* * *

Kate's next mind journey came soon after that meeting and although it was brief, it was amazingly vivid. With her Dad by her side, after a slow descent into a trance, she saw herself as a beautiful bird, a scarlet ibis. How extraordinary. This was an enormous change from her usual travels, and one she welcomed. She remembered from her history lessons at school that the ibis was revered in Ancient Egypt, as it was believed to be a god who protected people travelling to a promised land. Very symbolic, Kate thought. I wonder if that means me?

A voice in her head said, "Your position is at the top but you must descend to understand more."

To her amazement, she felt herself hop easily down what looked like a staircase, only made of twigs, leaves, and branches, balancing herself with outstretched wings of vivid red, feathers fluttering gracefully. Each step took her deeper into a trance, as she knew it would. She felt the energy increase, but couldn't see where she was going.

"Keep going further," the voice said.

Kate entered a large nest full of squawking chicks and the pungent smell of their guano filled her nostrils. From the swaying high branches of the large tree she looked out over a wide stretch of water. Kate held on tight as the branch she was on moved with the wind. She heard the fluttering of wings as other birds arrived at their nests. She looked to find a way through the branches and realised she was becoming human again and being transported elsewhere. The tree had vanished leaving her standing in a granite tunnel. She'd been here before. She knew the way and moved smoothly through a large passage until she came to the turning she expected to see.

She stopped and stared, incredulous, at what she saw. She hadn't expected to be back where she'd definitely been before, though she couldn't remember when and where. She stood by an open door to the business area where she'd worked in a distant past. Was this déjà vu, or was she visiting a past life? She saw there was much work to do. From the passage, she peeked inside and saw lots of papers on desks, many recording instruments and all sorts of contraptions and devices she couldn't put a name to. Some were hooked up onto the wall, ready to be taken down, and some were laid on a waist-high bench so she could work at it. She must have been very busy here. This had been her domain – she knew that, at least. She walked on.

At the end of the passage a glass door opened by itself, and she stepped through into a big open space with offices along one side of a narrow, green-carpeted passage. On the other side of the passage was an open plan layout where serious looking people worked in sectioned off cubicles containing computers, monitor screens and printers. Placed high at the far side of the open office space was a wall to wall television screen. In spite of all the activity, there was only a soft hum as people worked at their stations. Kate knew she was down deep. Nobody from the outside world visited, unless they had authority. All this was secret.

A tall man in a long grey robe stepped out from a side office and stood in front of her. Kate wondered what to do next. He resembled an aged sage, complete with a long grey beard. He studied her in silence for a moment before speaking.

"This is one of the secret caves which are referred to in the Ancient Mystery Schools. You should know that," he said.

"But this is very modern," Kate stared in disbelief at her surroundings.

"Do you think that we don't keep up to date? Of course, we do. We must be in keeping with the times where we work. Doesn't that make sense?"

"Yes, it does. So where am I going? Why the scarlet ibis thing?"

"It keeps your mind puzzling, so you are engrossed in the journey we give you. That way, you're less likely to have your thoughts wandering off, and not getting here."

"Oh, I see," Kate said, not really understanding.

"You're going to meet The Boss."

"The Boss?"

"Yes. You call him Master M."

"Oh, okay. I wasn't expecting that." Kate's heart began to beat harder. What could he want with her?

"Isn't it better when you get what you don't expect? Then you know you're not making it up. Is it a pleasant surprise?" He waved his arm in a circle.

"It's a confusing one."

All will be made clear. In the meantime, carry on with what you're doing. Do you not realise that we're feeding your mind? Will you allow it?

"I have done so far. What do I do now?" Kate watched the people working away at their desks and screens, and wondered if they could see her as they walked along past the desks. She was in a non-physical state and they certainly looked solid to her. Maybe this is what ghosts do, she wondered.

She brought her mind back to the sage waiting for her to give him her full attention. "You have an audience with Master M."

"I assume M is a pseudonym."

"Of course it is."

"What's his real name?" she asked.

"If he wanted you to know that he wouldn't be using a pseudonym, would he? You may go in now. He is ready for you."

Maybe it was magic, for suddenly the office surroundings vanished. All she could see what a door. Kate entered and was immediately blinded by the light and she remembered no more.

Jacob told her it was quite some time before she came back to earth in her own front room.

"Damn, damn, damn!" she grumbled. "Why can't I remember what happened after that?"

"Another part of you knows without any doubt. The meeting is in your subconscious and you will recall it when you are ready," said her father.

It was frustrating, but she knew she must trust that they knew best.

* * *

The following week at work, she didn't set eyes on Marco once. It seemed Adam had been true to his word. His desk had been removed from her office, as had the stationery boxes – it was as if his brooding presence had never been there. When Kate enquired to Helga where Marco was, she tapped the side of her nose and said, "That's on a strictly 'need to know' basis, Greene. But don't worry, he'll be back."

Not if Adam's got anything to do with it, she thought involuntarily.

Helga looked up from her desk inquisitively. "What did you say?"

"Nothing." Kate said truthfully, but realised instantly that Helga had picked up on her thoughts. She'd let her guard down and possibly compromised Adam. She could've kicked herself.

The weekend couldn't arrive soon enough for Kate, and needing to see Jacob and Adam more than she cared to admit, Kate got in touch with them suggesting they meet up for coffee on Saturday morning.

She watched from her front window as Jacob's Lexus pulled-up in front of her gate. She was so pleased to see him and eager to talk.

"Dad, I have something to ask you," she said as soon as he stepped inside the front door.

Jacob sucked in a breath, as if he'd been expecting something of this sort. "Go on," he said.

Kate closed the door behind him. "Dad, do you mind if Adam joins us? I've invited him too."

Jacob headed for his favourite chair. "It sounds as if you don't need my permission. I look forward to meeting this mysterious man."

Adam's arrival didn't go unnoticed on the street. Kate saw lace curtains twitching when his sleek black Mercedes parked next to Jacob's car near Number Six, and her neighbours peered out unashamedly at the tall, handsome, smartly dressed young man who emerged from the vehicle. They watched him stride up to Kate's front door and quickly slip inside. Clearly he was expected.

Jacob stood up as Kate showed Adam into the front room. "Dad, this is Adam,"

Jacob grinned broadly as he grabbed Adam's hand and shook it with enthusiasm.

"Sit down, sit down won't you Adam. Kate will get us some coffee, I'm sure."

"Not yet, Dad. I want to tell Adam about my latest mind trip, first. I know you think the meaning will unfold, but I feel it's urgent, so I'm hoping that two heads will be better than one, so to speak, and that maybe we can shed some light on what I was doing in that other office before I went in to see, or rather, not see, Master M."

"You went into an office and saw Master M?" Adam looked puzzled, but at least his response acknowledged that he already knew of the existence of Master M.

"I did, but I'm not sure why – I wish I knew. You'll have to listen to my story and then hopefully you and Dad can shed some light on the matter. Let's get started."

Both men did a quick check through the room for bugs before settling down. Was it her imagination or were they getting edgy? Jacob looked at Adam knowingly as Kate related all that had happened in her last mind travel. Outside the sound of lawnmowers filled the air, just a normal Saturday for normal people. A long silence followed while they digested what she'd told them.

Kate fidgeted. "Well? What do you think?" she asked when she couldn't contain her impatience any longer.

Jacob spoke first. "This is partly symbolic. The ibis part, as least."

"Yeah, I got that bit, Dad," Kate retorted. "Don't think you're getting your coffee just yet!" They all laughed, and the tension eased a little.

"They were trying to tell you something, Kate."

Kate cut him off. "Oh, give me strength please," she groaned. "What were they trying to tell me?"

Kate saw Jacob give Adam that look again, as if he knew Adam had the answer as well as he did but that they didn't know how to tell her.

Adam just shrugged. "Over to you Pops."

"Pops? What?" Kate asked, confusing the friendly nickname Adam gave to her father, with that she gave to her best friend. Then something else dawned on her. The term seemed too intimate for two men who'd just met — or did they know each other already? Was that a flash of recognition she'd seen in his eyes when Adam had first met her father?

Jacob turned to Kate and held her hands in his. "What they were trying to break to you gently is that you're a hybrid. Do you know what that means, darling?"

Kate frowned. "I know the word of course, but I don't understand the inference. A hybrid with what exactly?"

"You are part human and part Sirian, from the star Sirius, specifically part of the Bird tribe. Hence the ibis experience," he said. "It was to introduce you to the idea of being part of two worlds."

Kate's eyes widened. "You're kidding me!" She looked from Jacob to Adam and back again. "You've hatched this up between you for a joke." She stood up to go to the kitchen. "I'll get you that coffee now, but please can we stop all this nonsense. It's just too weird…"

The two men looked helplessly at each other. "She doesn't understand," Adam said.

"Understand what?" Kate whispered.

"Sit down and listen for a minute," Jacob said. "The coffee can wait."

"It must be serious," Kate retorted, but she saw the gravity of it all on his face and promptly sat, her heart beating hard over the implications of what he'd already said.

Jacob knew it was time for him to explain. "Your mother Francine and I were used for this purpose. I was taken on board a spacecraft and, well I won't go into details, but I was introduced to a female member of the Bird Tribe, her name translates as Joslene. The result was a fertilized egg, which was harvested from her then implanted into your mother in her sleep. You see, I was already a hybrid, but they needed someone from their race to mate with me, to continue the line on Earth. Your Earth mother Francine doesn't know about this, but she was chosen because of her many attributes: her physical strength to carry you through to full term, her intelligence, her ability to detach from relationships..."

"I can't take this in...I'm a *hybrid*? I'm not human…? And you're a hybrid too? I don't believe it," Kate said. "Why haven't you told me before?" Her insides churned at the implications. If it were true it meant her mother was a surrogate for a creature from space, and she was the result.

Jacob took his glasses off and cleaned them with his handkerchief. Then he continued. "This is why you and your mother don't understand each other. She never intended to become pregnant and took precautions to prevent it, so she never understood how you came about, and consequently, she resented you from the very beginning – but not only that, her natural instinct was to reject you because you're not of her kind. She doesn't know that she was in fact a surrogate mother. You mustn't tell her, Kate as she wouldn't believe you and what little relationship you have with her would be destroyed for ever."

Kate frowned. It actually made some kind of sense. "Poor Mum…" she said, for the first time feeling some compassion for the woman. "It was hardly fair on her, was it Dad?"

"On an individualistic basis, perhaps not – but on a planetary basis, she has been of great service to humanity, and she's been repaid in ways that are meaningful to her. A rich husband seems heaven-sent to Francine."

Kate looked at her father in a different light.

"But I don't look any different from anyone else," she protested. "Nor do you, for that matter."

"Don't you? What about the funny looks you get from time to time?" he paused for emphasis. "Actually, it is very clever genetic engineering on the part of the Sirians. You're meant to fit in. Have you never wondered how or why you have such advanced gifts of far sight and mind travel?"

Kate thought about this and she had to admit, he had a point. And perhaps this explained the feelings of longing, almost painful, that she felt when she heard birdsong. Then she recalled what Sechem had said when she first met him, about aliens arriving via DNA. She didn't realise then the significance of what he was saying. She certainly didn't realise he meant her. She remembered comparing this transfer of genetic material to that of a parasite, and cringed.

"Where do you fit into all this?" she asked turning towards Adam. "You seem to have psychic ability too."

"I'm a hybrid too, and I'm part of your soul group. We've had incarnations together before this one. Don't you remember? You felt there was some connection when you first saw me, didn't you?"

Kate felt herself blushing and hoped it didn't show. Fortunately, Adam didn't acknowledge this and continued. "Kate, our task is to prepare and alert any who'll listen to the beneficial presence of our space family here on Earth. The Dark Hat agenda, as Sechem calls it, is to make the world fearful of any intelligent beings from other worlds."

"And they're doing a good job too," Jacob said. "It's no accident that the majority of sci-fi programmes, books and films have negative, apocalyptic portrayals of aliens. But if they wanted to destroy human beings, why would they break up a meteor heading for Planet Earth so that it caused little damage? They've done this more than once, you know. And why would they be interfering with nuclear weapons and making them inoperable? A close watch is being held on all nuclear establishments for a reason, and it's so that humanity cannot destroy itself. It is humanity itself that humans have most to fear."

"This is so much to take in," said Kate, and finding herself parched with anxiety, she got up from her chair and headed for the kitchen to make coffee. Once there she rested her head against the wall and tried to calm down. Despite the fact she was part-alien herself was momentous news, somehow it sat quite comfortably with her. She suddenly remembered the swooping bird she'd seen – it must have been a clue, a way of familiarising her with her heritage. She felt herself ease into her new identity.

When she returned with the coffee tray she asked: "Where do Helga and her cronies come into this?"

Adam looked up in surprise. "I would've thought knowing you're a hybrid was enough to deal with, yet here you are surging ahead to the next question. But I'm glad to see you're taking it in your stride. Helga is what you might call a 'dark hat' I suppose, but she doesn't realise it. She has been put in her position in SatData to track you and make sure information that the world's secret government wants kept undercover is not divulged to the public. Data Sat is a front for the dark hats' operations, which is why I've been planted in there – to keep an eye on what's going on. SatData, do not know I work for the other side! But, back to Helga. She too has the 'Sight' although nowhere near on the same level as you Kate – but she caught your thoughts the other day and I did too – you have to be more careful. That's why she's been employed within the company: because she's been marked as a 'seer' and therefore, she's a key member of their team."

Jacob broke in. "Don't judge her too harshly though. She has no idea she's helping the dark forces of space with their plan. She simply thinks she's doing her job by protecting her government from hostilities, blind creature that she is." He sighed, a sadness etched on his face. "Each person involved only has a tiny part to play and never really sees the big picture. If they did, they might change their minds about the work they do."

Kate thought about it for a moment. "You're right. If all those individuals trudging to work every day to manufacture weapons saw first-hand, face to face, what it did to people — little children and whole families — they might look for alternative jobs. But they might actually think they are just manufacturing components, without knowing what they're for. They don't have the bigger picture.

"I suppose the people Helga is working for – the 'secret government" are still human beings, despite what they're doing. They're still on the journey through life like we all are. I could still feel love for them as individuals, even though they knowingly do dreadful things. Is this wrong? It doesn't mean I condone it, but I can see the humanity inside, the vulnerability, the doubts, the fears and all those things that drive them on. It's as if they can't help themselves, as if something has taken hold of them. Helga is a misguided soul. I just wish I wasn't working alongside her."

Adam grinned. "Watch out, you're letting your human side show."

Kate smiled. "And what about the other two: Marco and Silas. Where do they come into all of this?"

"Marco is just muscle, with not much between his ears. He's there to put the frighteners on people and I'm sorry I wasn't able to help you when he did that the other day, Kate. I was at HQ, so not even in the building."

"What's this?" Jacob butted-in.

"Nothing for you to worry about, Dad. Adam's sorted it. And Silas?"

"Watch him Kate. He's a big cheese in SatData's Washington office, where I sometimes work. He is not a good man, but you will see me working closely with him. I have to do that to maintain my cover, but don't doubt me Kate. I am there for you."

Kate smiled again at his words, hoping that he meant a little more than just work-wise. "I still can't believe that half of me isn't even human." If only he knew how much she wanted to reveal her human side in another way. If he did know, he wasn't showing it.

CHAPTER EIGHTEEN

DREAMS OF SALVATION

'There is no love that does not become help.'

Paul Tillich

Kate's mind was now constantly filled with thoughts beyond this world – space, other planets and what it meant to be in contact with Master M and Sechem. And now she knew that she was part-Sirian, she yearned to know more about her heritage. It wasn't enough to be simply told this fact, she had to fully explore it. Discovering her psychic abilities had been an incredibly steep learning curve, and it felt like as soon as she had got to grips with mind travel, she discovered that she had an adversary who could see into her mind – Helga. She had demonstrated her psychic ability to tap into Kate's thoughts way too efficiently for comfort.

Kate decided to be more diligent and find extra time to go deep and explore her heritage, but she knew she couldn't now always rely on Jacob to be around when she felt the need to make contact. He had his life too. She had to take responsibility for herself.

That evening after work, Kate turned off the phone, dimmed the lights and drew the curtains. She asked that whatever was given to her would be for the highest good for all. She took herself into a deep relaxing place within.

A voice she hadn't heard before came into her mind, loud and clear.

"Training is taking a new step forward," it said. "It's now on a need-to-know basis. Until then, we will maintain radio silence after this job."

There was no mistaking the authority in this voice. Kate stiffened at the formality of it.

"Understood," she said. She realised immediately that the threat levels had ramped up, and felt a surge of anxiety. Trying to quell her nerves, she focused on her breathing and following the voice's suggestion, went into a deep trance.

She found herself standing in front of a whole row of missiles, lined up and ready for action.

"They are intended for space but we do not wish for these warheads to enter the upper atmosphere."

Kate frowned. "I don't know how I can help you."

"Use your mind to direct them to malfunction. Create a picture where they collapse and fall among themselves and are not effective for any purpose. Even though you are not near them physically, and even couldn't even find them if you tried, you can still disarm them with your mind."

It seemed most bizarre, but Kate then fleetingly recalled reading about how atomic particles operate differently when they are being observed. Don't doubt it, just to it, she said to herself, and set about imagining the computer chips melting and motherboards crumbling, causing malfunction of the missiles. It took concerted focus and effort to do this, a level of concentration that was utterly draining. She felt herself wane as she continued to 'dismantle' the warheads.

"Well done," the voice said when it was over. But it had not finished with her yet. "We need to harness your mind powers again, this time to communicate with those from the cosmos who are on Earth, and who in some cases are restrained by your governments. Though they came to assist your planet, in many cases they've now been held against their will."

"But… why can't you communicate with them yourself?" asked Kate, astounding herself that she had the audacity to ask this authoritative being such questions. She still underestimated her contribution. The knowledge that she was different, powerful, a hybrid, still hadn't properly sunk in.

"This we do, but we are not physically in a position to affect their situation."

"That means I am? That doesn't make sense."

"You are a citizen of the Earth, like it or not. We need you as a citizen to do these things. It is called taking responsibility.

"Your energy is powerful enough to do this. It is known to us that when you take yourself into a higher vibration, you can still affect third-dimensional physicality while remaining invisible. You can change or move things which are physical. Another reason for you to make contact through the mind is that psychically, you may discover information that would otherwise be restricted. Others, outside government, can then have access to it through you. Does this make it clearer to you?"

"It makes some kind of sense."

"We would like to take you now where there is more information to share with the public. Do we have your permission? Are you up for it, as they say in your world today? Are you in your comfort zone?"

Kate laughed at his attempt to be up to date with the lingo.

"Yes, I'm up for it."

She soon realised that she'd entered a new area and somehow, she knew instinctively that she had to mask her psychic light so she couldn't be seen. She wasn't exactly sure she knew how to do this; she just did it. So much of what she had learnt recently was like this – she just had to accept that she had certain abilities and let herself do them without examining the whys and wherefores too much.

Kate looked around. Not much to see, just a big tunnel. She wore a closefitting silver suit that also enclosed her feet, padded so as not to make a noise. Kate chuckled at the absurdity of it all. Despite the gravity of the situation, part of her still struggled to immerse herself totally.

As she walked, the tunnel narrowed so her shoulders could touch both sides and then widened again, like an hour-glass shape. She walked through the narrow part and out into a massive, brightly lit space. She followed a walkway clearly marked with white lines until she branched off down a path leading to an enclosure that looked rather like a Faraday cage. Inside were many small alien figures – which she believed were called 'Greys' – with round heads and big eyes, all shoved together inside. They saw her and called out to her. Though she couldn't make out what they were saying, they were obviously trying to get her attention. She smiled at them and willed herself inside the enclosure. They swarmed around her and she felt huge beside them.

They stared intently at her. Everywhere she turned, she saw their big eyes looking back at her, as if trying to communicate with her, desperately trying to tell her something, so many clamouring for attention. They were so small, like children, and very vulnerable.

She knew she was there to help get them out, but they were physical and she was not, she was just inter-dimensional. Maybe her energy alone would do it.

Without knowing how she knew, she knew she had to deliberately increase her energy field until it covered them. She spread it further and further until they were all completely encased in a blue bubble of energy, then she walked out of the enclosure and back through the hourglass tunnel, with all of them in tow. Getting them through the tunnel was like squeezing a balloon through a drainpipe, but her energy field remained intact, and they all came through with her. Some even clung to her.

Kate climbed back up the steps dragging the load to the surface. Both she and the beings inside the huge energy field were protected and invisible as long as they remained inside. She finally made it to the surface, and to her surprise, just like in science fiction films, a light beam came down from the sky. The Greys scrambled wildly, almost in a panic, to gather inside the beam. Kate watched, stunned as they zoomed up the light beam, as if sucked up by a giant vacuum cleaner.

When the last one had gone, the beam dissipated and Kate was able to bring her energy back to normal size. The little ones had been rescued and were safe, but Kate was left with a massive headache. She held her head, utterly spent. No one is ever going to believe this, she thought, but it happened. It really happened.

"Well done," the voice in her mind said. "You may rest now and recover your strength."

* * *

A few days later Kate was called on again. At least they never disturbed her while at work, and for that she was grateful. When it happened the pull to get in touch was overwhelming, so strong she could hardly resist. This time, the urge to connect came after dinner when Adam was with her. He'd got into the habit of visiting on a regular basis.

"It makes sense to maintain regular contact," he'd said.

Kate didn't mind one little bit.

"Are you up for it?" The voice boomed in mind.

"I'm ready," she replied, trying not to laugh. The modern lingo sounded so strange coming from him. "I'm not alone, though."

"Perfect. Just what we want," came the surprising reply. "We know him. We want you to relate to him what happens as it happens, so he can listen to the journey. Can you do that? This is another rescue. Be in the moment."

"I'll try." Kate briefly explained the procedure to Adam and went into her self-hypnosis routine. She fed through the images to Adam as they happened.

"The steps are very steep, like going down into a cellar. Narrow with walls on either side. I can't see the bottom... Going down. The bottom steps are missing. I'll have to jump down. I land on a hard earthen floor. It's a very small area and sweltering hot. I'm looking for an opening. There's one, off to one side. It's very dark. It reminds me of being in an underground burrow of some animal, just wide enough for a creature. Some of the openings on the right don't go anywhere, as if a living thing had tried to go there and came up against a brick wall.

"I've come to an entrance which is clearly meant to be seen because it's glowing pale yellow. I'm going into this. It leads into a totally different area. Oh my God! It's huge, and very high tech, like the Tardis, with a lot of instruments and machinery. It's not a natural space. It's an underground base set up by some sort of official organisation. It feels like it could be nuclear. I have no idea what country though. It's hot – it could be anywhere.

"I realise that all the instruments, wires and pipes are just for maintenance, and this is only the perimeter of the base. I'm looking around for another door. There must be one. At last I see one with a big bar on it like a fire door. I lean on it and it opens inwards, not outwards. There's a threshold like you'd have on a ship. I step over it. Inside there are lots of corridors going off in all directions. My God! There's so much here. I can't take it all in.

"This is clearly a military installation, though I can't tell you how I know. I just know. I don't know how deep I am though. There are far too many things for me to understand. I get the feeling that this is truly massive. I keep walking. It has a solid floor. There are so many doors, where do I go? Please tell me where I'm supposed to go.

"Then I notice another similar door, it's almost like an airlock. I'm going through into the next room. It's enormous. I'm reminded of an aircraft hangar. There's something in here I must go to but I don't know what. What shall I do?'

The voice says, "You're to pull the plugs with your mind."

"I feel the voice turning me round to point me in the right direction. I am to pull the plugs with my mind. I see a long row of blue plugs with ring pulls, too many to count, and they have a glow around them as if they're being highlighted especially for me. Are you sure it's safe? I feel nervous about this but I walk down the line pulling. They come out very easily. Each time I do this there's a click. It deactivates them, the voice tells me. I say to the voice, 'Deactivates? Well if it's so easy, then it'd be easy to activate again, wouldn't it?'

'No, because they don't know what you've done. They cannot see you. It'll take them a long while to realise what has happened, by which time it'll be too late. You have completed this task, well done,' the voice says to me.

"I feel really scared, fiddling around with nuclear weapons. 'Are you sure this is right?' I say to the voice.

'We have more work for you to do,' the Voice says.

'I trust that what I'm doing is for the good of everybody.'

The voice confirms this. 'Please be assured in your heart that this is a requirement to help the planet and the space around it. You are helping to keep space safe.'

"I'm now in another large area. I see a lot of extra-terrestrials, I suppose you would call them humanoids. One in particular turns and looks at me. I feel an affinity with him. He has an ovoid head, a broad sloping nose. It looks a bit like a bird's beak, but looks soft, not hard. There are so many diverse kinds, some closely resembling humans, others not.

"They're all working. I don't know if they can see me or not. I stand and watch. They're working on something on tables. Some are at controls and some are walking about. They take no notice of me, so I assume they don't all see me, but I don't know.

There's not much flesh on them; they don't get tubby ones down here!

"The voice is saying to send them blue light. So, I project clear blue over the whole area. The blue is more comfortable and natural for them than the artificial light they had before, and they feel renewed. What else can I do? One of them, a tall one sees me and points at me. He tells the others and they all turn to look. For the first time they all see me. Why it only took one for the others to see me I don't know.

"He puts his arms up, indicating up, and he circles his arms, as if to say, all of us. Again, he points up. Telepathically I know I have to mentally enclose them in the huge bubble of blue, just like before. They stop working. They're still now, and waiting. I mentally lift the bubble with them inside and lift them all the way up. It rises and passes through the layers overhead. I'm rising with it to maintain the energy. It's a long way through all the layers to the surface, and I still have to maintain the bubble of blue. I keep pushing it upwards, up, up, up, until they disappear. I don't know where they disappear to but they've disappeared from my view."

'Well done!' the voice said. 'You can leave.'

"That's a relief, I feel quite tired out now."

Kate took some time to come back to normal. Eventually she opened her eyes, feeling very fragile.

Adam stared at her gobsmacked. "Wow, how did you manage that? No wonder they're watching you closely. You are incredibly powerful."

"Thank you. It's all very new to me..." Kate replied faintly. She longed to chat to Adam but was so utterly drained that she just sat limply in her chair. "I'm so sorry, I'm completely exhausted from that..."

"Of course, of course," Adam said. "You need to get some sleep. I'll see myself out."

* * *

When Kate was fully rested, she kicked herself that she didn't have the energy to spend longer with Adam, and get to know him more. Whenever she saw him at work he seemed to avoid eye contact, but she knew why. He had to maintain his cover. Kate mentioned it to him over a cup of coffee one Saturday morning.

"I know it's best that we pretend we don't know each other socially – in view of how we were put in touch with each other and the nature of our experiences together, but I find it so hard. I don't have many friends in that place. A friendly face after a day of Helga and Silas is such a joy."

"Likewise, Kate. But walls have ears and we have to be careful. Just know that it won't always be this way."

After a few moments silence, Kate answered him. She put her cup down very carefully before trusting herself to speak.

“Yes, you’re right. It’s absolutely the right thing to do,” Kate tried not to reveal her bitter disappointment at Adam’s apparent zero romantic interest in her.

“Helga doesn’t know the work you’ve been doing, and she mustn’t know. I’m not open like you, Kate. She can’t get into my mind, thank goodness.” Adam leaned back in his chair looking relieved.

“So, it’s better all round if there’s no hint of any familiarity between us,” Kate said, determined to remain dignified. “For someone of your position and standing, it would not look good for you to hobnob with a mere office worker in any case.” She sniffed and raised the tip of her nose with the back of her finger to make her point.

“It was a joke,” she said when she saw Adam’s horrified face.

* * *

Back at work, Kate kept her head down whenever Adam was around. Strangely, whenever their paths crossed either Helga or Silas were nearby, and occasionally, the dreaded Marco would be flanking Adam, which made her guts churn. It hurt Kate to suppress her natural urge to speak to Adam, and one day she couldn’t resist it. On her way to the photocopier Kate rerouted in the direction of Adam’s office. It was empty. But she turned away just as he walked around the corner. They collided and burst into laughter. At that moment, Silas saw them.

“No work to do, Ms Greene?” he asked. His voice was as cold as ice.

Silas watched the girl blush, then scurry away, while Adam gave him a curt nod and returned to his office. Silas had her under surveillance at all times, and despite Kate's best efforts, her feelings for Adam had not been missed.

Silas decided it was time to pull Helga and Marco aside for a meeting, ignoring Adam's request that Marco was needed for other things.

"Come into my office," he commanded. They filed in after him and stood like naughty children before his desk.

Silas looked them over with distaste.

"Sit down."

They sat, looking uncomfortable on the edge of their chairs.

"Have either of you noticed a friendship between Adam Fenshawe and Kate Greene?"

Blank faces met his. Marco's temple twitched several times.

"As you know, Colonel Fenshawe has been sent by HQ. He's supposed to be looking at our developments on satellites. But I smell a rat. We need to know what he's really up to. Keep a watch on his movements. There's something going on between him and Kate Greene. We don't want them getting together without surveillance. I don't trust either of them. Keep your wits about you, if that's not too much to ask. Marco, it seems your new position as Fenshawe's right-hand man may come in handy after all. Make sure you let me know what he's up to. Dismissed."

They both nodded and looking somewhat bewildered, left the room.

* * *

When Kate next received a call to mind-travel, she phoned Jacob. These days, whenever he had the time, Adam replaced her father in monitoring her when on her inner journeys, and despite enjoying his presence she missed her Dad. What was he doing all on his own, she wondered, and was he looking after himself?

"Hi, Dad, are you all right?"

"Yes, why wouldn't I be?" he said.

"I miss you, Dad. Can you come over tonight?"

He sighed. "Not tonight, darling – I'm sorry. I've got some work of my own to do. I'll be able to again soon, never fear, but for now you need to have Adam with you when you journey. He'll be most important in the events to come."

Kate had to be satisfied with that, but it didn't stop her worrying. Sometimes her father seemed to be so lonely. She wondered if he missed his own planet, and his own kind.

* * *

She took her father's advice and phoned Adam, and again it wasn't long before he was making himself comfortable in her front room.

"Same system?" he asked.

"Yes, I'll tell you as it happens, whatever it is. You are to record what I say. That way you'll have evidence that may be useful in days to come," Kate replied. "Off we go!"

She settled herself in her favourite chair and went into her special state. Adam clicked on the recorder and waited.

"I'm going down what appears to be a bamboo ladder, the sort you get attached to a hut set high in the trees in the jungle. It's not very steady. I reach the ground. I'm in a clearing of flattened earth. Where do I go? I wander around a little bit, but I can't see anybody.

"There's a pathway out of the clearing. I take the path. It leads into undergrowth, like in a rainforest. I keep walking and step over a line of bright green leaf-cutter ants. I can't see much on either side. The vegetation is quite high and almost impenetrable. I come to another path on the right through the trees. I am following that one. I don't know where it's taking me. Very quickly I come to a huge open space where the ground is well trodden down. It's been cleared for a specific and important reason.

"I see a craft and men surrounding it. These men are nothing to do with jungle people, they're clearly military. They're watching the craft, patrolling and guarding it. I'll try to describe the craft, but it's difficult. I call it a craft because it's not an aeroplane. An aeroplane couldn't land in this jungle. It's not a helicopter either. It could be a flying saucer. It's humming and active. That's the word, alive. It's not dead. It can move at any moment.

"I walk past the guards. They don't see me, or don't appear to. They're clearly military because they're wearing camouflage uniform; they're all around this thing. I walk straight through them and go up to the craft. A portion of it opens. It opens and I walk straight inside. I feel okay, a little scared but also safe too in a funny way. It's a bit cramped in here. The beings inside see me. They're not from this world; they beckon me over with long thin fingers. They're tall and gangly and have long limbs and a slim torso. They're chalky white, as if they never see any sunlight. They're not the short tiny Greys. Amazingly, I feel very relaxed with them, very comfortable. They show me to a seat. I lie down, almost prone, but I feel okay. I feel fine.

'What is this all about, please?' I ask them.

They telepathically tell me. 'You are to go on a trip. You are to go outside of your world and see the bigger picture. This is why you are here. You are here to see a wider perspective, not the little events that everybody is concerned about. So many on your planet are concerned about their own part in their existence, their own private worlds, and are not truly bothered about the big picture. They may say they are, but when it comes down to it they are not. As long as they're all right, as long as it doesn't touch them, then the rest is unimportant, or so it appears. That's how it seems to us.'

"So, I'm in. I'm lying down. It's odd, because I know we are travelling, but I also know that this craft is still there in the centre of the clearing. I just know that. To those guards outside it appears as if nothing has happened. Yet I know it has. Very odd! What I'm doing now is looking through a screen, a wraparound screen. I look closely and can see our beautiful planet but it looks different. Some areas are muddy and grey, and I realise that these are places that need help; that need healing.

"I'm not sure if I am seeing reality or an illustration of what can be, because the planet is entering a beam from the sun and from other influences. I don't know the words for them. Rays, particles, waves of energy. We are entering a field of all manner of interferences and influences. The whole planet is in this, going deeper and deeper in, until it's totally immersed. It'll come out the other side of the beam, but will take a long time. Somehow, I realise that it's a regenerating beam. While we're in it things are going to change. It's not an overnight process because the beam is very wide and vast. I'll be long gone by the time we come out the other side.

"They tell me, 'We're showing you this so that you know that this is just a period in your Earth time. It is an age it goes through. When you come out, you humans will be more responsible. Whatever happens in your future you will be more mature than before. You will take greater charge and care of the entire body of your planet, instead of being self-interested to the extent that you ignore events external to you.'

'I think this is already happening now on the planet.'

'Yes, people are being shaken up, which is as it should be. They've been complacent and stagnant for too long. We need agitation to get things moving. To change things we need you to become alive and put things where they are meant to be.'

'Put what where? I don't follow you. What am I supposed to do?'

'You are already working very effectively. Don't give up. Don't give up.'

"They release me from the seat and point to the door which is opening. I go down past the guards, who amazingly have not noticed a single thing happening. They continue to patrol. As I go back down the path, the whole thing disappears. It has been a time journey. I didn't get a chance to ask all the questions I should have."

After a few minutes of silence, Kate came back to reality. She opened her eyes and said, "There's no other word for it: I feel spaced out."

"Very apt," Adam replied laughing, "considering where you've been."

CHAPTER NINETEEN

AN INVITATION

'One thorn of experience is worth a whole wilderness of warning.'

James Russell Lowell

Francine carefully set her wine glass on the expensive marble fireplace in Helga's home. Whilst her hostess was busy seeing other guests out, Francine looked around the elegantly furnished room. The tall windows adorned with silk Roman blinds complemented the armchairs with rolled backs and soft curves. The carpets were of a deep velvet pile that Francine sank into as she walked and wondered, not for the first time, where all the money came from. Helga's position at her firm was not so elevated that it could command a salary high enough for all this luxury, and she wasn't married, so it couldn't be her husband's money. Wherever the money came from, Francine wanted some of it.

Helga strode in on high heels. They made her look even taller and more imposing than usual. "The evening's bridge went reasonably well, don't you think? Some of them really need to sharpen up though." Helga poured herself a whisky from the Georgian cut-glass decanter, and followed it with a cursory dash of soda from one of those 1970s soda syphons that now look so chic, in a 'vintage' way. She looked at Francine without offering her a refill.

"Thank you for staying behind to help clear up, dear. But you needn't have, the cleaner would do it in the morning." She sat down and patted the seat beside her. “Come and sit for a bit. Bring your glass over here.”

Francine winced at being called ‘dear’, but nodded and did as she was asked.

“Now, tell me about your daughter,” Helga said when Francine had settled. “She’s such an intelligent young lady. What does she do in her spare time, I wonder? I’ve always been interested in my staff. It helps with good relations, you know. Does she have a boyfriend?”

Francine bathed in the glow of Helga’s interest. She really did want to be friends with this class of woman, but sadly she didn’t have that much to share, never having been remotely interested in her daughter. “I don’t really know, Helga. I haven’t seen much of her lately, and you know how secretive daughters can be.”

Helga stiffened. “No I don’t, actually. I don’t have any children. Surely you must know something. Does she play bridge?”

“No – that’s one thing I can say for sure,” Francine replied, realising how little she knew about what was going on in her daughter’s life. It’d never bothered her before, so she couldn’t imagine why Helga was asking. “Why are you so interested in Kate’s life?”

“I told you. I like to establish good relations with my staff.”

Francine smiled, a tight, clenched-teeth smile. It stung that Kate was the topic of conversation and Helga hadn’t asked one thing about her. She got to her feet. “Well, it’s getting late. I’d better be leaving.”

Helga showed her to the door. Francine stepped outside, turned back to say a final goodbye and caught Helga already shutting the door and smiling to herself. What was that all about?

* * *

Although when Kate next went to work everything seemed much the same, she knew something had changed. There was an air of urgency with people rushing here and there, for no apparent cause. Had another satellite tracking gone astray? Had their systems been hacked into once again? While she pondered this, she glanced up and was startled to see Helga's gaunt face staring at her. She raised her upper lip and the penny dropped: The stick-thin woman was actually trying to smile at her.

Feeling a little unnerved Kate asked, "Um, is there anything I can help you with?"

"Yes, I was wondering if you'd like to join us at our bridge night?" Helga asked.

Kate just blinked, taken completely off guard. She didn't know how to respond. What was behind the invitation? She knew her friendliness couldn't be genuine.

"I'm so sorry," Kate said with a set smile. "It's very kind of you, but I'm no good at cards, let alone bridge." No getting around that, she thought.

"Well perhaps you'd like to come just for a drink?" Helga's fixed smile didn't slip one iota. "Bring a friend if you like."

Taken aback by the surprising invitation, Kate fought off a frown. From downright hostility to trying to socialise with her? Kate didn't buy it. She knew Helga hadn't been able to get into her mind recently – since the Adam slip-up, Kate kept her thoughts carefully cloaked – and her house, phone and car were regularly checked by Adam and Jacob for bugs. So what now? Was this another tactic?

"I really will have to check my diary," Kate said, looking her boss straight in the eye.

Helga sniffed. "Surely you know what you're doing without reference to your diary. How about next Wednesday? I'll tell you what, I'll invite a few friends along, make it a bit of a party. Your mother says you don't get out much. It would be good for you."

Kate gave a barely concealed sigh, shrugged her shoulders and agreed to go. She knew she had been backed into a corner.

"Oh well, yes, that would be…nice, thank you." She knew her boss was used to getting her own way and wouldn't be put off.

* * *

The following Wednesday came all too soon and Kate riffled through her wardrobe looking for something appropriate to wear. Nothing too dressy but then nothing too plain either. In the end, she wore a deep blue jersey dress, a contrasting scarf, some lovely heels that she'd been saving for a special occasion – not that this was it, but at least Francine would approve – and slicked on a flash of red lipstick. Maybe power-dressing would help her to feel less intimidated by the whole event? When Kate arrived she was surprised to see at least ten or so expensive cars parked outside Helga's handsome, rambling house.

Kate pressed the gold doorbell and heard a faint musical chime. A maid, who Kate assumed had been hired for the night, opened the door into a grand hall leading to a sweeping staircase. After taking her coat, she ushered Kate into a room packed with people she hardly knew. The first thing that hit her was a waft of heavy perfume. She knew that brand anywhere. Francine. She wasn't in any rush to talk to her mother and instead grabbed a glass of champagne from a passing waiter and headed for a large, leather settee. Before she got there, Helga caught her arm. She looked down her nose at Kate's outfit for a moment before speaking.

"Oh, my dear, I'm glad you could come," fake sincerity oozing out of her. "You must meet Adam Fenshawe. But you know each other already, don't you?" she said archly and drew her over to him.

"I've seen him around the office, and also when he comes in for meetings with Silas Pearce," Kate replied mildly.

Helga introduced him, and Adam shook her hand and nodded coolly.

"Pleased to meet you Ms Greene," Adam said. It was all Kate could do not to laugh. Kate realised, as she looked around at the crowded room, that he wasn't the only one invited from the office.

The dreaded Marco stood by the door looking more like a bouncer than ever, and Kate also noticed Silas moving among the guests, head and shoulders over everybody, his eyes constantly scanning the room. His unappealing, narrow face and superior expression put off anyone considering chatting to him. Ugh! This was going to be a trying evening.

An air of waiting for something to happen pervaded the room and Kate couldn't shrug it off. It felt like the lull before a storm. What on earth was Helga up to?

Just then, Francine noticed Kate that had arrived and came over, the fine silk of her simple yet elegant black dress shimmering as she walked. Seeing Adam with Kate, her eyes lit up.

"Oh do please introduce me to this handsome man," she gushed, piling on the charm.

"Adam, this is my mother, Francine." Kate said, knowing it would infuriate her, then impishly, she added, "Mum, this is Adam, who holds an important position where I work, doing exactly what, I don't know." She chuckled.

Francine glared at her, but kept her cool over the 'M' word. She opened her mouth to say something, but Adam got in first: "I'll go and get you both a drink."

As he passed Kate he muttered to her in an undertone, "Second sight. Use it now." So, he too sensed something about to happen.

Kate excused herself to go to the restroom, but she'd only just stepped out of the room when she sensed the air begin to crackle. She rushed back to Adam, grabbed Francine by the arm and pulled them both down the hall and into a passage. Quickly she found a cellar door. Yanking it open she turned to them. "No arguments," she said, "just get down there as fast as you can."

They read her urgent expression and mutely did as she told them. As Kate pulled the door shut behind them a wall of wind headed straight for the house. Like a tornado, it shook everything in its path.

A powerful voice boomed out above the howl of wind, so loud it hurt her ears, *"This is what happens when you mess with the ionosphere. You're upsetting the natural balance. This is a taste of what can happen if you persist."*

Adam and Kate stared at each other in shock, but it seemed Francine hadn't heard the voice. She just said, "They usually forecast storms like this on the local news, but I didn't hear anything today. I don't know what all the fuss is about."

The wind died down as suddenly as it began and an uneasy calm returned. They cautiously retraced their steps to the party and opened the door to see a scene of devastation. There was broken glass everywhere and the guests all looked as if they'd been dragged through a hedge backwards. Some had been knocked off their feet by the blast of wind and were picking themselves up and brushing themselves down, looking very shaken and scared.

"What was *that*?" someone asked. "We don't get tornados in this country, do we?"

"It was like a freak storm," another said. "Only I heard something else...an intense sound like someone was speaking through a megaphone…"

"I didn't hear that, but I've cut my hand when I stumbled. Look at the blood on her carpet."

Silas, Marco and Helga seemed to be the only ones who'd noticed that Kate and co had made a swift exit.

"How did you know? What was that voice?" Helga snarled, all sweetness and light gone now, her hair like a scarecrow.

Kate ignored her and along with Adam, set about ensuring that the other guests were alright. It seemed there was nothing more serious than a few cuts and grazes, and broken glasses, although all the beautiful tall Georgian windows had blown open, clattering the blinds against the casements.

The truth was, Kate didn't really know how she knew but she did, like a lot of things that were happening to her these days. And she didn't really know what had just happened, other than it was a warning that some people with heightened awareness could perceive where others couldn't. She knew her own perception was due to her awakening powers and the fact that she was part-Sirian. When she had first learnt this, it was too huge to process, but now she was seeing what she could do, how different she was from ordinary humans, she was beginning to enjoy herself a little more.

They learnt from the local news the next day that Helga's was the only house affected by the freak storm. When Kate phoned Jacob, he told her it wasn't as unusual an event in England and Ireland as they'd thought. There'd been a tornado in 2005 in Birmingham and over London in 2006, and more recently in 2012 they'd had tornados in Guernsey, Ilfracombe, Swansea, Belfast and Central Dublin.

"Yes, but Dad, even so, how does that explain the voice?"

"I think you know Kate that this is our interplanetary guides warning us of things to come, if we don't mend our ways. Certain, more spiritually attuned humans will have heard that message too, although not necessarily in that room!"

Kate laughed. "Well, that may be so Dad, but I think it also confirmed to Helga that Adam and I are in cahoots. I'm not entirely sure it was the most timely of interventions."

* * *

"Dash it, so I missed all the fun!" Jacob said next evening after Kate retold the story of the previous night's events. "I'd loved to have seen Francine's face," Jacob chuckled. "Well the cat is definitely out of the bag now." He slapped Adam on the back. "She knows you must see Kate outside the office, otherwise why would she have taken you with her and Francine to the cellar? Anyway, it's clear to anyone who has eyes to see. So, what are you going to do about it?"

To Kate's combined delight and embarrassment, Adam blushed. Then it dawned on her. "You knew, didn't you? You knew something would happen," she said. "Why didn't you tell me?"

"Look, I wasn't sure Kate. I was told a warning would be sent, but I promise you I didn't know how or when. Jamère said he would deal with it."

"Hold on. Jamère? Who's that?" Kate demanded. "I've a right to be kept in the loop, don't you think?"

"Don't get all worked up, sweetie," Adam replied in jest.

"Don't patronise me!" Kate retorted, but was secretly pleased about being called sweetie, regardless of the context.

"Sorry." Adam seemed contrite enough. "But honestly Kate, I didn't know that was going to happen."

Jacob who'd been watching the sparring with amusement broke in. "Oh, you would like Jamère," he assured her. "He's good at . . ."

Kate exploded. "So *you* knew too, and you knew about this, this Jamère person. You didn't think to tell me?"

"Your human mind is still too open to Helga," Adam explained. "She'd have picked it up. We couldn't take that chance by telling you. And even I didn't know that they'd do what they did."

Kate sighed, mollified by his words. "Well if she didn't know before, Helga clearly knows there's something going on now. So, I'm not sure Jamère's great plan hasn't actually backfired. So who is this Jamère anyway?"

"Oh, you'll like him," Adam said.

"Dad's already said that," Kate snapped.

"He has a whole box of tricks he can use if he has to, as you saw last night. Boy was that something!" replied Adam, beaming.

"Glad you enjoyed it. I was frightened." Kate grumbled.

Adam straightened his face. "Jamère's position is as intergalactic interpreter. He works across many languages within the space family. He's a 'Light Hat', you can be sure of that, and he's amazing. He can change accents within many languages, but he loves the Irish and Scottish accents best of all – isn't that funny! – and he does the Indian accent to a T." Adam grinned.

"You're joking right? An alien who speaks with an Irish accent!"

"Oh, for heaven's sake, do get on with it," Jacob said. "Tell her why he's coming in on the battle against the Plot."

Kate broke in. "What use is an interpreter when contact is telepathic?"

"Goodness, my sweet, I thought you were brighter than that," laughed Adam, playfully punching her arm.

"Clever clogs," Kate retorted and punched him back. "I'm brighter than you any day." She had to admit to herself that there was a bit of flirting going on here.

"Definitely more powerful, not sure about cleverer though!" Adam then put his sensible face on. "How many people do you know who are telepathic? Not many, and least of all those who are in power. We've tried to get through to them, but they're too entrenched in heavy energies, so we just can't make contact – hence the dramatics last night. This is where Jamère comes in. He can project an actual voice."

"But not everybody could hear him..."

"True, but those who could will speak about it and even those who couldn't hear him knew on some level that there was more to the storm than just high winds. It will create greater awareness every time it happens, a domino effect of knowing."

"Will I see him sometime?" Kate asked.

"He's been assigned to you for your mission when you act as an intermediary between the Galactic Order and the Human Races. He's been waiting for you to wake up in this lifetime. You were a student with him in past lives, when he was a translator between Egyptian and other cultures who were trading with star people. Because of that work, he became an ambassador to the stars and had to understand intercultural connections. You were also his friend and learnt to be a translator yourself. This knowledge will come back to you now. You learnt various star languages and he's returned to connect you with that memory and help you with your translating skills, so you can work in that way again. He's told me that your own work as an ambassador is coming into action now. He's very humorous and engaging to be around. Like we say, you'll like him."

"There's so much to learn about myself it's hard to keep up. I wonder when it will seem normal to me to know all this? 'Waking up' is quite a challenge," Kate replied.

"A lot of people are waking up right now, and it's about time too," Jacob said, dipping his biscuit into his tea.

"Will I actually see him when I meet him?" Kate asked.

"Have you noticed that your eyes sometimes change? They become an intense blue, much bluer than normal. It happens to you much of the time nowadays," Jacob said. "And when it does, it's the Sirius part of you revealing itself, and that's when he'll appear in your mind. He bears the insignia of a branch of the Galactic Command. And as for his appearance, he has his head in the stars and looks spaced out." Jacob broke off laughing. "Oh, that was a good one. Joke! Get it?"

Kate grimaced.

"Whenever you feel or see him you will receive and speak any number of space languages," Adam said.

"Oh! That's already happening," Kate exclaimed. "I woke up the other night and realised I was speaking a strange language. I didn't know what it was though."

Jacob looked from his daughter to Adam, then hauled his big frame out of his chair. "Well, I'd better be off. I'll leave Adam to fill you in on the rest." He gave Kate a peck on the cheek and left.

Alone at last with Adam, Kate leant forward and said: "So, tell me all." As she waited for his reply, she wondered if he'd ever show any feelings towards her. He was friendly, sometimes even a bit flirty, but nothing more. She was aware he held a high rank in SatData and that the business was deeply involved with the world's secret government, (something she still found hard to comprehend) and she was, after all, only a humble clerk. Maybe that was why he kept things so business-like? What they were about was hardly normal though, was it? Surely that counted for something.

Kate realised Adam was staring at her. She flushed in embarrassment. Oh god, I mind-spoke that didn't I?

He didn't answer, instead he said, "Look, your eyes are changing again. You may be about to meet the famous Jamère and learn how to speak ET."

Kate felt a strong urge to retort, but what came was no language she knew or could understand. It felt extremely good to speak it, though, and she let it flow from her mouth with an ease that delighted her. Sheer joy filled her, and when Adam joined in she almost burst with happiness. The flow of words soon finished, and they found themselves hugging each other in delight.

Adam drew back, flustered. "That was Jamère's doing," he said as if to excuse himself. "Did you see him?"

"No, I only saw you." Kate flung herself down on the sofa, deflated at Adam's reaction. It had felt entirely natural – and wonderful – to hug him and now he was distancing himself.

Adam replied all in a rush, perhaps to avoid mention of the hug. "He's such a colourful character with brown eyes, a small beard and a moustache. He likes to dress in white with a broad gold band across one shoulder and stars all over, which I suppose is appropriate given his job. He enjoys symbols too. You'll know him when you see him."

"I can't wait to meet him," Kate said somewhat sarcastically. "It sounds as if you know him very well," Kate said. "And what was that we spoke anyway?"

"It was our mother-tongue, Kate. Sirian. That's why it felt so joyful to you – to us. You will start to recall it from now on, and in times when you need me, or if you need to cloak a thought for me, use our language. I will know it is you."

"Oh, wow! That will be such a help in keeping our distance from Helga."

"Tonight has been a big step forward for us. We will be able to keep one step ahead of the Dark Hats now we have our language in common, but part of your work is to learn lots of other languages from Jamère so that you can be an intergalactic ambassador, and you'll interpret for those who can't receive information in any other way."

"Why can't Jamère do that himself, like he did the other night?"

"First of all, he can't be everywhere. And that was a special occasion that called for dramatics, but Jamère needs help now that we are ramping-up our work to help humanity awaken. It's going to be necessary to have many interpreters handy when our space friends come visiting, and others like you are also being prepared all over the planet." He looked at her for a moment, then added, "I'd probably better be going now."

He stood, gave her a farewell kiss on the cheek and let himself out.

Kate frowned. She couldn't help feeling that his quick exit had something to do with that hug. She was sure he'd enjoyed it as much as she had — or was it just that she'd been able to speak in their mother-tongue for the first time?

CHAPTER TWENTY

INNER EARTH

'You are children of the Creation. You are created so that the purest energy in existence may continue to expand, through experiencing all. You cannot help but be affected by all things, even when unaware of this. Open yourself to possibilities, even existence in form other than the human body. Open your mind to other realms, other dimensions, other worlds. You are bound together forever by the purest energy, that of love. Hold love in your being and you will know all.'

The Universal Brotherhood

A loud chuckling woke Kate up. There was no mistaking it. She opened her eyes and sat up in astonishment. Someone who could only be Jamère stood at the foot of her bed in full regalia blazing with amazing colours.

"You must be Jamère. It's nice to meet you," said Kate, hastily pulling up her covers. Emboldened by his cheery demeanour she added: "Don't you knock before you enter a lady's bedroom?"

"Och, forgive me, wee lassie," he said in a broad Scottish accent. "You know full well I can't knock."

Show off, Kate thought.

"I've come to show you much more of your planet," he said in a different, lilting voice that Kate found extremely pleasant to listen to. Even though he had not given her much time to ease out of her sleepy state, she realised he was now speaking to her in Sirian – her mother tongue. He launched straight in.

"There's much more to planet Earth than you know or have experienced. Even you. There's another branch of the human species that your scientists have never imagined, not even in their wildest dreams. Think how excited they'd be if they knew. It's high time you explored another part of Earth you've never entered before. You need to know all parts, not only those which are obvious on the surface."

Fully awake in his energy now, Kate saw the reference. "Are you talking about Inner Earth?"

"Yes. We're going to explain Inner Earth to you and by that we don't mean within the soil, within the rock structures or caves. There's another world within your known world."

"That sounds intriguing."

"If you open your mind I'll explain it to you."

Kate relaxed against the headboard of her bed and entered a state of meditation. After a moment, she heard Jamère again, as if in the distance.

"First of all, as you know, there's the crust, then the Earth's mantle down to the core. It accounts for the largest portion of the Earth and is about 1800 miles thick. That's all true."

"I see," said Kate, trying to grasp the complex geology. "So how can there be an Inner Earth?"

"The inner world as I prefer to call it shares these same layers, just in a different realm, a realm of great peace and harmony amongst the inhabitants. You might call this a true paradise, an Eden.

“Yes,” Kate hesitated, “but it’s a bit difficult to comprehend.”

“There are entry points into the inner world, but they’re well and truly hidden. We don’t wish for the mixing of inner and outer worlds, though there are records of journeys into the inner world. You may find more if you care to research. They too have the north and south poles, and these are the main entry points. They’ve been cloaked from prying eyes for the most part, but there’ve been signs for those who are watching and aware.”

Kate remembered the film footage of space craft entering volcanoes, such as in Jaime Maussan’s excellent DVD that she’ recently bought. So that was where they were going? Kate felt Jamère’s enthusiasm as he continued, his words flowing, as if unstoppable.

“Certain volcanoes are used as safe entry points, but these are not ones to be taken by humans. To say the inner world is populated by space beings would not be quite accurate, but it’s true to some degree. Space beings from your outer galaxies and universes have been there and still visit regularly. Understand that they’re able to travel inter-dimensionally where third dimension physicality is not a barrier. They can and often do travel through entry points, using volcanoes such as Popocatepetl and its neighbour volcano Iztaccíhuatl in Mexico.

“The engine that drives your planet and keeps its place in the solar system lies in the centre, inside the ring. For obvious reasons, given the hostility and truly aggressive nature of surface humans, the entry points to the inner world will never be disclosed to them. You however, can go if you wish, by using your mind. It is a fact that the inner world is affected by the goings-on on the upper surface of the ring. It is true to say that the actions of the human race are important to both.”

“I would love to go.” Kate replied, “but I’m feeling overwhelmed at all this new information I’m trying to assimilate it, and now I have yet another mission! My mind can only take so much. Have a heart."

"Oh, I have a heart, lassie" he said, laughing softly as he patted his chest. "We all have hearts, don't you know. Even the little people have hearts." Jamère changed his accent to a soft Irish brogue. "I will tell you about the little people, if you'll listen," he said, smiling.

Kate almost expected him to say 'begorrah' but it didn't come.

"They do exist – all of them: what you call pixies and leprechauns and fairies, as do the mythical creatures such as sasquatch, dragons and the Australian Bunyip."

Kate yawned, her attention waning in spite of herself.

"Oh, I see you're exhausted," Jamère said quickly. "Enough!" and he whisked away, leaving Kate reeling.

So, he did have a heart after all, and he knew Kate was struggling from so much information to take in, despite it being so fascinating. She loved learning all about the hidden aspects of Earth – it was like putting pieces of a jigsaw puzzle into place. But boy, she could do with a holiday – just a long weekend, maybe a girlie weekend with Poppy?

At that moment, the phone rang, and realising it was the landline downstairs, Kate shot out of bed and dashed to answer it before it rang-off.

"Hello stranger," said her best friend without malice.

"Poppy! I was just thinking about you," Kate laughed. 'What's up?"

"Not sure... I something strange just happened. It's knocked me sideways a bit to be honest."

"Oh yeah? Sounds like you might need a holiday too... What was it?"

"I got a phone call from some bloke who wouldn't give his name. He just said, 'No more lectures, no more talks, no more fliers, no more radio shows. Mark these words. Desist.' And he put the damn phone down on me! What's that all about Kate – whose toes are you treading on?

"Did he have an American accent?"

"Dunno... It's hard to say really. I think so."

"I have my suspicions. There's this guy at work, Marco – do you remember I told you he gave me the creeps? Well anyway, he just seems to hate me for some reason. He's just trying to put the frighteners on you."

"Yes, but why?"

Kate couldn't tell her best friend the real reason why Marco was getting heavy; that he worked for the Dark Hats who wanted to retain the Earth for their own greedy purposes. Poppy was still on the fence about all that. "He's just a bully Poppy, don't worry about it. Look, I haven't got a talk scheduled for a couple of weeks, have I, so that will keep him quiet for a bit, and then we can have a chat about what to do next. Maybe we should think about going 'underground' a bit: you know, extend our email database or maybe use What'sApp or something, and have invite-only meetings so that we don't have to advertise?"

"Or you could just stop doing it altogether and just be like Kate again?"

If only she knew who Kate really was. "I tell you what Poppy. Let's try and arrange a long weekend away, sometime soon, eh? A spa break in St Ives or something?"

"God yes! Sounds good to me. Okay, so we'll keep a low profile, and I'll get the email database up to date. Then we'll discuss where we go from here. Do you think this Marco bloke's dangerous?"

"He could never outwit you, my friend, but keep your eyes peeled eh? Best get off to work. Let's try and catch up at the weekend."

"Love ya."

"Love you too."

* * *

Next, Kate quickly rang Jacob. The phone rang and rang and rang. No answer.

"Oh please pick up!" She was about to give up when Jacob answered.

"Where have you been?" she shouted. "I'm sorry Dad, I didn't mean to shout."

"If you must know the delivery man was just dropping off my weekly shop. I have to eat sometimes, you know. Now what's this all about?"

"I think we have to hurry, Dad. Can you come round this evening for another journey? I think the Dark Hats are tightening the screws on us. Jamère has been, and I don't think we have much time. It feels important that you listen in and record."

"What about Adam? He's used to this by now, isn't he?"

"He's away for a few days. I'm not sure when he's back. You know how he gets summoned by HQ and goes off without a word."

"Am I invited only because Adam is not available?

Kate picked up on his peeved tone. "Oh, don't be like that, Dad. I need you."

"Fine. Would 7pm be alright for you? I can't get there any earlier."

* * *

That evening Jacob arrived dead on time and without much ado, Kate took her usual route into a trance and started speaking, telling him what she saw and felt as it happened.

"I'm going down. I feel all eyes on me so I'm ducking my head to avoid drawing attention to myself. At the bottom I can see people of all nationalities, as well as energies, balls of light and intelligence. Some of them are interested in me, some are just going about their business. We're in a big square surrounded by shops and buildings. It's absolutely packed, like a bustling market. I work my way through the crowd until I come to a passage on the left. I slip into it. Nobody seems to notice.

"It's calm, quiet and dim; there's just enough light so I can see where I'm going. The narrow passage feels like a crack or fissure in a rock. I have to feel my way along. I hit a dead end. The only place I can go now is down a ladder I can see fixed to the rock. I climb down. It's well hidden for safety and security.

"At the bottom is a well-lit big, open space, it's dazzlingly bright. There are a lot of people here – humans, and those who I can tell aren't. The place is very busy. Everyone's doing something. There's technology with lots of dials and controls. It's been here a while because it's orderly, and well used. What am I supposed to do here?

I hear a voice: "You are to observe and know that this exists. Know that we have plans to accommodate many."

My question is, 'how are people going to know about this? It's so far down. I don't even know the way here in real life.'

The voice replies, 'When it's important for others to know there will be an opening which will show them the way.'

My next question is, 'who gets to see this place?'

'We will show the way to those who genuinely wish to assist planet Earth and wish for a better world for all, not just for themselves. Those who feel they have earned a place only because of position or power will not know of this entrance.'

'Why are you showing me this?'

'So you can make it known. So that others will look to their soul condition and take heed of what we say. We know it is safe to tell you this for you do not know how to enter this place on a physical level. It will only be clear when the time is right.'

'Why are there only men are down here, no women or children?'

The voice says, 'These are the operators, those who are maintaining this in good order. The time is not ready yet.'

"They show me to another part, a different area where there are beings who are not humans. I can't say extra-terrestrials, maybe inner terrestrials, for they're of the Earth, but not the same as those on the surface.

'They too belong to the Earth and it is they who have assisted in the project you see being prepared here. Without these beings from inside the Earth this would not be possible.'

Jacob fidgeted in his chair, witnessing changes in his daughter's face and form that he could not control or understand. Another's face transformed over hers that became longer in the chin, had pointed ears and was more extra-terrestrial than human. She was changing into some other being. It unnerved him more than he cared to admit. Even if she hadn't had enough, he had.

"Kate, bring your mind back to this room," he said. "Feel the weight of your body on the chair. Give your toes and fingers a little wiggle."

Kate slowly opened her eyes. Jacob watched her shake her head as if to clear it, then she sat bolt upright.

"How was that Dad?" she asked. "Did you understand it that? What are we supposed to do with this information?"

"I really don't know darling. I suppose the more people know about the Earth the more likely they are to respect it and look after it. We continue to spread the word I suppose." He sighed at the prospect.

* * *

The next morning Jacob got up early to bright sunshine. He drew back the curtains and thought about last night's revelations. He felt unnerved. Were they getting in too deep? He couldn't keep an eye on Kate as much as he'd like and witnessing his beloved daughter morph into her Sirian side as she journeyed had shaken him. She must be getting more familiar with it for it to appear like that. She seemed to be discovering new abilities daily. It could cause her a real problem if it happened in her everyday life, and she didn't seem to have any control over when it happened.

Jacob was right. Kate discovered that this was a concern the very next day when a colleague, Jane, approached her.

"Call me crazy…Oh I can't believe I'm going to say this…but are you all right? This sounds ridiculous but I'm sure you disappeared yesterday," she said, brows furrowed and blushing slightly.

"Yesterday? Oh yes, I popped to the shop at lunchtime," replied Kate.

"No, I mean, *really disappeared*. You vanished. Only for a second, but you definitely weren't there. What was that all about? I can't get my head around it – I've been thinking about it all night. Is it some sort of illusion or am I going mad?"

"Don't worry, Jane, I'm sure it was a trick of the light or something? I have no intention of going anywhere. I wish I could disappear and get away from Helga's scrutiny – but I can't!" joked Kate.

Jane looked relieved but walked away shaking her head. Although she'd made light of it, Kate's stomach lurched at her colleague's claim. She wasn't even aware that it had happened. The notion that her physical presence was being compromised alarmed her, she already felt she was out of her depth.

* * *

Jacob worried that Kate was coming to rely more and more on Adam. He knew that Adam was himself a double-agent, but if Helga knew the depth of his relationship with Kate, they may start to put two and two together. If they discovered Adam was a Trojan Horse, Kate would be in even more danger. His frown deepened. Were they taking too many chances?

Nonetheless, their team was growing and strengthening. With Jamère alongside, Kate found her role a bit clearer. An interpreter, eh! Was the time getting nearer for public landings of spacecraft and the appearance of Intergalactic beings, she wondered? Her pulse quickened at the thought. She also realised that both Jacob and Adam had different roles to play: Jacob was solely focussed on spiritual matters and raising consciousness. His own work meant he was constantly mind-traveling the world over; whereas Adam's concern was what was going on unnoticed and concealed by an ill-intentioned power behind the façade of SatData Consolidated. He wished for disclosure. Kate was somewhere in the middle, with Helga and her cronies circling like vultures on the periphery. It was time for a meeting.

The nights were drawing in and it was getting dark in the street when Jacob parked his little car by her gate. Shortly after, Adam drove up and parked opposite. As he got out of his car, he looked towards Kate's house and saw faint blue lights playing over the roof. They were in good company. Nobody saw the two men arrive, or so they hoped.

Kate drew the curtains to shut out any prying eyes.

"Right then, my darling, what's this gathering all about?" Jacob asked as soon as they were inside. "You sounded so serious on the phone. Have you checked for bugs?" He looked around. Adam was already doing just that, roaming about the house looking and checking. Kate found it strange that they were concerned about government spies whilst they were dealing with much bigger, extra-terrestrial fish. Who knows? Perhaps they were right to be worried?

"Well, it is serious," Kate said. "Time is rushing by and it doesn't feel as if we're getting anywhere. I think we ought to be more organised."

"Oh, do sit down, Adam," she said as he walked into the room, satisfied that the house was not tapped.

She took a deep breath. "First of all, I know you're friendly with Sechem, Adam, which is why I've trusted you with my journeys. You've been a great help. And I know you're also from Sirius like me and Jacob. But I need to know more – it helps me to get my internal jig-saw puzzle together."

"Well, you know I have been sent here from Sirius, because we both speak the same language – that much, I'm sure you've gathered?"

Kate gave a nervous laugh, recalling the hug that had meant so much to her. "Then why are you not in ET form? How are you in human form?" (And, cloaking the thought this time, she said to herself, *and such handsome human form*.)

"If you'll give me time I'll explain further," he said.

Jacob interrupted him. "Please ignore me if I drop off. I might snore a bit. This is going to be lengthy, and I've heard it all before." With that he snuggled down in his chair and closed his eyes.

"What do you know about walk-ins?" Adam asked.

"Not much, I've read a little but I want to hear it from you," Kate said.

"A walk-in is a soul that has evolved sufficiently to be allowed to carry out a mission by exchanging places with an already incarnated person."

"Isn't that possession?"

"No, certainly not. A walk-in can only take place with full agreement of both outgoing and incoming souls. The incoming soul inherits the cellular memory of the physical body of the outgoing soul, with full recall of its life and appears to be the same person to others around. There are many reasons why a soul departs early. In my outgoing soul's experience he wanted out, to quit his life, but didn't want to commit suicide."

"What happened to him?"

"He has moved on to other experiences in non-physical worlds and will re-incarnate when he's ready; life had become untenable for him and he was happy when the contract for exchange was offered. A walk-in or an exchange is only allowed when approved of by a Higher Spiritual Council. It has to be shown that the walk-in has a sufficiently worthwhile mission to be allowed to do this, and is adequately evolved to carry out its task. There's no karmic debt incurred by the outgoing soul for having departed early. It simply ends this life earlier and then carries on in the normal cycle of life and death."

"So, who are you now? Whose life did you take on?"

Adam's took a deep breath. "Now? I am who I am, as you know me. The one who departed was an Air Force Colonel working in Aerospace Technical Information Command. He had secret knowledge and personal experience of the interaction between military departments and some extra-terrestrials they were keeping. He couldn't live with his conscience when he knew what their plans were for entire populations. His credentials and top clearance allowed him to go into deep underground bases crisscrossing the United States. He didn't know how to continue living with this knowledge and yet do nothing about it, so there seemed no way out except death to him. He could not disclose anything – he'd seen what happened to those who did. I've taken his place."

"Wow," Kate said, stunned by the revelation. "So, you have all his knowledge, but as a walk-in you have your Sirian knowledge too. That puts you in a powerful place. What are you able to do that he couldn't?"

"I'm a different soul and have different connections with space. I'm what you might call a Trojan Horse. No human, apart from you and your father knows my real identity. How could they? Others have come down from star systems as walk-ins, so I'm not alone, and we know of each other. Remember we have direct lines to the Galactic Command. Our collective plan is to help smooth the way between visitors and Earth, easing cultural integration and tutoring star visitors such as the Tall Whites residing at Indian Wells Valley. We've already achieved great things: regular humans are learning to accept their own star children, or Star Seeds as we call them, whose advanced abilities just aren't like other kids. We're hoping that people will learn to accept visitors from space in the same manner. Then they'll be more open about who and what they are without enduring the usual rejection, ridicule and avoidance that too many humans dish out to anyone who's different from them.

"We are what you could call 'spies' working within but not for either side. We have our own agenda, as I have stated, but it is important to us that humanity evolves quickly and stops the production of nuclear weapons and other destructive practises. Earth is too precious to all intergalactic beings to be destroyed by ignorance. So we are working for the good of humanity and of all in the universe. However, because we are working in what you might call the 'Secret Programme', we have insider knowledge and can do what is necessary to prevent or change such unwelcome projects. This is where your abilities come in. You've proved invaluable, and that's why The Galactic Command sent me to find and safeguard you. Master M, Sechem and Jamère are responsible for me being here now."

"Thank you so much for explaining all that to me, that's really helped me puzzle it out," said Kate. "I'm starting to get my head around things now."

"I knew you wanted to know, but I had to wait until the time was right to tell you in detail. It would have been too much to take in previously," replied Adam. "There's so much more I need to fill you in on too. You need to get to grips with alien politics for a start! There are groups of ETs who are happy to work with the secret government on Earth, but others don't wish to be involved or caught up in their programmes, hence the term, 'Dark Hats' and 'Light Hats' is most accurate. Some from Sirius A are assisting in building a suitable ecological system for human evolution on Earth by altering the 'bio-magnetic energy grid' of the planet. We need them. Those from the Pleiades, such as Sechem, are helping humanity find freedom from oppressive structures through raising consciousness. I could go on and on, but you get the picture. The ETs that you helped rescue were caught between the two factions."

Hearing this suddenly triggered something in Kate. It was like a subconscious bolt in her memory had been drawn and a door opened, unlocking suppressed memories. Her eyes lit up with excitement.

"Oh my god, I've just remembered something. Way back in…well it must have been 2003, late 2003, November I think, I received a mind communication from ETs held within a force-field in the Earth," she said. "I've totally blanked it out until now but weirdly I remember clearly what they said.

"They told me that they could only be released from their entrapment by dying, by ending their physical incarnation. But they do not choose this. They had taken hundreds of years to reach their present level of knowledge in this one incarnation. If they were freed they would continue for many more hundreds of years, as they do not age as quickly as humans. What would appear to us to be a lengthy passage of time on Earth would be much shorter if we were travelling in a space vehicle as they do."

Adam waited, fascinated, as Kate dredged her mind for more. The memories emerged like panning for gold.

"They told me, 'We are one type only. We are the workers. There are others different in form to us who are considered to be the thinkers, the organisers, those who have greater wisdom. We simply carry out our duties and are not in a position of great authority. We are useful in that we are regarded as such. We have technology, and this is the reason for our presence within this Faraday type field that prevents us leaving. The technological advances that we have are being used by your authorities. We were taken advantage of, you might say. We were willing to help.'

"Oh yes, I remember them saying that about their technological advances being used by our authorities. Specifically, the ability to time travel and to escape the gravitational pull of Earth by using Zero Point Energy – no wait, Zero Point Field. They also mentioned a particular energy source that does not originate on Earth. It has an element that does not exist in Earth matter.

"You know, Adam, they had the ability to instruct in its use and have been beneficial to those in authority in this way. They were not unkindly treated, but were not allowed to leave. That is what they told me."

"Wow, that's incredible. All this time, you knew this but had repressed it!"

"I know," replied Kate. "I'm so glad it's coming back to me now. I remember asking how they were captured and they said they didn't see it as such at first, because they crash-landed and were rescued. It was only when they realised that they weren't allowed to leave that the relationship changed from friend to prisoner. Their trust was broken. They were experimented on and some of them died. They were held in an environment which, after some experimentation, was suitable for them to maintain a healthy body. They are not as we are and do not have the same organs." Kate finished. "Sadly the survivors were kept captive for years."

"Did you see them?" Jacob asked.

"No, it was mind communication only. I felt them and sensed their immense sadness and desperation. It was heart-rending to listen to them. They had families they could never get home to. Can you imagine that? I wonder if they're the ones I rescued recently?"

"And you did it brilliantly too," Adam said.

Kate shrugged, wishing she'd been able to rescue them way back then.

Adam put his arm around her. "Anyway, I hope you're feeling better now about my role and who I am. Can you see now how it would've been impossible to tell you all at our first meeting?"

Kate nodded. She wanted to hug him, but restrained herself. Now she knew his background, she loved him even more. She felt a real connection with him, it was new and wonderful. They both had Sirian blood. He understood her more than she understood herself.

Adam took Kate's hand in his. "We need to talk about what you're doing when going into underground bases and why. What you're doing in your mind travel is very similar to remote viewing, except you don't need to follow protocols. You seem to be directed by a higher spiritual group of beings."

Kate said, "I'll be careful, but I can't stop now and I never know where I'm going to be taken anyway. It's not directed by me. Makes it interesting, don't you think?"

It felt good be here in the same room with two of her favourite men, although one of them was fast asleep.

CHAPTER TWENTY-ONE

DANGER APPROACHES

'When did the future switch from being a promise to a threat?'

Chuck Palahniuk

The next morning Kate pulled into the office car park and locked her car. As she walked towards the entrance she heard the distinctive cold click of a gun being cocked. A jolt of adrenalin surged through her as she ducked behind a pillar. She held her breath and looked around, but saw nothing unusual. She breathed again but didn't dare move until someone else arrived in the car park, then she walked with them into the building.

Did I just imagine that? she thought. Am I getting paranoid here?

The rest of the day was odd, to say the least. When she walked into the office, instant surprise registered on Helga's face, but she was quick to cover it up. Was she expecting Kate to have been shot?

Silas walked by a bit too often to go unnoticed. Was she being ultra-sensitive or was it pure coincidence? She knew he enjoyed preening in front of the window by her desk but she was sure that he had another motive too. Each time he passed, he stared at her, making the hairs on the back of her neck stand on end, and her second sight registered fear. Marco was also back in the East Wing today, probably because Adam had to take a day-trip to the London office. When she looked across to where he was sitting, he seemed as on edge as she was.

The long day ended at last with no further cause for alarm. Kate made sure she left with a crowd of other office workers, returning to her parked car with them as they fanned out across the parking lot to theirs. She knew she wasn't just feeling insecure, there were forces against her, and she was in grave danger.

Kate called Adam as soon as she got home and told him about her fears.

"I'm just pulling into Bournemouth station now. I'm coming straight round Kate. I'll be with you in ten minutes, then I think we'd better ask your unseen friends what's going on."

As Kate saw the lights of his Mercedes swing into her road, she felt a huge sense of relief. Jacob was right, she was not alone, and here was one of the people she realised she trusted most in the world.

She opened the door for him and they kissed each other on the cheeks. But then Adam held both her hands in front of him and gazed into her eyes. It was like an instant download of emotions – they didn't have to say much more.

Adam sat in Jacob's chair whilst Kate settled in on the sofa and soon entered a trance. Once again, she told Adam what was happening.

"I'm standing on a ship's gangway in long flowing white robes. I walk down the gangway. A car's waiting for me, a black shiny one. I get in, pulling my long clothes in after me. I don't know what this is or where we are going.

'You are going to The League of Nations,' the voice says.

'I didn't know it still existed. I thought it was dissolved after the war.'

'It's a different one. This is the Galactic League of Nations. It's been formed because what's happening doesn't affect only one country, but all countries and all of the universe. You and others like you have been called upon. It's recognised that you are the ones who can communicate with non-human beings on the planet. You're able to understand the thoughts and intentions and are not fazed by odd appearances.'

"We drive along a secluded gravel road with trees on either side and arrive at a check-point set in a reinforced chain-link fence. The driver flashes his credentials and an armed guard raises the barrier and waves us on. A bit further on we pull up in front of a large, flat roofed single story building with a guard blocking the entrance. The driver runs round to open the door for me. He salutes as I get out of the car. A tall uniformed man escorts me past the armed guard.

"We walk across a foyer and into a large lecture hall filled with seats arranged in rows. No one is sitting yet; they're walking around, communicating with each other in their own languages. Attendants are seating different humanoid species on the lecture stage. It's an incredible sight. Some are extremely tall, about 15ft, with huge insect-like eyes protruding out from either side of their heads. One has a golden-orange mane of hair like a lion. He has such a beautiful soft face, with cat-like eyes. One has enormous wrap around eyes with no iris, yet another is so tiny it is carried on the arm of a larger being. I watch as another takes a seat, a star visitor with a series of deep creases along the top of the head which slopes down towards the front, and with a strongly pronounced brow above the eyes.

"It's fascinating watching as the others begin to take their seats in the hall. Some are wearing long robes, their faces concealed by hoods. Others wear sleek bodysuits in shining colours. A small star visitor walks past. He has a large head with dark oval eyes, spindly frame and limbs, and his hands have three long, cartilaginous fingers.

'What am I doing here?' I ask the voice.

'You'll act as an interpreter, an intermediary, relaying to those in power the concerns of our intergalactic brothers and sisters.'

I am asked to stand in front of the rows of seats and the proceedings begin. Being after being stand up to speak of their concerns and I simultaneously translate their words into many different ET languages. I don't know how I am doing this; it is just an ability that seems to have been latent in me. What I do know is many beings feel that humans have outstayed their welcome on Earth; that they are fundamentally flawed and are not able to evolve to love and respect the planet in the ways that will be necessary to redeem her from the current malaise. The High Council of the League remain impassive, hearing all voices but making no judgement. The time for that is not now.

"Oh, the scene has changed. I'm being transported somewhere else," said Kate.

Adam mind-spoke with her. "Are you sure you're up to it? You've had a lot to take in." He was concerned.

"Yes, I'm fine," Kate replied, pleased that he cared.

"I'm on some stairs. They're covered in lino, broken in parts and uncared for. I'm in a derelict place. It echoes as I go down. There's a wall on either side, painted a horrible green. At the bottom it opens out into a big, empty space like a disused warehouse. I can sense it is deep underground. Gosh, this is not a nice place. It's old and uncared for. I come to a door that's been boarded up. I tug at the boards and they come away quite easily. The door inside is rotting on its hinges. I push and it falls over.

"I clamber over to get inside. There's something glowing. Not a celestial glow but radioactive. It's not safe. I suddenly realise this is why this place has been boarded up. It's because there's unsafe radiation in it. Nobody would dare go near. Well, I'm only a mind so I can go near. I move to a fairly large box. It's difficult to see through the reddish haze over it. Again, I pick up waves of radiation.

The Voice says, ‘What we are showing you is not an isolated place. There are other areas, other houses, other buildings that contain unsafe elements within them that we have isolated and forbidden entry to. That is, the authorities have forbidden entry. This is much more widespread than this one building. The general public have no idea. These are in many areas of the world, such as Eastern Europe, Russia, China, Japan, even the Philippines.’

‘I want to know what I’m doing here then. What can I do?’

‘We want you to use your mind. When you complete this one task it will have an effect on all those other places. Lay both hands on the box. As you do, with your mind see the glow subside. Send your thoughts so that the dangerous element in this box is neutralised. It reduces the radioactivity. This you must do. Create a mind picture of other aspects of yourself doing this in many other places. You are not restricted to one place when you use your mind.’

“I see holographic pictures of me in many places laying hands on similar containers. I see the glow diminishing, fading, and leaving the box completely free. I see pictures of me everywhere doing the same.

‘When this is done, we can use these buildings safely. All these areas will become safe as a result of your action.’

‘Why couldn’t you do this yourselves?’

‘If change is to come about on your planet the change must come from those who inhabit the planet, whether they use their minds or their physicality. Earth dwellers have to make the changes, not us. You can now leave with our thanks.’”

Some moments later, Kate opened her eyes and blinked a few times to clear the fog, then turned to Adam with a smile.

He returned the smile. “Welcome back. How do you feel?”

"Fine, a little tired, but I'm okay."

"Good, I'll make some tea in a moment. So, it's clear there's much concern from our guides about radiation and nuclear pollution and weaponry. Maybe that's why UFOs are more often seen over nuclear establishments? Don't you think? Kate, we're getting into deep waters here."

She laughed, making a pun: "Nuclear submarines too, then? They're really in deep waters."

"Ha ha! Funny. It's no laughing matter, though" Adam responded thoughtfully. "If the CIA finds out what you've been doing they'll target you. You'll be on their hit list. This is getting serious."

"But, I'm a nobody, just a clerk. How could they know it's me? There again, might this have something to do with the gun that was pointed at me this morning?"

"No. I think that was Marco, trying to scare you again. He's such a fool – but a fool is a dangerous person too. I'm sorry I couldn't take him with me to London, but there was no need for him to come and Helga's on to us like a hawk."

"But the CIA, Adam? How can they possibly know about all this?"

"Have you not heard of HAARP?" Adam said. "That's what Jamère was referring to when he gave his message in the wind storm. But that facility does much more than the public are told. The acronym stands for High-Frequency Active Auroral Research Programme and is based in Alaska well away from prying eyes. I've got to lend you Jerry E Smith's book of the same name, you'd be horrified. Individuals could be mind-targeted using the wavelengths produced by the HAARP array of signals, sometimes called the 'death ray'. Jerry Smith says he's convinced that HAARP has the potential to create an ecological disaster that would make an atomic bomb seem like a sparkler."

Kate's eyes widened. "Oh no…"

"I know, terrible isn't it?" said Adam. "HAARP uses scalar waves; I've heard they can be used to provoke an earthquake, ultimately even control the weather. Think what that means.

"Now you're really scaring me." Kate shuddered and turned pale. "It rings a bell though. I think I may have been sent there on one of my travels. Maybe I dismantled something...? Helga's small fry by comparison. I don't like the idea of being mind-targeted one little bit." Kate paused, thinking back. "But in a way, that's what she did when she psychically attacked me. You know, when she tried to push me down the stairs, and when that guttering nearly fell on me. That was her, I know it."

Adam nodded, his brow furrowed. "Look, we're committed to this work, because if we don't do it, the consequences are terrible. But the net is closing in, so we'll have to be more careful in future and make double sure the house is bug free."

CHAPTER TWENTY-TWO

SPREADING THE WORD

'My life is my message.'

Mahatma Gandhi

Coloured lights continued to play over Kate's house, and Mrs Thomas from across the street continued to keep watch. Since they didn't come from a black helicopter overhead, she figured it must be her friends protecting Ms Greene — and if Ms Greene needed protecting for any reason, then Mrs Thomas would do whatever she could, even though that wasn't much more than being a good neighbour. Even so, it gave her a comforting feeling. She was grateful they were standing guard over Kate's house where who knows what work was going on, but if the coloured lights were present, Mrs Thomas knew it was good work. Kate's other neighbours remained respectful and didn't ask questions about the regular comings and goings of smart cars and all manner of men and women. Maybe they preferred not to know.

Kate was now running her psychic development and mediumship circles back at home. After the warning that was sent to Poppy, they couldn't take any chances. Kate and Poppy had decided to downsize but invite a select audience from those who had filled out feedback forms from her previous talks. These were people who were truly interested in Kate's work, who could keep quiet about the meetings and who were intent on developing their own abilities. Kate loved these evenings. She felt she was doing something really tangible for the cause.

Nonetheless, the more research Kate did about HAARP and the CIA, the more disturbing facts she uncovered. She called Jacob and Adam round to discuss her findings the evening after her weekly meeting.

"I don't think I'll be going on any mind journeys this evening," she explained. "I need your feedback on what might be going on behind the scenes in the struggle for world dominance. I've been trawling the net and am finding out heaps, but is it to be believed? Is it true or not?"

Jacob grunted. "Oh, you can believe it alright. I've also been checking the credentials of those who've speaking out, the whistleblowers. They're all coming out of the woodwork now, aren't they? Remember what you said about safety in numbers when whistleblowers all get together? Maybe they're taking heart and encouraging others to say what they know and believe?"

"Maybe that's true…but we need to understand more of what's ahead for us all," Kate said once they'd settled down in her sitting room.

Adam spread his long legs out before him and leaned back. "Checked for bugs?" he asked, ever cautious.

Kate nodded. "Of course."

Adam sighed. "From what I know, the space visitors' understandable interest and concern with nuclear establishments puts them at risk, because such places are well monitored. News of frequent landings elsewhere is quickly squashed, and never makes the headlines. So the general public remains in ignorance and, worse still, dismisses it as fake news. Anyone talking about the subject is quickly labelled as odd and is discredited. It hardly encourages people to come forward, does it?" He sighed again. "If only they realised."

Jacob broke in. "Yes, the media are manipulated to a large degree when it comes to topics such as sightings of UFOs and crop circles, but the internet is playing a large part in helping to spread awareness of sightings that would never make the news any other way."

"In fairness to them," Adam said, "the media does occasionally air documentaries where they interview someone who's psychically gifted, or who has had some experience of 'off world' encounters. But anyone brave enough to be interviewed soon discovers there's always one person invited, who's more than happy to disprove or ridicule at great length, so nullifying anything that might otherwise be taken seriously."

"True," Kate said, "but the internet is changing all that by showing video footage that's hard to disprove. I've noticed that much authentic and verifiable evidence is now coming to light from people who have little lifespan left, or who no longer care about losing their jobs because they're retired."

Adam looked at her. "What did you discover? Anything we don't know already? I know that in remote areas of South America there are escalators large enough to take craft deep underground. I know there are interplanetary beings either held against their wishes deep underground, or working voluntarily with the shadow government control system. You, Kate have tapped into this on your journeys; which is why you need to be careful."

"No need to be nervous Adam. Haven't you noticed that there are coloured lights playing over Kate's house all the time?" Jacob chipped in. "We're protected by our allies."

"Of course I've noticed, but it doesn't mean she's safe." Adam looked from one to the other with wide eyes. "You haven't had to go to a dentist or doctor recently, have you? I know all about spyware implants due to my work."

"It's easy for us to get paranoid," Kate said, "but we need to remember where we've come from. Do you really think they'll allow us to be harmed? We have Sechem, Master M and Jamère watching out for us. Don't forget the high status of those who've sent us here for this work, The Galactic Council."

"You've *no idea* who you are dealing with. It's time you got a reality check, Kate. Remember I do know what they are capable of. Don't underestimate them."

"Well if Marco is anything to go by, I don't have much to worry about, do it?"

The furrow on Adam's forehead deepened. "You're being naive. He'll do anything his superiors tell him to. If bumping you off is required, he wouldn't hesitate. He'd even enjoy doing it too. They don't have to get their hands dirty, and Marco is expendable. We do have protection from our spirit friends, but the Dark Hats are ruthless. Utterly ruthless and you need to be aware of that. You need to use your second sight constantly – scan for danger, Kate. Keep alert at all times."

Kate didn't like the worried looks on both men's faces.

"Okay guys, now you've scared me to death, it's time you both left so I can get some shut eye." she said.

As Jacob left, he gave Kate a warm, extended hug. He looked into her eyes. "I love you," he said. As Adam left, he gave her a look that she could've sworn said, "I do too."

It bought a tear to her eye.

* * *

Kate continued to arrange talks at local venues to get her message to as many people as possible. Holding them at Number Six was by no means ideal, but it did help to keep the meetings below the radar, as no advertising was necessary. It placated Poppy's concerns too and her email database was working a treat: Nearby they invited a new audience each week and held the meetings on different days.

On this particular night, Kate gave her usual talk, which was well received, but towards the end she let forth a stream of ET languages. Gasps of surprise and astonishment rippled through the gathering. Suddenly to their greater amazement, a member of the audience stood up, walked up to Kate and replied, using the same language. To the people present this very act confirmed the language's authenticity. The atmosphere was electric as the audience processed what had just happened. Kate returned to normal speech and thanked the man from the audience for his contribution.

"This happens involuntarily," she explained as the elderly man returned to his seat. "It's always a real pleasure when it comes. I got the gist of what you said but can't quite interpret it exactly. I don't decide to speak in this way, but I have a feeling when it begins. I love it. The ETs are speaking through you," she said to the man. "You can work on the techniques I've talked about today to encourage them to use you as a conduit. You can be so helpful to the Great Work we are doing to secure the future of the planet."

"Do it again," a man shouted from the back.

"I can't do it intentionally. It seems to come when my space friends want to speak."

Kate finished her talk to an enthusiastic round of applause. People gathered around her asking questions and sharing their experiences. Kate was thrilled when a man came up to her and said, "My wife speaks exactly the same language in her sleep." What wonderful reassuring confirmation.

The message seemed to be spreading. People were relaxing enough to admit that they too had experiences like Kate's. The scepticism and distrust were fading and support for Kate was growing. She remembered too what she'd been told: that speaking these languages communicates to DNA. When she'd first heard about this, it had creeped her out a bit. Now she felt nothing but warmth and positivity when the ET language came through her – she found it totally energising. After all, she was a hybrid and this was her heritage. Yes, it was a bit scary, but it was truly amazing too.

* * *

The next day, Kate set off for her office much earlier than usual to have a look around Silas's office before anyone else got in. She wanted to find out more about this anonymous man if she could. The early morning cleaners were driving off as she parked, and the vacant lot told her no one else had arrived yet. She let herself in to the empty office and as she reached his desk, she looked around nervously, even though she was the only one there. His desk drawers were locked except for the bottom one. She opened it cautiously and rummaged in the mess of pens, post-it notes, rubber bands and other bits and pieces. Near the back of the drawer her fingers touched a hard, round flat disk. She brought it out and was about to study it when she heard the lift ping, telling her someone was on their way up to the first floor. She quickly stuffed the disk into her pocket, pushed the drawer shut and went to her own office, booted up her computer and tried to look busy.

All morning she kept thinking of the disc she'd found but didn't dare bring it out. It'd have to wait till she got home. She hoped he wouldn't miss it. Kate's nerves were on edge all day, and it seemed that everybody was staring at her. Why on earth had she done this? As if she wasn't in deep enough already! Occasionally, she glanced up to see Silas at work in his office – he didn't seem to be in any way concerned. The guy gave her the creeps – in a different way to Marco. Marco was a bully and a misogynist, but he was just brawn; she could outwit him, but Silas Pearce was a different kettle of fish altogether. He exuded an air of menace, he had no compassion in his soul. Silas made her afraid. He was dangerous.

Finally, at the end of what seemed like an extraordinarily long day, she turned the key in her front door, stepped inside her home and breathed freely. Here she felt safe. She wondered if the coloured lights were at play over her house – it was still light so they wouldn't be visible, but Kate had never seen them herself anyway. She just trusted that her sweet neighbour and Adam and Jacob were right. That it was a sign of protection, of solidarity.

Her house seemed extra quiet, eerily so. Why…? Kate listened, ears alert, heart beginning to race. Then she realised that her antique clock on the mantelpiece had stopped ticking. Hmmm – unusual. Kate held her breath. What else was wrong? With her inner senses on high alert, she slowly checked every room. Nothing appeared to be out of order, but then she saw scuff marks on the windowsill and a pot plant moved from its usual position. Somebody had been in the house, maybe was still inside. Kate's heart thumped, and for a moment she couldn't think what to do.

Then it dawned on her. The clock! She rummaged through the drawer in her office and with trembling hands found a small screwdriver. Still shaking, she unscrewed the back of the clock and saw a tiny, flat, metal disc that didn't appear to be part of the mechanism. With a shock, she realised that it was some time since this clock had been checked for bugs, let alone the clocks in her other room. She phoned Adam and Jacob in turn and told them that something was wrong, something she daren't tell them over the phone.

They came straight over. Kate waited for them on the drive and kept them outside the door while she told them what she'd discovered. Then they entered the house silently and turned the house upside down looking for anything that might constitute a bug. To their relief, it seemed only the clock on the mantelpiece had been bugged.

"It has to be recent if the clock was working yesterday," Adam said. "Was it?"

Kate nodded.

"And have you checked to see if anything's missing or out of place?"

Kate shrugged. "Actually, I think my desk's in more of a mess than usual!" she laughed apologetically. "I can't say for sure if anyone has been there, but things do look a bit different... I'm not sure. Hang on a minute – if someone's been in here without my knowing, what's to say they've not done it before? I think my Contract of Employment was stolen, you know. Do you remember? When I tried to hand in my notice, and couldn't find it. It's got Marco written all over it, hasn't it!"

"It has," said Adam. "And he can't even get that right!"

Kate then remembered the object in her pocket and fished it out. "See what I found at the back of Silas's drawer." She handed it to Jacob.

He took a quick look and passed it to Adam saying, "I haven't got my glasses. See what you make of this inscription."

Adam glanced at the small disk and took a step back in alarm. 'Kate, for God's sake. Why did you take this? This is a CIA badge, but not the usual kind. It's not given to just anyone, only for those on a special mission. And only people in the know would recognise it for what it is. No wonder he pushed it to the back of the drawer. Let's just hope he doesn't need it and discover it's missing." He looked at Kate in dismay. "It's good to know that's what he's involved in, but you took a huge risk doing this. Do you think you can get it back where it belongs? Like, tomorrow?"

"Yes, yes. I'll go in early again. So, he's CIA. One of the men in black. I knew it. He's faceless; he's soulless. He gives me the creeps. I've got to get out of that place, Adam. I know you said about keeping my enemies close, but I feel they're actually closing in – that can't be good, can it?"

"It won't be forever Kate. Remember, we're part of the bigger picture that we can't quite see, but one thing I know for sure: nothing stays the same forever. Just hold on for as long as you can. Okay?"

Jacob lowered himself into a chair. "What neither of you have realised is that if the CIA is involved then we are all in real trouble. How much do they actually know about Kate's mind-walking activities? I think it would be a good idea if we asked Sechem what to do about this latest development, the sooner the better. What do you say, Kate?"

"I'm willing if you are. It's getting late but I don't think any of us will sleep if we don't do something. Agreed?"

The two men nodded.

After they'd cleared the table and settled themselves in their chairs, Jacob said, "Do your usual thing, Kate, and just say what's happening."

"I'll start by asking for clarification. You know I never know what's going to be given, don't you? No guarantees." Though feeling a little nervous, Kate settled and went down into herself.

"The stairs are of polished wood in a nice rich colour. Somebody looks after this place. I'm going down, feeling the wood as I go. I'm dressed in what looks like protective clothing, an orange jumpsuit that rustles when I walk. I know I'm going somewhere deep because my head is starting to hurt. This usually happens when I go into a state that's much deeper into my subconscious than usual. I continue down, trying to keep focus, but oh, the pain in my head is increasing all the time. I must keep going and go through that barrier.

"I'm at the bottom now at the entrance to a passage that slopes gently down. I can only go one way. The walls are clad in wood. There's lighting and I feel I'm very deep underground at a sort of secret headquarters. I sense cameras watching as I go. Very weird! I know I'm being observed by eyes somewhere else, perhaps in a control room.

"I keep walking. This passage is endless. I come up against a blank wall. No, not a wall, it's an entry. I feel around for something that will open it and notice a pad on the right side. I sense I've been here before. It's a hand-print scanner. I put my right hand on the pad and the door slides into the wall. I step through.

"I'm in a very busy area, well lit, very bright. Lots of human beings working away in blue uniforms at their particular jobs. Some have orange jumpsuits like mine. There are monitors, screens, lots and lots of screens and wall charts. It's a hive of activity. I wonder what I'm doing here? Nobody takes any notice of me. I'm familiar with this place, and people seem to know me, though I can't quite get my head round that yet. I go over to what's obviously my desk. I sit down and start playing with the keyboard and watching the monitor. I haven't got a clue what this is about, but it's almost as if I'm watching another me doing it.

"I realise that this is an observation room for space activity. They're monitoring and co-ordinating space ships and satellites. Although the ships may have come from other dimensions and can go invisible, they're physical now, and all the space junk up there is dangerous for them. There's so much of it! If you saw it, you'd wonder how anybody could navigate their way around the stuff orbiting this planet. What we're doing here is Space Traffic Control, like air traffic control, assigning each object its own lane, making sure ships don't bump into each other. We have to be sure nobody is in danger. We're keeping it safe.

"I still have no idea why I'm here. Maybe I'm just here to learn. There are all sorts of currents, rays, energy waves and magnetic influences around the Earth which could interfere with these instruments. Somebody just said 'Scalar' – I know about that! The waves that can control the weather.

"We also have to deal with interference from governments doing their experiments in space, completely ignorant and uncaring about the detrimental effect they're having. They're inexperienced, like children playing cars. So, this is a control system to make sure they don't do too much damage.

"How peculiar this is! I'm Kate observing this other me who knows exactly what she's doing. I can't tell the difference. I had no idea about this part of me that works here – it must have been kept separate from my day-to-day consciousness for my own sanity. Is that right?

"The voice says, 'Yes; at a later stage you'll come to consciously interact with both levels and operate well. It's yet another level of understanding, one you previously have had no conscious record of. This is for you to process when your brainwaves have been reactivated.'

"My ears are aching. I must come back. There's definitely a physical change when I do this, at least while it lasts. The whole thing begins to fuzz now. It's fading out. Clearly that's the end."

"Well they never said anything about the CIA, did they?" Jacob said as soon as Kate opened her eyes. "But well done, my darling. You must need to rest now."

"I think you need to ask questions when I go deep. Otherwise they just give me what they want me to do or know."

Jacob nodded. "I agree, we have to ask for information – only then can it be provided."

Kate yawned and reclined back against the sofa.

Jacob and Adam nodded to each other and quietly made their way out, leaving her in peace.

CHAPTER TWENTY-THREE

CLOSING THE NET

'Nothing makes us so lonely as our secrets.'

Paul Tournier

Kate decided to get Silas's badge back as soon as she could, but the next morning when she arrived at the office bright and early she found a group of military police going through *her* desk and collecting her papers.

"What on earth are you doing?" she demanded, her insides shaking. The stony-faced men didn't reply. They simply continued boxing up her things.

One eventually looked up. "We have orders to confiscate your work."

"But why?" Her colleagues looked on, muttering among themselves. Her job didn't give her access to any sensitive information. She wondered if it was somehow linked to her mind-travelling work. She watched in silence as they boxed the contents of her drawers and took away her computer. It felt alarming but at least it wasn't her home computer. She had nothing to worry about as far as her work was concerned."

Helga and Mr P appeared out of what had been Silas's office. He looked flustered, and as bewildered as Kate, his face still showing the remnants of his recent stroke.

"Mr Peters…You're back! How are you?"

"Well, this isn't quite the fresh start I'd hoped for Ms Greene. I think you'd better go home."

"But why?" Kate asked.

'Orders." He said.

"Do as you're told and go home Kate," Helga said, looking smug and pleased.

"They're wasting their time," Kate retorted. "There's nothing to find." Nevertheless, mindful that she still had Silas's badge in her possession, Kate left the building and drove home. And where was Silas, anyway?

As she pulled in to her street she saw three men in dark clothing run down her path, climb into a black van and drive off with a screech of tires. She quickly parked her car and with a sense of foreboding, ran to her front door. Entering, she realised her house had been completely turned over. She stared in shock at the mess. They were quick – she'd only left a short while ago. Afraid to use the phone or her mobile, Kate hoped and prayed that her father had psychically picked up what was happening.

Apparently Jacob had, because soon after, Kate heard his car park by her drive. She let him in, but as she did so she saw another car pull up in the street and a tall, suited man get out. He walked up her path and knocked politely on the open front door. Kate stepped into the doorway. He eyed her up and down, then spoke in a soft, calm voice:

"Would you mind coming with me to the station to answer a few questions, Miss?" He flashed a badge at her, and though Kate didn't see in detail, it appeared to be official. It's like a scene out of a film, she thought, not believing it could be happening to her. If it hadn't been so serious she could almost have laughed, but she didn't feel like laughing. The whole situation terrified her.

The man took a step forward. For a moment, Kate thought he'd grab her by the arm. Jacob quickly moved to her side and the man in the dark suit held up his hand up.

"We don't need you, sir. Please stay here."

Kate turned to Jacob. "Dad, will you mind the house for me, please? Lock the doors." She reached into her pocket and in the pretext of giving him a door key passed the incriminating badge to him. At least they'd find nothing if they were to search her.

Kate knew it was imperative that she keep her mind firmly closed. That this situation was contrary to her mind journeys where she was told to reveal everything she knew. This time, she had to keep shut down. This couldn't possibly be related to her journeying – could it? Was Helga or Silas behind this? She walked quietly to his car and climbed into the back, where there was another dark-suited man.

As the car drove out of town into open countryside, everyone remained silent until Kate could bear it no longer.

"Where are you taking me?" she asked, her heart thumping. "This isn't the way to the police station."

"You'll find out soon enough," was the only reply.

Scenes from TV dramas flashed through her mind: kidnap, torture, worse... She couldn't let that happen, she was needed elsewhere, but she couldn't risk opening her mind to the others to ask for help, in case that incriminated them all.

Suddenly, without thinking, Kate lunged for the door, wrenched it open and heaved herself out.

"No you don't," said the man sitting next to her, grabbing her arm fiercely and yanking her back in the car. He produced a pair of handcuffs and roughly put them on her, then, to her horror, he produced a blindfold and tied it tight around her head.

"Keep quiet, don't struggle and don't try anything like that again," he said.

The car sped along stretches of heathland covered with gorse, but Kate saw nothing. Not the KEEP OUT sign warning of firing range activity, not the rolls of barbed wire on top of tall steel fences. Eventually they arrived at a gate in the perimeter fence. A man in army uniform with a rifle over his shoulder approached them. The driver flashed his pass, and the guard waved them through. The car stopped outside a plain, two-storey building and Kate was manhandled inside, where they took off the blindfold, but left on the cuffs.

Clearly, they weren't at a police station, rather, a military establishment, just like the ones in her mind-travels. The policeman who'd come to her door took her into a stark, white, windowless room. Strip lighting glared overhead. The room was empty except for a small table, two chairs and a large mirror on the wall. Kate had seen enough detective shows to know it would be a two-way mirror. Somebody would be watching her on the other side.

"What is this place?" Kate asked. "What do you want with me?" Adrenalin and fear coursed through her.

"Wait here. We'll come and get you when we're ready." He then left closing the door behind him. Kate fought the urge to run to the door and drum on it with her cuffed fists. She was terrified.

Through the glass panel in the door, Kate saw a guard station himself outside it. What now? When nothing happened and no one came, Kate was forced to wait. She felt terribly vulnerable and alone, but wouldn't under any circumstances uncloak her thoughts, just in case there was someone – Helga? – who could pick up on them. She would not involve her loved ones in this, not Jacob, not Adam, nor Sechem or Master M. She tried to control her jagged breathing and pounding heart and closed her eyes. Breathe, breathe...

An hour or so later the guard opened the door and escorted her to an office several yards down the corridor then un-cuffed her wrists. The relief was immense. The smartly dressed man she'd seen before sat behind a large desk and stared at her as she walked in. Kate noted that this room also had a large mirror. She stood facing him and saw on his desk, her notes for her talks on UFO landings, ET presence on Earth, military bases on the moon and underground bases in the US.

"How did you come by this information?" the quietly-spoken man asked.

Kate could see that in spite of his soft approach, his grey eyes were steely.

"Can I please sit down?" she asked. In truth, her legs were so shaky she was afraid she'd collapse.

He ordered the man at the door to bring a chair, and she gratefully sat down.

"All the information is simply preparation notes for my talks." Kate tried to control her trembling, but her quivering voice betrayed her. "Everything stated there can easily be found on the Internet."

Kate spent time going over each topic, explaining where she'd found it and that it was publicly available. The quiet man looked her up and down again, his expression less than happy.

"But why are *you* giving talks on this subject Ms Greene? What's it got to do with you?"

"Oh, I'm just an interested lay person really," Kate said, trying to make light of it.

"Really? So why, don't I believe you? One of our undercovers said you were 'talking in tongues' at one of your recent meetings. That's a bit...weird isn't it Ms Greene? You don't look like a charlatan to me...you don't look like a fraud."

"I...it was..."

"Go on."

"I can't explain that," Kate mumbled, totally out of her depth. What could she say? That it was alien language? That really would rattle him.

"You can't explain it, eh? Well let's just take you back to the cell and let you think about that for a little while longer, shall we?"

The door opened, and a uniformed man escorted Kate back out down the corridor and into the cell. He shoved her in and slammed the door shut. It was the last straw. Tears spilled from Kate's eye as she plummeted into the depths of despair. Why me? I didn't ask for any of this, she thought. I was happy with my quiet life and shitty job, and now it's like I'm in the X-Men or something. She let go of all the emotion and anxiety that had been pent-up for weeks and luxuriated in full-blown sobbing, her nose and eyes running her breath ragged. She curled up in the corner of the room, on the cold floor, with not even a blanket for comfort, until the emotion subsided. She felt infinitely better.

Some time later, the door opened and the steely-eyed man walked in.

"You may go," he grunted. "Take her home." He gestured to the door where a different uniformed man was waiting to escort her out.

As she walked past him, he put his arm out and barred her way.

"Take this as a warning Ms Greene. Stop meddling in things you know nothing about. Stop holding those ridiculous meetings and stop putting your friends and family in jeopardy. Do you hear me?"

"I hear you," she said.

As was the case on the way out, not a word was spoken on the return journey. Kate felt badly shaken.

It was late afternoon by the time she arrived back home to find dear old Jacob still there, minding the house. He was obviously worried out of his mind, and welcomed her with a hug as her legs turned to jelly. She made her way to the armchair, shaking like a leaf.

"How could they have known about your notes?" he asked after she told him what had happened.

"Marco?" she said. "I think he's been making a habit of snooping about my house while I'm at work. It's not like Adam needs him all the time. He's still working for Helga, isn't he...It all adds up to me."

"Do you really think so?"

"I do. And that dodgy bloke at one of the meetings... He's one of them too. It's a good thing Adam's away while all this is going on. He might have used his position to intervene, and that would've looked very suspicious and made things even worse."

"I don't agree Kate. We can't have you being subject to such danger in future. You have to be able to call us for help, even if it's just to let us know you're okay. I've been worried sick – you could've been hurt. We need to devise a series of mind-words – Sirian – that you can use, so that Adam or I can help you. We're skilled in these matters Kate. I will speak to Adam about it when he gets back from Washington."

"How can I do my work if I can't hold the meetings? Kate grumbled.

"We'll find a way," Jacob said softly.

"I could hold my talks further away from here, away from gossiping tongues," Kate suggested.

"You'll never find the time," Jacob said. "And anyway, I think it's too dangerous."

"I'll make time," said Kate, even more determined than ever. "They won't scare me off what I've pledged to do – whoever 'they' are." Although she was worn out, she wasn't beaten. Kate set her chin defiantly, blue eyes glittering.

* * *

Back at the office the next day, Kate ignored the stares and murmured comments and returned to her desk where a new computer awaited her, and horror of horror, Marco too, his desk once again shunted up next to hers.

Marco leered across the table. "You look tired, Kate. Late night?"

"Not at all. Everything turned out amicably. It was a case of over-reaction."

Helga popped in to see her, but as expected, it felt more like she was gloating rather than sympathising about her ordeal.

"I don't know what you get up to in your spare time Greene, but we have to be exceptionally careful, given what we do here," she said. "I would advise that you take this as a shot over the bows, and stop whatever bunkum it is that you're getting into." She stalked off, but then turned back. "Oh, by the way, as you know, Mr Peters is back at work now, so Silas is working more closely with me now, and Marco has also rejoined us, at least while Colonel Fenshawe is in Washington. So, the old team's back together again." She looked at Kate straight in the eye, daring her to respond.

"Lovely," Kate said.

The net was closing in.

* * *

Life returned to some semblance of normality over the next few weeks, or so it seemed on the surface. Adam returned from DC and was devastated to hear of Kate's incarceration, feeling personally responsible that he wasn't around to help her. Adam, Jacob and Kate agreed that it would be safe for her to uncloak and mind-speak with them in Sirian if anything like that happened again. It made Kate feel somewhat safer, although despite her best intentions, she had stopped giving her talks for a while. If truth be told, she was terribly rattled by what happened. The mind-travels had also abated considerably. She thought it was maybe Sechem and Master M's way of showing they cared, but in fact Kate would rather get on with it and do more – it literally took her mind off things.

"I have to go away again," Adam told her one evening as they sat across the table in the kitchen eating fish and chips. "I have to attend a meeting in The States."

"Oh. Right." Kate couldn't help but feel upset, although she tried to hide it. Despite their relationship being nothing more than friends, she had begun to hope that he might care about being away from her, as she did him. "What meetings are they that are so important?"

"It's better you don't know," he said, cuffing her playfully under the chin.

She missed him when he was away, and missed his support during her mind journeys.

She hadn't heard from Sechem, or Master M, or Jamère for a day or two, either. Maybe they felt she wasn't up to strength right now?

Maybe, maybe, maybe! Feeling a little uneasy about Adam going away again and the recent lack of contact from her spirit guides, Kate was flat and grumpy. She felt that something was up, but she couldn't but her finger on it.

Jacob's visit lightened her heart. When he arrived early one chilly Saturday morning, she hugged him so much he drew back in surprise and delight. He checked for bugs, as he always did, then they sat in the front room before a roaring gas fire.

"I don't know how to move things forwards," she said. "I know all this incredible information – the existence of aliens, the fact that world leaders know too but have hushed it up. I want to tell the world as so many people are oblivious, but it's becoming more and more dangerous. And then, some people are so open to the existence of aliens, and others are utterly freaked out by it and want to harm those who speak out. How can humans be so different?"

Jacob took a sip of tea then he took his glasses off — an indication that he had something to say. "I know it's frustrating my dear. But you can't force people to listen if they don't want to. You're not alone in your views, but not all can mind travel as you do. Not all have direct experience like you."

Kate frowned. "My job is to get people interested. There's so much on the internet if they only knew where to start. I wish they'd look and discover things for themselves. It would make life a lot easier for me! Although my talks have been popular and people seem to take on board what I'm saying, there are still millions out there who would dismiss me as a crank or a...what was it that man called me? A charlatan, a fraud." She sighed as she thought about the cruel words he threw at her.

"It doesn't help that I can't make contact with anyone anymore. I mean with Master M or Sechem or Jamère. You'd think they'd have something to say after all that has happened?" She sniffed and blew her nose hard. "I'm coming down with the flu too, I feel all shivery and I'm aching. I'm a bundle of laughs, aren't I!"

Jacob nodded in sympathy and hugged her. She smelt his familiar aftershave. It made her sneeze.

"Being held by the military like that wasn't funny. I was really frightened, Dad." Kate's lips trembled and tears threatened to spill over.

Jacob took off his heavy framed glasses and wiped them clean. It was his turn to blow his nose.

"I know, my darling girl. That was awful. You're doing so well, you really are."

"It doesn't help that I keep reading about other people who made contact with aliens, went public and then disappeared – mysterious deaths and so-called suicides." She reached for a tissue and blew her nose again. Tears started to flow.

"Oh Dad! This is so hard. I don't think I want to do it anymore," she snivelled.

"Stay strong, my sweet. Don't read anything into not hearing from Sechem for a while," Jacob said. "You're feeling rotten because of your flu, but that will pass. And lay off the Internet for a while. Just take it easy and rest. Take some time out and regain your energy."

Kate sniffed and wiped her eyes.

"I think they just want you to lay low for a bit. This could be why you're poorly. You're right to lay off giving talks for a while so those responsible for that interrogation will think you have heeded the warning and backed-off. They wanted to frighten you and they succeeded, didn't they?"

Kate thought about his words. "You're right, Dad, and to be honest,

I really need some time to myself. I haven't seen Poppy in weeks. I'll phone work and tell them I have the flu, which is not untrue." She reached for another tissue. "But I can't help wondering what's going on at the Galactic Council..." She blew her nose again. "What are the Lords of the Universe doing, and where do the human species fare in their current deliberations? How's the battle going between the Dark Hats and Light Hats? Should I try to contact them, Dad?"

"I'll leave that too. You know they can't come through if you're agitated or not well?" Jacob replied. "Your energies will be low now. Focus on getting better first and we'll give it a go when you've recovered, eh?"

Kate nodded and smiled weakly. "I'll go to bed now Dad, if you don't mind."

"Of course, my darling. Shall I make you a hot water bottle and a cocoa and bring it up? Like I used to when you were a child."

"Would you, Dad?"

"I'd love to!"

"Oh, thanks, that'd be so lovely."

Kate hauled herself up the stairs feeling absolutely worn out. This was what she needed. Some time off. She clambered into her pyjamas, lit her scented candle and crawled under the duvet.

Jacob brought up her hot water bottle and put it under her feet and left the cocoa by her book on the bedside table. She thought he was even going to tuck her in!

"I hope you'll feel better in the morning, my love," he said, then kissed her on the forehead and quietly let himself out.

Kate fell asleep, and the phone ringing the next morning stirred her back into life. It was Poppy.

"Your dad told me you weren't well and might need some company," she said. "I'm coming over right now." The receiver clicked down, ending the call.

Kate was delighted. She struggled out of bed and freshened up a bit, but was still feeling absolutely washed out. She was brushing her teeth when there was a knock on the door.

"Hello, stranger,"

"Hello Poppy"

"I've just got one thing to say to you," Poppy said as she stomped in." Poppy was never one to beat about the bush and Kate blanched, thinking she'd done something to upset her.

"You ought to be in bed. Straight back there, now."

Kate laughed. "Oh Pops, I've missed you!" she said and went to give her friend a hug.

"No you don't sunshine," said Poppy backing off. "Whatever you've got, I don't want to get it. Bed."

Kate could hear Poppy bustling about in the kitchen, and eventually she came upstairs carrying a tray on which stood a glass of hot honey and lemon and a bowl of porridge with yoghurt and raspberries. She sat down on the bed and watched as Kate ate her breakfast.

"So, what's this I hear about giving a talk outside the district?"

"Ah, so Dad mentioned that too, did he?"

"Yes, but he didn't say why."

"Right. Well…well, I was arrested – I think – and interrogated about giving the talks. I was put in a cell for about five hours and... God, it was horrible."

"Oh my God Katie! When did this happen?"

"A few weeks ago."

"Why didn't you tell me?"

"It just knocked me for six Poppy. I don't know why – I think I was in shock, actually. Anyway, they warned me off and told me to stop giving the talks.

"Who's they?"

"Good question. I don't really know. Dad and I thought they were the police when the first arrived, but I was hand-cuffed and blindfolded, Poppy, can you believe that? And then I was in this awful military place..."

"And you intend to carry on giving talks after all that? Are you off your trolley or something?"

"But I HAVE to, don't you see? It's important. It's bigger than just me and you, this is about raising consciousness so that we can care properly for this beautiful planet and live in harmony with our space brothers and sisters..."

Poppy was silent for a while as she was taking in what Kate said. Then, carefully choosing her words, she replied.

"You know, I was really sceptical at first about what you were doing, but of course I helped you because you're my bestie, right? But then, those times when you just started speaking in that strange language... Well, your face changed, your expression changed, it was coming through you... I just don't think you can fake that. And then, well... you know the last meeting? When I parked outside your house, I saw these beautiful coloured lights hovering over the roof and in the garden, and I just knew it was your space friends. You don't have to persuade me any more Kate. I'm with you."

"You can see them? That means you're receptive Poppy! Oh, that's the best news. Are you sure I can't give you a hug?"

"No way!"

* * *

When Kate had recovered from the worst of her cold and was well enough for mind-travel again, Jacob decided it was time to make contact, and help her to recover from the trauma she'd experienced. He drove to her house, got his own tea, put another log on the fire and made sure she was comfortable in her chair, well wrapped up in blankets.

"Ready?" he asked.

She nodded and went into a trance almost instantly. As usual, Kate shared her journey with him as it occurred.

"My pathway has a tropical feel with rattan matting underfoot, making it easy on my feet. I'm walking through a jungle. I keep going down and feel the energy increasing. At the bottom is a village. It's a hive of activity, smoke coming out of low huts covered in broad leaves. The people are small, with ebony skin and glistening with sweat. People are running about between the huts. A couple of small children point me in the direction I need to go.

"I follow the track and walk until I'm alone. It's extremely quiet, not a single sound anywhere. I come to a flimsy barrier, like a camouflaged stockade. I walk through and there's a big clearing at the bottom of a slope. Flying insects irritate my nose distracting me from what I can see. A flying saucer is quietly sitting at the foot of the slope. I slide down the bank.

"Men are guarding the spaceship. It's big, maybe 40-50ft across. It's hovering above the ground. The men can't see me. Oh, at last I understand. I have to think myself in. It takes a bit of doing, but I think what it might be like inside, and with that thought I'm there. This is interesting because it doesn't feel familiar. There's nobody inside, just narrow passages and activated coloured lights. Beautiful colours, all moving. I understand now. This is one of theirs, manmade, human, not space-made. It's one they've reversed engineered, but they don't quite know how to use it yet. How daft is that? Strange they should choose here to trial it, not in some highly-secure military base.

"There are lots of problems with how it's built. For a start, it's much too big. They should've started with something smaller, and there should be some accommodation. What am I supposed to do? Touch it? Feel it? It's smooth, very smooth. But there are far too many corners. There shouldn't be any right angles; it should all be round. Energy gets stuck in angles. Where's the propulsion? I don't know. This is making my head hurt."

Kate was becoming distressed, so Jacob encouraged her to come out of her journey. He'd forgotten to ask any questions, but was satisfied that she could still mind-travel.

"That was a good one my sweet. How do you feel?"

Kate yawned. "Fine."

Jacob smiled held her hand. "Good. It's clear you've seen one of the reverse engineered ships, made by copying a genuine UFO. I should've asked for markings so we could know who it belonged to. Never mind, another time perhaps."

Her hands were icy. "I'll get some more tea. You stay still and rest now."

He stood and turned to the kitchen, feeling heartened by the fact that Kate was back on form.

* * *

Kate's flu kept her off work for a week, which was a blessing since she still found it daunting to face her colleagues after the visit by the police. Deep in her heart she knew that they were, CIA or whatever the UK equivalent was, and that they weren't just worried about her talks, but more so her ability to remote view and whether she could or would tap into activities they definitely wanted to keep hidden from the public. But it wasn't within their abilities to determine that, not yet anyway. Was this bound up with the presence of two opposing forces of humans and space beings that were battling for Mother Earth? Kate put the question to Jacob on his next visit.

"Dad, I feel well enough to go for a walk. It's a lovely day – shall we?" she said. "But somewhere we talk properly" she added, nodding to the mantelpiece where her antique clock stood, indicating to him that she wanted to speak of 'classified' things. Somewhere there'd be nobody to tap into her mind, where she'd feel safe.

He agreed and she decided on Badbury Rings, an Iron Age hill fort in East Dorset. The Rings were occupied 4,000 years before the pyramid at Giza was built. It later became a main crossroads for the Roman Empire whose road network cut across Dorset. Kate loved it there and immersed herself in the ancient energies whenever she could. It was not too far away and had no houses nearby. They'd be completely isolated.

They travelled in thoughtful silence along an impressive mile-long avenue of ancient beech trees. After parking the car, they began to walk the several circles of the Ring, climbing as they went up to the top. It was a fresh but bright day, one to blow the cobwebs away.

"What am I really doing, Dad?" she asked. "Am I making any

difference? And how does this tie in with swinging the balance between the Light Hats and the Dark Hats? I'm having journeys and making contact yes, but am I helping?"

"But, of course, don't you see?" he said. "The more you discover the more you are likely to tell others. Have you forgotten that Jamère is going to teach you how to be an interpreter for space visitors when they arrive in their own form? And you've already rescued many. Had you forgotten?"

"I suppose you're right. When I'm in a trance it's so different from reality that what I do doesn't seem real."

They'd reached the top of the rings, sheltered from the wind by the trees, and Jacob was a little out of breath. "Let's sit here for a bit. I'm not as young as you."

They sat together on a fallen tree trunk and allowed their thoughts to wander. Kate got a flask of coffee from her bag and poured some for them both, then she sat back and watched a lone walker making his way along the ring below them. He stopped every so often to take a picture of the magnificent scenery.

"You know, Dad, we may be hybrids from Sirius – it still sounds very strange saying that - but as far as I am concerned this is the best place to be. I love Planet Earth, and don't want to see it damaged in any way, by any outside force, or our own foolishness. We must do what we can to keep it safe from ill-meaning species and their plan to dominate the human race."

"Oh, I agree. And luckily, we're not alone in our work," Jacob said. "Don't forget the space family who want to help us." He smiled. "They're truly magnificent. Remember the wonder and love you felt when you visited the meeting with the Planetary Lords? You know they're with us 100%."

Kate brightened at the memory. "Oh, I do." She just hoped that they would give humans the benefit of the doubt. It seemed a tall order when most of what was portrayed on the media was bloodshed, terrorism and fear. She knew humans were capable of much better. She prayed that the Lords of the Universe did too.

The weak sun slowly dipped into the horizon, and a cold haze rose-up over the land. "Time to go home, Dad. I'm tired too." She kissed him tenderly on the cheek, then took hold of his hand and helped him get up. It had been good to talk, and she walked back to the car park with more vitality and enthusiasm. She noticed the man with the camera watching them. He still had his camera out, but the light was almost gone. He couldn't be taking decent shots now, surely?

* * *

A few days afterwards Kate's spirit friends finally contacted her again.

"We would like you to link in with us this evening," The voice told her as she was getting ready for work. Kate grinned with excitement. It was too long since she'd heard from anyone in the spirit world. She called Jacob as Adam was still not back from the US, and he was more than willing to come and be with her. They arranged to meet after dinner.

Kate heard him pull up. The evening was drawing in and a light mist was forming as he got out of the car. Kate stood in the lighted doorway waiting for him to come up the path. A black car sat on the other side of the road in front of Mrs Thomas' house, and Kate frowned but didn't go over to it. She knew she was being monitored and resolved to be extra careful during her trance.

Once inside Jacob took his heavy coat off and dutifully hung it on the hall stand. Kate smiled. She liked to keep things tidy. They walked into the front room where she had a good fire going. The room was warm and cosy.

When they were settled Jacob said, “Let’s get going then, shall we?”

Kate relaxed and felt her mind slide into the familiar trance. She was soon in and speaking.

TWENTY-FOUR

CONVERSING WITH THE BIRD TRIBE

'Birds are a miracle because they prove to us there is a finer, simpler state of being which we may strive to attain.'

Douglas Coupland

"I've been given a tight-fitting silver suit," Kate said. "Very unusual and most attractive. How different, it makes me feel quite a lot younger. I don't mind this at all."

Jacob smiled at her broad grin, but he didn't interrupt.

Kate's voice deepened and took on the far-away quality that Jacob recognised as belonging to 'the voice' whoever was to be her guide today.

'It's a glimpse of a possible future,' the voice said.

In her own voice, Kate settles into the mind-travel

"I wonder what that means? Then I get a shock when I check out who's with me. He is a humanoid, but 8ft tall at least. Its face is incredibly bird-like, the mouth more like a soft beak than lips. It has blue skin, and extraordinary sparse hair which goes backwards into indigo-blue feathery spikes. Its eyes are piercing, eagle-like.

"I go to a console and sit. It's my own seat and has a large screen in front of it. I press some buttons and a scene of other times appears. It's a familiar scene, a landscape with trees but no people, just clouds and trees and a strong wind blowing. The wind is growing in strength. It's turning into hurricane force. Things are being blown across the ground, trees, hedges, all sorts of things. Where are the people? Where are they?

The voice answers me. 'Those that remain have buried themselves in places underground, they have barricaded themselves in strongholds. They are clinging on for dear life, fighting for survival. They do not wish to relinquish Earth for they do not believe there is anything more.'

'Why am I seeing this?'

'You are watching the last of the old kind, the old thinking, of past beliefs and ambitions for power. The new ones that come will have insight, and minds will turn in new directions. They will know that there is no need to fight for survival, and there will be peace.'

'How am I seeing this? What method are you using?'

'We use a device called The Looking Glass which can see into possible futures that may await Earth.'

'Possible futures? So, nothing is fixed?'

'You all create your future by your thoughts, dreams and actions. Make sure these are the highest ideals for good.'

Jacob leaned forward, remembering that Kate had suggested he ask questions to help them make sense of the session. "Who are you?" he asked.

In response to his question, a blue haze surrounded Kate, and a tall blue humanoid form appeared in it.

'Although I have been given the command to speak,' the voice said through Kate, 'I'm not a superior being, even to those who work under my command. I have a field of experience that places me in position where my knowledge can be used to the full.

'I am here to help and guide humans. You are responsible for your futures, each and every one of you. We do not wish any soul to enter a state of inaction and stagnation. This would be of great detriment to you. How you act now has an effect, will have an effect on what is to be. So, do not feel you have no control. We state this most firmly.

'We work as a team which is vast, much greater than you can imagine. Our team is larger than all your experts put together. It will give you some idea of the scale of the operation. We work under a higher command.'

Jacob watched in surprise as the hazy blue that had been over Kate separated from her and moved around the room, apparently investigating. The voice continued to speak through Kate.

'Our next project is to re-adjust the conditions upon which you live. We will make some fine-tuning to enable the smooth running of your world. We are making adjustments so that it revolves more smoothly and not erratically, so that the flow within it is even. Your planet is out of kilter, out of balance between the negative and the positive energies. We wish to set it in balance, as one would balance a wheel on a vehicle.

'You may be aware of some of our untangling, a teasing-out of difficulties. We have already begun, by introducing new blood. A life-saving injection you might say, for that is what it is: a life-saving injection of fresh souls. Indeed, some of them are fresh to your planet, though not fresh to other worlds. To some it is their first experience upon your Earth, volunteers to see what they might do to assist. You will meet many of these souls and those who have taken upon themselves the form of your being, your human form. You are all blessed by this infusion of fresh blood.'

Jacob wondered if this meant the Star Children. Jacob knew that today, Kate's mind could not be tapped into by unwelcome human psychic spies like Helga, since this kind of information held a higher energy that could not be reached by an inferior and denser vibration. Her journey here was not invading any sensitive military areas, where remote viewers patrolled. He was relieved and felt able to ask yet another question.

"Who are the Star Kids?"

'We have told you of the infusion of new blood. This should explain. Some are on your planet as a result of merging genetically with our kind. This you should know since your own daughter is one such.'

"You mean as the result of the abduction I experienced?" Jacob had not expected this to come up in one of their sessions. It was too close to his emotions for him to be comfortable hearing this through Kate, and yet the question came involuntarily. In spite of himself, he still had those memories and he still had feelings for Kate's real star mother. He quickly asked another question to divert the very personal experience away from him.

"What's your agenda with abducted human beings? We hear of them often in the media."

Was it his imagination, or were more coloured forms taking shape in the room, surrounding them both? He watched in awe as they gathered. A tall vibrant-blue column appeared and Kate disappeared behind it. Then the column slowly morphed into a vaguely recognisable human form almost twice her height. Jacob just made out long pointed ears and a narrow face with a sharp chin. Entranced he didn't dare take his eyes off where his darling daughter sat behind the form. Should he speak? Jacob wasn't sure. He leaned forward, eyes straining.

The form spoke through Kate in a soft but clear voice. 'Do not fear us. We mean you no harm. You asked about abductions. This is a complicated matter. The word is misleading since it implies being taken against one's will. The majority of those who come aboard with us had already agreed to do so as part of their life plan. It can be frightening at first for they will not be aware of the agreement. Once they have been a few times they settle down and look forward to spending time with us and the journeys we take them on. They form a bond with us. The connection usually runs in families down through the generations. Experiencers often find they have gained enhanced psychic abilities and gifts of healing. Our message to them is simple: we warn against environmental abuse and the dangers of nuclear weapons.'

"Usually ignored by all governments, unfortunately," Jacob said.

'Alas so. They fail to understand that advanced extra-terrestrial civilisations visiting your Earth are not evil, demons or devils. Either you grow spiritually with advanced technologies, or you fall victim to that technology. However rogue elements exist within these civilisations just as they do here on Earth.

'We have always warned that not all contact would be of a friendly nature because of the inferior and destructive natures of some. They have access to the technologies of their own civilisation, just as the rogue elements on your planet have access to your technologies. The cartels and mafias do not manufacture their own vehicles, guns and ammunitions.

'It works the same way with the advanced ET civilisations visiting Earth. There have been abductions carried out by friendly ETs, and they took added precautions to ensure that no harm came to the individual. In general, they invoke amnesia so that it's forgotten, but this doesn't always work. We no longer need to carry out these practices.'

Jacob wasn't entirely sure whether to be pleased at this news or not. After all, hadn't his own abduction resulted in Kate?

'We're hoping to save you from yourselves. You are your greatest enemy. During the Cold War your nations that had nuclear weapons conducted open-air testing in total disregard of the effects of the radioactive fallout and the extent of the area it might cover. We now know that the fallout from these tests covered the entire planet, and even now we are not sure of the effects it had on your world population.'

"Is this why there is so much cancer, not only with humans but with animals too?" Jacob asked.

His question was not answered. 'The greater threat lies not with us, but within the many nations of your Planet Earth using mind-control technology for use against all humanity. If you should find yourself becoming a victim of abductions, might we suggest that next time you ask questions of your abductors? You might be surprised at the response. You might discover that they are carried out by your own Earth people.

'If our visits were hostile or meant you harm, if our visits were bent on taking you over, with our technology we could indeed take you over in a day. We could do this simply and quickly, without the need or aid of anyone, or any group of powerful, greedy humans. Frequently those abductees have implants, so that they can be tracked. These you can call 'dark hats'. Abductions by cruel and unloving intergalactic beings did take place in the past, but have been forbidden in recent years by the Intergalactic Council, or they will face penalties. Those that occur in recent and present times are conducted by your own people, not us. Their objective is to create fear and control.

'We are also concerned about the many nations of your Planet Earth using mind-control technology, creating memories that are false. The damage that you are doing to yourselves and your planet is complicated by the fact that there are members of space who do not have your best interests at heart. These you can also call 'Dark Hats."

"You are 'Light Hats' then?" hazarded Jacob.

'We are the Bird Tribe, sometimes called Blue Avians. But yes, we are what is known as Light Hats.'

The shapes in the room gathered around Jacob. He felt warm, very warm. He took his attention off Kate and looked at them.

'Your Earth is under a quarantine that prevents most negative ETs from being able to enter your airspace. Without it, negative ETs would have invaded and taken over your planet eons ago. This quarantine came after many of the planetary infiltrators had already arrived on Earth to carry out their plan. It's maintained by a vast network of super-advanced, indestructible satellites surrounding the Earth. These satellites keep humanity locked in and everyone else locked out. The Quarantine protects you from the Dark Hats except from those already on Earth.'

Satellites? This confirmed to Jacob that this was why Kate and Adam had been placed in SatData Consolidated. They were there for a reason, that much was obvious, and even though Kate longed to leave, her role there would become clear.

The overshadowing on Kate began to fade until he once again clearly saw her as herself, but still the lilting voice continued to speak.

'There are certain orbits between Earth, the Moon and other planets called 'Nodes' which are neutral in gravity. These Nodes are used by mother ships orbiting 165-170,000 miles from Earth and are the equivalent of docking berths such as those used by your ships. They could be called space stations or way stations, if you like.

'Please make a note of the current Galactic Planetary Census. There are 7.5 billion planets that have human life, 44 million of which in your galaxy alone have evolved human form, that is to say humanoid, of which there are 340 different species. Remember this when you consider your own humanity. I will leave you now. Please take care of her.'

With that he left, and the other blue shapes went with him.

Kate slowly returned. Rubbing her eyes, she said, "That was so weird. I knew that the voice was speaking through me but I was still present, if you know what I mean."

"That was amazing, wasn't it?" Jacob said. "That was very different from your previous journeys. It's really helped me see the bigger picture."

"Me too."

"Now, we must think what we have to do with this information..."

"You're right, but I'm so tired," Kate said with a yawn. "Do you mind if we wrap it up? Have a discussion later?"

"Of course not. Speak later my love. Sleep well."

With that, Jacob slipped out of the house. He was so deep in thought he didn't notice that the black car was still there.

Kate began to ponder the enormity of what she'd just learnt. There were so many things to digest, and the discovery of the Quarantine and alien satellites was certainly food for thought.

CHAPTER TWENTY-FIVE

A SCARE

'Really important meetings are planned by souls long before the bodies see each other.'

Paolo Coelho

Kate decided to walk to work. It was a fair distance and would take her the best part of half an hour, but she felt she needed to clear her head and for her, walking was always the best way to do that. The streets were quiet in the early morning. Lights flicked on in people's houses as she walked — alarms would be sounding, showers turned on and breakfasts got ready. A sleek grey cat strolled across the road in front of her. It turned to look, and then sat watching as she passed by, curious as cats so often are.

"Puss, puss," she called to it. The cat wandered over and as she bent down to stroke it she caught sight of a man ducking behind a garden hedge, such an obvious movement by someone trying not to be seen.

She walked on, a little more quickly now, slightly unnerved and wishing she'd taken the car. Several times she heard footsteps behind her, but each time she turned to look she saw nobody. Was it just her imagination? Her heart rate quickened with panic but she refused to break into a run. Whatever was to happen, she would deal with it. At last she reached the large gate leading down the long drive to the building where she worked. Several other office staff were arriving in their cars and Kate felt safer by their presence.

The day dragged on with little to mark it as out of the ordinary. She resisted the urge to join in Marco's staring match. When he first arrived he'd scared her. Then when he'd tried to molest her, Adam had helped her out so that she could avoid seeing him wherever possible. Now though, she'd begun to notice what a scruffy idiot he was – a buffoon. She realised he always had at least one button undone on his shirt. His bulging torso made it hard for any of his buttons to stay done up. His habit of pulling on one ear and feeling for a pencil that wasn't there amused her. And his propensity to wear dark glasses in doors just made him look like a pretentious jerk. She'd see him leer at her female colleagues as they passed by, then laugh at their discomfort. Underneath the bully's façade, Kate could see there was an insecure little man who lacked the intelligence to be anything but a hired hit man. Kate had lost her fear of him. She knew now she had the measure of him, she could outwit him any time.

Silas, however, was quite another thing altogether. Every time she was near him her psychic powers flared-up, an internal voice screaming, 'Danger, danger'. She sensed that he was highly intelligent and capable of a cruelty that would be calculated and vicious. His dark eyes were as cold as steel, and she doubted there was any warmth in him at all. What had happened to make him the way he was now? It was clear to anyone but a fool that both men were there to keep a watch on her. She longed to know how they were connected with her secret work.

At the end of the day Kate tidied her d
drawers and said cheerio to the few pe
to do overtime. She regretted having w
had to walk home, and that prospect v
the dark afternoon's wintry chill. She ho
again. She stepped out of the door, wr
her neck and set off at a fast pace. A

lamps were turning on and cast a dim light, but also many shadows.

The lighted windows of the houses she walked by comforted her. Cars were pulling into their drives after a day at work. People were at hand if she needed them. She had nothing to worry about. There was nobody following her, she told herself.

Two streets from home, she was crossing the road to make a turn, when she heard the roar of a car coming straight towards her. She spun round and leapt to one side just in time. Hadn't it seen her? She breathed deeply through her mouth and out through her nose, trying to calm herself.

It was dusk by the time she turned into her own street. As she got closer to her house, she saw that same black car parked opposite. She stopped in her tracks. The dark shape of someone sitting inside moved slightly, as if he or she was getting out.

Kate's second sight went into action. 'Get indoors quickly,' it said to her. She legged-it down her street and through her gate, but in her haste, she fumbled and dropped her keys on the path. She pulled off her gloves and felt for the keys on the ground. It was too dark to see clearly, and she couldn't find them. Footsteps sounded behind her, coming closer. Panic was just setting in when she located the keys. She raced to the door and managed to get them in the lock. The owner of the footsteps was nearly on her when a car pulled up and honked its horn twice. Whoever was behind her turned and fled. She didn't stop to look, just got inside and leant against the door in relief. The world felt malevolent, like everyone was out to get her.

The next moment a sharp urgent knock sounded on the door. She
ze and held her breath. The knocking resumed, harder now. Heart
ding, she inched to the window to see who it was. Recognising
pe of her father, she let out a sigh of relief. She opened the
ulled him inside, sobbing hoarsely.

k you so long?" Jacob asked, then he noticed her

expression. “You’re trembling. What’s wrong? What’s happened?” He wrapped his arms around her.

“They’re ramping up their intimidation techniques, Dad,” she sobbed. “Didn’t you see that man running down my path?”

“No… I was searching for my mobile. It’d slipped down between the seats. I accidently sounded the horn twice with my elbow when looking for it. I hope it didn’t frighten you?”

“It was the horn that scared whoever it was off,” she said, regaining her composure, “so you saved the day, Papa!” She then told him about the way she’d been followed to and from work. “It was definitely not my imagination.”

“Well, I think it would be wise to only go by car in future,” Jacob said. “They’re just trying to frighten you.”

“Well they’re doing that all right,” Kate said. “It’s strange though, because when I see them – I mean Helga, Marco and Silas, who are the ones behind this, I’m sure – I don’t feel frightened of them. I kind of feel sorry for them. But it’s when I’m being followed or threatened that the old human ‘flight or fright’ syndrome kicks-in. I suppose I’m only human! Well, part-human,” she joked, more at ease now her father was by her side. “Anyway, why did you come?”

“Second sight!” he replied, grinning broadly. “Now let’s get a brew on. Dammit, where’s Adam these days? He’s never here when he’s needed.”

“I couldn’t agree more. I miss him, Dad. He can’t text or communicate with me in the normal way, as we have to maintain a professional distance, but I do get the odd connection with him in Sirian, assuring me that he’s okay. I get a feeling he’ll be back soon.”

“Let’s talk about something else then, shall we?” Jacob said as they wandered into the kitchen together. “It’ll take your mind off things. I was thinking about what you said some time ago regarding underground bases and I started thinking about the undersea bases too."

Kate laughed. "That's supposed to take my mind off things? Dad, you are funny!"

At least she was laughing.

"They call these bases DUMBS which is an acronym for 'deep undersea military bases'. There's an undersea version of Area 51, the US Navy's Atlantic Undersea Test and Evaluation Center (AUTEC), on Andros Island, in the Bahamas. Did you know that? I've been doing my research!" Jacob looked pleased with himself.

Kate nodded, not looking up from warming the teapot. He'd got the bit between his teeth and there'd be no stopping him now he got going on his favourite subject –anything to do with the sea.

"It's one of the world's deepest sea trenches, over 6,000 feet, which is amazing considering the shallow seas surrounding the Bahamas. Officially, AUTEC is an instrumented laboratory that works on undersea simulated warfare and research.

"Get this Kate! A whole bunch of UFO hunters are drawn there because of testimonies by local witnesses of Unidentified Submerged Objects (USOs). They'd heard of a bizarre time-travel experience by a pilot. They interviewed a US government psychic, and a French spook who each alleged that the area, located at the tip of the Bermuda Triangle, is an inter-dimensional portal populated by underwater aliens, and that the Navy is doing experiments with these energies and entities."

Kate perked up at the mention of experiments with underwater aliens. Perhaps this would be one of her next mind journeys? She poured hot water over the tea leaves. Jacob was correct. It had taken her mind off things.

* * *

Kate's spirit friends were keen for her to mind-travel again, and as Adam was still unable to return to the UK, Kate asked Jacob to sit with her. His presence reassured her that he was keeping watch on the outside, as she journeyed inwardly

They both settled, quietened their minds and waited – and waited. Where were her space friends? They'd especially asked for this contact to be made. The seconds ticked by and they were just about to give up when Kate jerked to attention as the voice began.

"'Sorry for the delay –Master M here. We needed to get permission from the Galactic Council to tell you more about our bases for the planetary family. I'll let them speak for themselves. Transmission about to begin. Are you ready?'

Kate started to shiver uncontrollably, not from fear but because a wave of cold air suddenly surrounded her. Her breath appeared in a cloud as the temperature plummeted in the room. A different voice channelled through Kate. It was emotionless, almost mechanical.

"'We're a special branch, a task force you might say. We use the Antarctic a great deal. There are many of us but you'll not see us since we operate on a different vibration. The cold climate has no adverse effect on us at all.'

It's having an effect on Kate though, Jacob thought.

'We leave no mark or sign that we are in Antarctica, but it's helpful for us to have a base there since it's a good jumping-off point. We carefully observe the hardy souls that make up your Earthly teams of researchers and arctic experts. They'll be called on in times of need, for they have skills many others do not have.'

Kate, numbed with cold, intervened. "Master M, can you do something about this temperature please? See what's happening to me?"

"'We'll close that transmission,' Master M's voice replied through Kate. 'That should do it. He's said what he needed to say.'"

Kate began to warm up immediately, for which she was grateful. It was strange how she was affected physically even though it was psychic communication.

M picked up on her thoughts straightaway.

"'You forget that when you communicate in this way you are halfway to being wholly with us. We merge the vibrations. The higher in vibration you go the colder you'll get. There can be some distortion but usually we manage. Warmer now?'

"Yes, thank you. Please continue."

"'There is much talk on your planet among those who believe in ETs. We wish to let you know that there are at least 165 species of what you call 'Greys'. These are not supposed to live on your planet, though they visit often in order to carry out our work. We point this out because there are some species of Greys who have taken up with what you call the secret government or the negative movement within the military.'

"Would they have anything to do with Kate's recent interrogation?" Jacob asked.

"'They might have,' Master M said. 'They were involved with the reverse engineered spacecraft Kate saw and are involved in other secret negative activities such as abductions. However, in general, the tall Greys are helpful and benevolent, and they use the short Greys for their work. It's the tall Greys who've had meetings with important people on your planet. They also have prevented some disasters, and will continue to do so.'

His next words gave both Jacob and Kate a shock. 'Helga is a mind-controlled ET/human hybrid. This is why you have such trouble with her.'

"Really? Helga is the same as me? A hybrid? That's unreal!" Kate's eyes widened with shock.

'It's true, but the difference is that she's mind-controlled and you are not.'

"So, when she reads my mind, is it her or someone else doing it?"

'Someone else. She has no power over it. Realise it's not her human side that invades your mind and knows about your journeys. We are trying to do something about it.'

"Well, make it quick, will you please? I don't think I can stand being around her much longer."

'Jacob, are you still listening?' Master M's voice continued through Kate.

Jacob smiled. "Hello, Master M. I'm unused to being addressed directly, but I'm pleased to be included and acknowledged."

'I need you to take notes, are you ready? Our purpose this evening is to give information on several counts. Are you ready for that? Jacob, are you ready to take this down?'

Jacob nodded vigorously. "Yes, yes. Ready and waiting."

'First of all, there are thousands, no, millions of humans living on other planets that are similar to Earth. The majority of them have absolutely no idea of your existence, in the same way that humans on Earth have no idea of them. Bizarre? No, it makes sense if you remember what we told you a while ago, that the main objective of all species is to expand and grow. Earth was not the only planet considered suitable for this expansion of human form.'

Jacob sensed that Master M spoke with pride. "Does this mean we can visit and interchange?" he asked.

'We are sorry to say that humanity on Earth has not yet reached the required level of spirituality to be allowed to travel to uncontaminated spheres. You could say you are in quarantine. You are too warlike and aggressive.' He heaved a big sigh.

Jacob shrugged. "So, what can we do about it?"

'You have heard that like attracts like? Of course you have. The aggressive and negative natures among you are attracting those space beings that have designs on your world. Their low vibrations would be extremely comfortable and at home in the current environment on your world. No opposition to overcome, you see.'

Jacob nodded. "Is there a solution?"

'These 'Dark Hats' species would not be comfortable in your environment if people started to treat each other and the creatures on Planet Earth with love and kindness. Their dense and heavy vibration could not enter a lighter, more loving sphere. You and Kate would be safe from any plot against you, as would every other person of love and not hate.

'This is why we are contacting you. Make it known to as many as you can what is at stake if attitudes do not change. Continue to let it be known that we do exist, and we will be presenting ourselves openly very soon. Pass the information we give you to all who will listen. You will be challenged of course. Does that bother you?'

"It bothers me that my darling daughter is finding herself in perilous waters. Can you keep her safe?"

'Her soul is forever safe,' Master M replied.

"But what about her day-to-day life?" Jacob felt his anger rise. He expected more reassurance than that. "If you can't ensure her safety I'll tell her not to mind-travel."

An uncomfortable silence descended on the room. After a few minutes, Master M spoke again. 'You are aware that she will mind-travel, whether you want her to or not. Without you she'll be put in greater danger, but from a source you cannot see. How would you like that? Be assured, we've her best interests at heart and will do what we can.'

Jacob saw his point. He nodded. "All right, proceed."

Kate inclined her head in agreement.

After a few moments, she said: "I'm in a big hall. I see great floor-to-ceiling windows. It's a public place, or one that's hired out to the public. Various doors lead off to little rooms. I take one door to the left that is quite easy to open, and step into a corridor with doors all along it. It's a bit like an adult education building, or a college with a lot of things going on. I continue until I reach a door painted in bright red. I step inside.

"It's a conference room with a big long table. People from different planets are sitting round it. Human beings are here too, representing different countries. I can tell by the clothes they wear. They're pretty much all men. These are the ones who control, or dictate roles and strategies, not just for Earth but also for other planets and their interactions.

"They beckon me to sit down and I find an empty seat. I sit down with them but don't hear clearly what they're saying. Do the humans represent their own countries?"

Master M said, 'No, individual countries fight their own corner. But when an event is seen to be more global, things won't happen in just one country, it will happen in all sectors of the world, which will encompass all the countries within that sector. To avoid conflict, the men sitting here have been chosen from spirit. They are spiritually higher than your elected representatives, such as ministers, presidents and so on, those who run their country's affairs.'

Fascinated, Jacob asked, "What are they meeting for?"

'We are telling you that we have in place, in all corners of your world, our human representatives for the highest good, to counteract the deeds of those who would do harm. They have a difficult job to do, but we are hopeful they will manage to turn the tide.'

"This is not interference then?" Jacob said.

'Indeed not. Each has decided to be incarnated as human for this role. As such, they now have a right to choose what they do. As you do. We have frequently stated that citizens of Earth have to put matters straight themselves and not expect others to do it for them. But this is our way of giving support. Would any of you object?'

Jacob had to admit it was a good way to tackle the mess that humans had got into.

"What did you mean when you said earlier that you would be presenting yourselves openly soon?"

'We will be arriving and walking the streets as ourselves among you. This is why we're asking you to prepare everyone to be ready and not to panic. We ask you to make it clear that there's nothing to be afraid of. If we'd wanted to harm you we could have done that eons ago. Instead we have helped you many times over, and still are.

'We feel that is enough for the moment. We do have quite a lot more for your daughter to do, so please continue to maintain your watch over her. Do not worry. She does enough for both of you. We have a plan!'

With that intriguing comment, he left Kate. She slowly began to return to herself and to the room. She opened her eyes and stretched her arms.

"It's so great to be moving forwards with this, I feel that something is finally going to happen," she said, smiling broadly.

Jacob nodded. He shared his daughter's enthusiasm but still couldn't help but temper it with some trepidation – were they up to the task they'd been given?

* * *

Next morning, there was a knock at the door. As always, Kate's heart leapt: Adam. But no, when she opened it, it was the postman. "Sorry to bother you but it would take ages to post these through the letterbox. I thought I might as well give you the whole sack," he said, smiling.

"Whole sack? What on earth...?" replied Kate, looking at the grey hessian bag bulging with letters. She hefted it inside and opened the top one.

> *Dear Ms Greene, I just wanted to say how impressed I was with the talk you gave recently. You have touched something in me I never knew existed. I believe everything you say and I am telling all my friends too...*

Fan mail!

Kate couldn't believe it. Her talks *were* doing some good then. She opened the next few and they were all the same. Full of praise and the promise to spread the word. She noticed that the majority of the letters were actually printed-out emails and were from all around the world – and it wasn't long before she cottoned-on to who was behind this. Poppy. Oh, bless her! What was it she said, when Kate was ill with 'flu: "I'm with you." What a wonderful thing to have done.

A quick check online told her that her talks had been uploaded not just to YouTube but to hundreds of websites, ufology ones and general interest too. There were even fan sites devoted to learning the alien language she'd spoken, with contributions from others who had become able to speak it too. Kate smiled with delight when she remembered that this was one way that the extra-terrestrials were going to join the human population – their language is linked to DNA.

She marvelled at how things had really taken off, but could it really have happened all without her lifting a finger?

Kate picked up her mobile, but at that very moment it rang, and to Kate's sheer delight it was none other than her best friend on the line.

"Well you're full of surprises, Poppy!"

"You got them, then?" Kate could almost feel Poppy's smile through the phone.

"I can't believe it!"

"Well, you know that email database I've been working on? I just sent a round-robin to all the people who'd seen your talks and videoed them on their phones, and just asked them to start sharing the information through Facebook and Twitter. And Bob's your uncle."

"You are amazing!" Kate said.

"No, you are."

"No, *you are!*"

They gigged as they lapsed easily back into their childhood banter.

"I have to see you soooon," Kate moaned. "It's been too long. I'll ring you and fix a date okay. Love you."

"Love you too"

Kate practically skipped into work, buoyed up by the cheering news that she was actually fulfilling her duties – people were taking her message on board. Her mood was soon dampened however when she saw Silas. For the whole day, he hung around Kate much more than she was comfortable with. During a break, she was sitting in the canteen having a quiet coffee when he pulled up a chair and sat opposite her. There was no, "May I sit here?" She mumbled a polite 'good afternoon' – he was a boss, after all – but he ignored her, didn't speak and stared at her with cold blank eyes and a scowl on his face. Since she could hardly get up and move to another place, she continued to sip at her coffee. But his strange behaviour unnerved her and made her anxious for the rest of the day. She wondered if, like Helga, he too was not human at all.

That evening, just as she was settling down to a rare night of television, a loud knocking sounded on her front door. Slightly peeved at the interruption to her evening, Kate went to open the door. Adam stood there, smiling broadly. She wanted to rush into his arms and kiss him all over, but instead gave him a friendly hug.

"Can I come in? Am I still welcome?" he asked.

"Of course you can. It's so good to see you." Heart pounding, Kate stepped back and gestured him in.

Adam frowned and scratched his head. "Everything okay? What's going on?"

Kate shut the door behind him. Nothing, she said, but felt her cheery façade crumble. "It's just that – well, what keeps you in DC so long and so often? Things have been so tough here. Did you know I've been ill? Did you know I was arrested and followed? Do you actually care?" To her utter dismay, Kate started to cry.

Adam looked at her in astonishment. "Do I care? What's going on here? Please don't doubt me Kate. Come here, sit next to me and I'll tell you." He sat on the couch, and Kate sat beside him. He gave her another warm hug, which genuinely felt like he did care.

"I have to be in DC because that's where I work, and I have to report back or I'll come under suspicion. You wouldn't want that, would you? I told you about my work, Kate – it's important."

"I know, I know…It's just that. Well, do you have a house there? Or a social life? Have you got a girlfriend there…?" Her breath grew shallow as she knew she didn't have the right to ask these things. She felt ridiculous and embarrassed, particularly when they were just friends, but she had to know.

Adam turned to her and gazed at her steadily. "Naturally I have a house there. What do you think? That I'm at my office desk day and night? But no, I don't have a girlfriend – at least… I don't think I have."

She looked up at him and saw longing in his face. He reached for her again and wrapped his arms tight around her, then his face drew close to hers. She closed her eyes and tilted her face up towards his. Soon they were lost in kisses. Kate felt sensations she she'd never experienced before.

"I hope you don't have to leave again until tomorrow?" she whispered.

"And I hope tomorrow never comes," he replied.

The next morning dawned bright, both in weather and mood. Kate stirred, her heart full of joy. She rolled over and discovered that Adam was already up, dressed and straightening his tie in front of the mirror.

"I'm sorry to dash off so soon, but I have to be in the office, your office, early this morning. I'm only here for a few days, but let's try and make the most of them, eh?" He kissed her. "See you later, sweetie," he teased.

As Kate dressed for work she felt her euphoria bubbling over. She knew she was glowing. Finally, something had happened between her and Adam and she was walking on air.

CHAPTER TWENTY-SIX

FUTURE CHANGES

'The future belongs to those who believe in the beauty of their dreams.'

Eleanor Roosevelt

Kate's week flew by as she spent much of it with Adam. Despite their best-laid plans however, Adam had to return to the States after only being back for four days, and most of those were filled with interminable meetings. But when they could, they spent every moment together and her memories were now keeping her warm.

On Saturday morning Jacob arrived to have coffee with his daughter. He looked around her small sitting room, straightening a framed picture on the wall and running his finger along the top to remove the dust.

"I spend so much time in your house, perhaps I should move in and do your housework?"

Preoccupied, Kate wasn't really listening. "Ah, well, I've got more important things to do!"

"Things are really hotting-up, aren't they?" said Jacob.

Kate smirked but hastily covered it up when she realised he wasn't talking about Adam.

"There's a definite sense of urgency about Master M's communications," Jacob continued.

"Too true, I'm even dreaming about it now. Last night in my sleep I called on the Blue People from my childhood and asked them what they needed me to do. They said that they had a mission for me and guided me towards a storage basement. In it were lots of packages all containing what appeared to be bullets or little bombs. At first I thought they were small missiles, but not ones shot up from the ground like missiles, these are dropped from aircraft.

"I was told, 'We want you to alter the DNA of the contents so they're rendered completely harmless. Each one is a capsule containing biological toxins. In altering the DNA of one then all the others are automatically altered too. DNA communicates with itself even if it's divided. If you do this, whoever owns these, and we are speaking of more than one country, will not know that what they intended will have no effect, or rather no harmful effect. Wherever these capsules land they will fail at the job that some military government organisations intended. They will wait for results and will wonder why nothing happened.'

Dad, I didn't know where they intend to drop these. It felt like places we're not thinking of."

"Chemical weapons! Biological warfare! It doesn't bear thinking about. No wonder Master M is concerned. Did you do the change, darling?"

"No, I woke up, but I can try again." Kate's heart began thumping at the thought of it. "So, it wasn't just a dream, then?"

"I don't think so." Jacob replied. "I hope this isn't a pre-warning of something that could happen."

"But that wasn't the only dream last night," she said. I had another just before I got up. I made notes because I needed to tell you before it faded. This may be an additional way of giving me information."

"I hope it had a more pleasant tone," Jacob said. "What was it?"

"I was led underground, down a ladder to the bottom of a well or conduit. The water was pure, beautiful and fresh. Sweet. I followed it to where it was coming from, and as I moved along I knew that nobody knew it was there. Eventually I came to the source, a spring-fed well hidden by bushes.

"I was told, 'This must not be discovered. The source of all spring waters must be kept hidden from governments, councils, official bodies, water boards. If they discover a new source of fresh water, they will commandeer it, use it, steal it, take control, pollute and use it for all manner of things for which it was not intended. So, these natural springs need to be protected. Anybody knowing about fresh springs of water can use it but keep its whereabouts to themselves. You need to keep this information away from governing bodies, which as we've said will commandeer and misuse, and very soon it would disappear. This is part of the message you must put out. The peoples of the world need protection from their own rulers. They need protection from those who are supposed to look after them, from those in power.'

"There, what do you make of that, Dad? It's sobering, isn't it? Mind you. It was just a dream. Maybe I'm simply bringing up my own fears, and manifesting them as dreams. I hope it isn't a true state of affairs."

Jacob looked appalled. "Are those in power really that bad? Surely they can't all be? But I've never known Master M or Sechem give false information, so why would they do it now through dreams? You must trust your own judgement."

"I know, we'll sit and ask them this evening. How about that for an idea?" Taking action made Kate feel better.

"Yes, that's a good idea."

Kate stretched. "The momentum is really picking up if my dreams are being commandeered now too! I need some fresh air, let's go for a walk."

Jacob smiled. "Another good idea."

Kate drove them to Hengistbury Head, along the Dorset coast, with the sea breeze ruffling their hair through a chink in the car window. The air was a bit nippy, but the winter sun kept the chill off, and they wrapped up warm. She parked the car and they set off arm in arm.

There were not many people on the exposed coastline who were brave enough to take a walk along the headland in the wintry weather. The only sound was the scream of seagulls, dipping and diving as they wheeled around the grey sky and scudding clouds. Even from the car park Kate could hear the thundering crash of waves on the shore below the cliff. Kate loved the smell of the sea and the crunch of dried heathland under her feet. It seemed they had the entire countryside to themselves. She breathed in deeply and smiled in contentment.

"Dad, can I talk to you about Francine?" she asked after they'd walked the short distance across the dried scrub to the little café. "She's been calling in on me unexpectedly, on the off chance of seeing Adam, I suspect. If I leave her alone in the room she pokes around in my things. I can stand that, but I know she reports back to Helga. It's that I don't like. I feel really uneasy about her. Uneasy knowing what I know about her being just a surrogate, not my real mother, uneasy about her relationship with Helga. It's hard to know where I stand with her. Is she someone I should be careful around or what? I thought she was my mother, my real mother, for years and now it's all been turned on its head."

"It must be hard for you Kate, after all these years to have learned that Francine isn't related to you genetically. And it's true to say that Francine hasn't a psychic bone in her body so she won't be able to see all the ghosts and ghouls in your room when she comes around!" His big frame shook with laughter.

"Dad, take it seriously," Kate said, punching him affectionately on the arm.

"Sorry, darling. Well, Francine has always been an enigma to me, even when we were together. I did love her in my own way, if only because she gave birth to you – but she chooses to suppress her consciousness. It is easier to keep her mind busy with superficialities rather than realities and that's what she does. All I can say is trust your instincts about her."

"I also wanted to ask..." Here, Kate hesitated. She didn't want to hurt her dear old dad but she had to know. "Do you think Francine was so cold with me because she must have sensed deep down that she wasn't my biological mother?"

"I don't know, Kate, I really don't. You were an adorable baby and I could never understand why she didn't fall in love with you like I did, regardless of whether you were related by blood."

"But Dad..." Kate bit her lip. "Why did you stay with her for so long? Why did I have to grow up with a mother who hated me? She really was awful to me. Locking me in a cupboard, refusing to let me have friends home, barely looking at me, let alone talking to me. Why didn't you do anything?"

"Oh Kate, that is the one question I don't know the answer to myself. At the time, I hoped that I could make up for her coldness. I tried to give you as many cuddles as I could when I got home from work – and even then, I was on mind-travel missions so was absent from you in other ways. I felt terrible leaving you with her when I went off to work but I couldn't see any other way to make things work. Now I hugely regret that. I wish I'd left her the minute she turned her back on you. Please forgive me. I was weak and indecisive and I regret it deeply." He gazed beseechingly at his daughter.

"Thank you for telling me that, Dad. I feel a lot better. I wish you had too but then hindsight is 20/20 isn't it?" Kate felt a weight lifting from her. Discovering that Francine's rejection of her was not her fault had been deeply healing. Now that her father had been honest about how he had been too, she could start to move on.

They'd reached the little café. It all looked run down, closed-up and left to fend for itself over the winter season.

"I'll just nip to the loo," Jacob said. "Won't be long." He disappeared into the toilet block.

Kate wandered up and down for a bit, stamping her feet to keep warm. She tried the door of the café, but it was well and truly locked, so she stood in the doorway to get a little shelter from the chilly wind. Then as she looked about her at the spread of gorse leading to the sea she heard a car pull up on the gravel of the deserted car park. Two burly men got out.

Suddenly she remembered that time – it must've been nearly a year ago – when she'd had that hallucination of clouds and the image of being abducted. Except this time, she knew it was really going to happen and she was powerless to change it. It was déjà vu in action. What should she do? Run? Hide? Scream for her dad? Before she had time to do any of these, she felt the cold steel of a gun pressed to the back of her neck.

"Stay quiet and you won't get hurt. Scream and you die," said a rough voice, then a leather-gloved hand was clapped over her mouth.

They dragged her away from the doorway and over to the car park. Kate didn't dare resist as they roughly pushed her inside the car. Another black-suited man sat in the back. He pressed a gun to her ribs while a blindfold was put on her. Kate felt the urge to kick, fight, claw her way out but she didn't move a muscle as the unforgiving muzzle of the gun was still jammed in her side. The gloved hand held a foul-smelling pad of cotton wool firmly over her nose. Everything went black.

* * *

Kate surfaced alone, in the dark, with her mouth feeling like sandpaper. She opened her mouth to call out, but only a croak came. Where was she? How long had she been here unconscious? Terrified, she tried to piece together what had happened, but her mind was fuzzy, unable to string thoughts in place. Unbidden memories of the cupboard under the stairs came to her – again she was in a cold, dark enclosed space controlled by another. She began to shake, both with the cold and with fear. She knew it was no good screaming; she knew there would be nobody to hear her.

Grateful that she still had her winter coat on, she rummaged in an inside pocket and found her phone. Salvation! She switched it on. No signal. Her heart crashed into her boots again. She used the dim green glow to look around. The narrow beam revealed a cellar-like space — no windows just a low bunk, a blanket and a bucket. Obviously, a makeshift prison cell. She looked for ways to escape but the walls were unforgiving concrete.

What did they mean to do with her? How long was she to be kept here? At least she was unharmed, but who knew for how long? Was she going to be tortured? Kate sat on the low bench, put her head in her hands and prayed, not to God, but to the higher beings that she'd met, to Master M, to Sechem, 'Please, please save me'. Then she uttered a mind-plea in Sirian: '*I don't know where I am*, but I am in danger. Please help me.'

She turned her phone off. She had to save the battery. She could be here a long time. She passed out again.

Hours passed. It has to be dark outside by now, she thought as she woke. She was desperate for something to happen, anything – but nothing did. The waiting was awful, not knowing where she was, why she was here or what they wanted from her. She worried about Jacob too. What must he be going through?

Kate lay on the bench, staring into the pitch black when she heard a scraping sound on the cellar steps. The door opened and shut again quickly. She turned on the phone and saw that food and drink had been left on the top step. So they, whoever they were, didn't mean to kill her, then – unless it was by poison, she thought wryly. She reached for the sandwich and gulped it down, so ravenous that she didn't care if it were good or bad. She had to keep her strength up for whatever was ahead.

Despite her torment, she somehow drifted off and awoke hours later to the sound of the cellar door slamming shut again. In the phone's light she discovered a candle and matches alongside more food and drink at the top of the steps. At least she had some light now. Though comforting, it also meant they intended to keep her there, which filled her with dread.

Hours went by. Where were her blue friends? Fat lot of good they were now, she thought, after all she did for them. Kate clenched her teeth and shouted into the stale air.

"Where are you now when I need you? Some friends you are!" She finished up the remainder of the food and drink and feeling groggy lay down on the bed. Her thoughts grew dull, and her head felt thick. She fell back into a deep, drugged sleep.

The next time Kate awoke, she tried to piece together what was happening. I'm being drugged by the food, she thought. So, I won't eat the food – and I can't connect with Spirit because the drugs are dimming my powers. Oh god! She tried to focus enough to make contact.

"Sechem! Adam! Daddy! Can you hear me? Can you feel me?"

Nothing.

Hours ticked by and Kate phased in and out of consciousness. Whatever it was they'd laced her food with, it was powerful. It was rendering her powerless. Did she even know if they were doing anything to her when she was out of it? She checked her arms, her thighs. She couldn't see any bruises, any marks of violence, in the dim light of her phone.

She crouched by the door, so that the next time it opened, she could spring out and make a run for it. But when the door opened whoever had brought her food was ready for her and pushed her roughly to the floor.

"Please! Please help me," she cried.

A slammed door was the only answer she got.

She stared at the food and a bottle of water. God, she was thirsty, but what if it was the water, not the food that was laced? She lay back down on the hard, wooden bench, shivering with cold, despite her winter coat. She made the most concerted effort she'd ever made in her life to connect with Spirit. Still aware enough to project in Sirian she sent out a powerful message: "Help me now! I am here." She spread her psychic energy into every nook and cranny of wherever it was she'd been incarcerated, then imagined it flowing out into the world, like a tide, connecting with Adam and Jacob wherever they were.

Exhausted, she eyed the bottle of water. She was so thirsty, but so afraid to drink it. No, stay focused, Kate, she said to herself. But as the hours ticked by she could think of nothing else except that bottle of water. Who knows how many hours later, she crawled over to the bottle and gulped down the refreshing liquid. A black curtain enveloped her mind.

* * *

Kate woke to find herself out in the open, lying in a ditch by a field. Dumped. Finally she was free. Why had they let her go? It didn't make any sense. Her head thumped so hard she could barely think. It was rapidly getting dark and she'd no idea where she was. She staggered to her feet and looked around. She reached into her coat and found her mobile phone.

Please have some battery left, please. Opening it, she was delighted to find she now had a signal. She quickly phoned Jacob and prayed hard he'd answer.

"Hello?" came a voice after it connected. To her shock, it wasn't Jacob. She threw her phone to the ground, horrified and stared at it like it was a dangerous animal. What the hell? She could hear a voice still speaking on the other end.

"Hello, hello?"

Gingerly she picked it up. "Who are you? Where's my Dad? What are you doing with his phone?" Kate began to cry. Maybe they'd got him too. She could hardly bear it.

"Where are you, Miss? Tell us where you are," the man said.

"I don't know where I am. I'm in a field. WHO ARE YOU?" Tears ran down her face.

"It's all right, calm down. Your father is right here, with us at the police station. I had to answer because we're tracing your call. He reported you missing three days ago. We've been out searching for you. Look around you and tell us what you can see."

Three days...? Kate looked into the dusk and made out a church spire on the horizon. Through sobs, she told them what she could see. "It's getting dark," she added. "You'll never be able to find me." Her phone beeped, it was about to run out of battery.

"Stay calm and focused. The trace has nearly finished. Start walking towards the church and wait there. We'll find you, even if you don't get to the church. We will find y..." Kate's phone went silent. The battery used up. She was on her own now.

The edge of the field wasn't far so she headed that way. She tore her way through a bramble hedge and fell into another ditch before reaching a small road. Sobbing with relief she trudged on heavy legs towards the church steeple that she could make out over the rise in the road,.

Night had fallen by the time she reached the church, but the lights were on. Sobbing and exhausted, she pushed open the heavy doors and walked in. A small group of people turned, their eyes widening in surprise. A woman rushed forward to help her, followed by the rest of the group. Muddied all over and covered with cuts and bruises, she told her story. One of the group phoned the police and gave the address. She was miles away from Hengistbury Head in a small village on Salisbury plain.

A police car arrived half an hour later. Jacob raced into the church and wrapped her in a hug.

"Oh Kate, thank goodness you're safe."

She sobbed into his chest, unable to speak.

Two police officers walked in after him and stood in front of Kate. The older one said he needed to ask some questions. Jacob released her from his embrace but kept one arm around her shoulder.

"I don't know who they were," she told the officer back at the station. "I hardly saw them. I was blindfolded and drugged."

"And, were you assaulted?" the officer asked — rather bluntly Kate thought.

Kate's face flushed. "I was unconscious for most of the time, so who knows?" she replied sharply, thinking he could have been more sensitive. She glanced at Jacob. He was very pale and looked exhausted, as if he could break down in tears any moment. She realised he'd been to hell and back too. She was taken into a side room and examined by a female doctor, who was thankfully more compassionate than the police officers.

"I can't see any sign of physical or sexual assault," she said, putting away the swabs.

"Well, that's a relief," said Kate weakly, putting her damp and muddy clothes back on.

She returned to the main office. "Is your car here?" she asked Jacob after she'd signed her statement.

"Yes," he said in a whisper, so faint she barely heard him.

"Let's go home."

She rummaged in her coat pocket for a tissue and discovered a piece of paper. Written in clear bold lettering were the words.

STOP WHAT YOU ARE DOING OR THERE WILL BE WORSE TO COME.

"Dad, look...Should I show this to the police?" she whispered to Jacob.

"On no account. They will ask what it is you have been doing to get this reaction. You can't tell them," he said wearily. "Let's go home."

* * *

In a top secret office in Washington DC, the monstrous figure of Gork raged at his subordinates.

"What do you mean, you can't get access to her mind? She is a mere woman. Young and weak. She is no match for you!" he roared.

"No sir, I mean yes sir..." Silas stammered, avoiding his dreadful eyes. "We've tried everything but it was like a solid steel fortress. Even unconscious, she was resistant to everything. She's obviously getting help."

"You idiots. You morons! *Of course she's getting help*. We have to find out what's going on; she is the key. Use all the resources we have – throw everything you have at her. Don't give up until you are successful. Double your efforts, triple them and find a way, or suffer the consequences."

* * *

What had happened was obviously meant to frighten her, not kill her. And it'd succeeded. Whilst Kate was physically and psychically intact, emotionally she felt like an empty husk. She'd been badly frightened. What should she do now? Actually, she couldn't face doing anything. All she wanted to do was to curl up into a ball. She phoned work and faked a tummy bug to get a few days off. Jacob spent every day with her, afraid to let her out of his sight.

As she recovered from the trauma, she tried to regain a sense of calm and control, but it didn't help that all she wanted was the one person who wasn't there. Why hadn't Adam replied to her calls? She missed him so much it hurt. Why didn't he come back? He was meant to look after her. Maybe he'd been found out and was in trouble himself? That thought did nothing to ease her mind.

"I was so drugged-up, I couldn't get through to you, to any of you," Kate lamented. "And Adam – they're keeping him in the US, away from me, aren't they Dad?"

"I fear so, Kate. I think he would do everything in his power to come back, if he could. But he has to be so careful that we are not compromised. His not being here is a sign of his love for us." Jacob smiled.

"You think so?" That thought helped a little to heal her heart.

"They clearly meant it when they said stop what you're doing," Jacob said at dinner later that evening. "I think we should give it a rest."

Kate shook her head. "Not a chance. It's doubly important that we continue, especially now we know that they want us to stop." Although she still felt like hibernating she plucked up her courage and forced herself to be proactive. "Dad, will you join me for a session?" she asked tentatively.

There was a lengthy pause while he paced the room thinking. Then he sighed.

"Alright, if you think you're strong enough – but I'm not convinced it's the right thing to do." He marvelled at her resilience. He wasn't sure he would be as brave as her.

Kate drew the curtains and locked the door.

"I love you, Dad," she said and kissed him warmly on the cheek. Once she was settled she was soon in and speaking.

"There's a little street on the left, an alleyway with houses and buildings on either side. My head's beginning to hurt, which is a good sign that I am going deeper. I come to another tiny alleyway with a bollard at the end. No vehicles are going to go down here. It's really narrow, just a gap between two buildings. Anyone leaning out of a window could hold hands with someone on the other side.

"Clearly it must lead somewhere or it wouldn't have been built in the first place. I see a small boat. I step in and cast off. The current carries me past deserted warehouses and broken-down docks.

I'm drifting along quite steadily until a man on the right bank brings in the boat with a boat hook. He helps me out. He's an ordinary looking guy, and yet there's something extraordinary about him. I do a double take as I notice that his eyes are much larger than you'd expect. I'm quite happy to go with him. I remind myself this is just a mind journey. I follow him up a slope and at the top different kinds of beings from the stars are standing behind a long trestle table, covered with a cloth. They have notes in front of them and recording equipment.

I have to look at each contraption and examine it, although I haven't the faintest idea what they are. I start at one end. There's a tiny little guy here, clearly extra-terrestrial. I pick up what he shows me, and then put it back down. I move along to another contraption and do the same. I do this all the way along, handling each object. I sense that it's important that I hold them first. It is not enough just to look. There's one very tall being in white robes and a hood at the next space, and he hands me something, I don't know what to call it. I handle that too. With this one I press a few buttons. I don't know what it does, but the buttons are there so I press them. He's quite happy with that. I put it back down and move on.

They seem anxious for my approval. I don't understand any of it. There are loads of them. I keep walking down the line. Some are very animal-like, and all of them have amazing eyes. I look into the eyes of each one before I pick up whatever it is they're showing me. What's this about?"

Kate's tone changed to the familiar voice that accompanied her mind travels.

'The purpose of this is that you receive the energy and knowledge that is contained with each device. Not only that, you have now put your own energy into it, creating a link that will not be broken. You have now connected with many different species from the Galaxy. You've received an electromagnetic connection, an energy connection, as a result of you holding their devices. It's like leaving your fingerprint, but it has imprinted you too. It's not the same as having an implant. It's imprinting. You now have a strong connection both mind and electromagnetic with many different species from the Galaxy.

"Transformation is coming. Another heavenly body will approach your planet. As a result of its density, it will have a gravitational pull and this will have an effect.'

"What effect exactly? It sounds worrying," Jacob asked.

'We speak now of physical changes, by which we bring about transformation. This heavenly body is solid but will not collide with Earth. It is a dense body that passes by. We call it a heavenly body for it has been sent. It has been directed in its course to bring about the necessary changes. You speak of the grand cosmos as the heavens in general, but we say this has been directed by the force of Creation, to bring about the necessary adjustment to one of the members of that Creation.

'It is not to be feared, for it has been sent, and we do not conceive of a destructive, vengeful God. This is no vengeance. This is merely adjustment, correction. You are already aware of the changes in your atmosphere. This is a progressive, consequential change brought about by you on Earth. It is this bringing about a change in your atmosphere that we are attempting to correct. We are speaking on two levels here: preparation for mankind and adjustment to the physical form of your planet, two considerations. Both are necessary: adjustment to humankind's thinking, which is necessary for humanity, and adjustment to the planet. Remember your planet is but one minute entity within the grander cosmos. We have consideration for all of creation.

'I am without personality, for I am but a representative of The Voice of Creation. I have been sent through the mind. I do not come from a civilisation with an identity to which you might form an attachment. I come from beyond that time. I am larger than the whole of your own galaxy.'

Kate started rubbing her head as if in pain. Jacob realised the strength of the communication was too much for her.

“Kate, wake up. Bring your mind back to this room. Feel your fingers and toes. Come back.” His instinct was to bring her back quickly, to get her out of it, but he knew that would be foolish. Her journeys were similar to deep sea dives and she had to avoid decompression sickness. So, Jacob brought Kate slowly out of her deep trance, even though she appeared to be stressed.

“Are you all right, my darling?” he asked watching her closely as she slowly opened her eyes. She stretched and yawned.

“Yes fine, I’m starving. Shall we have a sandwich?”

Jacob smiled, relieved that it was over and she was all right. As she sat and munched, she mused over the latest message.

“My connection with our space friends is growing stronger and stronger. I’m beginning to understand the way the wider galaxy operates. Our methods of communication – talking, email and so on – are so rudimentary by comparison. Theirs work on a much deeper level, molecular even. They understand philosophical truths as part of their make-up. They see the bigger picture and share this over their whole population. It’s wonderful Dad, really inspiring. It’s an honour to gain an insight into their world, to be included in it.” She beamed, back to her old self, then took another bite of sandwich.

CHAPTER TWENTY-SEVEN

ESCAPE

'It is time to be the light that you know yourself to be. Time to be the pioneer, to go where the majority do not have the will to go.'

A spirit guide

Jacob had chosen his house on the outer fringes of town because of the small river that ran near the end of his garden. He spent many hours in solitude there, contemplating his life and how it could have gone. The best thing to come out of it was Kate. However bad his marriage to Francine had been, Kate could not have existed without her, even though she'd been created elsewhere. He looked around his sparse living room and felt lonely. Just a few books, a chair or two, a battered settee and a television set. Not much to show for a lifetime, he reflected sadly.

The doorbell broke his mood. He opened the front door and his jaw dropped in surprise. Adam stood there breathing hard.

"Oh, it's you," he said absent-mindedly. "I thought you were in America?" Jacob invited him in and Adam sat down. Jacob frowned, clearly something wasn't right. "What's happened?"

Adam finally found his voice. "Sechem alerted me that Kate was seen on one of her journeys. She must get away from here. Now!"

"So why aren't you telling her this?"

"Nobody knows I'm here, Jacob. I daren't go to Kate's house. They're watching it."

Jacob poured him a whisky. Adam took it with shaking fingers.

"I've never seen you so agitated before," Jacob said.

"I've never been in love before," Adam admitted. "It changes everything."

Jacob's eyes twinkled – he was delighted for them – but before he was about to comment he heard a car pull up and froze.

Jacob peered out of the window. "It's all right, it's Kate." He opened the door and she walked in. Her face lit up when she saw Adam.

"Oh Adam, you're back," she spontaneously hugged him and kissed his lips, not caring what anyone thought. He returned her warmth ten-fold. "But why are you here at Dad's?" she asked looking into his eyes, drinking in the reality of him.

"Kate, my darling, listen. Adam has something to tell you," Jacob said.

"No, me first. What I have to tell you is important. I recorded my latest journey. Don't you think that's clever!" Kate placed her mobile phone on the table and switched it on. "Listen to this. I took this one alone." She sat down and pressed the play button.

Adam groaned and tried to speak but Kate held up her hand to stop him.

"Listen!"

The two men sighed and listened. Static came through at first, then her voice clear and firm.

"I'm in a very broad concrete tunnel. The air is extremely fresh and unusually sweet. Fragrance of apples? There's a rush of it, like a gentle breeze. Something's powering it or there wouldn't be a slight draught.

"I'm here as myself. Oh, surprise! There's some sort of rail track off to one side. I can't see any carriages, but a rail track clearly means transport. If I take my mind and see myself at the end of the track I won't need to walk it. So, I just think of destination and in the blink of an eye, I'm there. Some vehicles, like capsules are sitting there. I see seats inside, through the transparent walls. There's a door. I must go through. What am I supposed to do here?

As usual I get a response to the question. The voice tells me I'm to make notes for future reference. The tunnels go in all directions and are firmly anchored to the sea floor. So, we are under the sea?

Kate's voice changes on the tape as she speaks in the voice of her guide.

'Yes. This has to be firmly anchored; otherwise it would be at the mercy of the elements. We can't have that.'

"When you say, *we*, who are you referring to?"

'There's a combination of us here – those who wish for preservation, and those who would choose these places purely for secretive reasons. It's a combination, a mix. Nothing is cut and dried, black or white.'

"That's intriguing. So, what am I doing here?"

'As we said, you are observing and noting. Look around you.'

"Oh, another surprise. Flags of different nations are painted on the wall depicting a truly international affair. This is not just American, Russian, English, Chinese or French. There are a whole lot of national flags. An occasional flag denotes a religion too. So, the various religions have come together on this as well. This can't be a bad thing, surely?"

The voice says, 'All things have two sides to them. We wait to see what happens when they are challenged. When there is a need for this facility, what then? How will each nation or creed react? Will it be for the benefit of all, or for their own particular interest? That is the big question. It's a big question on the surface as well. Do people really come together, or do they look out for their own and disregard the others when a crisis comes?'

"That's not a question I can answer. Time will tell I suppose."

'Yes, time will tell. It would benefit everybody if they were to pull together and not consider just their own particular sector. That would be the ideal.'

"You could get lost down here, it's quite a labyrinth."

'If you look closely, you'll see arrows and signs pointing the way to various parts, like an underground train station where you have maps of where you are and how to get to where you want to be. We're not too deep, so the pressure is not much of an issue. We know you're thinking of water pressure. We've taken that into account. We are not so deep where it would cause a problem, but deep enough.'

'We feel your thoughts, and you were thinking, what if the air above is contaminated in some way. How then can we breathe air down here? The answer is that we have incorporated a filter system, which is similar to how you use gasmasks. Air is being ducted down and filtered so that when it arrives to be breathed in, it is pure. Some would say purer than the natural air above, when it is not polluted of course.

'We hope and pray that it will never be needed. It's a safeguard, a contingency plan should your governments, those in power do what they appear to be intent on doing.'

"Why are you showing me this?"

'So that you can promote the fact that we really do have the interest of your planet and the human species at heart. We do not wish to see you destroy each other. That is why we are showing you this. You have now witnessed it. You are a witness for the record.'

"How many know about this?"

'Quite a few. Obviously, those who are invested in this and those who have arranged it.'

"What about the public? How many in the public arena know of this?"

'Only a few. Naturally it is not common knowledge.'

"I feel that's quite enough. Thank you for bringing me here."

Kate switched off the recording. Total silence followed.

"Well say something, do," she implored. This was not the reaction she'd expected. Kate looked from one to the other, noting their grim faces.

Adam turned to Jacob. "*That* was why then."

"Oh, for heaven's sake, tell me what's going on."

"You'd better sit down and have a drink," Adam said. Kate did as she was told. Clutching her glass, she steeled herself to hear what could be serious news.

"Kate, listen, you have to pack up and leave at once. Adam found out something in the US that makes it imperative that you go. Adam, explain it to her please." His expression brooked no contradiction.

Adam took a deep breath and took Kate's trembling hand in his. "First of all, as you know, I am what you'd call a 'spook' in that I work for intelligence, infiltrating covert operations concerned with space projects."

"Yes, I remember you saying," replied Kate said, thinking: *As if I'd forget that, I think about you all the time.* If either of them picked that up, they ignored it.

"I was recruited because of my abilities to see and feel what others cannot. As you yourself know, anybody who is an experiencer, that is, had contact with space beings, has an increased psychic ability. It was discovered that I had this ability. I could communicate with the planetary beings at special facilities, unknown to the public but known to the military. I was told about you and asked to locate and recruit you. You were popping up everywhere on the psychic screen. My bosses thought you could be useful to them." He paused, gulping the rest of his whiskey down in one go.

"You were just using me?" Kate's voice rose and snatched her hand away from his.

"No, no, it wasn't like that," he protested. "First of all, I care deeply for you."

"Well, why don't you just show it sometimes!" she demanded, a surge of anger colouring her words. "I've had to deal with so much on my own, and you're supposed to be helping me."

"I am always helping you, darling," he said. "Always."

A glimmer of a smile reached her lips and the tension in his face relaxed.

"Get on with it!" hissed Jacob.

"Kate, what they didn't know – but of course I did, given our heritage

– is that you are a hybrid and work for the Galactic Command. You could never, ever work alongside the secret government, and since you haven't joined them, they're keen to suppress your activities."

"Yes, I guessed that from the abduction," Kate replied. "But why should I listen to them now?"

"Well, that last trip, the one you mentioned just now, was too close to what they want kept secret. To them you're a loose cannon. To put it bluntly, they definitely don't want you proclaiming to all and sundry what you have just learnt. Many don't know they have a choice to make, or know of the contingency plans in place, like bunkers." Adam sighed.

"So, why do I have to leave?"

"They're not now satisfied with just monitoring and frightening you. They want to stop you altogether," he said grimly.

"How?" she asked.

"Don't be naive. You know what happens to those who get too close," he retorted.

Kate gulped. "Oh. I see...Well, I'll certainly be glad to leave that hell hole at work."

Jacob cut in. "Don't you realise, my darling, that as you talk about these things, you're changing people's minds, their opinions and attitudes. You're galvanising them into action. Little sparks igniting a bigger fire and momentum is gathering. Think of all those e mails Poppy got."

Kate frowned. She knew that her talks were being shared worldwide now, thanks to Poppy and her genius with information technology. She'd noticed even the media was changing its attitude towards extra-terrestrials. The dismissive 'little green men' phrase had been swapped for 'space visitors' in much of the coverage, and the negative judgments had become much more balanced. Not just in her local paper, but national broadsheets too. Her message had begun to spread far and wide and had gathered momentum, even without her input. She was certainly on the radar now.

"You have done what Sechem and Master M asked of you, but in doing so, you're now in the firing line," Jacob warned. "You have to lie low."

"It's just seems so drastic. Where would I go?"

"I can't tell you that right now but I have a plane standing by, ready and waiting," Adam replied. "I think it's too dangerous for you to go home and collect your things."

"A plane? Good grief. How long am I going for? And what about the bills and mortgage, how will they get paid if I'm not there?" said Kate.

"My darling, you might never come back to your old life," explained Jacob gently. "I'm coming too," he added. "I couldn't let you go on your own."

That stopped Kate in her tracks. "This is for real, isn't it? I'm in mortal danger."

"You are. Adam's right, you have to leave for your own safety."

But Kate pulled a face.

"Hold on. Not so fast. I have a few questions before I turn my life upside down. First of all, where are you going to take me, without even a toothbrush to my name? If it's abroad, won't I need my passport? Or won't I be going through the usual passport control?"

Adam sighed in frustration. "Kate. Don't you trust me? Time is running out. We have to act now. Right now!"

Kate turned to Adam. "You're working as a spy, a spook. Why should I trust you? What if you're discovered? What happens to us then? You work in the States, you're never here. And I certainly don't want to go there. How do I know you won't take me to one of the secret bases, like at Groom Lake?"

"I wouldn't do that." Adam shook his head. "You'll have to trust me at some point. Look, we want you. We, The Galactic Command have recruited you. You know that. That's where my loyalty lies, you know that."

That did it. Kate exploded. "So, this is what it's all about? This is all it has ever been about, isn't it? Recruiting me?"

Jacob had been looking at his watch and listening in silence, but at last he could hold it no longer.

"Damn it girl! The man loves you. He told me himself. You *have* to listen to him."

A log burst into flame in the fireplace, sending out sparks all over the carpet. They all turned their attention to damping them down, giving Kate time to draw breath as she took in what Jacob had said. She stared at Adam, willing him to say something, anything.

"It's true, Katie. I love you. You are my first priority, which is why I'm here now, risking my life to save yours, for God's sake. If my absence is noted from work, then sparks will fly, just like they have here."

Kate laughed, despite herself.

"And Dad can come too?"

"Yes, of course" he said, smiling. "I wouldn't hurt either of you for the world. Now will you two kindly hurry up. I can feel them coming."

Kate beamed, her face lighting up like a diamond, but after a beat Jacob said,

"Into Adam's car, now!"

They ran through the pouring rain to the waiting vehicle. They barely had time to shut the doors before Adam was powering down the road and drove to her house to collect her things. She threw what she thought she'd need into a suitcase.

"We must hurry," Jacob said. "I feel them coming."

Jacob glanced back down the street as they drove off and saw several black limousines draw up to her house. They'd cleared out just in time. He wondered how long it would be before they could return, if ever.

As they turned left to get to the main arterial road, two black sedans with blacked-out windows turned right into their lane.

"That's them," whispered Adam. "Hold tight." He wrenched on the steering wheel and ploughed into the traffic dodging oncoming cars like a lunatic, his hand on the horn blaring for everyone to get out of the way. But before they knew it, he turned off, down a side road and through a maze of residential streets, constantly checking his mirrors. He was trying to outmanoeuvre their tail.

"Can't see them," said Kate, looking out of the back window. "Where are we going."

"There's a small private airfield on Salisbury plain, ex-military. It's one I've been using to get to Heathrow quickly for my flights to Washington. There's a small plane waiting there for us. When we get there, just make a run for it, okay. They're not far behind, I'm sure."

CHAPTER TWENTY-EIGHT

SPACE TRIP

In less peaceful times, interact with others and put into practice the solutions you have found within yourself. Know that *both* these opposite experiences are of major importance throughout your journey.

The Universal Brotherhood

Adam raced through the rolling countryside at great speed and made it to the airfield without mishap. He flashed his credentials at each check point, and they were whisked through in no time at all.

"You really do have some clout, don't you, Colonel?" Kate said, impressed. "I'll never doubt you again," she said, squeezing his arm.

He flicked a flirty smile at her.

A small Cessna Citation Mustang waited for them on the tarmac. They climbed aboard in the pelting rain.

"You know, all this excitement is making me hungry," Jacob said, once inside. "I hope we're going to be fed?"

"Don't worry," the pilot said, "provisions are already waiting for you."

Without further ado, the plane taxied onto the runway and in minutes, they were airborne. At last, they could relax.

"That was a close call," said Adam. "But actually, I don't think they were on to us. I think we lost them." He grinned.

"You lost them you mean!" Kate replied. "Thank you, Adam. I know I can be a bit demanding sometimes, but thank you." She kissed his cheek, but he pulled her to him, needing to prove that he meant every word of what he said. He did love her."

Jacob grunted, and looked out of the window at the blackening sky, munching his smoked salmon panini with relish.

By the time the pilot was preparing to land at Tingwall in Lerwick, they had all nodded off into a deep sleep, Kate with her head resting on Adam's shoulder, he with his arm around her.

When they touched down, Kate readied herself for what was to come. The flight had been a brief but delightful respite from the reality of her situation. She stepped out of the plane and stared at the desolate landscape.

"Welcome to the Shetland Isles," Adam held her arm protectively. The hills were still covered in snow and the chill wind whistled over the sparse scrubland around them.

"A far cry from Dorset," she commented dryly.

"Don't worry, this is just for starters," Adam said and guided them to a waiting car which whisked them away from the airfield and into the countryside.

Two hours later they drew up in front of a stone cottage. A low wall skirted a rundown front garden, and a scattering of sheep munched on scrubby grass. Apart from a few trees and seagulls swooping and diving in the semi-darkness there wasn't much to see. It was getting too dark to take a look around, but Kate saw the cottage was high above the sea, and she could just hear the sound of waves crashing on a beach.

"Let's get you inside and settled comfortably," Adam said as he carried their bags inside. Kate heard in his words the inference that he could not stay with them. She stepped into the front room and was pleased to see that somebody had lit a roaring fire to keep them warm. She held her hands to it to warm away the chill, then turned to toast her back and take in the room. The rough stone walls had been rendered and painted white, and small embroidered pictures hung at regular intervals. Someone had made an effort to make it homely. A wooden table, its top scrubbed smooth by years of cleaning, stood in one corner with four wooden chairs around it. The cottage was basic but cosy.

"I'm sorry, but I have to leave you for a bit – things to arrange," said Adam. Won't be long." He deposited the bags, then he kissed Kate firmly on the lips as if to say, 'No questions', and drove off.

Kate sighed. "Fine, let's see what we have." She explored the cottage and found two simple but clean bedrooms. The tiled bathroom was surprisingly large for such a small cottage and boasted an old cast-iron bath with clawed feet. Kate's shoulders and back were aching from being so on edge for so long, and she hoped there would be enough hot water to have a long soak. She wondered if she should be letting herself relax, though, was she safe? The kitchen, like the rest of the cottage, had all the basic necessities — simple and functional, in tune with a country cottage style — and the larder had been fully stocked. Kate wondered who else they'd hidden away here before them.

"No television, no phones, no wi-fi, no signal – we're completely cut off here," Jacob observed when she returned to the main room. He stood warming his back at the fire like she had. "What have you got us into, Katie?" he asked, with a twinkle.

Kate remained quiet. Although she knew he was teasing, their predicament was all because of her mind journeys, and she felt responsible. Guidance, that's what she needed. Guidance and reassurance.

"No bugs to search for here, Dad," she said. "Why don't we see what Master M, Sechem and Jamère, are up to? It is about time they put in an appearance, don't you think? After all, they're supposed to be looking after us."

When Kate spoke next, it was in Master M's voice, surprising even Jacob at the ease with which she now connected to both dimensions.

"'Transmission about to begin. Master M here. Are you listening? We understand you've had quite a time of it lately.'

"You could say that again," Kate retorted, in her own voice.

'Say that again? Why should we repeat? I don't understand you.' Master M said.

"Oh, forget it. What do you have to tell us?" Jacob said as he recovered from hearing his daughter speak in a man's voice.

'How are you? A lot has happened since we last communicated. We are quite prepared for the changes happening now.'

Kate said, "What do you mean by changes? I thought it was us on Earth that had to be prepared, not you."

'We are affected by everything you do down there. Don't you know that? The irresponsibility of those in charge of your planet puts us all in danger. We would have to pick up the pieces, so to speak. Changes! Oh yes, changes.'

"Master M have you been drinking? You don't seem quite yourself."

'Drinking? Me? Never. It must be the strange cosmic rays flooding through the energy field that the solar system is in right now. It affects everything, even us. We are in flux just as you are on Earth. The Galactic Council's negotiations have reached crisis point and it could go either way. Either the forces for good will win, or Earth will continue to spiral downwards, as it has been doing.'

His voice had grown a little blurry and indistinct by the end.

"Master M? Are you all right?"

'Yes, I'm fine – well the cosmic rays flooding through the energy field that the solar system is in right now are getting to me, but I can manage. Solar Cycle 24 affects everything, even us. I will pull myself together.'

Kate dimly remembered reading about Solar Cycle 24 – the activity of the sun and its electro-magnetic field. It only just occurred to her that of course anyone in a spaceship would be in range of the cosmic waves too. Even if they were stationed on a Node in a mother ship they might be affected. It was obviously a massively powerful wave to impact even the mighty Master M. Then she remembered the mind travel when she learnt about how the Earth was due to be reconditioned. She wondered if this was connected. It was time to have some refreshment after which she would connect.

A little later they sat in front of the blazing fire and waited for Kate to trance.

Suddenly he reappeared in her mind, and she let him speak through her so Jacob could hear.

"'Master M here, back loud and clear. The changes on your planet have started already. The changes on your planet are to come about in a variety of ways. The changes you feel to be the most obvious are not the ones to look out for. Let us explain. First of all, there will most certainly be a change as a result of a cosmic body nearby. This does not mean catastrophe, simply disturbance and upheaval. Have you noticed how people are no longer willing to accept the status quo? That will create a certain amount of chaos, while people re-stabilise and re-establish order.

'What will happen then, will be diverse, in respect of the thinking and subsequent behaviour of the peoples. You might say there will be division. There will be those who prefer to continue to think in heavy, demeaning ways. Others will prefer to focus their light in a better manner for all, even if it involves sacrifice, which it will in many cases. The end result will be separation into two time lines. It's not as clear cut as you might think. The most important thing is to decide which side you wish to be on. Shouldn't be too difficult, should it?

'People are rising up and demanding justice for all. This is excellent, and a direct result of your work. You introduced them to the concept of star beings, and opened their minds to a new way of thinking. Just as they have become receptive to the existence of aliens, and even welcomed them, they have become alert to their own potential, in a positive way. This has trickled down into the collective consciousness, and the immense electro-magnetic activity of Solar Cycle 24 is reinforcing it, cementing it in their minds. People have become aware that they can make a difference, they no longer need to be passive victims. They have realised that it's their Earth, they need to look after it. Not just for them but for the whole galaxy.'

"Oh, but that's wonderful," interjected Kate in her normal voice.

"Extraordinary. Well done, Kate, I knew you could do it," Jacob said. "Does this mean she doesn't need to go on her mind travels anymore?" he asked M.

'No, there is still work to be done. Unfortunately, there are still dark forces that want to sabotage all this good work. But only one mind travel is possible until this electro-magnetic waveband passes. It is very strong just now.

Kate go ahead and tell him,' Master M said.

"Okay," said Kate. "I'm on a pad, larger than a helicopter pad, but like a take-off platform. There are people standing around. Older thick-set, white-robed people. They remind me of big Russians.

They're all in white and have long white hair, almost albino white, not even grey, no colour at all. What are they waiting for? They're standing around in little groups expecting something. A shaft of energy comes down over me and onto the open space around me. You can't see through the shaft. It's like dust particles in a beam of sunlight, and the particles are agitating, like dancing molecules. They're moving rapidly in the column. There's an opening in the shaft, and I step out of it. I'm walking along, but not on anything solid. There's nothing around me. Somebody's waiting up ahead, somebody unlike anything or anybody I've ever seen before. I'm going towards him."

Master M stepped in and said, 'It's been arranged. It's the link between you and them. They're not like you. You wouldn't recognise them in the form they're in now. There's a lot I mustn't say to you.'

"I feel I'm merely being used here. Their eyes are strange," Kate said.

"What's this all about?" Jacob asked, concerned.

Master M replied, 'It's a precursor of an experience that is coming. Kate's mind is being prepared so it can cope with an enormous task…'

The sound of a car pulling up on the gravel road outside alerted Jacob. He had time to bring Kate back gradually, so she wouldn't be damaged by whoever was arriving. The time they'd forgotten to unplug the telephone before had given Kate a swift return from a deep place and it had given her a bad jolt.

The car door slammed. "That must be Adam," said Kate excitedly.

Jacob opened the front door to see a uniformed man. Disappointment washed over Kate.

"May I come in, sir? It's blooming freezing out here," the man said. Jacob stood aside and let him pass. "Oh, that's better. Any tea going?"

"A man after my own heart, I see," Jacob said. "But first . . ." his eyes narrowed, "can you tell us who you are and why are you here?"

"Yes, sir. Sorry sir." The man almost saluted, but apparently thought better of it. He seemed unsure of his position. "Hello, I have a message from Colonel Fenshawe. He has been called away. He says to tell you not to worry about him. I've brought provisions for a week, Sir, and Miss, and a change of clothes for you both. I hope they fit..." He turned to Kate. She sat still, like stone.

The man stood erect and alert. "You are to wait until he comes back," he added.

"Permission to sit, sir?"

Jacob shook himself. "Where are my manners? Of course, please do, and no need to call me sir."

The man took a chair and immediately appeared more relaxed, though his posture remained upright.

"What's your name?" Jacob asked. "It's a long drive to get here, we know."

"It's Jim. No rank to be given. Orders."

Jacob turned to Kate. "Would you like some tea, darling?"

She nodded bleakly, not yet over her disappointment at the visitor not being Adam.

Jim relaxed in the warmth of the fire, but Kate remained silent and focused on her thoughts, whist Jacob busied himself with tea for them all. He turned to Jim. "After your tea you'd better unload those provisions you talked about. Then it might be wise to stay the night. It's much too late to drive all that way back at this late hour. You can sleep on the couch."

"Thank you. That's very kind of you."

Kate smiled; comforted by Jacob taking charge.

Next morning they awoke to discover that Jim had folded his bedclothes neatly and left before they'd surfaced. Adam had said it was only for starters, but a week of sitting around was more than enough in Kate's view. They were in the middle of nowhere.

CHAPTER TWENTY-NINE

THE CUSTODIAN

Friends upon the Earth are we,
who wish to share the Earth with thee.
Join with us in our joy
and use the methods we employ
To unite us all as one great Soul,
To bring us back into the Whole.
We are all of one Divine Creation,
All worlds and every nation.
We are not meant to be apart.
Unite with us with loving heart.

ET Osishoo

Their first day dawned bright but was a bit chilly. Kate wrapped up warmly and stepped outside to explore. Seagulls wheeled overhead, squawking.

"Come and see, Dad," she called. "We're close to the sea, and it is breathtakingly beautiful, quite different to Dorset. There's a little path leading down to the beach." Kate turned and scanned the countryside. "Look! There's smoke over there. We're not as isolated as we thought. There must be some houses around." It was comforting to know people were nearby.

"I'd like to know how long we'll be stuck here," Jacob said, his breath pluming in front of him in the cold air. "Let's go in and have a coffee." He turned and went back inside.

Three days went by with no news from any quarter. So much had happened over the last few months, and now here they were, miles away from everyone with no clue as to what was ahead of them. Worst of all there was still no news of Adam. Not a word. Still, not having to go to the dreaded office and face that numbskull Marco was a relief, and actually, wasn't this a bit like a holiday? The only difference being they didn't know where they would be going next. Kate thought of her little house, Number Six, and of Poppy and all the connections she'd made in her life in Dorset. She'd been happy there, but she knew that life was in the past. Kate passed the time slipping and sliding down the steps to the beach and taking the long climb up again. At least it was keeping her fit. She wondered if her mother missed her and doubted it.

Over lunch on an overcast day Kate said, "Dad, shall we try to contact Master M or Sechem again tonight?"

"What about Jamère? Doesn't he get a look in now?" Jacob chuckled. "We could do with his humour."

Kate grinned. "True."

"Okay, but we don't know if the electro-magnetic field or whatever it's called has passed. I suppose the only way to find out is to try."

So, that evening they settled down to wait for contact. In spite of a howling gale tearing at everything outside, indoors the roaring fire kept them warm and cosy. After entering her trance, Kate felt an extremely high vibration coming in, and to their surprise, instead of Master M announcing himself, a completely new voice made its presence. Kate sat up straight and listened intently.

"'I am extra-celestial Azeus, The Custodian," he announced, his voice booming through Kate's vocal chords. 'We wrap your Earth, indeed your entire Solar System in our protective colour and energy field," the Custodian continued. 'We acknowledge the work done by the Ascended Masters, The Universal Brotherhood and by so many on your planet. They and you are a powerful conduit to channel the positive energies of humans. It is with this acknowledgement that we have decided that your Solar System will upgrade, to use a modern term, and be elevated into a greater family within your galaxy, and within the greater part of the Universe, for which I am responsible.

'We are custodians to ensure that those of good will and good intent continue and are encouraged. At the same time, we take care of those who still have some way to go in their growth. Those particular groups and individuals we will allocate to other planetary bodies, more suited and more comfortable to their energies. It is dispersal, a reordering of those who are not suitable to your new Earth.'

'We can divert harmful magnetic influences from your planet and have done this several times already in your history. Be aware that our energies are strong. We can quite easily divert what is known as a solar ejection. However, we do allow some ejections to take place when this is for the good of the planet. They are for recharging Earth's energetic field and its magnetic and gravitational force. Although at times it is uncomfortable, some solar ejections are necessary for the planet. Human beings may feel the effect of this.

'Do not worry about mood changes. We know you have them. We work with many who are aware of us. There is no need for reverence, merely acceptance of the different roles we play in your Universe. Many give us names just to satisfy their need for understanding. We do not mind, but it limits the mind because you restrict yourselves to your own conceptions. Think big and you will be big. Think small and you will be small.'"

Jacob dared to ask a question. "I'm interested in why, when an off-world being or space visitor is seen they're usually wearing silver suits, at least the humanoid ones do. Even Kate on her visits to other worlds sometimes wears a silver suit. What's the reason?"

'That's a good, sensible question. Silver suits are worn as protection against the various radiations that come from many other species that visit the mother ships, the way stations. Not everyone is compatible with those radiations, so the suits protect them and they can intermingle. This is also applicable when we meet humans on Earth. It is a protection on all sides, very similar to your astronauts' suits, which are very bulky.

'Regarding the new Earth, your own behaviour and actions will position you with like-minded souls who also behave in a similar fashion to yourselves. You will never be alone or singular, for the whole purpose is to bring unity. There are several levels depending on the quality of vibration and status of soul. If through actions you have achieved an advanced state of vibration and a purer level of thinking then you may ascend into a higher state. You will be grouped with others who have achieved the same degree.'

Jacob was buzzing with more questions but forced himself to remain quiet.

Azeus carried on through Kate. "With those who are resistant to change, or who do not comport themselves in a loving manner to others, or who deliberately damage others, then their vibration will hold them into a separate grouping. They will not feel alone for they will be surrounded by similar-minded souls. Each level will be totally unaware of the other levels, each in their own time frame. In your present time frame, there are many different levels of being, such as those who are speaking to you and others who are operating at a lower level.

'The purpose of our interaction is to engage each and every soul no matter where level they are at, to raise them to a higher state. The higher states will be varied. What you might consider to be a high level would be different to what another might consider to be high.

Quite a task, is it not? We wish them to continue and so they will.

'It is a difficult concept for those on Earth to realise that levels and states of being all occur at the same time. Currently there is a mishmash of those who are not operating very well, and those who are operating beautifully. It is a time of great transition. With this evolution you may have a slightly different form to the one you have now. You already have a different form to early man, more upright, with a different capacity of brain. Your facial features may change. Earth will be a different place.

'We are concerned with the soul that takes on the form. The soul will always continue and embody a form that it likes, that it wishes to and chooses to have. It is the soul that makes its form.'

Jacob took a sideways glance at the fire hoping it would last. "Another question please," Jacob asked after a prolonged spell of silence though the energy of Azeus the Custodian was still strong and filled the room. "Will ET races show themselves en masse soon, and will they be accepted by humans?"

"'They are already showing themselves in many areas of importance, areas that should have some effect in the running of your world. They have not been secluding themselves to the extent that you might believe. Soon they will be doing much more. Even those of you who find it difficult to accept their presence will have to acknowledge them. It may take some adjustment, but they will soon settle down. Greater numbers will be arriving, and will be more noticeable than the previous visitors. We wouldn't come where it would cause chaos. We are fortunate in that we are able to assess an area beforehand, before we make a decision to appear or not. We try to be kind and gentle wherever we can.

'It is difficult for your governments to silence entire populations or to deny them privileges, or whatever it is they do to individuals. It would be difficult for them to do that to whole towns, would it not? So mass showing is important. It will be soon, sooner than you can imagine.

We are looking forward to it.'"

A torrent of extra-terrestrial language burst forth from Kate's mouth and sent ripples of energy throughout her body. She laughed with sheer delight and Jacob smiled cautiously.

The Custodian continued. "'As Kate knows, life is to be enjoyed. We aim to improve the experience of existence, through humour, pleasure and joy. The end result is always up to you, if you are receptive to it. Whether you enhance your quality, or whether you degrade your quality, it is always up to you.'"

The energy of Azeus the Custodian faded from the room.

Kate stretched and rubbed her eyes. They were always the hardest part of her body to return to normal, as if they'd gone elsewhere.

"Well that certainly wasn't Master M, Jamère or Sechem, was it?" Jacob said looking at Kate.

She shook her head. "I miss those three," she said. "That was the most powerful energy I've ever felt. It was hard to stay focused. But what incredible things he was saying! It's lovely to hear that the impact of my talks reached even the Guardians of the Solar System. And what about this division on Earth? It sounds a bit too much like apartheid to me."

"That's what I thought too, although it's probably because we don't understand the concept properly. I trust him and believe him when he said he wanted the best for us so we'll just have to wait and see."

"I trusted him too. It wasn't just his words, but his energy too. It was just so… good. It was profoundly good. I feel like I've been in the presence of a god or something…"

Kate shivered and Jacob bent down to pick up a log stacked by the side of the fire and throw it on the dying embers. Kate gazed into the fire as the new flames started to lick around the log. "I can't wait until our space visitors make themselves known to us on Earth," she said, her eyes shining. "It's going to rock the world more than all my talks put together." Her thoughts turned to Adam, as they so often did. She imagined the future and hoped that it included him. She willed that their vibrations were the same so they wouldn't be separated. She loved him so much she felt sure that they must be.

CHAPTER THIRTY

HIDDEN IN PLAIN SIGHT

'Make haste and act before it is too late. Give of your best in all things, with hope and trust in a perfect outcome. Now is *not* the time for sitting and waiting in spite of all you have been told. Complete your unfinished projects and step forth. **Now** is the time for action.'

A Spirit Guide

The next morning dawned bright and clear with a pale blue sky. The air had an unexpected and unseasonal warmth to it, which made Kate feel alive and so much more positive. Azeus' incredible energy was still rippling around her and she felt impatient for something to happen. It was difficult to stay so far from the action in this remote cottage.

"I'm going for a walk," she called out to Jacob. "I won't be long." She took some binoculars and set off to a viewpoint she'd discovered a day before, a place where she could see the bay and the occasional fishing vessel setting out to sea. After a short walk, accompanied by seagulls crying to each other and the sound of the waves gently breaking on the shingle beach down below, she felt at peace with the world. She was grateful she was far from Helga and her cronies and men in black cars. She breathed a sigh of satisfaction.

When she reached the cliffs she stood and scanned the bay. After a moment the powerful lenses honed in on something out on the horizon. What was that? A whale? A fishing boat? No… it was moving too fast. Her heart jolted with fear as she realised it was a motor boat, heading directly for the beach. She adjusted the binoculars to zoom in closer. There, standing and looking her way, were Helga with Silas and Marco behind her. There was no mistaking them. How on earth did they know where she was? Helga raised her binoculars to her eyes and trained them back on Kate.

Oh my God! Kate scrambled to her feet and ran back to the cottage. The boat still had to land and then there were the steep steps to the cottage. That would give her and Jacob some time. But where would they go? They had no car, not even a telephone to call for help.

She burst into the cottage where Jacob stood fully dressed and waiting.

"You forget, my darling, I too have the sight," he said. "We must get away quickly."

"Where can we go?" gasped Kate, breathless from running.

"Into the trees for a start. Then we'll head for the village and find somewhere to hide." They set off at a run. Kate soon heard her Dad's laboured breathing and it grew rapidly worse. They wouldn't be going anywhere fast, that was sure.

"Look, it's you they want, not me," Jacob bent over trying to catch his breath. "You go on. Leave me here."

"Stop trying to be the hero," Kate retorted, angry at him, but she heard the stress in his voice. She could also hear the strident voices of the boat party getting closer.

"No, I let you down as a child, I'm not going to let you down now," he said firmly, standing stock-still.

"Dad, I love you. I always have and I always will. Come on, I'm not going without you!" She grabbed her father's arm and held on tight. There was no way she was going to leave without him. They ran on, looking around desperately for somewhere to hide.

Kate became aware of a soft humming noise coming from above, then a shadow was cast over them. She and Jacob looked up. Her jaw dropped, and Jacob let out a low whistle. Above them in an aura of blue light, two glowing counter-rotating rings spun at incredible speeds. Unbidden came a memory from one of her mind-travels: 'This is one of ours'. The spinning disc glowed white, and Kate marvelled at the brightness and beauty of it. It settled slowly on the snow a dozen or so feet away.

"Come forward." Kate heard in her head. It was a voice she recognised, but because it was coming from a spaceship, she couldn't quite pin it down. Whose was it?

She took a tentative step and Jacob moved forward with her, so she assumed he'd heard it too. She held on to his arm as they ran. An opening appeared as they drew close. Jacob stopped a few steps away and shook his head. "Leave me here, they want you, not me."

Kate looked at him. "Dad, for God's sake! I'm not going without you, and I have to go inside, so you do too. This is one of ours. I can feel it. You do too, don't you?" She glanced behind.

She yelled, "Dad!" and he looked behind too.

Helga, Silas and Marco had reached the top of the steps and were running towards them, shouting. Helga's face was thunderous, she was pointing a gun at them.

Kate and Jacob ran up the ramp. She pushed him inside and fell in behind him. The entrance closed silently. She heard gunfire.

They sprawled on the floor of a dome-shaped room with a central seating area. Around them was an enormous screen filled with stars, like a planetarium. A control panel of lights flashed as they lifted off. It was an incredible feeling – like that you get when a lift first starts to ascend, only magnified a thousand-fold. It was amazing!

One of the seats by the control panel swivelled around and to their enormous surprise, Adam was sitting there.

"Did you really think I would abandon you?" he said with a grin. "You should see the looks on your faces!" He pressed a button and the screen changed to the view below. As the spaceship ascended, they could make out Helga, Silas and Marco, astonishment and fury mingled on their upturned faces.

Kate opened her mouth, but nothing came out. Disbelief left her at a loss for words. She helped her father up from the floor and towards a seat.

"This is just amazing! Thank you, thank you so much. How did you know?" Jacob asked Adam. Then the adrenalin, exhaustion and stress caught up with him and he broke down in tears.

Kate put her arms around him and gave him a big hug. "It's alright now, Dad. We're safe." She turned to Adam and playfully beat him with her fists. "So, Captain Kirk, you didn't tell me you could fly a spaceship! And where've you been all this time?" Although she was trying to look strong, her eyes were brimming with tears too.

Adam put his arms around her and held her tight. Then she collapsed, all her pent-up emotions finally bursting loose. He held her until she stopped crying. She dried her eyes on her sleeve and looked up at him, sniffling. "Well?" she said. "Any chance of an explanation?"

"Some thanks I get. I've been putting myself at risk, pulling strings and making excuses for my absence at work. They were getting suspicious, and I couldn't risk getting caught. I still have a lot of work to do there. I couldn't tell you before, because it might have been detected." He smiled fondly. "You would've been thinking about what I was doing, and Helga would have picked it up in an instant. As it is she discovered your whereabouts. Have you still been blanking your mind to her?"

"I didn't think it was necessary here," Kate confessed.

"My goodness, Kate. You still don't realise that distance is no obstacle to remote viewing, do you?" Adam sighed in frustration.

Kate hung her head. It was true. She'd forgotten to put up her shield against Helga.

"I'm sorry – and thank you, Adam. From the bottom of my heart."

Kate looked around her. It was quite compact – she'd expected a spaceship to be larger for some reason.

"This is just a scout craft. It'll take you to our way station," Adam said, guessing her thoughts. "You call them Mother Ships. One of those is sitting in a Node 165,000 miles from Earth, in an orbit in neutral gravity between Earth, the Moon and other planets."

Kate nodded, suddenly too tired to even think. Now she was safe, and Adam was guiding her and her father away from Helga, she could allow herself to let her guard down. The trauma of the day had taken it out of her. She sank onto one of the seats and nodded off, lulled by the gentle hum of the spacecraft.

All too soon she was being gently woken by Adam. Jacob sat in the chair next to her, rubbing his eyes. It looked like he'd also dropped off to sleep. Adam stood in front of her, dressed head to toe in a silver suit.

"Here, put these on," he said and handed them each a silver suit of their own. "You'll need them. They help protect against radiation – remember like in that mind travel you went on?"

Kate nodded. "I thought it was a strange question for Dad to ask, at the time, but now it makes sense." She slipped out of her coat and pulled the suit over her jeans and T-shirt, while the big screen showed them docking with a ship so large that it took up the whole picture. Kate watched Adam at the controls, impressed by his calm demeanour. Her respect for him grew enormously.

"I'm excited and nervous at the same time," she told him. "But it's odd," she said, "I didn't feel we were travelling at all. No movement."

"Earth itself can be considered a spaceship travelling around its star at 65,000 mph, and yet nobody feels that speed. It's the same when you're on board an aircraft."

"Of course, that makes sense."

The craft glided into the docking bay and the gentle whirring sound slowed and finally stopped. Kate clutched her father's hand as they waited for the door to open. Her stomach churned with apprehension. She'd never physically been on a Mother Ship before — at least not as far as she knew. It seemed a long way from her quiet street in Dorset.

Adam moved to the entrance and pressed a button beside the door. It slid silently to one side, and he stepped through. Kate and Jacob followed. Their jaws dropped in surprise, not just at a huge area full of disc-shaped scout craft, consoles and screens but at the beings in full splendour standing ready to greet them.

"Sechem, Jamère?" Kate said, gasping with delight. Seeing them 'in the flesh' was quite spectacular, their beautiful swirling colours and vibrant blue skin. The third being, who she'd guessed was Master M, wore a ground-length golden robe trimmed with white and turquoise, and a thin golden band circled the long dome of his head. All three towered above her.

"You're right, I am Master M," he replied. "Welcome to the Mother

Ship. We are so glad you could join us. We have much to do."

Kate gasped again, suddenly realising that Master M was none other than one of the visitors she'd played with as a child. A bird man. "But I've known you for years," she said. "You're Osishoo, at least that's the name you gave me then. Why didn't you tell me? Why say you're called Master M?"

"You're right, I did visit you when you were younger. I didn't reveal who I was because your enlightenment had to be a gradual process. A child's brain is very fragile, very malleable. We had to be careful how you remembered us. You have progressed so well that you are ready for most of the pieces to fall into place."

She looked back at Sechem and Jamère. "It's wonderful to see you again. You're real. You're solid," Kate exclaimed, trying to get her mind around seeing them in the flesh before her. "I'm so used to seeing you as a vision in blue. Sechem, you look so like a human being, I could pass you in the street and not know who you really are, except for your colouring of course. That would give you away. I don't think anyone has seen a blue skinned person before." She laughed in delight.

Master M waved his hand in the air. "But of course we're real. What did you think? That we only existed in spirit form? We were often holographic when we communicated with you down there." He indicated downwards with his long finger. He turned to Jacob. "And how nice to meet you again," he said, patting him warmly on the arm. "You have been so vital to our programme. Without your support of your daughter during her mind travels, much of the information would have been lost," he said. "You helped her process it."

"And you've kept her safe for us, too," Jamère added.

Kate smiled as these beautiful, stately creatures embraced her father. She turned to Adam and took his hand. "So, what's happening next? Where do we go from here?"

"Always questions! You're right, there's no time to waste," he replied with a smile. "Back down there the others are scratching their heads and wondering what they can do next. They haven't finished with us yet."

Jamère moved to her side. "Kate, we have a lot to teach you about the vibration of sound. Each sound we utter vibrates and activates the DNA, so it's important you speak all languages of space." He said this so seriously that she knew this would be no light task.

Sechem bubbled with laughter. "Oh, Jamère, don't put her off before she's even begun.

"I think we'd better get started straight away," Master M said. "We must hold a meeting at once. Time is running out. You can take those suits off now since we'll not have time for a tour of the ship this time. I'm sorry. I know you'll be disappointed, but there will be another opportunity later."

It took a short while for them to remove the suits, then Master M indicated they should follow him. He led them past people busy at their consoles to an oval table off to one side and gestured for them to sit. Large star charts covered the wall behind them.

"I feel it's better if you continue to call me Master M to avoid confusion," he said.

As she sat down opposite him she couldn't help but stare, fascinated by his appearance. His pharaoh-shaped head, huge eyes and sweeping nose; his mouth with lips like a soft beak. She felt quite overwhelmed.

Suppressing her emotions, Kate forced herself to focus. "So, what's to be done? How long will we be here?" she asked. "What's the urgency, and why is Helga so determined to get me out of the way? I've left my job so that should satisfy her, don't you think?"

Sechem drummed his fingers on the table, apparently impatient to respond, but he waited for the Master M.

Master M nodded at Sechem. "Go ahead. Lay it out for her please, before she asks any more questions. Or perhaps Adam would like to say something."

Adam glanced at Sechem for permission and Sechem nodded.

"The secret government have manufactured a new satellite that can mind-control from space, and they intend to use it. Orders for it have already been submitted. Think what that means." Adam looked around the table with a grim face. "Mind-control is already in use but it's not as widespread as it will be if this satellite makes it into orbit. Have you noticed how there's been such an upsurge of random, unspeakable cruelty amongst people in their own nations? Fathers inexplicably murdering their children? Shootings at schools and supermarkets? The government says it's terrorism, but it's not. And it's only going to get worse with this mind-controlling satellite. We have to do something and quickly."

"Helga is part of this, isn't she? So, the company I worked for is mind-controlling people?" Horrified, Kate looked from Master M to Sechem then back to Adam. They all nodded. "What can we do?"

"It's more a question of what you can do, Kate," Sechem said. "There's a lot of space junk surrounding your planet. Remember, one of your jobs was Space Traffic Control, making sure that our ships wouldn't crash into the debris that circles the same orbits? Well, we want you to make sure this particular satellite has a collision with a sizeable piece of space junk, making it inoperable." That took Kate's breath away. How would she be able to do that?

"You have done similar things before, deactivating nuclear weapons, for example," Jamère said.

"We can't do it. You know our rule," Master M said. "Changes must come from citizens of the Earth, or what we do is regarded as interference, and we're not allowed to do that. You'll have to do this back on Earth, not here in space."

Kate felt a wave of anxiety. "But what if I can't? What if they get to me before I manage it?"

Jacob reached over and patted her arm in reassurance. "Darling, don't worry, you can do this. We'll help you. Just see it as another of your mind journeys, but this time you know what you're going to do. All of your mind journeys may have been preparing you for this one."

Kate turned to Adam. "What about you, Adam? Will you be staying here or do you have to go back?"

"Oh, Kate," he sighed. "I do have to go back. If I'm missed, many more questions would be asked, and it could jeopardise the whole thing. Helga has no idea I was on the craft that rescued you."

"But where will we go?" Jacob asked, practical as usual. "We can't go back to our homes? When's this satellite due for launch? How much time do we have?"

"Sensible questions, Jacob." M replied. "We have about four days before it goes up."

"Four days?" Jacob looked staggered. "But where will we live, and what about Kate's job? What about our passports, our finances..." He started to pace up and down, like a distressed lion in a cage.

"Calm down, Jacob," Master M said. "It has all been taken care of. We have moved all your things and Kate's to a house near Aldermaston in Hampshire. No one knows your new address."

He turned to Kate. "Not even your mother Francine or Poppy. We've given them both a plausible reason for your absence, so they'll not seek you out. You will have to come to terms with that I'm afraid."

Kate frowned and her heart sank. “Is that forever?”

“Nothing is forever Kate.” Master M turned to Jacob.

“There is a place of work and an interesting job for Kate nearby. The papers on this are in the new house. She can take this up if she wishes and has one month to decide. Jacob, you are retired, but you may continue your mind-travel work as you have done in the past. One of us on the ground has arranged all this.”

“And you don’t call this interference?” Jacob exclaimed. He was rattled at how his life had been turned upside down and that he had no control over what’d happened or what was to happen.

Master M looked at him with sympathy. “I understand your feelings, but this is not interference, for you agreed to the process right at the start.”

Jacob grunted.

“When do we go?” Kate asked.

“Now,” came the surprising reply. “You will need time to adjust to your new surroundings, before you’re settled and calm enough to do what has to be done in four days’ time. We’ll be assisting you and we will put a shield around you when you do this work. Remember this satellite is capable of mind control, but only when directed by those on the ground. It’s imperative they do not know beforehand where you are. Kate, do not under any circumstances have a mind journey before this one. If you do, they could pick it up. Helga will be scanning for any sign of you so we’ll put an extra barrier in place against her. No contact please with family or friends, no matter how tempted to do this you may be.”

“Now you’re frightening me,” Kate said. “I hope I can do it.”

CHAPTER THIRTY-ONE

THE FINAL PUSH

'Look for the way forward. If you are looking you will see it. It is not at all hidden. Seek out the Wisdoms of the Ages which lie within you. If you look far enough, you will also see far into the future. All is the same, no past, no present and no future separation. It is all together in you.'

Erasmus

They returned to Earth at night in the woods near Aldermaston. Nobody saw the small space craft silently land, disembark its occupants and take off again immediately.

Kate looked at the car that waited to take them to their new home and gave a huge sigh. "I don't know if I'm up to this, Dad. It's dangerous ground."

"Think about the consequences of the mind-control satellite if you don't," he said. "You have no choice. Let's get in the car."

After a short drive, they arrived at their new home. Their driver handed them the house keys and wished them luck. A warm fire, flowers and a well-stocked fridge greeted them inside. There were no packing boxes; it appeared that all their belongings had been neatly put away.

"I don't understand it," Kate said. "How could they do all that in such a short time?"

"Remember, my darling, they had this planned from the moment we left Dorset," Jacob explained. "You forget that more time has passed here than where we've been."

Kate nodded and looked around her new home. Documents for the cars and credit cards in new surnames were stacked on the coffee table. It seems they were in a district of Tadley on the fringes of Aldermaston.

"I assume they've chosen Aldermaston because of the Atomic Weapons Establishment there," said Jacob. He glanced at his daughter and saw how drawn she looked. "You've got a big day coming up, you'd better go to bed."

"I don't know if I can sleep, but I'll try," replied Kate, finding her way to her bedroom. Despite her anxiety, after she climbed under the soft feather duvet she was asleep in an instant.

Kate woke to daylight streaming in through a crack in the curtains. It took a while to realise where she was and take in all that had happened in such a short space of time. She jumped out of bed and drew back the striped curtains and saw her bedroom looked out over a small garden. A jolt of adrenalin coursed through her as she remembered the huge task that lay ahead of her. She found the bathroom, quickly had a shower and got dressed. Going downstairs, she supposed she should have some breakfast first, to keep her energy up. Munching on muesli, she saw Jacob coming downstairs.

"Morning, sleep well?" he asked. "It's amazing! All my clothes are here and stacked neatly away."

"Yes thanks, surprisingly well. I'll be raring to go when I've finished this," replied Kate.

"That's good to hear, but remember there's another three days until the launch, there's not much we can do until then."

"Oh yes," said Kate, shoulders sagging. "I'd forgotten. What are we supposed to do until then?"

"I think we should have a stroll around the area if this is going to be our home," Jacob replied. "It'll be good to stretch our legs before the mission."

As they set off after breakfast, Kate discovered they were in Pinks Lane. "Such a lovely name," she commented. The road was lined with semi-detached houses and as they walked they discovered it was part of a larger estate with many cul-de-sacs branching off. They wandered along, discovering that the village had a charming stream meandering through it. They strolled by the side of it, taking in the pretty cottages alongside.

"They'd have a job kidnapping us from here without being noticed," she remarked to Jacob, who was puffing a bit at the exercise. "Shall we head back?"

Jacob nodded so they retraced their steps to the house. As they drew near Kate's eyes lit up. Adam stood at the door with his finger on the doorbell and a grocery bag in his other hand. He turned to greet them.

"At least this one has a bell that works," he said grinning.

Kate unlocked the door and welcomed him inside, wondering how long they'd be in their new home. She supposed it all depended on what happened over the next few days. She marvelled at how easily Adam flitted about – spaceship, government office – he was never in one place for very long. That's probably what made him such a good spy. Not such great boyfriend material though.

"I've been able to wangle things at work so I can stay close by and help with your mission," Adam said once inside. "I've booked a room at the Broomsquire Hotel off the Silchester Road. It's only ten minutes' walk away."

Kate wanted to suggest that he stay with them, but felt embarrassed to – especially in front of Jacob.

"Do you know yet exactly when the launch is?" she asked coolly, trying to match his demeanour. "It's no good trying before the satellite's up there, and we need to know the launch is successful first."

"Not yet, but I'll let you know as soon as I hear. I've brought lunch for us all." He indicated the grocery bag he'd placed on the floor beside him.

"Thanks," Kate said, "lovely." She led him into the kitchen where he unloaded fresh bread, cheese, salad and fruit pastries for dessert. They spread it on the kitchen table and sat down to eat.

"What do your bosses say about you skipping off every so often?" Kate asked, her mouth full of salad. "Surely they're curious about where you go."

"That's when being a Colonel comes in handy. Just say 'Top Secret' and you're covered." Adam carried on munching as if he hadn't a care in the world, but Kate didn't miss the anxious frowns that flitted across his face every now and then. She sensed he was worried about the danger she was putting herself in and hoped for his sake as well as hers that she wouldn't be discovered. She had to put all her faith in Master M that he'd created the protective shield around her like he'd promised. She could change identity, move house, but she could never change her psychic energy and that's how Helga tracked her. She knew she must put worries about her own safety to one side. Protecting the minds of the nation from Helga's satellite was more important. It had to be stopped, whatever the cost.

"Thank you for all you've done, Adam. We really do appreciate it,"

Jacob said. "Kate would've been in deeper trouble without you. You've saved our skins so many times, diverting attention, blocking signals, not to mention rescuing us in a spaceship!"

Adam smiled back. "No problem," he said, then changed the subject as if uncomfortable with all the praise. Shall we watch TV tonight? And yes the licence has been paid."

"Some mindless entertainment is just what we need," Kate said and Jacob agreed.

* * *

Days passed and nothing happened. Everyone was on tenterhooks, waiting for news. Jacob paced a lot, and Kate couldn't settle to anything for long. They still hadn't been told the exact date for the satellite launch. But without contact they had no way of knowing, and Kate was afraid to link in with her spirit connection in case the Dark Hats found her. Adam popped in every now and then never failing to bring flowers or chocolates, which pleased Jacob, seemingly more than Kate – but he couldn't update them. One afternoon they were listening to the radio when the phone rang.

It was Adam. "Get ready this evening," he told Kate. "We have the green light. The satellite went up this afternoon. I'll be round at 6pm."

After she hung up, Kate felt a huge surge of panic. "What if I can't do it?" she cried. "What if I hit the wrong satellite? There are a lot of them up there."

"Stay calm. You've never failed," Jacob said. "You're not alone. You'll have help. Have a nap and then you'll be ready."

"I'll never sleep," she wailed and started to pace the room.

Jacob did manage to get her to rest for a while and at six o'clock exactly the doorbell rang. Jacob hastened to answer it.

"Come in, come in Adam," he said. "We're as ready as we'll ever be. Kate's a bit anxious, I have to tell you."

Adam walked into the room and took Kate's hands in his. "You know what you have to do, don't you, Kate?" he said.

"I've thought of nothing else since we got here."

Jacob closed the curtains, while Kate dimmed the lights. Then they sat quietly together and waited while Kate took herself into a trance. Time passed. Jacob watched her closely, hardly daring to breathe.

"She's changing," he whispered. "Watch!"

Both men stared, eyes like saucers as Kate morphed into a cloud of blue. Her physical form had completely disappeared and been replaced by a dreamy, swirling mist. A giggle emanated from within it – clearly Kate's distinctive giggle. Jacob had no idea what she was laughing at, but he was forced to just wait, hoping she was okay.

Then they heard an unfamiliar alien language, which made Jacob sit up. Who was this? Were they friendly? Had she been taken over by the Dark Hats? Then the penny dropped. He recognised the voice, if not the language.

"That's Sechem," he said. "I'd know his bubbly musical tones anywhere. Sechem's with her. She'll be alright." Jacob breathed easier and they continued to watch.

"I'm floating in a cloud of blue," Kate said after a few moments. "It's great up here, a bit like my previous mind-travel when I lifted up above the city. I'm not alone. Sechem's here with me.

"There's so much stuff flying around up here. Oops! The satellite's coming into view, the one I have to damage." Kate giggled. "Something nearly hit me as it passed by." She laughed.

"Jacob, why does she sound so relaxed? She's not taking this seriously," Adam said in a worried voice. "This mission is vital; we can't mess it up now."

"She's just feeling her way, I'm sure," replied Jacob his voice uncertain.

The tone of Kate's voice changed abruptly. "I'll get on with it now. I must find the perfect chunk of debris." Jacob shot Adam a pleased smile. Seconds ticked by. "Ah, yes that will do. I know what I have to do. Use my mind and send it crashing into the satellite. Yes, that's it. I need to put all my energy into this and move the chunk into its path."

They heard no more from Kate for a few minutes. It felt like an eternity to Jacob and by the look on Adam's face, Jacob guessed he felt the same.

Suddenly they heard Kate heave a sigh. "It's no good, I can't do it! Somehow being weightless is hindering me. I can't get any purchase on my energy. What shall I do?"

"Try again my darling," said Jacob, hoping she could hear him.

"That's what Sechem's saying too. I'll give it another go."

Both Adam and Jacob stared intently into the blue mist, trying to make something out. As they watched, a dot of magenta appeared on the cerulean blue, then a dot of turquoise; it was becoming speckled with other colours – just here and there at first, like the first drops of rain in a storm and then the dots increased until Kate's cloud was a wonderful swirling rainbow.

"What's happening? I can feel different energies around me!" Kate screamed in surprise. "There's hundreds of them, no it must be thousands..." Kate's voice was breaking with emotion. "I know who this is. It's my followers. I can even recognise individual energies.

There's someone from the Spiritual meetings, loads of people who came to my talks… Oh my goodness – there's Mrs Thomas! There's Poppy!"

Jacob looked at Adam and frowned. "Poppy?"

"They've come to help me. Oh, it's wonderful – how did they know? I feel so much more powerful. Thank you, guys!" she called out. "Right, I'm trying again, I feel good about this attempt."

Silence followed.

Jacob and Adam didn't dare stop looking at the multi-coloured cloud, but with all their energy and love they willed Kate to be successful, adding their considerable support to that of the rainbow energies before them. Suddenly they heard Kate shriek with delight.

"Wow. Bang! Did you see that Master M? Woo hoo! Right on target! The satellite is spinning out of its orbit. There are parts flying off it. It's breaking up. It's disintegrating. It's gone! We did it! We've only gone and done it!" Kate's voice was ringing with triumph.

"Fantastic work, my darling, you can come back now," said Jacob and both men watched as the rainbow cloud dispersed, leaving their beloved Kate sitting there, rubbing her eyes.

"That was amazing! I never thought I could do it but then I had this sudden rush of energy from all the people helping and it was easy!" Kate's eyes filled with tears at the memory. "Right back when I started the talks, I never really believed that people were listening, were taking on board what I was saying, but they were, they really were!" She gazed at Adam and Jacob, cheeks flushed, looking radiant. "How did they know?"

"You must've called to them with your mind. And they responded. Oh Kate! You're amazing!" Jacob was crying tears of joy and relief.

"That was something else. You should've seen all the rubbish that's up there. Somebody ought to clean it up."

"That's my Kate." Jacob said. His heart could stop pounding now. "You have done something unbelievable. You have changed the hearts and minds of hundreds, maybe thousands of people. And towards what's right, what's good. Towards a better future for us all. That's my Kate. I'm so proud of you." Jacob hugged her tightly. "Time for a little celebration, I think," he said, heading to the kitchen and the kettle.

"Yes, you were incredible. That was impressive," Adam said, drawing her to him and taking the opportunity to give kiss her passionately, whilst Jacob was busy. When Jacob came back in, instead of the customary tea tray, it was laden with champagne and glasses. They broke apart, but kept hold of their hands.

"Come on you two lovebirds, come and have a glass of bubbly," he said with a twinkle in his eye, setting down the tray.

The first bottle quickly disappeared and a second was opened. None of them could stop marvelling at the success of the mission, and the evening was spent recalling all the events that led up to it. By midnight the fridge was empty of bottles and they were trying to do impressions of Sechem, Jamère and Master M, to much hilarity. The early hours saw Adam nodding off on the sofa, whilst Jacob and Kate staggered to their beds.

The next morning one by one they surfaced with aching heads and the need for strong coffee. Adam moved slowly and tried to avoid bending over. He winced and pressed his hands to his head whenever anyone spoke too loudly or he moved too fast.

"Never again!" he was heard to lament.

"So that's that, I suppose?" Jacob said as they sat around the kitchen table sipping coffee. "We can relax and start to live a normal life."

Adam peered at him through half-closed eyes. "You what? No, I don't think so somehow. This is when the hard work really begins. Kate has to continue to get the messages out. Don't think we've finished with Helga either. She'll be looking for any chink in our armour, you can be sure."

"I'm on it with Helga," Kate said. "I'm getting better at cloaking so she can't get to me, so I can still have my mind journeys and be directed by our space friends. They'll know what to do. Anyway, she has to find us first."

"Don't underestimate her, darling. She has friends in high places," Adam said. "But don't let this talk spoil your success. Anyway, I'm sorry, but I really have to be off in a moment. Business."

"What, again? So soon?" Kate moaned. She was fed up of him rushing off, especially since her major achievement was only yesterday.

Kate swung round to face Adam, but taking one look at the concern on his face she melted. "Yes, duty calls, of course, my darling. I understand. I don't like it, but I understand – and I'm proud of you, Colonel Fenshawe." She kissed his forehead and cupped his face to look into his eyes.

"Always," he said to her in Sirian.

"He'll be back, my darling," Jacob said looking at her stricken face.

"He will," Kate smiled.

CHAPTER THIRTY-TWO

REMEMBERING OLD FRIENDS

'Acceptance looks like a passive state, but in reality it brings something entirely new into this world. That peace, a subtle energy vibration, is consciousness.'

Eckhart Tolle

Since Adam had returned to work, Kate decided to follow suit, and start at the job that had been lined up for her – sales and lettings agent at the local estate agent. It wasn't quite what she expected – she thought it would be something a bit more high-brow – but then she reckoned, it would leave her with plenty of energy for her real work; for her spiritual work. The manager had been expecting her call and welcomed her in the next day. It was an interesting job and she found it much more stimulating than she expected and her previous role at SatData, and thank goodness there wasn't a whiff of a Marco-type anywhere.

Jacob had struck up some friendships with their neighbours and they were introducing him to all the delights on offer to the retired community, so he was in his element. One evening after Kate had got home from work and was sorting through some paperwork, she heard a buzzing in her ears, so insistent that she couldn't ignore it, and soon after a voice rang through the sitting room where she had her papers laid out on the sofa.

'I'm after talking to you, me darlin.'

Kate recognised the voice immediately. “Oh, it’s you Jamère! Nice Irish accent you have there. It’s good to hear from you.”

‘We’d all like you to join us tonight. Can you link in then?’

“Yes, definitely – it will be good to catch u…” but he was gone.

As soon as Jacob returned from a stroll, she gave him the news and he seemed as pleased as her at the thought of the reconnection. That evening they sat together, and Kate slipped into a trance and soon began to speak.

“I’m in the great hall where the Lords of The Universe and The Galactic Command Council have gathered. Ooh! Sechem, Jamère and Master M are here with me. I can see the same great seating of a triangle with all those space beings I told you about before. It’s amazing; they’re glowing in stunning arrays of colours and lights. I wish you could see this, Dad. But I must hush now. They’re speaking. You’ll hear them. Listen, Dad, you’ll hear them yourself.”

Kate was right, though he couldn’t see what she saw, he sensed the layout and different light qualities in different parts of the room, and he heard the voices.

A Lord of the Universe from the brightest side of the triangle spoke.

‘We have watched and heard much of what has been happening on Earth and see that there is great endeavour on the part of the humans to put right the wrongs on their home planet. We have seen those who speak out against tyranny. We have seen bravery, kindness, love and forgiveness. Therefore, we have decided and agreed to put into place a restriction order on all interplanetary species who do not wish to work with and for the benefit of the ongoing programme for Earth. There is to be no restriction of non-invasive and well-meaning interplay between humanity and those from other spheres.’

Loud applause erupted from two sides of the triangle.

'We have noticed this too and are happy with the arrangement,' another voice said.

"The Galactic Command representative is standing to speak," Kate said in a whisper. Then she gasped. "What a surprise – it's Master M."

'The prospects for Earth look good,' Master M said through Kate, 'for there are many more positive and enlightened souls than there are those who are irresponsible and profit-seeking. The balance has been swung towards an enlightened perspective, even if it is not always apparent. We have seen the right impulses and intentions and a level of urgency regarding these that is promising.'

As Kate watched, she discreetly made gestures with her arms, as if collecting energy. She'd learnt this during her satellite-destroying mission and now here was such a rich source – it was streaming all over the room – she wanted to take advantage of it.

'There are many good souls already in place on the planet to point the way, to act as guides. Even those who have acted out of order, even they will turn and pray for assistance. Help will be given there also. So, the situation is looking a lot brighter for Earth. But it needs to maintain momentum; people still need to feel the situation is urgent. Only when man feels there is nowhere else to go will he get down on his knees and sincerely and honestly turn to a Higher Source. We have seen this happen and because man has and will continue to request help, it will be given. If we thought that there would not be this change in outlook and behaviour then we would be in despair, for the outcome would be bleak for the human race and the planet Earth.'

As Jacob listened to this glorious news, he watched fascinated as Kate once again used her arms as if she was manifesting forms. He saw swirls of light coming from her fingertips. He felt his heart lift at both the wonderful ruling by The Galactic Council and by his daughter's ease and ability to work amongst these super-powerful beings.

'Because we know that when there is nowhere else to turn, humanity turns to the Divine and will have open ears at that time. It matters not what religion covers this plea, for all is one and all are covered. Even those who have brought about the difficulties on your planet will seek assistance, and it will be given. All that is required is that it is asked for. There are so many waiting to assist when the requests are made. We see the future ahead for humanity. We see far into the future, beyond this lifetime. We see a flourishing planet, a flourishing species of humanity. All will become harmonious again. So much help is waiting, so much.'

"Oh, what brilliant news. Jamère and Sechem are clapping like mad," Kate said.

'Jacob. Look after her, won't you, she's not finished yet. And don't worry about Adam, he's not finished yet either. He'll be back with you very soon.' It was Sechem's voice, speaking to Jacob.

Jacob listened with tears streaming down his cheeks; it felt like the end of an era, with an outcome that he'd only dreamt of. As he watched Kate slowly resurface from her trance a great sadness in his heart stirred.

She'd been with such great ones as The Lords of the Universe, and he envied her ability to have so many amazing journeys. The time when he had played a vital role with these space beings was long forgotten. He yearned to be properly reconnected with them, to revisit the place he had once called home and to see Kate's true mother, Joslene again. He felt a connection with her that far surpassed any he'd ever made on Earth and he was lonely, very lonely. Although he had tried to love Francine, they were just too different, he could never understand her and their hearts had never fully joined.

Kate rubbed her eyes, then looked at him and frowned. "What's the matter, Dad? I thought you'd be happy after all they said."

Jacob looked at her. She was glowing. How could he tell her of his longing? His home was not planet Earth but Sirius and as he got older he missed being there more and more.

"Come on, Dad, something's troubling you. I can tell. Don't make me use my 'sight'," she threatened with a chuckle.

"It appears we've been successful," Jacob said. "There'll be no more use for me now. What am I going to do with myself? I'm past my use-by date." He laughed in a vain attempt to appear light-hearted.

Kate shook her head, took hold of his hands and held them tight. She looked intently at him. "But there's something else. Tell me."

He sighed. There was no getting out of it. "Do you remember I told you I was a hybrid myself? Well thoughts keep surfacing in my mind. Places I can remember seeing keep popping up in my head, places from my youth, from my time with your real mother. I don't know where I belong anymore. I had to marry Francine because we needed a human woman to act as surrogate for you. But I wanted to stay with your mother, your true mother."

Kate stopped him. "Do you regret this, Dad. Are you so unhappy?" Her chin began to wobble.

"Oh, my darling girl. I'm overjoyed to have you as my daughter, and I love you more than I can say. I'm so proud of you and all you have achieved – how could I not be –but I yearn to meet your real mother again. I can't help it. Ever since the spaceship rescue, it has brought all these feelings to the surface; feelings that I thought were long forgotten and they are getting stronger and stronger. It must have triggered something within me."

Kate squeezed his hand. "Dad, I'm sure something could be arranged. Why don't we ask?" Then her face fell. "Would you leave me if they arranged for you to return?"

"You don't need me anymore, sweetheart. And you have Adam."

"No, I don't. He's never here. He's always somewhere else." Her voice broke. "I know he can't help it, but he's never here."

Jacob was torn between his love for his daughter and his desire to reunite with her star mother. In truth, his love for her had never diminished. He put his glasses on again and got up from his chair.

"Look at the pair of us, emotional wrecks. Why are we so miserable when we should be celebrating! You've just diverted one of the most devastating plots to control humankind in years, if not ever. Never forget that, my darling. With all that drama, it's no wonder we're feeling a little disconsolate."

Kate smiled blurrily, amused by his old-fashioned word.

"We'll see what tomorrow brings, Kate. A goodnight's sleep is what we both need right now."

After a peck on Kate's forehead, he left the room.

* * *

Jacob stood by his bedroom window and stared out at the dark night. Nothing moved out there, and he felt a stillness in him that he rarely experienced these days. At fifty-five with many years ahead of him, he was a relatively young man, but apart from Kate, he had nothing. He felt empty. He sighed. Time for bed.

As he drifted off to sleep he noticed the room getting lighter, but dismissed it as someone's car headlights. He kept his eyes closed and the day's happenings faded away. How long he'd slept, he didn't know, but when he opened his eyes again he was no longer in his bedroom. He was lying on a couch in a circular room with coloured lights playing on the walls; he recognised that it was a spaceship.

He sat up cautiously and looked around him. He adjusted to the brightness and stood up, wondering how he'd got there. At that thought a panel slid open and a beautiful glowing female walked in.

“Don’t you recognise me, Jacob?”

“Oh, my goodness! Joslene, is it you? Is it really you? You’re even more beautiful than I remember.” Jacob moved towards her taking his time to admire her radiant beauty and fell to his knees at her feet. He felt awe-struck by her majestic power and energy.

“Hello, Jacob, yes it is me. No need to be down on your knees, we’re equal here.”

Jacob stood up and gazed at her. She continued to speak. ‘We’ve been so impressed with how you’ve raised our daughter. She’s already surpassed our expectations and I can’t wait to see what lies in store when she’s fully realised her powers. And a lot of that is down to you. We are all in love with you and what you do.”

“I don’t think I do anything special,” Jacob bowed his head remembering, how Kate had suffered with her surrogate mother Francine. What Kate had said recently was still raw.

“Come,” Joslene said and waved her arm at the panel opening. “We’ll spend some time together.”

For the next few hours Jacob felt he was in paradise. They talked a lot, about Kate’s childhood, how the surrogacy hadn’t been straightforward and his guilt about Francine’s treatment of Kate. They also discussed global issues – the future of the human species and its home, Planet Earth. Jacob felt enriched by the conversation. Then Joslene showed Jacob around, walking down the many tubular corridors. They arrived in one room to find a panel of viewing screens on one side showing the stars outside, and on the opposite wall, a cascade of lights. Joslene led him through these into what appeared to be countryside.

“Where are we?” Jacob asked.

"We're on what you call a Mother Ship."

"Are you taking me back to Sirius?" Jacob's blue eyes sparkled at the thought.

"No Jacob, you can't go home yet. You still have years ahead of you. You're still a young man. This will have to do."

"But this hasn't been long enough. I want to stay for longer; for ever," he replied mournfully.

"But Jacob, my love, you have to return to our daughter."

"She doesn't need me now. She has Adam." His heart began to pound. "I want to stay with you. I can't leave now."

"Remember how worried you were when she was kidnapped? You were beside yourself with worry and fear. That's how she would feel if you were to leave her." Joslene said. "Also, she doesn't yet have Adam. He has his work to do, which takes him away from her." Joslene patted his arm, then held him a tight embrace. "We all have to do things we don't want to do that take us away from our loved ones," she said, gazing deeply into his eyes.

"So, I have to go back?" Jacob's eyes filled with tears.

"Come, my darling." She led him back to the room in which he had arrived. "Lie down, my love. We will meet again."

Jacob settled back on the bed, tears leaking from his closed eyes. It was painful to accept it, but he knew she was right.

* * *

The morning dawned bright. Kate bustled about in the kitchen feeling refreshed. Minutes ticked by and then hours. What was her father doing staying in bed so long? Should she be worried? When she couldn't wait any longer, she knocked softly on his door.

"Dad? Are you awake?" No answer. She knocked again, louder this time. Still no response. Fearing the worst, she entered his bedroom and discovered his empty bed. It'd hardly been slept in. Her heart plummeted. Thoughts raced around in her head. Had his wish been granted and he'd been taken? She stood stock still in the middle of the room, frozen. She had no idea what to do next, but she had to do something.

Shaking herself free of all terrible thoughts, Kate decided to drive to the place where they'd been set down in the woods near Aldermaston. If Jacob had been taken she might find signs on the ground where a spacecraft had landed.

She drove like the wind and soon arrived at the woods. Now where had they been? It was hard to tell. The ground was squelchy and wet from the rain the night before. Although she had no idea what she was looking for, there should be some marks if anything had been there, even just flattened grass. Thankful there were no dog walkers or anyone else around, she began looking over the ground, but she couldn't find anything helpful. She was about to give up when she heard a faint sound. She listened hard. It came again, like a sniffle. Not an animal, more like someone with a cold. An enormous sneeze close by in the undergrowth made her jump. She turned in the direction of the sound and relief flooded over her.

Jacob waded out of the undergrowth grinning from ear to ear. She ran towards him and he opened his arms wide and engulfed her in a huge embrace.

"I saw her, I really did! I saw your mother again. I feel wonderful, like a new man," he shouted. "Except for a cold I seem to have picked up. Probably while waiting for you to turn up," he teased. "What took you so long? What about using your special sight?"

"I was so worried about you, I totally forgot. But instinct led me here in any case. Oh, Dad I'm so happy to see you. I thought I'd lost you. Let's get back to the house. I can't have you going down through a mere cold, can I? I want to hear all about what happened." She bundled him into her car and drove off.

Once they were safely back indoors she asked him to tell her everything.

"Not before a cup of tea," he replied.

"Dear old dad. You haven't changed a bit."

"That's where you are wrong, my darling. I'm a new man."

Kate supplied him with tea, biscuits and tissues for his now streaming nose while Jacob looked around as if seeing everything with new eyes. Kate waited impatiently for what he had to say about his visit.

"They did it," he said again. "They listened to my plea to reunite with your mother. She's wonderful. You wouldn't believe how amazing she is. One day you'll get to meet her. They came to get me. I was feeling really down and prayed so hard for a solution to my dilemma. I must have dropped off, then I realised I was no longer here but on a Mother Ship. It was huge.

"Anyway, waiting for me there was your beautiful mother. We spent time together and talked everything over. She loves you as much as I do and told me I had to return to you. There's much more for us to do together. I must admit I wanted to stay there but I now realise that it's not my time. We've achieved great things but there is still work to be done. She told me that the human race on Earth still hadn't managed to avert disaster through their actions. I had to come back."

He was right. Helga would not have given up on finding them. She may have lost that particular battle, and Gork, that malevolent creature with his death-wish eyes, had punished her soundly for it, but the war was far from over.

“I wish I’d been there, Dad,” Kate said wistfully.

“I had to go alone. If you’d seen her you too would want to quit your role here and return. That can’t happen, not yet. You do understand, don’t you?”

Kate nodded just as the doorbell rang. “Go and answer it, my dear,” Jacob wiped his eyes and blew his nose. Reluctant to leave him, Kate went to the door. She opened it to see Adam standing there. Her heart missed a beat.

“Hi gorgeous,” he said and swept her into his arms. “Missed me? I’ve got two weeks’ leave. I’m all yours.”

Locked together in an ecstatic embrace, they were unaware that high up in the sky, barely visible, were twinkling dots, spaceships. Were These the first fleet of visitors, waiting for clearance to enter Earth’s atmosphere? The future had arrived.

* * *

Dawn light was just beginning to break through the curtains when Richard finished. He wiped his brow. What if any of was true? He realised what he had read was only the beginning. He had to find the old woman. Who was she and what more could she tell him? Richard knew he could not rest until he knew what happened to them all.

THE END

APPENDIX

COVER UPS - THREATS - WHISTLEBLOWERS - EVIDENCE

Allan Rex Sandage, born June 18, 1926, and Brian Geoffrey Marsden, an American-British astronomer born August 5, 1937, both specialised in observation and research of comets. The American government threatened them with death if they revealed their discoveries concerning the trajectory and real size of the Elenin comet. They wanted to reveal the facts to the general public, but in vain. Those two astronomers died with five days of each other of the same illness (acute disseminated encephalomyelitis), which is an extremely rare illness. Too much of a coincidence?

Dr. Michael Wolf stated, 'I met with extra-terrestrial individuals *every* day in my work, and shared living quarters with them while doing research at underground government research laboratories. Zetas work in underground facilities as requested by US Government – but governments have broken treaties by mistreating ETs and by trying to fire on UFOs."

Dr. Brian Clifford of the Pentagon announced at a press conference in 1982 that contact between US citizens and Extra-terrestrials are strictly illegal, according to a law still on the books (Title 14, Section 1211 of the Code of Federal Regulations adopted on July 16th 1969). Anyone guilty of such contacts automatically becomes a wanted criminal to be jailed for one year and fined. A NASA administrator is empowered to determine, with or without a hearing, that a person or object has been extra-terrestrially exposed and can impose quarantine under armed guard for an indefinite period. **This can't be broken even by court order.** The legislation is buried in a batch of regulations. Probably very few members of the government bothered to read it in its entirety, and it was slipped onto the books without public debate and without informing the public. In its infinite wisdom, the government of the United States seems to have created a whole new criminal class: UFO contactees.

At Mt. Perdido in the Pyrenees, between France and Spain: there is a famous set of caves in the Pyrenees that have ancient drawings of astronauts and flying spacecraft, and there've been a number of sightings there.

REMOTE VIEWING

Remote viewing is a mental ability that allows a perceiver (a "viewer") to describe or give details about a target that is inaccessible to normal senses due to distance, time, or shielding.

A Former CIA director described a remote viewer, Pat Price, who was one of Stanford Remote Viewing Institutes as a man who could see what was going on anywhere in the world through his psychic powers. One day in 1973, Price walked into an office, tossed a file on the desk and said, "You might be interested in these UFO bases." Price believed that ETs had established four underground bases. He had remote viewed them and provided Puthoff, his boss, with descriptions of their locations and functions.

Price reported that the main base was protected around a two-mile perimeter with detectors. Several craft were in the launch recovery area and had what looked like an electromagnetic field propulsion system. A third site was at Mount Hayes, northeast of Anchorage, Alaska. The fourth site was at Mount Ziel, in Australia's Northern Territory. This base had the most personnel, including many from the other three sites. While viewing this location, Price thought he was detected, so he 'left,' but then returned. He noted the base was also the *homo sapiens* introduction point. On one occasion Price felt slightly disoriented and decided they had detected him, so he led them to Melbourne instead to put them off.

Price returned to the site and noted that the site should be approached with caution. He didn't think aliens limited themselves to four bases; he also sensed bases on the Moon, Mars, and under Earth's oceans.

Hal Puthoff, Ph.D., founded and directed the CIA-funded Remote Viewing programme at Stanford Research Institute from 1972 to 1985. Price died under mysterious circumstances in 1975. He was believable and had a proven RV track record with neither agenda nor any axe to grind.

BOOK LIST and VIDEO/DVD - ETC

http://www.youtube.com/watch?v=MPRN0kuaYio#at=93

Mary Rodwell web site : ETs, Souls, The New Humans, and a coming global Shift

https://www.youtube.com/watch?v=7i_SqOkpanE

'Being Human' by Shirley Battie **ISBN: 978-1-4500-6491-0**

'Spirit Speaks' by Shirley Battie **ISBN: 978-1-4500-6110-0** www.amazon.com or local bookstore.

'Beyond the Stairs' by Shirley Battie

'Windows of Opportunity' by Sherri Cortland

'Keepers of the Garden' by Dolores Cannon

'The Source Field Investigations' by David Wilcock

Millennial Hospitality by Charles James Hall. His experience with ET living here on Earth in social family groups.

Holographic Universe by Michael Talbot

The Missing Times by Terry Hansen on media cover up

The Keepers by Jim Sparks – ET influence

Raechel's Eyes on ET girl living in USA- get through Granite Publishing Group

Jaime Maussan http://www.tercermilenio.tv/

http://www.youtube.com/user/littleowlorg

www.little-owl.org

https://www.facebook.com/shirley.battie

ACKNOWLEDGEMENTS

So many thanks to Mike Forte for his encouragement throughout. Without him I might never have persevered. Thanks to Emily Cunningham for helping me get my writing in order. Thanks to Lorna Howarth for editing.

Thanks too for the patience shown by my friends who listened to me banging on about this book over a long time. And thanks to YouTube, Facebook and the Internet for the massive evidence found there proving much of my experiences to be real.